A LONG JOURNEY HOME - LALANI

A Long Journey Home - Lalani

Melody Lavrakas

This book is dedicated to best friends everywhere.

To Peggy for what will continue to be a lifelong friendship of joy and laughter and Thursday morning breakfasts.

To Ginny for all the encouragement and love we have shared over the past sixty years and will continue to share, no matter how far apart we may be.

To my husband John for loving me for who I am. For all the patient hours while I write and his gracious hours of editing. He is my best and truest friend, and my forever beloved.

Contents

1

The Return to Home

Lalani stood at the rail waving to Charles as the steamship SS *La Bourgogne* pulled away from the dock at Le Havre, France heading to New York. This was not her first time crossing the Atlantic. She had done it many times in her thirty years of service to wealthy ladies. But this was the first time she was only responsible for herself. She walked down the long promenade deck of the ocean liner, her long wool beige skirt and matching westkit fluttering in the breeze; Brandy, a six-year-old Gordon Setter, at her side. Lalani was returning home to America after being with her friend, Katherine and her husband, Clay, who had gone to England on business and then on to France to visit with her dear friend, Charles Duvaneau. Lalani had stayed in Paris at Charles', while Katherine and Clay went on their honeymoon throughout Europe. Charles had been very gracious to show Lalani the sights of Paris. She was feeling quite proud of herself for climbing to the first level of the newly built Eiffel Tower, and was amazed at the grandeur of Versailles. After being away for over six weeks, Lalani was anxious to get back to her home in Oak Ridge, California. She wanted to get the spring vegetable garden planted, and she missed the small ranch and Jim Baker, the ranch foreman.

Now on a crisp day, Lalani strolled down the promenade to one of the deck chairs and sat. There was no urgency to unpack clothes. She was on her own and could do things as she wanted. Lalani was now thirty-eight years old and had that warm Hawaiian beauty: her long dark thick black hair pulled back but down, her deep dark brown almond eyes twinkling out from a slightly oblong full cheeked face. Her full lips looked like they had spoken years of wisdom. She sat petting Brandy, watching the ocean looming up in front of her. It was March 1892, and she hoped for a smooth crossing, but the clouds off in the distance didn't look like they would dissipate.

Lalani sat searching her memories for the first time she was on a ship, just a month before her twelfth birthday. It was the mail ship *City of Melbourne,* another steamship bound for Sydney, Australia. Lalani had been forced into service by Horace and Edith Crocker to be Edith's travelling companion and personal maid. She was far too young to be either, but Edith had known Lalani since she was four years old. Lalani's mother Leia had come to work in the Crocker house as a maid. It was 1859, just after Lalani's father had died of the measles, brought by the Europeans. Most of the native Hawaiians died of the diseases brought to the island by 1880. Lalani's father had been a fisherman, and the family village was near the east side of Honolulu Bay. Lalani often played and watched her father bringing in the nets full of fish, even wading into the bays to help at the age of three.

As more missionaries and European and American businessmen came to the island, the Hawaiians lost their land due to the 1850 Alien Land Owners Act that allowed much of the land around Honolulu Bay to be bought up by foreigners, including Lalani's village. With nowhere to go, Lalani's mother sought out the missionary school to see if she could get work. She didn't want to work on the newly established sugar plantations, which would take her away from Lalani for eight to ten hours a day. She hoped the school would hire her as a cleaning lady. Leia was in luck. The Royal School for the chief's children did not need help, but Edith Crocker, one of the English teachers, was in need of a new maid for her home on Queen Street. Edith Crocker liked Leia's eagerness and there was something about Lalani, not quite five at the time, that sparked an interest in Mrs. Crocker. Lalani was inquisitive, pretty, and eager to please, like her mother.

Leia came to work for Mrs. Crocker as a maid to clean and wash clothes on a daily basis for $1 a week, plus room and board for her and Lalani. Lalani would help her mother empty trash bins and clean the fireplaces and take on more duties as she grew older. Leia dressed in Mrs. Crocker's old dresses and tried to take on the English ways, but deep down she was always Hawaiian. Edith made sure Lalani had a work dress and a dress for Sunday church as well. Attending church was part of the agreement for work. When Lalani was eight years old, Mrs. Crocker arranged for her to attend the Royal school and learn to read and write. The school also taught the Hawaiian history and culture along with Christian theology. Many of the students eventually became future leaders of Hawaii. Lalani found herself ostracized by the children of the Royal family, but her spunk and inquisitiveness allowed her to hold her own for the three years she attended.

By 1866, Horace was ready to retire. He had started one of the first mercantile businesses in Honolulu and in 1856 became a silent partner in a sugar plantation. After twenty-five years on the island, he and Edith were ready to travel and then return home to Boston. The Crockers knew they would not feel at home in Boston for some time, for they had been gone so long and were used to simpler island ways. Boston would seem like a foreign city with all its high society standards and traditions. Horace and Edith wanted to travel abroad and see Europe before truly settling down in Boston, and working their way back into high society life.

The Crockers never had children of their own, and Lalani filled that void. They had watched her grow up over the past eight years and Mrs. Crocker had become very attached to her. Edith wanted to take Lalani with them, to grow into the role of companion and personal maid. Edith wanted to show inquisitive Lalani a bigger world. Horace also wanted Leia to go to Boston, and to continue to work for them. Leia had taken on the English manner, but she was Hawaiian and the thought of the bustling new world was terrifying.

In March of 1866 Horace Crocker sat down with Leia and asked her to come with them. Leia reluctantly said no. But Edith did not want to give up Lalani, whom she now viewed as her own. Edith wanted Lalani all to herself to raise, and had changed her mind and now did not want Leia to go with them. Horace, desperate to find a way to please Edith, finally sat Leia down and told her he was invoking the Masters and Servants Act, that since Lalani had been under their roof the past eight years, been provided for and educated, that Leia needed to repay him for the costs of providing for her daughter. Of course, he knew she would not be able to do so and that she would be facing debtor's prison according to the law. Horace offered her an alternative. If she wanted to avoid imprisonment, she could agree to an indentureship, where Lalani would work for Mrs. Crocker as a companion and maid, for the next fifteen years or until the end of Edith's life. At that time Lalani would be a free woman, all debts fully paid. Leia was heartbroken, trapped, with no way out but to accept the proposal. Edith promised Lalani would not be treated like a servant but have all the privileges of a companion. Edith would encourage Lalani's eagerness to learn and fulfil her sense of adventure.

On March 2, 1866, Mr. and Mrs. Crocker and Lalani boarded the *Melbourne*. Leia knew Edith would keep her promises and Lalani would be well cared for, but she would never see her daughter again. Leia died the following winter of smallpox.

Lalani now sat thinking of that first trip on board the *Melbourne*. She was so unhappy. It was a miserably long trip. She missed her mother and friends, and held tight to the small box her mother had given her. She couldn't understand why her mother couldn't come with them. Mr. Crocker had promised they would return to Hawaii, and she could see her mother again, giving Lalani a bright thought to hold on to. Suddenly Horace's words came floating back to her. "We want you to have the opportunity to experience the world." *I've certainly done that.*

The *Melbourne* was set for a twenty-one day sail east to Sydney, Australia before they boarded another ship for Europe. With the civil war barely over and life still uncertain with change in America, the Crockers choose to travel for a year or two before heading home. On board the *Melbourne*, Lalani was lucky in one way, she was given a small pullout bed in the Crocker's stateroom, instead of being put into third class steerage. But on the third day a storm came up and the ship was tossed by high winds and waves. Mrs. Crocker became ill with seasickness. Lalani found herself constantly emptying the basket of vomit and scrubbing linens and clothes of the smell. She rarely made it on deck, but she had grown up with the ocean, and the rough motion only affected her when the ship was buffeted by the winds with a battering motion. Mrs. Crocker was so ill; she didn't want to eat the crackers and potatoes Mr. Crocker brought. Instead, they were given to Lalani. After the storm, things got better, and though Lalani wasn't invited to dine with the Crockers and other guests, she was well taken care of, as promised. She had free reign to wander the deck, and they often found her on the stern looking back towards Hawaii.

Now on the *La Bourgogne,* Lalani knew this crossing would only take eight days and hoped it would not incur that kind of storm. A steward came up and asked if she would like a cup of tea, interrupting her thoughts.

"No, thank you, I will wait until tea time."

Lalani went to her cabin instead. Charles had made sure she had a nice first-class cabin. Lalani was met by her cabin steward, a young Philippine girl, Samantha, and introduced her to Brandy. She didn't want Brandy growling if Samantha came to the room to turn down the bed when she wasn't there. The young girl helped Lalani put away her clothes and asked for her meal preferences.

"If you need anything, just push this button, and I will be happy to help."

Lalani felt strange having someone else do these things for her. *I've always been the one to hang the dresses and put things away for Katherine and Edith.* Lalani told her she wouldn't need much, as she had been in service and was used to doing things for herself. Lalani asked how long she had been on board.

"I've been in service for two years now. I send money home to help my family. Most of the time it's not too bad. Sometimes the signal men give me trouble, but the captain is a fair man and reassigns me if they become too friendly."

"Don't stay away from your family too long, you never know what can happen. I thought I would see my mother again, after I left, but never did. She got sick and died before I could return."

Samantha took one more look around to see everything was in order, then curtsied and said, "I'll keep that in mind."

The ship was good sized. There were about two hundred passengers on board, with about one hundred in the first-class decks. Lalani made her way to the first-class dining room for afternoon tea. She sat in a comfortable chair by a porthole and watched the other ladies, most with their husbands, a few with whom she assumed to be their daughters. Again, she felt strange being treated as a lady of wealth. Now in her own right she was a lady of means. Katherine had seen she was well paid for her work, and she had put most of the money away. She also had the ranch house. She had traveled the world and been in some of the most important houses in London and Boston. She could hold her own against any of the other first-class ladies. Yet, she wished Katherine was there. *I wondered where she and Clay are. I'm sure they are having a wonderful time.*

Lalani and Katherine Keen had been good friends and companions for twelve years. Lalani met Katherine when she was twenty-six. After the Crockers had died, Lalani had been hired to be the personal maid to Katherine, then only sixteen. Katherine had lost her mother and father and had come to live with her aunt and uncle, Mr. and Mrs. Shaw, in Boston. Katherine was from a small mining town in the foothills of central California. Lalani and Katherine bonded immediately, both having lost what they loved and been forced to live in what seemed to be a foreign country, so different from the places they were raised. Katherine's father was Madi Indian, and she had his darker skin and dark hair, and at first glance, one might think they were sisters. Katherine became a concert pianist and Lalani was her companion as she travelled. Lalani was like Katherine's big sister, and they shared everything: sadness, hope, dreams, laughter. Although Lalani worked for the Shaws as a maid, Katherine never treated her like one, at least when they were away from the Shaw house. When Katherine moved to London, Lalani went with her, continuing her role of companion and personal maid. Katherine inherited two large estates and became a very wealthy woman. Finally, she returned to her native California, and Lalani, then thirty-six, went with her. This time as equals, no longer as a personal maid, but as best friends. When Katherine married, she wanted to make sure Lalani would be secure, giving her the ranch house and a significant financial sum. As Lalani sat amongst the other first-class passengers, she was truly equal, in all ways: wealth, education and travel, yet she felt like she was only playing the role.

As she sat sipping tea, an older lady came up and asked if she could join her.

"Certainly," Lalani said and asked the waiter to bring more tea.

"I'm Constance Lang, and you're Hawaiian, are you not?" she asked.

"Yes, but I haven't lived there since I was a young girl."

"Oh, I see. Do you live in New York or just visiting?"

Lalani looked at Constance to size up what type of person she was. Constance was in her mid-fifties, with gray hair and warm smile. *She reminds me a little of Edith. She must not be too high society snobbish since she has joined me.* "Neither, I will be going on to California where I have a small ranch. But I've been to New York many times. And yourself, visiting or other?"

"I'm returning home. I have a home on Long Island. I have been traveling for the first time since my Albert passed. We loved to travel.

We were in your native Hawaii many years ago, beautiful place, but I found Honolulu too commercial. Yet the gardens were exquisite, the wild orchids and hibiscus were breathtaking. We had dinner with King Kamehameha, and the native dances and music were most provocative."

Lalani smiled, "Yes, I miss the music and dance. I've only been around symphonic music the past ten years, living in England for five years, and visiting the Paris and Vienna symphony orchestras, and before that in Boston and New York with their philharmonic symphonies."

Constance just assumed Lalani was from the royal family since she was well travelled. Lalani didn't see the need to inform her she travelled as a companion. They enjoyed talking about the common places they had been and agreed to meet up later for supper.

That evening the seas turned rough, and very few people were in the dining room. Constance sent her regrets. Again, Lalani thought of her first voyage and how miserable everyone was. She had been terribly unhappy about leaving her mother and home, and Edith was in no condition to console her. This time, as her bed pitched and rolled, at least she didn't have tears in her eyes. She did feel a little lonely and hoped Constance would feel better in the morning, so they could continue talking.

But the rough seas continued for another two days before the sun finally broke through. Now everyone was up on deck and wanting to complain about how badly they felt and how glad they would be when the ship reached New York. Lalani slipped away, not wanting to hear the complaints. She was sitting on the port bow enjoying the fresh air. Her thoughts now returned to the *Melbourne* and remembering her own feelings about arriving in Sydney.

She too had been glad to be off the ship that became smaller and smaller with each passing day. Sydney was a bustling port town, bigger than Honolulu. The port was cramped with ships from the orient with goods for England, and ships from England with prospectors hoping to find gold, or undesirable criminals from England sent to the prisons. She remembered, *clinging to Edith's hand and clutching my mother's box in the other as we followed Horace through the docks to the center of town. At first the streets were crowded, with wagons and crates lining the wooden walkways. Then we reached the Grand Hotel with its three stories of towering white-washed brick and arched windows. I was excited but felt very small and insignificant.* The Crockers had requested a nice suite in which Lalani was able to sleep on a cot just for her. They stayed in Sydney for three weeks before their ship to England departed. *I was angry at Horace for taking me away from mother. The night Edith and he went to the theater without me, I shouted out in anger at him for the first time. I always wondered why he didn't hit me or punish me for that. He did lock me in the room so I couldn't leave. Edith did try to make me understand that I was too young to go. I cried all night, I felt so abandoned. Yet Sydney wasn't all bad.*

The following week was Lalani's birthday. That day, she truly began to feel how much Edith cared for her. *It was the beginning of autumn in Sydney. On my twelfth birthday, Edith took me to the Royal Botanic Garden. The flowers reminded me of home. The correa with its trumpet shaped blossoms and the bright red bottlebrush were almost finished blooming. The eucalyptus trees with their minty smell and the Koala bears were a special surprise. But the orchids reminded me of home the most.* The kangaroos on the other hand, she found frightful, as everyone warned her how powerfully they could kick, and to stay away. *Edith took me shopping for a new dress and then we had afternoon tea at the hotel. That was the happiest day of the whole year. Edith wasn't always able to show it, but she did love me. Most of all she loved Horace and he her.*

She was lost in thought about the elderly couple when a slightly older gentleman approached. "Looks like we are the only two that the rough seas didn't affect," he said giving her a nod. "I saw you in the dining room last night, but you were just leaving. I wish I had come earlier, so we could have eaten together. Eating alone is … well lonely, I'm Roger Atwell, heading home to Virginia."

Lalani came back to the present, smiled, and indicated he should sit, while at the same time calming Brandy. "Yes, I think there may not be too many people tonight either from the way many of the women are talking. Growing up on an island, the sound of the waves is just part of you. It's the sound and rhythm of waves crashing that make some people feel seasick, not just the movement. But I love to feel the movement of the boat as it rises and drops with each swell."

They spoke for a while and then he asked if she would join him for supper. "I'm sorry Mr. Atwell, but I don't think it would be appropriate, besides I already have an invitation from Mrs. Lang. Perhaps we will find ourselves together at the captain's table." Lalani had never really had occasion to be alone in the company of a man, other than fellow servants. *I should be polite and accept, but I'm not looking for a man's company. Besides there are only three more days, and then we will be in port, and I'll be on my way to the ranch.* She pulled out her book and began to read, the thoughts of Sydney now gone. He stayed and quietly looked out to sea, but didn't try to engage in more conversation.

Lalani had Samantha bring her meal to her cabin that evening since Mrs. Lang again was not dining. On the following evening the two ladies did dine together and resumed a most pleasant *tête-a-tête*. Samantha took extra care of Lalani when she dined in her room. On occasion, if Samantha had free time, they would sit and talk about being in service. Samantha also brought Brandy scraps of meat left over from other diners.

On the last night, Lalani was invited to dine with the captain and found herself seated with Mr. Roger Atwell and Mrs. Lang. The captain regaled them with stories of rough passages and how this wasn't nearly the worst. Constance reminisced about sailing with her husband and how much more fun it was to play cards with him. Mr. Atwell was a bachelor and traded perishable goods. He had been in Holland and France purchasing cheeses for several New York restaurant clients. Mr. Atwell brought some of his cheeses for a course between the salad and main meal that would go along with the captain's wine.

"How do you like the *Comté?*" he asked Lalani.

"I like it very much. It is one of my favorite French Cheeses. The *Gruyère* is also nice. I have been in Paris for several weeks and had these often, but not with this wine. My friend has his own vineyard. The New York crowd should like your cheese selection very much."

Roger was surprised at her knowledge of cheeses and wanted to know if she had eaten other unusual cheese from other countries. She mentioned the goat cheese in Italy, but said that Holland and France were his best sources. Lalani thanked the captain for the delicious meal, and then she escorted Constance to her cabin. Samantha came and helped pack clothes into various cases for New York and those to go on to Oak Ridge.

"Samantha, enjoy seeing the world. It's the best education you can get. The memories will last a lifetime. But do return home when you can."

"I will have to work for another ship if I'm to get home. This ship is only to Europe, and Manilla is so very far. But perhaps one day."

The last morning, Lalani had tea on deck as New York, off in the distance, grew larger. *I truly have seen the world and Edith showed me how to maneuver within it as a woman. Edith had such joy in showing me new things, and I basked in the discovery of each one of them. And now I think I shall exercise my unconventionality and go by myself to the Symphony while I'm in New York.*

The ship came into New York harbor on a cold wet morning. Lalani asked that her trunk be delivered to Grand Central Station will call, as she would be going on to California within a day or two. Samantha had packed a suitcase with the gown and things she would need for the two days in New York. Lalani found Constance on the promenade deck watching the activities of the crew as they pulled into the dock. "Will you stay in the city tonight?" she asked Constance.

"No, my dear, my son is there (she pointed to a tall blond haired gentleman waving). We will have lunch at Delmonico's and then make our way out to Long Island, about a four-hour carriage ride," she replied as she waved to her son. "How about you, will you visit friends here before going on to your ranch?"

"I thought I would catch the symphony tonight. My very dear friend, Katherine was a concert pianist and played here several times, and I thought it would be fun to hear the orchestra again, even if she is not playing."

"Well, that sounds like a delightful idea. You should ask Mr. Atwell to escort you. He seemed most interested in you."

"Mrs. Lang, are you trying to matchmake an old spinster like me? Besides, I have a very dear friend back at the ranch that I'm very fond of."

"I see! Lalani, you are never too old for love and adventure. Until you have had both, you need to keep looking," Constance said with a twinkle in her eye. She gave Lalani a gentle hug and kiss to her cheek as they departed to fetch their things before disembarking.

Lalani carried a small case and Brandy on her leash as she waited in line to disembark. Fortunately, she was second in line for a carriage, and she pointed out her suitcase quickly to the driver amongst all the bags waiting on the dock. It was drizzling as the carriage made its way to the Waldorf Hotel. The bellman held out an umbrella for her as she stepped from the carriage. Brandy on the other hand, bounded out into the rain, getting wet while the luggage was retrieved and the driver paid. As she came through the door with Brandy, the hotel manager gave a disapproving look. Brandy's feet were wet, leaving paw prints on his clean floors, and smelled like wet dog.

"May I help you, madame?" he said as politely as he could muster in his perturbed way.

"Yes, I'm Miss Lalani. I have a reservation for a suite." *Thank goodness I have a reservation for a nice suite, otherwise I don't think he would let me in.*

"Oh, yes, Miss, we have your suite already." He escorted her to the desk where the young man continued to help. "Nice to have you back, Miss Lalani, you will find an extra towel in your room to dry off your dog."

"That will be helpful, thank you. Is the symphony playing this evening?"

"Yes, miss, would you like the concierge to arrange for you to attend?" He motioned for the concierge and he approached. "Did I hear you wanted symphony tickets for tonight?"

"Yes, please something on the mezzanine level if possible, and I will need a carriage for seven o'clock."

"How many tickets?" he asked.

Smiling, "Just one, I will attend on my own," she said, handing him a five-dollar bill.

"Certainly, I will send your ticket to your room and a carriage will be waiting with the doorman. Just give him your name."

Lalani followed the bellman carrying her suitcase to her room, Brandy's feet now dry but still smelling like wet dog. The bellman laid out the towel to use on Brandy and asked if there was anything else, accepting his tip with a smile.

Lalani dried Brandy, found her brush in her luggage, and sat brushing her coat, like she had done so many times before. Brandy was a beautiful heavy boned, broad-shouldered setter with the traditional red coat but a white chest. Lalani ordered a simple roast beef sandwich and a bowl of soup before she dressed for the symphony. The roast beef she gave to Brandy, and ate the bread with her soup.

She changed into a beautiful green gown, did up her hair, clasped a simple pearl pendant around her neck and grabbed her gloves and cloak. Her ticket had been delivered and she was pleased to see it was for a box on the mezzanine level. As she entered the Metropolitan Opera House where the Philharmonic performed, it didn't seem any different from the last time she was there. But this time she would not be backstage. She was one of the patrons coming to hear Brahms and Beethoven. She ascended the stairs to the mezzanine level and the usher escorted her to her seat. The stage looked so different from this viewpoint, where she could see all the instruments and several private patron's boxes. She shared hers with a couple from Connecticut in New York visiting their grown children.

She enjoyed the opening Brahms piece. There was no guest artist this time, but she recognized Maestro Thomas, the conductor, noticing his demanding style right away.

At intermission, she wandered down to the lobby. She recognized several people, the Griswalds and the Astors, who were busy talking. Suddenly she heard from behind her, "Is that Katherine's Lalani?" in a high feminine voice. She turned around as Isabella Gardner came rushing her way. "It is you! Is Katherine here?"

"Good evening Mrs. Gardner, what a delight to see you again. No, I'm here by myself enjoying the music. Katherine and her husband Clay Taylor are on their honeymoon in Europe."

"Honeymoon! Well, she finally went and got herself married did she, to one of those wealthy lords from England?" she said inquisitively.

"No, Katherine and I moved back to California a few years ago. She bought a small ranch and returned to raising horses. Her husband owned the neighboring cattle ranch."

She said this, being careful of how much Katherine would want her to know. *Word will spread like wildfire amongst the Braham elite.* Just then Mr. and Mrs. Cunard came up.

"Lalani, how wonderful to see you. Are the newlyweds back from their honeymoon?" Laura said, as she gave her a hug and greeting kiss.

"No, they're in Vienna at this point I believe. I came back on my own."

"We stopped by the school before we left. Sophia and Jessie have the old house in a major state of construction. But we think it is going to be well received. Sir Reynold says he has fifty applications already," Mr. Cunard added.

"What's this, a school?" asked Isabella.

"Yes, Katherine's opening a music school for future concert piano and violin professionals," Lalani explained.

Just then the gong sounded, announcing the concert would resume in ten minutes.

"Lalani, you must come to my little soirée after the concert. The Griswalds and Lady Astor will be there and will want to hear everything about what Katherine is doing. Meet me in the lobby and you can join me in my carriage. Laura and William, please join me as well. I didn't realize you were back in New York."

Mr. Cunard looked at Lalani, and seeing the look of hesitancy, asked, "Why doesn't Lalani come with us and we can make a brief appearance, just to say hello and catch up on what Lalani is doing. We can tell you about the school and then take Lalani back to her hotel."

Lalani gave a grateful nod and said she would meet them after the concert. Beethoven's Third Symphony was splendid. Lalani had not remembered hearing it before and was very glad she had gone. She wished the couple from Connecticut good night and then found the Cunards.

Lalani had stayed at Isabella's house before with Katherine and her uncle. It had not changed much in the five years since she had been there: a new rug in the entry and perhaps a new Ming vase on the dining room table. Isabella snatched her up as soon as she arrived, wanting to hear all about Katherine's time in London and why she left her career so abruptly. Lalani explained how she performed with Sir Reynold's Chamber Orchestra in London, the Ladies Vienna Symphony at the beautiful music hall in Vienna, and meeting Rimsky-Korsakov in St. Petersburg. At the moment they asked why she left, Lalani was confronted by Maestro Thomas.

"Yes, tell us why she ruined a brilliant career by not showing up to a performance with no warning. From what I understand she left the Bonn Symphony high and dry."

Lalani wasn't sure what to say. *Katherine wouldn't want me to say she ran away from her husband, and using the performance was the only way.* "It was an unfortunate miscommunication. It was to be her last performance in Europe as she wanted to return to the United States. Passage was booked out of France, for what she thought was after the performance. Instead, the ship was leaving three days before the performance. We had just arrived in France when we were informed the ship was leaving that evening. The next ship going directly to the States wasn't leaving for another two weeks. Katherine sent a telegram to Bonn, apologizing, but felt she needed to keep the ship reservations."

"Well, it certainly wasn't professional of her," Thomas spouted.

"Perhaps not, but Katherine was ready to retire and make a life for herself, which she has done. She has a wonderful and growing horse ranch and is happily married to a respectable cattleman in California."

Just then Freddie Wallace spoke up, "She always did love her horses. I'm happy for her. And what about you? Now that Katherine's married, your travel companionship will no longer be needed. What will you do?" He was trying to help change the subject off of Katherine, but unintentionally put Lalani on the spot. Freddie had been very gracious to Lalani at various parties she attended with Katherine, always asking her to dance and taking interest in her Hawaiian background.

"From the looks of it, she is doing quite well for herself as an independent woman," Laura Cunard chimed in.

Lalani smiled, "Yes, I'm no longer her companion, but we are best of friends and neighbors. I have my own house and I'm looking forward to getting home to my garden and chickens and a very dear gentleman friend."

"Ah, ha! That doesn't sound very exciting after all the places you have been. But do tell us about your gentleman," Isabella said.

"A lady never talks about her gentlemen callers, at least not in public."

Freddie whisked her away from the questioning and introduced her to his wife, for which she was most appreciative. "I must apologize, but it has been a very long day and I have the morning train to Boston to catch. I should say goodnight to Isabella and see if I can find a carriage back to my hotel," she said to Freddie.

"Let Esther and I take you. I think we're ready to go as well," he said.

She found the Cunards and said Freddie would take her to the hotel, then thanked Isabella, saying, "I'm sure Katherine and Clay would welcome you to their ranch in Oak Ridge, if you journey west." Isabella escorted them to the door and the butler summoned their carriage. On the way to the hotel, Lalani thanked Freddie profusely for coming to her rescue in answering all the questions. Freddie said he always admired her and hoped she would find happiness with her beau back home, as he had found with Esther. Lalani blushed and told them Jim was a good man, the foreman who helped with the horses. She was comfortable around Jim and having been away from him, she admitted she was very fond of him and missed him.

Lalani caught the morning train to Boston to visit friends. She still stayed in contact with Minnie who still worked for the Shaws. Lalani arrived at the Parker House Hotel and left Brandy in her room, while she went to meet Minnie for afternoon tea. Minnie was a few years older than Lalani and had work for the Shaws for the past twenty years.

Lalani caught a carriage to the tea shop on Commonwealth Avenue in Brighton. As she passed the Evergreen Cemetery, she called out to the driver to stop. She suddenly wanted to stop and pay respects to Edith and Horace Crocker. Edith had died in the fall of 1879 and Horace the following spring. Horace's brother had him buried with his beloved wife of almost fifty years. It had been twelve years since she had been to the site. The double headstone read, Horace Crocker 1810 to 1880, followed by, Edith Crocker 1812 to 1879. She had known them as long as she could remember. She had travelled the world with them, and they finally settled in Boston when she was fourteen. In Boston, Edith trained Lalani to be a lady's maid: how to help dress and take care of ladies' gowns, how to do their hair and keep a room. Edith taught her proper etiquette, how to prepare afternoon tea and the proper way to serve. In her early years with them she was more of a servant, but as Edith aged and Lalani came of age, she became Edith's companion and was treated more like a daughter than a servant.

Lalani stood looking at the grave with mixed emotions. She was angry at Horace for taking her away from her mother for many years. Yet loved Edith for the kindness she gave her. In many ways, they were her parents and she loved them. She was one of the lucky Hawaiian children to be taken from the island. She had been trained as a companion and not just as a downstairs maid, never to be seen. She was glad she stopped. *They were so cute together in their final days. Horace adored Edith and would sneak up behind her and kiss her on the top of her head or they would walk hand in hand in the garden.* Lalani couldn't be mad at Horace. She could only love them both in the end.

Lalani said her quiet farewell, then had the carriage driver go on to meet Minnie. It was like old times, when they would have a day off and go to the tea house. Minnie filled her in on all the goings on with the Shaws. Mr. Shaw had retired from the bank and Mrs. Shaw was busy playing grandmother to Irene's three children as well as her ladies club meetings. Minnie was delighted to hear Lalani had her own home and that Katherine was happily married.

"Mr. Shaw still has not told Eunice you are back in the States. I think perhaps it is time he did. Eunice often talks about Katherine, admitting she misses her piano playing and having her at the Cape Cod house. But I think Mr. Shaw misses her most. He often asks if I have heard from you."

Minnie asked if Lalani ever found a beau for herself. "I managed a few dates during my time off in London, but never let it get serious as I knew we would return to the States. If you can keep a secret, I am very fond of the ranch hand that helps with the horses. Jim is eight years older than I am, but still strong and handsome. Has a good heart and treats me like a lady." They whispered and giggled like school girls as they talked about the men they had known. After several hours of chatting, Lalani walked Minnie back to the Shaw's house in order to say hello to Mr. Shaw. Minnie said Eunice was visiting friends and he would want to see her. Mr. Shaw was delighted to see Lalani and gave her a hug as she came through the front door. Minnie gave her a hug and returned to her duties, bringing tea and cake while Lalani and Mr. Shaw visited.

He was glad she came and to hear how both she and Katherine were doing. Over the years he had been very grateful that Katherine had Lalani in her life. "You understood her better than any of us could," he said.

She smiled and said, "we came from simple beginnings and great loss, which has given us a great bond. She's like my little sister and I will always look after her and she me."

She asked how he liked retirement and not working at the bank. He said it was hard and he missed it. He then reminded Lalani of the trust account that Horace Crocker had set up for her just before his passing. That when she turned forty, she would be able to access the funds of $40,000 plus interest. She had forgotten about the trust and had no idea it was worth so much. Mr. Crocker was grateful to Lalani for all the years she lived with them and felt she was more like a daughter than his wife's indentured companion. He couldn't leave his estate to her, as his brother wouldn't allow it. Instead, he set up a trust account so she would have something to live off in her older years and not have to work. She would turn forty on April 8, 1894, in two years. She gave Mr. Shaw her bank name in Oak Ridge and the manager's name so he could send the funds when they became available. She told him Katherine had seen that she was well taken care of, giving her the ranch house. That she had her own savings, that she had enough for a comfortable life.

Eunice was due home shortly, so she took her leave. Mr. Shaw had his carriage driver take her to the hotel. "Do keep in touch and let me know how you and Katherine are doing," he said giving her hand a warm pat, then helping her into the carriage. As she sat watching the scenes of the old neighborhood, she thought *that was the first time I've ever felt like a guest in that house. I never realized how much Mr. Shaw appreciated me and it gives me a new warm feeling towards him.*

She had one more person to visit in the morning before leaving, that was Margaret Bowles, Katherine's old piano teacher. They had spent many afternoons together, all three of them and she wanted to see her before her train left for California. The next morning Lalani checked out of the hotel and had her things sent on to Central Station, while she and Brandy took a carriage out to Margaret Bowles's small estate on the edge of town. The house and stable with their red brick and white trim looked the same. Lalani knocked on the door and waited, Brandy at her side. A young woman dressed in a simple black dress opened the door. "Hello, may I help you?"

"Yes is Mrs. Bowles available for visitors?" she said apologetically, now realizing she should have sent word for an invitation.

"May I ask your name?"

"Of course. Tell Margaret it is Lalani, Katherine's friend."

Within minutes the door opened wide and Margaret stood smiling, reaching for Lalani to come in. Margaret had aged, her face more wrinkled, and she seemed shorter, but her eyes had the same eagerness for life. "Lalani, it is you. I'm so glad you have come. Come, come in," taking her hand and leading her to the sitting room. Margaret had retired from teaching at the girls' school and spent quiet days playing piano and taking a carriage ride every afternoon. She immediately took a look at Lalani, "You have grown into a real lady. Katherine has done right by you. How do you like ranch life and the west? And how is our dear Katherine?"

Lalani told her all about life on the small ranch, how she liked having her chickens and her own garden. How Katherine had begun to raise horses, but now that she was married, she would be living in the big house and she had given Lalani the small ranch house. The young woman brought tea and cakes, and Margaret explained how it was hard for her to ride a horse nowadays, since her hips bothered her. But she still had her black Friesian and took a buggy ride every afternoon. Lalani confessed she still preferred the carriage to horseback. Fortunately, Katherine had never asked her to go riding with her. Margaret asked if she wanted to walk down to the stable to see Chester and Prince George. Chester was the gelding that Katherine had ridden while in Boston. "She used to sneak him out for a ride, thinking I didn't know, but I always knew. She had a funny little way of looping his bridle back on the hook that gave her away. Plus by the end of the week, the carrot bin would be half empty." It was one of the great pleasures in their friendship. "And how many times did you have to come get her so she wouldn't miss supper or a dinner engagement? I used to watch you shooing her out the stable door and grabbing her hand and running down the path so she wouldn't get caught by her aunt. So many wonderful memories. And here you are a mature woman, but still young enough to marry and have children if you desire."

"Marry maybe, but children, I don't know about that. I may just settle for being Nana Lalani to Katherine and Clay's children someday."

Margaret slowly opened the stable door allowing the light in. Lalani spotted Chester immediately. Margaret grabbed a carrot from the bin and handed it to Lalani. "He's getting old, but still has enough back teeth to chomp on a carrot."

Lalani held the carrot out and he sniffed her hand and looked at her with a puzzling eye and then took the carrot. Lalani rubbed his forehead as he chewed. "Do you think he remembers me?"

"Sure, he does. Chester doesn't take food from just anyone nowadays."

"Katherine will be pleased to know he is still here. She has a beautiful chestnut mare and her own black Friesian carriage horse. Prince George and her Prince Philip must be from the same stable in Holland. Prince Philip is really my horse, since I use the buggy whenever I go anywhere." Lalani walked over and held out her hand to Prince George and rubbed his muzzle. That's when she spotted the old cowboy hat hanging on the nail. "You still have Katherine's riding hat?"

"Yes, I just haven't had the heart to throw it away. The mice got to her pants and shirt a long time ago, but the hat stays as a warm reminder of my favorite student and friend."

Lalani wanted to stay longer but time was growing short and she needed to catch the train. She would be sure to tell Katherine that Chester and her hat were still in the stable waiting for her, as well as her dear friend. "I'm sure she will write when she returns. She may even surprise you too with a visit. I know she would love for you to meet Clay."

Together they hitched up Prince George to her buggy and Margaret drove Lalani and Brandy to Central Station. Lalani knew her way around the station very well, as she and Katherine had gone through it many times. Lalani had a private compartment from Boston to Council Bluffs, Iowa. From there she would catch the Pacific Railroad line, which ran directly into San Francisco. She would get off at the Oak Ridge stop, five stops before the end of the line. It would be four more days and she would be home at the ranch. Her compartment was comfortable, with a pull up table for dining, and her seat pulled out into a bed. There was just enough room for her to step around Brandy sleeping on the floor. As the train pulled slowly out, she took in all the old red brick buildings. *It will be a long time if never before I see red brick again. California just doesn't have brick buildings. And Minnie says there's talk of a motorized buggy that will do away with all the horses. If I return, the city will be very different. I think I shall remember it as it is now.*

The train ride to Oak Ridge was very different from the ship crossing from France. There was no promenade deck and Lalani didn't find any single ladies in the dining car. She spent most of the four days in her compartment, reading, watching the scenery, or conjuring up memories.

2

The Men That Could Have Been

It had only taken a day to get to Council Bluffs, Iowa, where Lalani would catch the Pacific Railroad to Oak Ridge. The porter took her luggage from her old compartment and placed it in the overhead bin of her new compartment. This one was the same as the others except it was on the other side of the train. Brandy wanted to run and chase a small rabbit instead of boarding. Brandy had trapped the poor scared bunny between two crates, and the porter started to pull her away, when she turned and growled at him. Lalani quickly apologized and placed the leash back on her, scolding her as she pulled Brandy back to the train platform. Lalani didn't scold too hard as she felt sorry for the dog. Brandy had not been able to run for days and had too much energy. She wanted to play. Lalani reached into her handbag and found a dog treat and tossed it to the end of the platform. Having let go of the leash, Brandy raced after it, almost tripping a gentleman with the trailing leash as he walked onto the platform. The middle-aged man did a two-step to avoid the moving leash. As Brandy stopped to eat the treat, the man picked up the leash. "And who must you belong to, you beautiful, but menacing beast?" he said out loud. Lalani, seeing what had happened, came up behind him. "I deeply apologize. I wasn't thinking when I tossed the treat, that someone would come out at that moment. It's just she has been cooped up for so long she needed to run."

"No harm done," he said handing her the leash. "You have been traveling for a while then. May I ask where your destination is?" now looking at Lalani and thinking, what a lovely face.

"Yes, I've come from France and we're heading to California."

"I'm Harry Steinberg. I guess we will be fellow passengers. I'm headed to Cheyenne, Wyoming, to buy beef to be shipped to Chicago."

"I see. Miss Lalani and this is Brandy. My family is in cattle. They have a large spread in Oak Ridge. Perhaps you have heard of the Taylor Ranch."

"No, I can't say that I have, but most of the California ranches sell to Denver or San Francisco. We have a few minutes before the train leaves. May I be so bold to suggest a stroll to give Brandy a walk. Just down to town and back in sight of lots of people."

She smiled, "That would be acceptable."

Lalani did not take his arm, but they walked along speaking about where they had been. Harry was a broker for the Chicago's butcher's trades and was always looking for good meat at a good price. Brandy tugged at the leash wanting to go faster. As they got closer to returning to the train, Lalani told Brandy to sit, took off her leash and told her to stay. Harry and she walked onto the platform, as Brandy watched intently, then Lalani turned and motioned for the dog to come. Brandy came running to her. "Good girl."

"That's quite a dog you have," Harry said.

"Yes, she is! She's a good companion and guardian, when needed," Lalani replied.

"I'll keep that in mind," Harry said with a smile. Just then the train whistle sounded and the conductor called, "All aboard!"

Harry assisted Lalani on board and escorted her to her compartment. His was on the next car up. "I hope you will join me for supper, say six o'clock in the dining car. It's so much nicer to dine with some-one rather than alone."

Lalani wasn't sure about Harry but he behaved like a gentlemen, and Brandy didn't feel the need to stand between them. "Six o'clock would be fine, I'll meet you there."

Harry smiled, tipped his bowler hat and closed the door behind Lalani, then continued on to his compartment. Brandy was still in a playful mood, bouncing up onto the seat and back to the floor several times, before Lalani put an end to it. Brandy finally settled by the door as Lalani slid next to the window to watch the landscape slide past.

I haven't been strolling with a stranger in a very long time. Charles and Jim don't count, they're not strangers. I only sat with Mr. Atwell and briefly at that. Of course, a respectable young woman doesn't go walking with strangers. When was the last time I was so bold?

Lalani sat thinking about strangers she had met. The first month in London when she and Katherine had arrived, she had gotten lost on her way back from the milliners. *That's when I met Wallace for the first time. He was coming back from the tack shop with a repaired halter, when he spotted me looking confused and asked if he could help. I thought he was a handsome young man. When he said he worked for Lady Wycliffe, Katherine's friend, I was relieved. He was so kind and walked me back to the Cunards. Wallace and I became good friends and often took evening strolls once we moved in with Lady Wycliffe.*

She reached over and took out some stationery and began to write to Wallace. They had been very good friends and she realized she had been amiss in not writing him since she left. She wrote she hoped he would forgive her the oversight and that he was well. As she sealed the letter, once again she sat watching the scenery roll by.

Again, her mind came back to the question, when was the last time she had gone for a walk with a true stranger? It wasn't when she worked for the Shaws. It had to be when she was with the Crockers. Her mind wandered back to a trip to Marseille, France when she was twenty-one. It was the last leg of the trip that started in Amsterdam.

They were staying for a month along the Mediterranean, as it was cooler there in July. *It was such a beautiful city. The water was warm and the cathedral at the top of the mountain stood like a magic castle. The city of my first love.* They had been in Marseille for only a week and Edith was resting one afternoon. *I remember asking Horace if I could walk down to the sea shore. It was only two blocks, and he agreed. It was beautiful. The water was so clear and aqua blue, like the lagoons in Hawaii. It made me homesick, something I had not felt in years. I was sitting on a rock. I had taken my shoes and stockings off and had my feet in the water. That's when Philippe appeared. He was gorgeous: tan, muscular, with a strong square jaw, and blue eyes that I almost drowned in. He said Bonsoir in his deep French voice. I just couldn't help but sit and talk with him. Philippe was the first stranger I walked with. He took my hand and we strolled along the water. He was a waiter at the hotel where we were staying. We would sneak visits when we could get away. He was my first kiss now that I think about it. Of course, Horace put an end to it, when he found out we had been seeing each other unchaperoned. He was furious, and I thought he was going to kill me. Instead, we suddenly left for Granada, Spain the next day, I felt as if he had killed me. I cried for weeks. Poor Edith didn't know what to do with me. She said I would find someone someday. I always thought it be sooner than this.* Lalani shook her head, "That was so long ago. This time there is no one to object." She realized it was getting late, the sun had gone down. She washed her face and adjusted her hair and went to the dining car to meet Harry.

She spotted him sitting halfway down the car. He stood as she approached. "Right on time. I hope you don't mind, but I ordered a sherry for you."

Lalani smiled, "Thank you." She didn't often drink, and sherry was the only thing when she did. Harry was very interested in her travels and where she had been. He had to admit he had never been out of America, but he had seen a great deal of it. "Perhaps that is what I need to do, see more of the United States, now that I'm settling down here. I've seen very little. From the train you can't see much of anything other than trees or prairies," she said as she glanced out the window to the prairie, then back to Harry.

"Oh, there is so much to see. The bustling city of Chicago for one, and the gold city of Deadwood for another. Of course, there is Pikes Peak in the Rocky Mountains and Yellowstone geysers in Wyoming, and Niagara Falls in New York, so many places."

"They sound wild and powerful. I guess I have become the more civilized Boston, Philadelphia type. I like to think of myself as a lady rancher. I don't manage the horses. The foreman takes care of them. "

"A real lady of leisure," he quipped.

Lalani didn't like this remark. Apparently, he had no idea how much work keeping a house and entertaining required. *I do plenty of ranch work, planting and tending the garden and the chickens, milking the cow and even helping with turning the horses out to the paddock.*

Lalani did enjoy her meal of chicken and steamed potatoes. By the time she was finished, Harry seemed a little gruff and much more arrogant than he did when they walked at the station. She thanked him for the company and stood to return to her compartment.

"Let me escort you back," as he stood and started to take her arm.

"No, I 'm quite capable." But he cut her off before she could say more. "No, I insist a gentleman always escorts a lady." He stepped aside and let her go first.

They walked in silence through the narrow corridor of the three cars until they reached her compartment. She turned and thanked him again. "I hope you have a successful time in Cheyenne," and opened the door. He began to follow her in, when she turned and put her hand out to stop him. "Goodnight, Mr. Steinberg." The tone in her voice alerted Brandy to her feet and she growled as she came between the two of them. Harry looked at the dog and stepped back from the door. "That sure is a good guard dog you have. Goodnight, Miss Lalani. Perhaps we can meet in the morning."

Lalani didn't say a word, but just took a step back with Brandy, still quietly growling.

Harry turned and left, and Lalani quickly closed the door and locked it. "Good girl, Brandy, good girl," patting her on the head. She was now glad Charles had insisted she take Brandy with her instead of keeping her until Katherine returned. She'd only been away from the west for a few months and had quickly forgotten how forward and assuming the men could be.

The train would be pulling into Omaha around eight o'clock and then arrive in Cheyenne in the morning. She requested the conductor to bring her a lantern when they stopped so she could walk Brandy where she could do her business. She also hoped Harry wouldn't come looking for her. Just before eight, the conductor brought her a lantern and she took Brandy to the last train car to disembark. Just beyond the station was a stand of trees. She kept Brandy on the leash so she wouldn't run off if she needed protecting. It was cold and she didn't bring her shawl. Brandy took her time sniffing and checking out every tree. Finally, she squatted and pooped. Lalani headed back to the train and Brandy peed just before the steps. As she waited, she noticed Harry board a few cars forward, at her car. Now she didn't mind waiting, even though she was cold, if it meant missing Harry.

As the whistle blew, they climbed aboard leaving the lantern on the rear platform where the conductor said he would retrieve it. She walked up through the two cars and glanced through the glass door to her car to see if Harry was at her door. There he stood, waiting. *Darn! He didn't get the message from Brandy and me that I wasn't interested anymore.* She went back through the second train car hoping there was an empty compartment she could wait in, but no luck. *I will just have to confront him and tell him I'm not interested.* She walked back through the car and slowly opened the first door stepping between the two cars and reached for the other door. Harry was still there. She waited but it was narrow for her and Brandy on the landing. She opened the door, just then Harry turned away from her and headed back towards his train car. She put her hand on Brandy's head to keep her quiet. If she growled, he would turn around. She stood motionless, holding her breath, waiting until he had left the car. She then quickly walked to her compartment and entered, locking the door again.

She was cold and wished she had some hot tea. Suddenly, there was a knock on the door causing her to jump. Brandy stood ears forward ready to growl. "Warm towel for washing?" called the porter. Lalani gave a sigh, and unlocked the door and took two hot towels from the tray. They were warm and comforting against her cold hand and cheeks. She finally undressed to her undergarments and pulled the bed out and slipped under the blanket.

The train continued its steady speed through the night, lulling its passengers to sleep, to a rhythmic click, click, click and rocking motion as the wheels moved along the track. The train pulled into Cheyenne just after seven the next morning. She stayed in her compartment as long as possible hoping to miss Harry's departure. But she needed to walk Brandy. She slipped off the rear of the train and away from the platform. Brandy was quick about her business this morning, and as the whistle blew, they were back on board. Now it would only be two more days and she would be home.

She asked the porter to bring a light breakfast to her, if he had time. In about an hour he showed up with two hard boiled eggs, a biscuit and coffee. She gave the two eggs to Brandy and poured water into the basin for her to drink, while she enjoyed the biscuit and coffee.

Once again, she sat watching the scenery, as the train headed up into the mountains. There were snow-capped peaks against the brilliant blue sky and thick green pines. She sat petting Brandy's head laying in her lap. *I'm glad you were here last night. I'd hate to think what he would have done if you weren't... and yet there was Philippe and Marseille. There were moments when he had gone further than appropriate, putting his hands on my waist and kissing me in the back garden. I was so young and naïve, but it was so exciting to have his attention and he was beautiful.*

No wonder Horace whisked me away. Who knows what would have happened back then? At least I'm not naïve anymore.

When the train reached Elko, Nevada the next day, she wanted to send a telegram to Jim confirming her arrival time into Oak Ridge. The porter said Elko was no place for a lady. The many saloons were full of rude unemployed rail layers and prospectors that never made it big. She gave the young porter a quarter to send the telegram for her. She stayed close to the depot when she walked Brandy. She could see the dusty drabby little town and men idly milling around on the wood boardwalk outside every saloon. She was glad Oak Ridge had not appeared so hopeless when she first saw it. Now she would appreciate it even more when she got there.

Oak Ridge was a growing western town. The train station was at the north end of town, near the livestock pens. There was a doctor's office, apothecary shop and a dress shop. The lands records office and one of the big hotels were across the way on the main street. Another larger hotel was down the street aways. There was the saloon, busy mostly on Friday nights, and a local bank and general store across the street from each other. There was also a saddle and gun shop, next to the barbershop. The livery stable and jail were at the far end of town. There was no courthouse since Oak Ridge wasn't the county seat. The courthouse was two towns to the north about an hour by train. Local working people came and went in a civilized manner. There were two churches: the Catholic and the Protestant, and for the most part, the congregations got along well. The Catholic church had the organ while the Protestant church had a small grand piano. Lalani liked her town and felt comfortable walking alone there. The ranch was only twenty minutes southwest of town.

On the last day of travel, Lalani woke early and the porter brought fresh water for her to wash with and then returned with hot tea and a biscuit and a sausage for Brandy. She became excited, like a little kid, as the train pulled into the Oak Ridge station. She stood on the train landing, straining to see if Jim was waiting. There he was at the end of the platform, wearing his usual blue plaid shirt and his brown cowboy hat. He spotted her about the same time, and smiles and waves went in both directions. Jim met her at the landing step and taking her by the waist lifted her across onto the platform. Brandy came bounding down behind her.

"You made it safe and sound. I'm so glad to have you home," Jim said, giving her a friendly kiss to the cheek as he released her.

"I'm happy to be home and to see you too. I've missed you," she said smiling and taking his arm as they walked off the platform.

Jim had brought the carriage, and not the work wagon, thinking it would be nicer for Lalani. The porter brought her luggage, and Jim managed to tie the small trunk to the back. Brandy had run into the pens to do her business and was now jumping at Jim's feet for her greeting. "Yes, Brandy, I'm happy to see you too."

"There she is. Welcome home, Lalani," Morgan said reaching out and giving her a hug. Morgan was Kate's brother-in-law and Jim's best friend.

"Morgan, what a surprise. I didn't expect both of you," Lalani said.

"Jim said you would be home today and I had business in town, so here I am. Aren't you glad to see me? How was the trip?"

"Of course, I'm glad to see you, and the trip was long," she replied.

"Mother thought you would be tired and would like to have you both for dinner tonight. We are eager to hear about your trip and how Katherine and Clay are doing. Beside she didn't want you to have to endure cooking on your first night back."

"Great, there's not much food at the house. You've been away so long I ate what was there and I didn't know what to get. I've been living off beans and bacon the past two weeks," Jim beamed.

"Well, I guess we accept, but I would love to get home and clean up and rest."

Jim helped Lalani into the carriage and then joined her. Morgan headed off to complete his errand at the bank. Brandy jumped in the back next to the suitcase, holding her head out in the fresh air as the carriage moved down the main road out of town. Once on the road to the ranch, Lalani put her hand through Jim's arm and onto his big hand. She shouldn't be so friendly, but she couldn't help herself. She was so happy to be almost home and back in his company.

Brandy leaped from the carriage as soon as she saw the house from the hill and ran full out to the horse paddock and was soon barking at the mares. Jim pulled up to the house and lifted Lalani down from the carriage.

"I tried to clean the dust away and sweep the floors but I'm not sure I did much good, other than rearrange the dust," Jim said as he carried in her luggage. He returned with the trunk and carried it upstairs to her room. Lalani took off her bonnet and wandered around, opening the drapes and windows to let in the crisp April air. She walked into her kitchen and spotted the kettle, and was filling it with water when Jim walked in. He automatically reached for some wood and started the stove to heat the water. On the table was a basket of fresh bread.

"Mrs. Taylor must have sent it over. You know I can't make bread look that good," Jim said. He pulled Lalani's favorite tea cup and his large mug from the cupboard and set them on the small table.

She looked out the kitchen window and could see Jim had plowed the area for her vegetable garden, and the chickens were locked in their coop.

They settled at the table, not missing a beat, as if she had never left. She thanked him for getting the garden ready. She was most anxious to get it going. She wondered why the hens were cooped up.

"There has been a pesky coyote around the last week. I'm afraid she got a Rhode Island Red. I stopped her from taking the Plymouth Rock hen. I shored up the wire fencing so she can't get in. I only let them out around noon. Getting them back in the coop has been an afternoon chore. Hopefully Brandy can take over now she's back."

Lalani chuckled as she imagined Jim chasing chickens. They were her birds, and all she had to do was call and show them some grain, and they came running. They talked for a short while, then Jim said he needed to get some work done and Lalani wanted to unpack, bathe and rest before going to the Taylors. Jim put the large waterpot on the stove and then carried cool water to the tub so it would be there when she was ready.

Lalani watched Jim head to the barn, *I'm glad Jim's here at the ranch, especially after all the strange men I encountered on this past trip.* She was content with Jim and felt safe having him there.

Now that Katherine was no longer at the house and it was her house alone, she thought about changing a few things around to suit her. Katherine had taken two pieces of furniture from the parlor: a large wingback chair and her piano, which left a rather gaping empty space. There was still the French style settee and one wingback chair. *I've never had my own home to decorate or set up the way I want. I will want to get a smaller woman's chair and maybe a small game table where Jim and I can play cards in the evening. I would like to bring my rocking chair down from my room too. I should have brought a few more trinkets from France when I was there. My little Eiffel tower will look lonely by itself. But first things first – a bath!*

She spent the morning taking care of her own needs. She unpacked, airing out some of the dresses that didn't need washing and putting the things that did in a large basket that would wait until tomorrow. Then she carried hot water up to the tub and prepared her bath. She made two trips for water, wanting to fill it extra full. It had been five days since she had soaked and washed thoroughly. She had never had all the time to herself, to set her own schedule. Not having to hurry with her bath felt strange. She had to keep reminding herself there was no one else to look after. No one needed her now. *I don't know if I should be glad or sad. I feel sad that no one needs me anymore. Lalani, you just wait, when Katherine returns you will have plenty to do. Or maybe not, I don't work for her any more, but we are best of friends. You will just have to wait and see. For now, enjoy the bath and let things come as they may.*

Jim brought the carriage up to the house where Lalani stood waiting. She felt refreshed, and her clean dark hair glistened in the setting sunlight. She wore a simple green and lavender cotton dress with a gathered bodice. "You look lovely," Jim said as he came around and assisted her up. The Taylor's were delighted to see both of them. Jim knew it was Lalani they wanted to talk to the most, but was glad for the invitation.

Lalani told them all about the plans for selling and dividing up the big estate manor that Katherine no longer wanted. Also, about the conversion of the London house to a music school for concert pianist and violinist. How she enjoyed being at their friend's estate in the country. They all enjoyed going to the theater to see the Gilbert and Sullivan operas, especially Jessie. The operas were silly, lighthearted musicals, and fun. After a month, when plans were mostly settled, the three of them went on to Charles' place outside of Paris. Katherine and Clay only stayed for a few days and then left for Vienna. Lalani told them all about the Eiffel Tower, how the Parisians thought it was a monstrosity and how she climbed the 328 steps to the first level. From there you could see all of Paris. "It was so high up. I wasn't brave enough to climb the 674 steps to the second level. It would be like standing in the clouds.

"After two weeks of being spoiled by Charles and his mother and not having anything to do, but sightsee and read, I was ready to come home. So here I am," she said smiling. *I did enjoy visiting with Charles' mother.*

Dinner was then served. Again, Lalani felt strange sitting at the Taylor table without Katherine. Mrs. Taylor had prepared game hens, with wild rice and some of the last pickled cucumbers. Lalani told them about the amazing French sauces and patés, and that Clay was taken by Charles' vineyards, warning Morgan he would want to bring back some of the French variety of wine grapes.

After dinner, Mrs. Taylor wanted to show Lalani the house addition of the west wing that would be for Katherine and Clay. She and Morgan were glad to have it done. "The noise and dust went on for weeks," Mrs. Taylor explained.

Lalani graciously declined, "I would like to see it with Katherine and share in her excitement, if you don't mind." They then settled in the study by the fire. Morgan and Jim talked about spring roundup and branding, that if Clay didn't get home soon, Morgan was going to have to hire a new foreman. Jim added that Katherine needed to start halter breaking the yearlings soon, if she didn't want them completely wild and have twice the difficulty. The yearlings were ten-months-old and had been weaned for some time. Morgan teased Lalani about having to learn how to raise horses since she lived on the ranch. "I'll leave the breeding and training to Katherine and Jim. I'll stay with making mash for the foals and growing carrots for the mares." She admitted she loved watching the foals in the paddock outside the parlor window, but was afraid of Medianoche, the stallion.

The conversation then turned to planting the spring gardens and alfalfa. Jim had to buy the alfalfa for the yearlings last winter and didn't want to have to do it in the future. Morgan and Jim discussed alfalfa seed, while Mrs. Taylor and Lalani talked about lettuce and beans. The evening grew late, and it had been a long day for Lalani. She and Jim said thank you for the delicious meal and she said, "Katherine and Clay should be in St Petersburg, if Maestro Korsakov agreed to see them. If he was still mad about her not showing up for the Bonn concert and declined her visit, then they should be home in two more weeks. They planned to return to Charles for a few days and then back to London for a few more before boarding the ship out of Southampton."

Mrs. Taylor gave Lalani a gentle hug and said she enjoyed the evening and hoped she and Jim would attend the barn dance at the Olsens on Friday. Jim lit the carriage lanterns and placed a blanket over Lalani's lap and headed for home. Lalani snuggled up to Jim to stay warm, and he liked having her close, though he said nothing of the sort.

3

Taking Charge

Lalani found herself at home doing the things she normally did, washing clothes, airing out bed linens, and cooking, but this time it was for her and no one else. Jim washed his own clothes and kept the bunkhouse himself. Jim was glad to have homecooked meals again, sharing dinner and supper with Lalani. In the morning he fixed his own eggs and bacon, but came up to the house to see if Lalani needed anything and would join her for a cup of coffee before starting the day's work.

Now that things were clean, she wanted to move things around. Katherine had used the big master bedroom and insisted Lalani take it. Lalani preferred her bed to the one Katherine had. Lalani's was an English sleigh bed and the other a French provincial. Katherine had taken her dressing table and Lalani would need to get her own. Lalani liked that the master bedroom had its own entrance to the tub room, and she wouldn't have to go through the hall anymore. Lalani went through the house, making a list of things that needed to be moved and things that needed to be purchased.

First thing was to move the beds. Jim disassembled them and carried the pieces to their new room, and reassembled them. Doing Lalani's first, he moved her heavy rocking chair to the parlor, where the other wingback chair had been. By dinner time, Jim was ready for a hearty meal, and Lalani had roasted chicken and mashed potatoes waiting. With the big things moved, Jim went on to do his normal ranch chores.

Lalani went upstairs and proceeded to move her clothes and things to her new room. When she left Hawaii as a young child, her mother had given her a few family items, which she carefully moved from one place to the next. Now they finally had a permanent home, and she wanted to display them. There was her mother's blue and white Hawaiian breadfruit quilt, to bring abundance to her. She carefully washed it and laid it out to dry. This she would put on the top of her bed.

There were also two dark gourds that her mother used when she did the native dances and the conch shell her father blew at the beginning of harvest. A comb made from coconut shell her father had given her and a white piece of catspaw coral. Finally, a small battered woven basket, but inside was a Hawaiian printed white fabric her mother had given her to use as her wedding dress someday. Lalani took out the fabric and carefully unwrapped it. It was a silky cotton, still white. Around the base was a row of black ink chevron patterns, representing the mountains. Above them floated small flowers as if showering down on the mountains. Below were two rows of curled waves with patterned turtles and manta rays interspersed. This her mother had carefully made, and gave it to her daughter, right before Lalani was taken by the Crockers. Lalani held the cloth with great yearning. *I wish I had met a wonderful man and had made the dress. Now I am barren and too old to honor the fabric she made.* A tear came to her cheek as she tenderly folded the fabric and put it back in the basket, and placed it on the top shelf in the large armoire. She ran the comb through her hair and then placed it on her nightstand. She took the two gourds, conch shell and coral downstairs to the parlor and placed them on the mantle next to her Eiffel tower. She retrieved two English silver candlesticks and placed one on each end of the mantel.

She had so little to show how much of the world she had seen. She never brought trinkets from Sydney, Bombay, Cape Town, Granada,

Greece, France, Vienna, St. Petersburg, or Prague. All these places, she had travelled with Edith and Katherine. Suddenly she remembered the postcards she had bought. She had a small box of cards, up in the bottom of her night stand. She brought them downstairs and sat in the rocking chair, fondly looked at each one. There were eleven total: The London Tower, the Parthenon in Greece, the Sacre Coeur de Montmartre in Paris, the Alhambra fortress in Granada, the castle in Prague, and the Colosseum in Rome, and a Koala bear from Australia. The last card was the oldest. Edith had bought it for her. *I don't recall much, but I do remember the sleepy Koala and the Kangaroo they had at the Botanic Garden in Sydney. I begged to take a koala home, that I'd stop crying if I only had a koala. She bought me the card instead and I only cried half as much.*

One by one she looked at the pictures again. Bombay with an elephant and Cape Town with its harbor and sailing ships. She was in these places only briefly, as the Crockers made their way from Sydney to London. *The people in Bombay wore colorful clothes and it was so crowded. I wouldn't believe Horace when he said the elephants were real and so big, until we went to a nearby temple with elephant statues. In Cape Town, the servants, like the Hawaiians, carried their goods in baskets on their heads or shoulders. I had never seen so many people with darker skin than mine. I was quite afraid in those towns, and begged Edith not to leave me at the hotel alone. Fortunately, Horace agreed it was too dangerous.* Horace had bought these cards for Lalani, since the first card had made her happy.

She picked up the London card. It too was from her first time there with the Crockers. *Horace in a teasing manner always said he'd leave me at the tower, if I weren't good. Edith would get so mad at him.* She picked up the card of the Parthenon. *Now there were a lot of steps. It's hard to imagine it was built so long ago and yet still so impressive.* She laid it down and picked up the card from Paris. *Aww, the white church on the hill, you could see all of Paris from there. Neither Edith nor I were inspired to attend a catholic mass but it was beautiful inside. I guess Paris is a city you need to see from above. It seemed much bigger this time from the Eiffel tower.* She laughed, *Paris has far too many steps, but I have to admit it is one of my favorite places.*

As she picked up the card from Granada, it held bittersweet memories. *I never really appreciated Granada. I was so heartbroken over losing Philippe. Edith dragged me to so many places, trying to get my mind off him. I don't remember much. I do recall the Alhambra and the walled gardens with the long shallow pools. It was a type of garden I had never seen before. We did have a lovely afternoon tea there. That's where I got this card.*

She quickly looked at the card from Prague and Rome. *Prague square was so fun with its shops, and the pink marble cathedral was breathtaking. Rome not so much. The Colosseum was too old and such cruelty.* The card from Vienna was the newest, bought when there with Katherine. *Vienna was fun, a charming city.*

In the very bottom was a small piece of paper. It was a note from Philippe, written in French. She never knew what it said, but dreamed that it was a love note, a poem sent to her the night before she was whisked away to Granada. She sat holding the cards and notes, so many places, so long ago. *A lifetime ago and I barely remember being in these actual places. I wish I had written a journal to remind me of the feel and aroma of each place. Now I look at these photos and recall only vague glimmers of being there.* As the afternoon sun began to stream through the front windows, she stood, gathering up the cards. She went to the kitchen and found a small woven basket and put the cards in it and brought it back to the parlor, placing it on the small writing desk at the window. *This is an appropriate place for postcards.* She put Philippe's letter in her pocket to put back upstairs later. She looked around the scarcely decorated room. *It doesn't say much about who I am, but it's a start.*

The evenings were still cool. Lalani could hear Jim's evening knock at the kitchen door. He always knocked and never just came in, but waited for Lalani to open the door. Jim stood with an armful of wood for the parlor and smiled, then went and started the fire. He noticed right away the gourds and candlesticks. Lalani brought a tray with cold chicken and biscuits along with hot coffee. Jim sat in the wingback chair and Lalani in the rocker. They talked about the things she had set out and then to practical things, like how she wanted her garden laid out. He would furrow the rows for planting in the morning after feeding the horses. It would be ready for planting in a few weeks when the rains eased.

That night Lalani lay in her bed in the big north master bedroom. She could hear Brandy sleeping by the fireplace and was glad she was there. *I have become dependent on that dog being nearby. I will hate to have to give her back to Katherine when she returns.*

Lalani rose early the next morning ready to work outside in the chicken coop and helping with the yearling that needed moving from the barn corral to the south paddock. Jim had divided the large south paddock into two areas, in order to accommodate the foals weaning process. They needed to be separated from their mothers and still be able to see and touch them through the fence, but not be able to nurse. After a few weeks the mares would be moved back to the north paddock. When weaning wasn't happening, the two south paddocks would be used to separate the yearlings and the two-year-olds.

Lalani knew trousers would be more practical for working around the ranch, but she just couldn't bring herself to wear them. Even as a small child she wore the native Hawaiian shifts. She had two outdoor work dresses, for helping with the horses and working in the garden. They were sturdy cotton, the skirt not too full, and the hems were about two inches shorter than normal. This helped prevent stepping on the shirt and made working on her knees easier. Dressed in her simple brown dress and working boots, she set about her usual feeding of the chickens and collecting the eggs.

Jim milked Cleo and put the milk in the outdoor cooler. Then together they went to the corral to fetch the three yearlings. They would come to Lalani easily when they saw she had a bucket of oats. She sat on the mounting step with the bucket in her lap and would slip a halter around their muzzle and over their ears as each came to feed. Jim would then step up and clip the bottom strap closed. Ever since the yearlings had been two months old, this had been the routine. Jim clipped a short lead rope onto the first filly and now the tug of war began. Lalani had the corral gate ajar ready to open it when Jim got the first filly close. The filly whinnied and pranced against the lead, not wanting to leave the others. Jim's strong grip pulled her down, and with another hand full of grain, she stepped through the gate. Lalani closed it quickly so the others couldn't escape. Jim would walk the filly out to the south paddock, close the gate, and then unclip the lead. They would repeat this little routine until all three were down in the south paddock. The yearlings would charge up one end and back down the large paddock, now that they were able to run. They held their heads up sniffing at the air, getting acquainted with their new surroundings. Later in the day Lalani would go down with an alfalfa mash bucket and as they fed, she removed the halters.

When they finished, she was anxious to work her garden patch that Jim would plow after the noon meal. Six long rows were what she wanted. The outside rows she would plant with marigolds, lavender, and basil, all which repel most of the bugs. The four interior rows would be for beans, squash, cucumbers, carrots and radishes. She wanted to plant romaine lettuce and cabbage, but needed to figure out how to keep the rabbits out first.

Morgan dropped by to see how Lalani was doing and laughed when he saw her ankle-deep in mud, walking around the garden. He'd come to ask Jim when he planned to plow the large alfalfa and hay fields and would need to borrow the plow horses. It would be in a few days. The garden came first. Morgan also reminded them about the barn dance at the Olsens and that they would be expected. "Your bread pudding would be most welcome, too," he added, knowing she would add a little rum to it.

Jim was true to his word and had brought up horse manure to spread on the garden to be plowed in. By midweek the garden was ready for planting and Jim had brought the plow horses up from the

Taylor ranch. By Friday he had half the alfalfa field plowed. But now it was time to clean up and escort Lalani to the dance. Lalani, with her dark hair and skin, glowed in the soft light as she and Jim entered the Olsen's barn. She looked pretty in the soft lavender dress with lace around the neck. Mr. Olsen snatched up the bread pudding as soon as he saw it. Several of the ladies came up and welcomed her home.

The music began to play and Jim immediately asked her for the first dance. He wasn't the best dancer, but he did manage to keep his big feet off her toes. Morgan took his turn dancing with her as did a few of the other men, married and single. This was a delightful evening where she could be herself and not worry about stepping beyond her position as she often did at the galas in London. She was among friends, hard-working unpretentious friends. At one point she strolled outside to see the stars between the thunderclouds that were moving in. "Don't worry. It won't rain until after midnight, and I will have you home by then," Jim said as he came up next to her.

"I don't mind getting wet. I loved to play in the rain as a little girl. It would rain a lot in Hawaii."

"You seem to be thinking a lot about Hawaii since you brought out the gourds. Do you think you will go back someday?"

"I have been recalling the island, but it has been twenty-five years since I was there as a little girl. I may look Hawaiian but I can't say I think like a Hawaiian. It might be nice to go back someday, but there is no one there for me anymore. Even my village is gone, bought up by the Europeans. I'm not sure I would like the Honolulu that is there today. Oak Ridge is my home and I like being here, with these good people, with you," she said smiling and taking his arm. "I do miss seeing the ocean, and summer is way too hot. But tonight is lovely."

He patted her hand, "I'm glad you're happy here. I missed you more than you could imagine, when you were gone. I have become very fond of you. I know I work for you, but I feel I work more with you at the ranch."

"Jim, you don't work for me, you work for Katherine. You're simply with me at the ranch."

Before he could say more, Mr. Olsen interrupted and said they'd best come in for the last dance. Soon after, everyone began to depart. Miranda Taylor invited Lalani to join her and Evelyn for tea on the morrow, before Evelyn and Eric returned to San Francisco.

The next day was cloudy and threatened rain. Lalani kept the invitation to tea and arrived with homemade scones to add to the gathering. Evelyn invited her to stay with them, that she should come to San Francisco and order the furniture she needed. Evelyn knew of two excellent carpenters that made beautiful tables and wardrobes. There was a clap of thunder, and Lalani felt she needed to get home before it began to pour and the stream rose. Morgan brought the carriage with Prince Philip hitched and ready. "Are you sure you want to go now, maybe the rain will let up and it would be better to go late. Do you want me to go with you," Morgan said as he helped her up.

"No, the rain is not going to stop and if I go now, I can still cross the stream and get home. I'll be fine. A little rain won't hurt a Hawaiian like me."

She gave Prince Philip a tap with the reins and the carriage jerked forward. The rain was hitting the back of the carriage, so Lalani wasn't getting soaked. The dirt road was quickly turning to mud, so she gave Philip another tap and he picked up the pace, and the carriage wheels ran through the watery mud, leaving a muddy spray in its rear.

Lalani came to the stream that separated the Taylor Ranch from the Circle K. The stream bed was fairly wide but the actual water flow was usually narrow and more like a creek. Now as she approached the stream, she could see the water had widened to the width of the streambed and was flowing at a much faster pace. It didn't look deep at the center, so she tapped Prince Philip and he began to cross. He slipped slightly on a few stones but kept moving forward. Suddenly the right wheel dropped into a small pool and Prince Philip stopped mid-stream. Lalani tapped him several time to get Prince Philip to continue moving forward, but the wheel was stuck in the mud and rocks. She tried again to get him to pull the carriage out, but it didn't move. Lalani shook her head and frowned. *Just my luck. I don't think I can't get it out myself, I'm not strong enough. I'll just have to unhitch Prince Philip and maybe I can ride him the rest of the way home. Or perhaps I'll just walk him, it's only a little more than a mile at this point.*

She slipped off her shoes and stockings, as the slightly heeled shoes would be more of a problem than help. She climbed down into the cold water, that came to about the middle of her calf. Her dress clung to her legs, making it difficult to move. Holding onto the carriage whiffletree, she unhitched the horse harness on the left. Then making her way around to the right, she gave a pull at the wheel, but it barely moved. She slipped in the hole and went down, catching herself with her hand. The rain had already drenched her, and the cold stream water chilled her body. She grabbed the carriage whiffletree and unhitched the right side of the harness. Prince Philip moved forward pushing the carriage shaft towards Lalani, catching her on the side and causing her to slip again.

She grabbed for the carriage shaft as she went down. The flow of the water had deepened and she found herself being pushed by the carriage down into the rocky pool. Her foot slid into a boulder as the carriage slid sideways, sending a sharp pain to her ankle. She was parallel to the carriage and she grabbed the wheel in an attempt to push it away and prevent falling face first into the water. Her left foot went deep into the mud, bringing the boulder down on it, just missing her right foot which she had pushed forward to keep her from falling. She was still standing, mostly on her right foot, but she was stuck between the large rock and the wheel. The boulder wasn't huge but big enough that she couldn't move it. She tried pulling her foot loose, but her ankle ground against the unmovable rock, sending a cringing pain through her, yet the cold water quickly numbed the sting. The carriage had caught her at the wrong angle to be able to turn around or to move behind the boulder to try pulling from that direction.

She was cold, wet and quickly become tired and overwhelmed. The water had risen to her knees and she feared it would get higher. She leaned her head against the carriage, but the added weight put pressure on her ankle. There she stood in the middle of the stream soaking wet, chilled to the bone. All she could do was hope someone would come. She looked around for any sign of help, but not even Prince Philip could be seen. *Please tell me, the horse went home to the barn and Jim will find him. Horses always go home to the barn and not to the bar for a drink. Right about now, I sure could use...I could use an elephant from Bombay.*

The horse had taken off and indeed had headed to the barn. Prince Philip came walking into the yard, with the harness straps dangling. Brandy started barking from the house as she heard Prince Philip wander in. Jim came from the barn to see why Brandy was upset. Immediately Jim became worried, seeing only the horse and no carriage. He reached for Prince Philip and saw the harness, not broken, but unhitched. Prince Philip followed Jim into the barn. Jim grabbed his rain slicker and quickly saddled his horse, Buck, and headed out the main road to the Taylor ranch. Left unattended, Prince Philip wandered into his stall to feed on the hay. Brandy stood inside at the door barking, wanting to go with Jim.

Lalani had tried to free herself by pushing the wheel away, but it wouldn't budge. Her free leg was now numb and at an angle. There was nothing she could do. Finally, exhausted, she gathered her skirt around her free leg, and she kneeled down on that knee trying to take pressure off the trapped foot. It helped slightly, but now more of her body sank into the deepening cold water. The sun was still covered by clouds, but had not set. The air was warmer than the water and she rubbed her hands together in an attempt to keep them from becoming numb, too. It was all she could think to do. She knew she would be in trouble if help didn't come before nightfall. She had never been so trapped and helpless. Tears ran down her cheeks, but you couldn't tell them from the rain still falling. *I feel like an anemone at low tide, all I can do is curl up and wait to bake to death, or in this case freeze into an ice sculpture. Oh sweet Lord, send help, bring me Jim!*

Jim rode quickly searching frantically for any signs of Lalani. It only took him fifteen minutes to come to the stream. He motioned Buck into the water, and lighting off Buck, landed just behind Lalani. Lalani was too exhausted to reach up to Jim. Jim quickly realized the problem and wanted to pull the boulder back, but was afraid it would cause Lalani to fall, and then the carriage to fall on top of her as everything shifted. Jim took Buck to the other side of the carriage and tied a lanyard from the saddle to the carriage, hoping it would hold the carriage in place. Going back to Lalani, he kneeled down so Lalani could lean over his back. Then he reached down and pushed the boulder back and away, as the water buffeted him in the face. Lalani let out a small groan, and Jim could feel she was free. He stood, lifting Lalani over his shoulder and carefully walked back to the shore. Setting her down, she was shaking, though she seemed unharmed other than her ankle. He waded back into the stream and retrieved Buck, leaving the carriage as it stood.

Jim now had only one urgent thing to do, get Lalani home, to dry warmth. He lifted her up into the saddle like a bag of flour, as she was barely conscious. He swung up behind her and turned her into his arms and headed towards the ranch. Reaching the house, Brandy began barking again. Jim swung down off Buck and carried Lalani in and up to her room. Brandy following close behind.

Jim and Lalani were both drenched, and Lalani began to shiver as he set her on a chair. Jim knew he had to get her out of the wet clothes, and get her warm. He began to undo her dress and strip it off. Prim and proper privacy had to be done away with, as she was now violently shaking and too weak to do it herself.

Brandy pranced around them desperately, and Jim angrily told her to get out. Brandy obediently went and sat at the door. Jim was still wet, his clothes still dripping. He removed his shirt and proceeded to remove the rest of Lalani's wet clothes. Now she was bare, except for her pantaloons, and he grabbed towels and wrapped her up, pulling the final wet undergarments and drying her, before putting her into her bed. Lalani, now unaware of where she was and what was happening, Jim called for Brandy to come to him and patted the bed, encouraging her to jump up and lie next to Lalani, hoping Brandy's body heat would help warm her. Ignoring that he was still wet and cold, Jim made a fire in the fireplace. He then went and started the stove and put the waterpot on. If he couldn't get her warm, he would put her into a hot bath.

Back upstairs, Jim took a towel and wrapped her wet hair, and then began to rub her legs and arms under the quilt to try and warm her. Brandy lay quietly with her head near Lalani's shoulder.

Lalani opened her eyes and gave a slight sigh when she saw Jim there taking care of her. *Thank God, you found me.* She began to shake and her teeth rattled too much to be able to say anything. Jim went to the fireplace and retrieved two warming bricks, wrapping them in towels and placed them at Lalani's feet. She gave a wince of pain as he moved her left ankle. He carefully uncovered just her foot to see if it was broken. It didn't look broken but was quite bruised. He covering her back up, gently rubbing her arms and legs again, and she attempted a half smile. She could feel Brandy next to her as well.

Lalani nodded her head and managed in a shaky whisper, "Thank you, I'll be alright once I'm warm."

He gently stroked her forehead, "I'll be right back."

He went to the kitchen and took a dishtowel and tore it into long strips. The pot on the stove was now hot and he took a moment to make a cup of hot tea, adding a dash of brandy. He spotted one of his work shirts Lalani had mended, hanging on a hook by the back door. He snatched it up and partially put it on, then gathered up the strips and tea and went back to Lalani. He kneeled next to the bed, as his pants were still wet, and lifted her up enough for her to sip the hot tea. "Slowly, it's hot."

She took a sip and gave a slight cough, not expecting the brandy. It felt warm going down through her body. She took another sip, and she began to relax and the shaking faded away. Jim removed the towel from her wet hair, now much drier, and adjusted her pillows so she was upright just a bit. Brandy stood, circled once and lay back down close to Lalani's side.

Jim took the towel strips and began to carefully wrap her ankle to give it support. Lalani winced once or twice. Her feet were still cold, so she really didn't feel the cloth. Once Jim was done, he warmed his hands at the fire and came back and held her feet in his warm hands. He reheated the bricks and placed them back, finally tucking her in again with another quilt on top. The room was now warm and Lalani said she felt better.

She looked at Jim, standing by her bed, his hair was slicked back but drier, the shirt still unbuttoned, and his trousers, still quite wet, clinging to his legs. Jim at one point had removed his wet boots. His socks were soaked from the dripping trousers. "Jim, you're still wet, you must go get changed and warm up too, before you catch cold. What would Katherine say if she found both of us with pneumonia?"

Jim smiled and then felt her hands and feet. They were warmer. "Alright, but I'll be right back. I'll make some warm broth. Don't you go anywhere. Brandy, stay!" He said with a wink.

Jim headed out to change when he saw Buck still standing in the rain where he had left him. He grabbed his reins and lead him to the barn, where he found Prince Philip still in harness gear. He took care of both horses and rubbed Buck down with a dry towel, and gave them a small bucket of grain along with their hay. Then he slipped out to his place and changed. He had to admit his feet were pretty cold, and dry socks felt good. He put on his Sunday boots as his others would take a day or two to dry. Putting a dry poncho on, he grabbed some dry wood from his place and headed back to the house. In the kitchen, the pot of hot water was still quite warm. He took a piece of beef jerky from the pantry and put it in a bowl of warm water, letting it steep for a few minutes. He took a few biscuits and placed them in the upper stove warmer. Then he took the wood up to Lalani's room and stoked up the fire. Lalani was now sleeping. He wanted to check to see if her feet were warm, but was afraid of waking her. Instead, he felt her forehead, which was warm but not hot, and then tucked the quilt back up around her, patting Brandy on the head as she lay there too. He went back downstairs to retrieve the biscuits and broth.

With Lalani sleeping, Jim took a moment and made coffee and sat at the kitchen table holding a cup, as he thought about Lalani and how horrible it would have been if he had not gotten to her in time. When she was up and around again, he would have a good talking to her about going out in pouring rain. *She should have spent the night at the Taylors. I don't understand why Morgan let her go home. I knew it was going to rain, I should have taken her myself.* Jim was mad and wanted to take it out on someone, even himself.

Jim didn't want to leave Lalani alone, in case a fever arose. He carried her large rocking chair back upstairs and put it by the fire, then sat and watched her sleeping, dozing off and on himself. After several hours, Lalani began to stir again. He went back down and retrieved the biscuits and broth and brought it up. Lalani was now awake, and he helped her drink the warm broth. She wasn't interested in the biscuits, but was happy to see Jim eat them with great gusto. Lalani was now warm and realized she was only covered by blankets and not wearing a nightgown. She looked at Jim and then tugged at the blanket with a you-did-this kind of look.

Jim blushed and nodded his head. "I'm sorry, but it was necessary. I had to get you out of the wet clothes, you were so cold. No one needs to know but us."

"I think that's a good idea, I'll just say I managed to change. If you would be so kind as to bring me a nightgown from the bureau, I'll feel better," she said pointing to the top drawer. Jim opened the drawer and pulled out a soft pink gown, holding it up for approval. Lalani nodded. Jim brought it to her and gathered up the gown and slipped it over her head. Then turning his back, she managed to slip into the sleeves. Leaning forward was tiring, and the gown only went partly down.

"Jim, I'm too tired to get it down over me. Can you help me stand so it will fall properly?"

Jim blushed as Lalani reached up to hold on to him as he lifted her out of bed. She stepped down on her left foot and immediately crumbled from the pain into Jim's chest, but he lifted her back off it. The gown only slid half way down just past her buttocks, being caught up in his big hands. Jim looked down seeing Lalani's bare legs again as he adjusted his hands. Lalani put down her right foot, and Jim helped her balance as the gown slid the rest of the way down. He then lifted her up in his arms and laid her carefully back in bed. He couldn't help notice the softness of her body as he lifted her and laid her down. The cotton gown lay smooth against her body, as he covered her up, again noticing her feminine curves. Brandy returning to her spot on the bed brought him back to reality.

"You are a pretty woman, Lalani," he said blushing.

"Jim, if you tell anyone what went on here, I'll call you a liar and say that I managed all on my own," she smirked with a stern stare.

"It's our secret, I assure you," he said smiling. He made sure she was comfortable and warm, placing newly heated bricks near her feet. He swept her hair away from her face and felt her forehead for any indication of fever. She was warm, but not overly warm, and she wasn't coughing, which reassured him she would be alright.

"You get some sleep. I'll stay in the guest room tonight and check in on you." Lalani nodded and closed her eyes.

The sun had set hours ago, but her room was warm. He put another log on the fire and took the supper tray back to the kitchen. He took a moment and washed up the bowls and spoons. The fire in the stove had gone cold. Jim spotted Brandy's food bowl empty sitting on the floor. He went to the food bin that held her food and clanked her bowl against it. He filled it and put it back and put fresh water in the other bowl. Brandy did not come. He walked to the bottom of the stairs and called her. Brandy was hungry but didn't want to leave. Jim called again, and she finally responded. "Come on girl, you need to eat. Your mistress will be fine." Brandy followed Jim to the kitchen and gobbled down her food. Then they both went back upstairs, Jim sat in the rocker and Brandy curled up on the floor at his feet.

Jim watched the fire flames flicker as he thought about Lalani. He had missed her when she was in Europe. And now as he attended to her, he felt even a deeper love for her, thinking briefly about how pretty her body felt in his hands. They were not young teenagers and didn't look for great beauty. But suddenly he saw her splendor as a desirable woman. Feeling guilt for needing to put her into that compromising circumstance, he quickly squelched the thought of desire. He thought about her gentleness and her love for people that had drawn him to her instead, or at least tried to.

He rose and checked her forehead. She was warm and now running a slight fever. He took a wet cloth and laid it on her forehead. She woke and grinned at Jim. He helped her to drink some water, and then she fell back to sleep. He stayed and sat in the rocker for the rest of the night, checking the fever, but it didn't seem to be getting worse. Occasionally he slept.

4

═══════════

Katherine Returns

For the next few days, Jim was very attentive to Lalani, happy that her cold was gone and making sure she didn't overdo using the crutches. Lalani got after him for drifting in and out of the house to check up on her. Occasionally, he made comments about when they were married or asked what kind of wedding she wanted. But he was good and didn't go too far as to ask when. Most of the time Lalani politely ignored his teasing or said she hadn't taken the time to think about a wedding yet.

Lalani was just happy to be back in her kitchen, with help from the crutches. The doctor said it would be another week before she could go without them. Hattie continued to come help with heavy water-pots, sweeping, and the other things she had helped with.

Today, Lalani went about the house humming and secretly thinking about what life would be like having Jim in the house all the time. She was not going to move. She loved the house. It was really more her house than Katherine's, since she was the one who took care of it. And now that Kate had her things out, it felt like her home. *I wonder what things Jim has that he will want to put out.* Lalani clomped over to the desk at the front window and sat and watched the three mares with their fat pregnant bellies. She didn't mind feeding the three-month old foals. She didn't mind the horses, as long as she didn't have to ride them and she could be upwind from them. She did mind the horse flies that would be showing up soon.

53

She spotted Ben and Morgan coming up the road with the carriage on a hay sled. They had retrieved it from the stream. The one wheel needed replacing, but the rest of it didn't seem damaged. Jim wasn't sure the horsehair seats would dry out without molding first, but they could be replaced easily. Lalani was relieved it hadn't been destroyed. It had taken six months to get this carriage, and she didn't want to have to rent a carriage again.

Lalani took out some paper and wrote to her friend Minnie, telling her about the accident and how her life had changed from taking care of others to being taken care of herself, and that now she would marry Jim.

By the end of the week, she was able to put pressure on her left foot. Her ankle bone was still tender and therefore she was not able to wear shoes yet. Hattie and Miranda had knitted her some slippers to keep her feet warm and clean. But Lalani was eager to lay out her vegetable garden, and slippers were not an option.

Growing up in Hawaii, she had gone barefoot most of the time, and now standing in the freshly turned damp soil in her bare feet, it reminded her of her childhood. She brought the long hoe from the barn and used it to steady herself and then carve out rows, and push seeds one by one deep into the rich soil. As Jim came back with the draft horses from furrowing the hay field, he spotted Lalani in the middle of the garden. She was leaning on the hoe and had wiped her forehead with her hand, leaving a smudge of dirt behind.

Jim shook his head, "Is that woman ever going to slow down and take care of herself? She's trying to do too much too fast. Is she trying to catch cold again standing there in her bare feet?" He walked out to the garden, where she stood. "That's enough for today, future Mrs. Baker," and he swept her up in his arms and carried to the house.

She was smiling all the way, with her muddy feet swinging as he walked. He sat her down on the back step. "Just sit there – don't move, and yes I'm telling you what to do." He winked and grinned as he went to fetch water from the barn.

He tenderly washed her feet, being most careful of her tender ankle, and dried them. Then he lovingly wiped the dirt from her face. Once again. he picked her up in his arms and this time carried her up to her room.

"I like your pretty green cotton dress," he said as he pointed to her mud-covered skirt she was wearing.

"You do, do you?" she smiled back.

"Need any help?" he replied raising his eyebrows.

With that she pointed to the door, with a big Cheshire Cat smile across her face.

"Don't forget to put warm slippers on those cold feet," he said as he left the room.

~~

They had not set a date to marry or had told anyone. There was so much to do in the spring with the fields and foals coming due. They both agreed a wedding would have to wait.

A letter finally arrived from Katherine saying they would be home on the twenty-third of April, in nine days. Jim was relieved at the news, but was pretty sure two of the mares would drop foals within the next few days. Lalani's first instinct was to want to get to the big house (as she called the Taylor ranch main house where Clay had been raised), and make sure everything was ready for her return. But Jim reminded her that Miranda was there and her servants would be taking care of her now. She was no longer in her service, but was her best friend. It was all still too new for Lalani, even though it had been four months since Katherine's wedding and she had last taken care of her. It was a hard habit to break. Still Lalani as a friend wanted to make sure things were ready, *yet if I go over there to help ready things, then I will see the renovations before Kate. No, I'll wait. Katherine will want to see it first and then share it with me, telling me all about her plans for the spaces.* Instead, Lalani kept busy with making her own home ready to show Katherine. She hoped she would approve and not be disappointed that she had put away things that belonged to Katherine.

Katherine and Clay's train was due into Oak Ridge at noon, and Miranda had invited Jim and Lalani to join them for supper, knowing Katherine would want them there as they shared all the news about their trip. It was also time to take Brandy back to her real mistress. Lalani would miss having Brandy in the house and the clicking of her feet on the hardwood floors. They had become good companions over the last three months. Brandy had become very protective of Lalani as they traveled and when Lalani recovered from her injury.

Lalani dressed in a cotton floral blue dress and selected a simple flat pair of shoes she hoped she could wear. It would be the first time she wore shoes in two weeks, and she hoped her feet hadn't flattened out from going barefoot. Jim, like Prince Charming, slipped the right shoe on easily and then, oh, so carefully and slowly slipped her left foot into the other shoe. It was ever so slightly snug, but the sides didn't hit her ankle bone. Jim helped her up, and it felt fine. She took a step and winced and tried not to limp. She took a few more steps and then managed to walk more smoothly. "I'm fine, let's go see our friends."

Jim lifted Lalani up into the carriage to keep pressure off her foot and climbed up beside her.

Lalani called for Brandy to come, and she jumped into the back bench. Lalani held on to Jim's strong arm as the sun was just going down and gave their little valley a golden glow. Arriving just at sunset, Jim again took Lalani and lifted her down from the carriage. "I'm not going to break. I'm not made of porcelain. I'm fine. No hovering. Katherine intensely dislikes people that hover."

Jim smiled, extended his arm in a gentlemanly manner and said, "Yes, ma'am."

Morgan answered the door when he heard Brandy barking. Miranda was happy to see Lalani on her feet again. "Come, sit, and have some sherry. Clay and Katherine will be down shortly."

Morgan turned to Jim and said, "Scotch or whiskey?" then poured drinks for everyone.

As Katherine and Clay came down the stairs, Brandy sprinted to them, bouncing around them as they reached the bottom.

"Brandy, Brandy, yes, girl I'm happy to see you too," Katherine said patting the dog on her head. After a few moments, Brandy calmed and Katherine and Clay joined the others in the parlor, as Brandy took her favorite spot by the fireplace.

Katherine was radiant, beaming with excitement and overjoyed to see Lalani and share everything with her. Clay and Katherine had had time to unpack and explore their new rooms. Katherine was most eager to show them to Lalani, having heard she had not gone to see them herself. "You men just sit there and talk ranching, while I show Lalani our sitting room and spaces," Katherine said, taking Lalani's hand and pulling, rushing her to the stairs. Lalani winced as she took the first step, and Katherine turned, concerned. "What's wrong? What happened?"

"It's nothing, just a little bruised ankle, giving me a little trouble. I'll be fine if I go slow."

Katherine took her arm and they slowly ascended the staircase. Katherine showed her the new parlor, that once was Clay's large room. An archway led to a small alcove where the small grand piano from downstairs now stood. Katherine's grand was too big for the space and now stood in the family parlor. From the alcove she opened two double doors that led into their large new master suite, with its own private tub room. There was a small room attached to the master. This would be the nursery someday. For now, it was going to serve as Katherine's wardrobe for all her dresses. From the sitting room, there was a hallway that led down to two more rooms. These would eventually be older children's rooms or guest rooms. The two women returned to the private sitting room. "You and I are going to have so many wonderful afternoon teas here, and I will do the serving, not you. You can sit and quilt while I play piano, just like before. I've missed you, my dearest friend."

"That sounds wonderful. But I hope you will stop at the Circle K and have a cup of coffee as you finish your morning ride each day." Lalani didn't want to take away from Katherine's excitement by talking about the change to the little ranch house or about Jim's proposal. The ladies returned to the top of the stairs and started down. Jim spotted the wince on Lalani's face as she took the first step and immediately jumped up, and taking two steps at a time, reached Lalani. He picked her up and carried her down. Lalani blushed with embarrassment. Morgan understood but Clay was puzzled. Jim realized too late that his gallantry was embarrassing as he set her down next to Miranda. "Sore foot!" was all Lalani could think of to say. Jim knew he would get an earful about it on the way home.

Miranda had made a wonderful dinner of roasted duck and red potatoes. Katherine and Clay talked about their trip. Clay beamed with pride as he retold their time in Vienna and visiting the Grand Music Hall, where Katherine had once performed. After dinner the men retired to the study and began discussing ranch work. It was branding season, and new foals would be arriving. Jim began to talk about horses, then realized he best hold his thoughts because that was Katherine's business and not his. Discussing what he wanted to do with Clay probably would not go over well with Katherine. Meanwhile the ladies were sitting in the parlor discussing the latest European fashions and new furnishings for the house. Lalani finally told Katherine about rearranging the small house with a few of her things.

Katherine talked about wanting to go to San Francisco to see Joanna and to purchase some new furnishings for the new rooms.

"Katherine, would you mind if I came along? I want to get a few small pieces for the little ranch house. Now that the piano is gone and the Wycliff chair, the sitting room is a little sparse."

"Of course, you can, Lalani. You need to stop calling the Circle K house, the 'little ranch house' and start calling it your house. It was always as much your house as mine. I had Eric draw up a new deed while we were gone, putting the house into your name. So, no more calling it the small house. You should give it a name. The ranch land may be the Circle K, but the house is no longer. Don't the Hawaiians have a tradition of naming their houses?"

"Yes, a house is named according to its use and feeling. The *hale* is the word for house and *ohana* for family. So, for example this big house being Clay's family house you might call *Hale Ohana*. If a house is grand, it might be *Hale Nui* or known for roses it could be called *Hale Kan Loki* or just *Kan Loki*. I will have to think about a name for my house. But the ranch will always be the Circle K. Let me see what the house whispers to me and what I sense."

"That's beautiful, Lalani," Miranda said.

The men came out of the study wanting to know Katherine's plans for the horse ranch. "Kate, are you going to want to obtain more breeding mares this year?" Clay asked.

"I hadn't thought about it. I already have six mares. This year we will have six new foals but next year we could have more if we obtain more mares. The real question is do we want to sell horses that are saddle broke or not? It would be a handful, trying to break six or more five-year-olds in one season, considering I do it with a slow gradual method. I don't like breaking their spirit by brute force and slapping a saddle on and riding them until they give in. That does not build trust to make a good cutting horse or riding horse for that matter. Why?" Katherine replied.

"Jim just wanted to know how much work to expect, that's all," Clay said, as he sat down next to her.

"Katherine, you and I can handle the foals and mares we have now, but in a year or two if you increase breeding mares, we will need help. That's all. I was just trying to figure where we could put another paddock," Jim commented.

"That's a good question," Kate said.

But before the conversation got too intense, Miranda told them all work would have to wait until tomorrow and changed the conversation back to Clay's and Katherine's trip. They didn't see Maestro Korsakoff in St Petersburg and only stayed one day as Kate wanted to show Clay the colorful architecture of the Kremlin. Clay teased that Katherine was fine on the boat, but at a loss as to where the maid had put things, and that coming home on the train made her queasy. Lalani told them how strange it was for her too, not looking after Katherine these past months, and then diverting the subject by asking, "Miranda, I hope you still plan to do the cooking for a while. I'm afraid I never taught Katherine how to cook."

"I hope so too. With branding coming, we men are going to be hungry. Kate only knew how to make oatmeal when we were kids. It would stick to your stomach alright and then some," Morgan teased.

"No, no, I will continue to cook. I have to be able to do something around here. We may need to get a housekeeper, now that there are so many more rooms to clean," Miranda admitted.

"As long as it's not Lalani," Jim chimed in.

"Definitely not. She has spent a lifetime looking after others. Now I want her to look after herself and to continue to be my best friend," Katherine said leaning over and patting Lalani's hand. "Speaking of best friends, Charles has sent you a present, Lalani." Clay got up and left the room, while Katherine made Lalani guess. He came walking back in with an arm full of puppy.

"Charles saw how close you had become with Brandy and wanted you to have a companion of your own," Kate said as she and Brandy stood. Brandy sniffed at the two-month-old reddish-brown Gordon Setter.

"This little girl is from the same dame as Brandy. Charles said she wouldn't have any more pups and wanted you to have this one."

"Oh, my, I was going to miss Brandy tremendously. Now I guess I won't have time to miss her," Lalani said, as Clay put the puppy in her lap.

Brandy came and licked the pup and sat watching it. The puppy wiggled and tried to licked Lalani's face. The pup had a white crest like Brandy, but was a little browner than red. She stood about eighteen inches tall and weighed about fifteen pounds. Clay retrieved a large crate the pup slept in.

"She's pretty good, didn't cry too much on the voyage over. Charles made sure she was house broke before sending her. What are you going to call her?" Clay asked.

"I don't know. Now I have two names to think of, one for her and one for the house." Lalani was delighted with the wiggly bundle of fur. "I'm actually thrilled to have her. What a wonderful gift," Lalani said and then sat thinking for a moment. "How about Makana for her name? It means gift in Hawaiian." Lifting the puppy up and looking into her sparkling brown eyes. "Are you Makana?" The pup licked her face.

"I guess so with a response like that," Jim said. He helped Lalani set her into her crate and Brandy put a paw up on the edge as if taking charge.

The evening grew late. Katherine said she would come see Lalani's place tomorrow, and they could make plans to visit Joanna in San Francisco and do some shopping. Clay teased her about wanting to leave him so soon after getting home. Jim lifted Lalani into the carriage and handed her the sleepy pup. She was a lap full, but snuggled down on the seat with her head in Lalani's lap.

~~

The next morning, Lalani was busy getting Makana to follow instructions. The pup was bright and learned quickly to sit and stay. Charles must have been working with her. After morning chores and having Makana and Jim under foot, Lalani sent them both to the barn. Makana took to Jim and followed. Jim began to teach the pup to stay away the horses, as he didn't want trouble. Finally, Makana found a pile of hay and slept.

The conversation from the night before gave Lalani a lot to think about. The thought of giving her home a name kept coming back to her mind. She thought about her home as her forever house. which in Hawaiian is *hale mau loa*. She would still think about it and wanted to see what her spirits told her. Perhaps just white house would be best *Hale Ke'oke'o*, or *Kālua 'ana* for baking since she will someday be Mrs. Baker. Something that start with a K would fit with the ranch logo of the Circle K.

The more important thing on her mind was when to tell Katherine about Jim's proposal. Lalani sat at the parlor room desk, watching the horses in the paddock, something she did a lot of when she needed to think about something serious. The mares were very pregnant. They calmly stood and nibbled at the grass waiting for their time to come. *Has my time come to be a wife? I never thought I would get married. I'm still trying to imagine myself as a wife. I do love Jim and I am happy when he's around, at least most of the time. I don't want to be in this house alone. Though with Makana, I guess, I will feel somewhat protected, but it's not the same. Katherine will have a thousand questions and I'm not sure I will be able to answer them. Ulu Pono, Lalani, prosper on the right path!*

Lalani got busy again, making a noon meal for her and Jim. She felt the need to ask when they should marry, as Katherine would want to know. Jim wanted to say soon, but knew he would be very busy with planting alfalfa and the new foals, due anytime. "I think sometime in May, when I can give my bride the attention you deserve. By then the planting will be done and the foals will have arrived," Jim said, hoping this would be agreeable with Lalani.

"That will give me time to have a dress made of the fabric my mother gave me. Though I'm not sure Katherine will be in any condition to work with the horses," she calmly added.

"What do you mean?" Jim said surprised at her comment.

"Didn't you hear Clay say Katherine was queasy on the train ride home? She had a warm glow to her. We Hawaiians have a sense of nature, and it's telling me she is with child."

"Are you sure?"

"No, so don't go saying something you shouldn't. I don't think Katherine even knows at this point," Lalani smiled with a warm wise look.

Lalani then got busy making scones for Katherine's visit in the afternoon. Makana was underfoot and got scolded for trying to get a scone from the counter. Lalani knew she was going to have to draw a line in the kitchen that Makana would not be allowed to cross. This would keep her away from the hot stove and food sitting on the counter. Lesson one came today with a stern No! and putting her back on the kitchen table side of the room.

Katherine arrived about three o'clock and was delighted to be back in the house. It felt like home but different. The color accents Lalani had changed from blues to green and lavender. A large vase of early blooming wildflowers stood on the dining table. Katherine agreed the parlor needed more seating, something that reflected the Hawaiian trinkets she now had out. Lalani served tea and scones and they sat talking about going to the city to shop and seeing Joanna. Katherine sat on the settee thinking how nice it would look in her sitting room, that it went with the Wycliff chair.

"Lalani, I hope you don't mind, but this settee and the chair, being from Abigail's house were meant to go together. How about we get you a new settee, one you can pick out in the style you like. When it comes, I can take this to go with the chair."

"Well, I guess so. After all it is yours. Abigail left you her house and things when she died. Do you miss the London house?"

"I don't miss the house, but from time to time I miss Abigail a great deal. She was so good to me, taking me in and making me her family. I still can't believe she left everything to me. I want you to have some of the good fortune I have had. I want you to pick out the furnishings you want. I'm not sure we can get ratan or woven chairs. But you could probably find a French provincial with wood features. As for the house, Eric is working on the deed to the house, putting it in your name."

Lalani sat quietly thinking for a long moment. "What is it, Lalani? Please tell me you want to stay here, you want the house," Kate said nervously.

"Oh, yes, of course I want to stay, but something has happened." Lalani didn't know if now was the time to tell her about the proposal. "What's happened? Are you ill? What?" Katherine was now very concerned.

"No, No. Jim has proposed, that's all," Lalani quietly admitted.

"Proposed, that's wonderful. You had me thinking it was something awful," Kate .

"No, not awful, actually it is wonderful. I just never thought it would happen to me."

Katherine wanted to know all about the proposal. When Lalani told her about being stuck in the river during the storm, Katherine didn't know whether to be furious about her foolishness or grateful to Jim for saving her. "I guess I'm both." She had always been fond of him and now was even more. "The month of May will be perfect. We have even more to shop for when we go to the city."

Katherine could sense there was something more on Lalani's mind. Lalani would fidget with the nail on her left index finger. Both Kate and Jim knew this meant something was bothering her. "What is it, you do want to get married?" Katherine asked.

"I'm not sure what kind of wife I will make, I've never really been with a man before. And then there's the house. How will Jim feel if I own everything? Jim says he wanted to buy a spread of his own, but he would set that aside and stay here. He likes working with you and the horses," Lalani said rattling on in all directions.

"I see. First off, you will make a wonderful wife. I had no experience when Clay and I married. Jim, I'm sure won't be as needful as well as, let's just say, a young man." They both chuckled as Lalani blushed. "And secondly, if we talk to Eric about deeding the house, something can be worked out. You let Clay and me worry about that. If we all sit down and look at the ranch land survey, we will come up with an answer that won't hurt manly pride, or womanly. Just rest assured it is yours," Katherine said, patting Lalani on the hand and taking another scone. Lalani and Katherine made plans to go to San

Francisco at the end of the following week. Providing there was no trouble with the foals.

The next morning, as Jim joined Lalani for coffee after morning chores, Lalani wanted to know how Jim felt about staying at the Circle K or what kind of a ranch he wanted if he were to buy his own spread. Jim looked at Lalani over his cup, "I want to be where you are, and be able to do a good worthwhile day's work."

"No, Jim! Tell me about the kind of ranch you hoped to have someday."

"I never really thought I would have my own ranch. It was a young man's dream," he said looking at her, but seeing she wanted to know. "I always dreamed of having a small ranch. Something I could manage myself or with one or two hired hands. I wouldn't be able to pay for more. I admit I would raise maybe two hundred or more head of cattle, rather than horses. Cattle are easier in the long run and beef is always in demand. Don't get me wrong. I do like working with horses. I like working with Katherine."

"How big a spread would you need for two hundred head?" Lalani asked.

"Well, about five hundred acres, plus another fifty for winter hay. I guess it would be about a third the size of this place, the Circle K is about fourteen hundred acres. Most of the land between the main road into the house and the Taylor ranch isn't used at the moment. I'm not sure what Katherine plans for it. Anyway, I hope you're not disappointed with my boyish dream."

Lalani took Jim's hand and said, "Not at all, we don't need big things. I'm not a worldly person. I'm just a simple woman, grateful for a good-hearted man."

Jim chuckled, "Not worldly! I beg to differ, you have been all over the world, you have seen things and experienced people and places I will never see. As for simple, you have a wonderful mind that knows what it wants. I'm just grateful you want simple old me." And he kissed her hand.

"You're far more wonderful than simple," she said giving him a kiss. "But right now, I want you to go do whatever needs doing. I have my own work to do," and she got up and pointed to Makana waiting to go out and thinking, *A not so wonderful mind that can't make up its mind about being a good wife, about being loved.*

The next week was busy at the Circle K. Three of the mares dropped foals. Estrella had another fine-looking colt and two of the mustangs had strong fillies. Katherine was reluctant to go to see Joanna with three mares still due. Jim assured her Camille and Rosie would be another week yet. There was only the chestnut mustang due anytime, and this was not her first time, so she would be fine. He would bring her up into the barn and would be on hand if needed. Seeing the new foals were doing well, Katherine and Lalani departed for San Francisco on the Friday afternoon train.

5

The Proposal

Brandy woke Jim as the sun rose. She wanted outside. Lalani was sleeping quietly, the fever that came during the night felt cooler when he touched her forehead. Jim stood just looking at her, seeing how pretty she looked to him. After a moment he went downstairs and let Brandy out the back door. He lit the stove and put a pot of coffee on to brew and the tea kettle on to boil, knowing Lalani preferred tea. The rain had stopped and the sky was clear again. Jim went out to his place and took a moment for himself and cleaned up. He could hear Medianoche whinny, wanting to be feed. He went to the barn and opened his stall and lead him to the barn corral and turned him out. He tossed a few flakes of hay into the feed trough to pacify him, then took a few flakes to Duchess and the other horses still in the barn.

When he returned to the house, the kettle began to whistle and the coffee was ready. He found the bread and sliced a couple of pieces for toast. Brandy was back and wanted in. She raced up the stairs to Lalani's room and sat quietly at her bedside, waiting for her to wake. After a short time, from downstairs, Jim could hear Lalani talking softly to Brandy, causing him to bring a tray with the tea, toast and jam up to her.

"Good morning. How are you feeling?" he said, setting the tray on a table.

"Good morning. I'm a lot better than yesterday, but tired and very glad to be here in my warm bed." She was a little foggy on how she got there. She clearly remembered being trapped in the water and Jim arriving. After that, not so much.

Jim helped her sit up and put the pillows to her back. "I'd like to take a look at your ankle. Do you mind?" he asked.

She felt the pain in her ankle as she tried to move it, and remembered him wrapping it. She then remembered the episode of getting into dry clothes, and she gasped in horror.

"What? Does it hurt that bad?" Jim asked. He had only moved the covers partly back, but had not touched it.

"No, I'm sorry. It aches a little." She wasn't going to bring up his undressing her if he didn't.

Jim gently unwrapped the ankle. It was black and blue and a little swollen. "Can you wiggle your toes?"

Lalani slowly wiggled her toes, but it hurt to move her foot. "I think it's just sprained," she whispered, trying to speak louder.

Jim didn't want to wrap it again since it wasn't broken. He covered her back up and set the tray on her lap. "I brought this for starters, but you need to eat something hardy to get your strength back and to prevent a cold. Will it be eggs and bacon or hot oatmeal?"

Lalani had coughed a few times since she awoke and hated to think of a cold coming on. "Let's make it eggs and bacon. Make enough for yourself and join me. But first I need assistance getting to the commode in the tub room." She couldn't do it on her own, and she had to go soon. He had already helped her undress, so this would not be any worse. She wasn't sure she would be able to stand and balance on her right foot, feeling the way she did. Jim picked her up easily in his arms and carried her to the water closet. Setting her down slowly so she could balance on her one leg, she took hold of the wall to the closet, mustering all the strength she could to stand. "That's fine. I can manage from here. You go get the eggs and bacon." And she shooed him away with her hand before she fell.

She did manage, and when Jim returned with breakfast, he found her sitting on the edge of the tub waiting for him. He picked her up and brought her back to the bed, getting her settled again. They sat and ate in quiet at first. She could tell Jim wanted to say something about last night.

"Well, this has taught me not to go out in the rain. I'm so glad Prince Philip had the instinct to go home. Is he okay?" Her voice was stronger now that she had eaten.

Jim had moved the rocker next to the bed and looked up from his plate. "Yes, he's safe and dry in his stall. I gave him extra oats. But for you heading out in a storm, what were you thinking? Wasn't Morgan there?" he said sternly but trying not to sound too mad.

Lalani wasn't sure she wanted to answer Jim, seeing the disapproving look on his face. "Jim Baker, don't go telling me what I can and cannot do. I saw it begin to rain and thought I could get home before the stream rose. It wasn't that deep when I began across and I didn't expect the wheel to get stuck in the mud. As for Morgan he did offer to take me home, but I told him no. He apparently knows better than to tell me what I can and cannot do." She was about to say more as she took a deep breath, causing her to cough, breaking her line of thought.

Jim shot back with a stern look of concern. "I'm not telling you what to do. But do you know what you did to me when I saw Prince Philip and not you? My heart stopped and my stomach turned over. Last night when I got you home, you were so cold. I thought I might lose you." He got up and moved the tray from her lap and sat down on the bed. "Lalani, I never want to have that feeling again. Woman, I love you." He picked up her hand and kissed it.

Now she didn't know what to say. She caressed the side of his face with her hand and looked into his eyes, "I'm glad you do. I've missed you, too."

Jim looked at her. He was hoping for a little more than 'I missed you'. "I see, well then, right now probably isn't the time to ask you to marry me, since you don't love me back," he said rather disappointedly.

Lalani sat stunned in her tired state trying to comprehend what Jim just said. *Marry me, marriage?* She looked at Jim now expecting her to say something. "Oh, Jim, I am very fond of you too." Her head was fussy from her fever and she fought to clear her confused state of mind. "I'm so grateful to you for saving my life. You want to marry me? I..uh. It's just hasn't been something I thought would come my way. I'm pretty set in my ways, you know that. I ...my head's so foggy... I need time to think about this and what it all means."

"What it all means? It means I love you and want to marry you. I want to take care of you as a husband and not just as a ranch hand. Is that how you see me, as just a ranch hand?" Jim's dander was rising. He had never understood women and guessed he still didn't.

Lalani reached out and took his big hand stopping him from leaving her side. "Now, just you wait a minute. I didn't say no, I just need a little time. We need to make sure we're not jumping into this because of last night, me being saved by you and you seeing me, well, without clothes, vulnerable and helpless. When I'm well, and I'm not helpless. Jim, I thought of you all the time when I was in Europe, I missed your voice, your smile, your strength. I missed all of you. I guess I just hadn't realized until now, it meant I loved you. Let me get my strength back and my feet under me and ask me again. Please! Just a little patience." She then kissed his big hand gently and leaned back on the pillow, not sure the tiredness was from the emotions trying to rage through her or the exertion of sitting up and talking him out of leaving.

Jim smiled and teasingly replied, "Alright, I wouldn't want to be telling you what to do. I'll just have to take good care of you and win you over." He leaned forward and kissed her on the forehead and snuggled her back under the blankets. "Now get some more rest." He picked up her empty plate and trays and headed downstairs.

Lalani lay contemplating all that had just been said. *Jim is such a dear man. I truly did miss him and couldn't wait to get back with him. I haven't felt this way emotionally....well.... ever. Is this what love truly is?* Before she could answer her own question, her exhaustion took over as she cherished his words, "I love you," and soon fell asleep.

Jim was sitting at the kitchen table in a daze, also trying to figure out just what happened. He knew he loved Lalani, but had no intention of asking her to marry him at that moment. He thought he would be more romantic than that. *Perhaps that's why she didn't say yes right away. I should have gotten on my knee and asked her properly.* He tried to put it out of his mind for now, as he needed to figure out how to best help Lalani get around until her ankle healed. He wanted to go into town and get Doc Newell, yet he didn't want to leave her alone. As he sat worrying, he heard a pounding knock on the front door.

It was Morgan, and he had a look of deep concern on his face. Jim opened the door, but before he could say anything, Morgan blurted out, "Is Lalani safe? is she alright? I found her carriage turned over in the stream."

"Yes, she's here, she had quite an ordeal, but seems to have only a sprained ankle. She's sleeping last I checked." Jim's tone had an annoyed ring to it. Jim showed Morgan to the kitchen and offered a cup of coffee while he explained what happened.

Morgan felt more awful with every detail Jim relayed. "I knew I should have taken her home."

"You should have never let her leave," Jim said sternly, acting his senior to Morgan. Then he chuckled as he thought about what Lalani had said about not telling her what to do.

"What's funny? I feel terrible." Morgan was now confused. Was Jim mad or not?

Again, Jim explained. Morgan wanted to see her for himself, so they both went up and looked in on her. She was sleeping but her breathing seemed more labored. Jim felt her forehead and the fever had returned. Morgan said he would go for the doctor and hurried down the stairs. Jim took a cool towel to her forehead, and she woke coughing. After a moment she seemed better. Jim went back to the kitchen and made some hot water with honey, but could only find lemon drops, instead of fresh lemons. He stirred in the lemon drops and honey and brought it up to her. He held the cup as she sipped the warm tea. It felt warm and soothing as it went down. Jim told her Morgan had come and had gone to bring Doc Newell. She started to protest, but began coughing again. She took another sip of tea, and Jim settled her back down under the blankets. Her fever didn't seem too high, but he did worry about her being so tired.

Morgan and Doc Newell arrived back within the hour. The doctor put the men out while he examined Lalani. After about twenty minutes, he opened the door and let Jim and Morgan back in.

"She's lucky. The fever isn't too high. At the moment it appears it's just a cold running its course. As long as you keep her warm and give her plenty to eat and drink, it should pass within a few days. As for her ankle, it is badly bruised. She will need to stay off it for at least a week. I can send some crutches out in a few days, once she is stronger and her cold is gone. When she's well enough to get out of bed, she should be able to move around a bit. For now, young lady, you stay in bed, and let Jim take care of you for once."

Jim assured him he would do just that. Jim asked Doc Newell if he knew of a young woman that could assist Lalani with, "You know, personal things, like bathing." Doc said the Olsen's older daughter might be available to help. He gave Jim some laudanum, just in case the coughing got worst. It would cut the phlegm better than the lemon.

Lalani was resting quietly again. Jim showed Doc to the door and said he'd fetch the crutches in a few days. Morgan came down and said he would have his mother come over and help for now. The two men walked back to the kitchen and sat. Jim asked Morgan what kind of shape the carriage was in, "Is it salvageable or not?"

"The water carried it downstream slightly, causing it to tip over, but it didn't look too damaged. Of course, I didn't look at it too long, once I realize Lalani wasn't in it. I hightailed it for here. I'll have some of the ranch hands get it out and bring it up to your barn. Don't worry about that for now. You just take care of Lalani. Katherine will be very unhappy with us, if we don't take good care of her."

Morgan finished his coffee and headed home. He would bring his mother, Miranda, over that afternoon. Jim went back upstairs and checked on Lalani. She was still sleeping, quietly now. Brandy raised her head from where she was laying at the foot of the bed, but didn't move. Jim reached down and patted her on the head. "Well, girl, you will have to be my go between and come get me when she needs me. I have to get the southeast field planted if the horses are to have alfalfa or hay come winter. And there's Lalani's garden to plant. I don't want her out in that cold ground. Don't tell her I said that," and he laughed.

Miranda Taylor and Morgan arrived shortly after one o'clock. Lalani was awake and was just finishing the broth Jim had made. Miranda sent the men out to take care of ranch work, while she attended to Lalani.

Morgan felt terrible about what happened and knew Jim couldn't take care of Lalani and the ranch work, so he stayed and helped. Once Miss Olsen came and Lalani got stronger, Jim could go about his work during the day and care for Lalani in the evening. But for the next day or two, he would need help.

Miranda took charge now. "Lalani I'm sorry, I should have known the storm was heavier in the hills and would be sending a lot of water down into the stream. I've lived here long enough and seen it happen so many times. I don't know where my mind was yesterday."

Lalani tried to convince Miranda things were not as bad as the men let on. "I just need a little help until I get my strength back."

Miranda realized Lalani was still too weak to stand and she would need Jim to help carry her to the water closet. She started to leave to fetch Jim.

"Wait, Miranda, just send Brandy. When Jim sees her, he will figure out we need his help." Off went Brandy with a wave of Lalani's hand. Jim was at the door within minutes. "I'm afraid I need a lift to the tub room again. Too much dang tea and broth," Lalani grinned.

Jim picked her up as before and carried her to the closet, setting her down carefully. Miranda took over from there and Jim stepped out. They would send Brandy again when needed. Miranda changed the bedsheets, then washed Lalani's back with warm water, and helped her into a fresh gown. When things were set, they sent Brandy. Miranda and Jim could see Lalani was tired again. Jim put a log in the fireplace and stirred up the hot embers, bringing the fire back to life. Then they went to the kitchen and let Lalani sleep. Jim returned to working, while Miranda made a batch of lemon honey tea. She had brought lemon juice from her pantry and fixings for chicken soup.

Miranda took small pieces of chicken, cut carrots and a few pieces of potatoes and added them to a pot and set it to simmering on the stove. She took the main part of the chicken and heated it and made potatoes for Jim and Morgan's midday meal, which was several hours late.

The men came in to eat and sat talking with Miranda about how to manage things. "Clay and Katherine need to come home soon. Branding starts in a week or two, and I need Clay's help. Jim needs Katherine here to help with the horses. You can't do it all Jim, planting, taking care of the horses and Lalani. What if I send Ben over with the draft horses to help with the plowing and planting later this week?" Morgan said, as he picked up another piece of chicken.

"I hate to pull Ben away from your place, Mrs. Taylor, but if you can spare him, it sure would help. At the rate Katherine wants to grow this ranch, I think we will need to hire another ranch hand. I was just waiting for her to return before going forward," Jim confessed.

For the next two days, Lalani did a lot of sleeping. The fever didn't come back on the third day and her cough was not as deep and hard.

Hattie, Mrs. Olsen's daughter came on the third day and began to take care of Lalani's needs. By then, Lalani had enough strength to stand on her own. Hattie was a tall strong girl and managed to help Lalani get to where she needed to go. She was good natured and didn't mind running up and down stairs to fetch things. Emptying the commode was not a favorite chore, but she did it discreetly and without complaint.

By the fourth day, Lalani was tired of being in bed and sat in her rocking chair by the fire, hoping Jim would pop in to visit between chores. That evening, as she was much better, Jim carried her downstairs to the parlor where he had the fire going and a supper laid out. He told her about his day, planting alfalfa and how he thought two of the mares would foal soon. They sat and played one round of cribbage, and then he whisked her back upstairs and settled her back in bed. Sitting by her side, he took her hand and smiled.

"Have you had some time to think about my proposal?" he said softly. Then going down on one knee. "I love you. Will you marry me?" hoping for a better answer this time.

Lalani looked down at Jim's strong hands, then at his anxiously awaiting face and smiled, "Yes, I have, and the answer is Yes, but I don't want to commit to a date right now."

"Well, that's progress. I got a yes!" Smiling he stood and graciously kissed her on the cheek, then sat on the bed next to her. "Can I ask what's holding you back?"

She knew part of the answer but not all of it. "Like I said, I want to get back on my feet first." She hesitated and Jim knew there was more.

"What else? I can see there is something more. Is it because you don't want to give up the house or is it that I can't support you in the manner you're used to? Lalani, I have some savings, and I don't want to take you away from your home. I'd like to buy the ranch, but I'm sure Katherine won't sell."

Before he could go on, she put her finger to his lips. "Shh… I don't want fancy things, you know that. Katherine said she would deed me the house when they returned, so no need to buy it. And you're right. She will never give up the horses and land. I guess we need time to figure out how we're going to live here. I need a little time to adjust to the thought of having a man share my bed, as well."

Jim chuckled, "I assure you we won't be sharing this bed, it's too little for both of us. I'll buy us a beautiful new big bed, where you can have your own space when you need it. I just would like to think it won't be all the time."

Lalani began to blush and wanted to change the subject. "Well, like I said, we have things to talk about. That was at least a beginning and enough for now. Yes, Jim Baker, I do love you and deep down want to be your wife. But can we keep it just between the two of us for now? At least until we figure more out and I'm back on my feet?"

He took her in his arms and hugged her. The feel of her body through her thin gown brought a craving to him, but he hid it for the moment. "Alright, just between us for now. You get some sleep. Doc said he would bring the crutches tomorrow. So, you have a big day ahead of you." He snugged her down in the quilt, being careful of her ankle, and turned down her lamp. "I love you, Lalani," and he turned and left a happy man.

6

Close Calls

Joanna met Katherine and Lalani at the train station and was delighted to have both of them for the week. Joanna, Katherine's good friend from school days in Boston, was now married to a doctor, and had two little girls. Joanna was as fond of Lalani as Katherine. Lalani had helped both girls many times while they grew up at the boarding school. Lalani would come do their hair for dances, and often the three of them sat discussing boys, always assuming that Lalani being so much older knew all about men. Yet she had very little experience in courting or with men.

Joanna and her husband Richard sat in awe as they listened to Katherine tell about her honeymoon adventures and Lalani telling about the other amazing places she had been.

"Someday, Joanna, when the girls are grown, I will take you to those places," Richard said. "But not tonight. I have early rounds at the hospital, so I will say goodnight. Katherine please don't keep my wife up all night talking." He kissed Joanna on the head and headed upstairs.

Joanna wanted to hear all about Jim's proposal, which lead all of them to comparing their proposal moment. They agreed Joanna's was done correctly with Richard asking her father and then getting on his knee with a ring, while Katherine and Lalani's were done when their men thought they were going to die. Katherine had been extremely ill with a fever when Clay realized he couldn't live without her.

"Lalani, when is the big day?" Joanna asked.

"Lalani and Jim are waiting till after spring branding and planting. But I don't think they should wait. Jim's going to have most of the planting done in the next two weeks," Katherine explained.

"Just hold your horses, you two. There is a lot more to be done with spring planting now that there are so many more horses to feed. We need alfalfa as well as hay. I'm just getting back on my feet and have only planted half of my vegetable garden. I still need to get the cucumbers and lettuce seeds in. I'm not young like you two, and neither is Jim. Rushing into marriage isn't as urgent to us."

"Doesn't branding end by May, and the foals should have all arrived by then, Kate? I think Lalani's right about having a spring wedding. She will need time to have a dress made," Joanna smiled.

The three talked into the late evening and planned to see the dressmaker and furniture store the next day. Joanna and Katherine were eager to take Lalani to the dressmakers to discuss her gown. Lalani wasn't sure on the style of dress she wanted.

Almost before Lalani finished her morning tea, Joanna and Kate whisked her off to the dressmakers. Joanna introduced them to Mrs. Laurence, and Lalani confessed she wanted something simple in a Hawaiian style.

"My mother gave me a lovely Hawaiian fabric when I was little. I always thought I would use it and have a more traditional Hawaiian gown. But traditional Hawaiian dresses are wraps gathered just above the bust, with bare shoulders. As I have been raised in the Presbyterian church, I don't think the traditional style is appropriate. I'm sure it would raise a lot of talk and disapproval. But I would like to have the skirt of my dress made with the fabric."

"I think you're quite right about bare shoulders, though I'm sure that Jim and the other men wouldn't mind," Kate chuckled.

Lalani described the fabric to Mrs. Laurence who quickly sketched a simple dress. The top would be a simple bodice without sleeves, that wouldn't distract from the simple lines of the dress, but give the proper coverage the church would require. Mrs. Laurence suggested a small jacket that could be worn during the ceremony but be removed later. She also suggested a black satin ribbon below the bustline and around the neckline that would complement the black print of the skirt fabric. Lalani was pleased with the final design, and Kate and Joanna were already busy picking out a veil.

"Kate, there will be no veil. I will wear the traditional flower crown instead," Lalani announced.

Now that the dress was settled, the three excited ladies headed for Breuner's home furnishings. Katherine had a list of items she wanted for the new rooms. Lalani wanted a small game table and chairs, a small chair for her, and a new dressing table. They spent several hours looking at chairs and other items. Lalani was drawn to the wood and fabric of the Sheraton chairs, while Kate went more traditional with Chippendale. After an hour of looking at catalogs and selecting several items, Joanna suggested lunch before making the final orders. The salesman was most bewildered as they walked out without placing an order. Over lunch they discussed each piece of furniture selected. Joanne teased about the beds, but both Kate and say in selecting.

The clerk gave a sigh of elation when the ladies returned and each placed a sizable order. As for the beds, he provided them catalog drawings to show Clay and Jim.

"I'm not sure Clay will give up his big bed. It's quite sturdy and plenty big enough for the two of us. I wish it just a had a little more feminine look to it," Kate confessed, as she placed the drawings into her bag.

Lalani blushed as the two married women talked about making sure there was room for a man in their beds. *I hadn't given much thought to sleeping with a man, with Jim. But he has already seen me without clothes.*

Kate looked at Lalani deep in thought. "Lalani! Are you afraid of sleeping with Jim?"

"Katherine, a public store is no place for that kind of discussion," Lalani scolded. *Oh, my, we need to leave. Jim and I again are not as young as you and Joanne, but we're not that old either.*

Lalani picked up her receipts and drawings and hurried towards the door, Joanna and Kate scurrying behind her with girlish grins.

In the morning, Kate and Lalani were headed back to Oak Ridge, but Kate had one more stop for them at Eric's law office. Eric was Clay's older brother, a lawyer, married and living in San Francisco. To Lalani's surprise, both Clay and Jim were there when they arrived.

"What is this?" she said, as she greeted Jim with a smile.

Katherine explained Eric had drawn up a new deed to the Circle K ranch. That the deed would be in both of their names as husband and wife, therefore Jim needed to be present. Kate let Eric explain the layout of the property she and Clay had decided would work best for everyone involved. The Circle K sat on about two and a quarter square miles, just over 1,450 acres. On the north was the main road, and on the south, just past Natoma Creek was about a 200-acre strip from the east property edge to where the road into the ranch cut the main property in half. Kate and Clay agreed the 100 acres that held the northeast paddock, house and barns should be kept intact. This would be gifted to Lalani and Jim, with the understanding Katherine could use the paddock for horses. The 400 acres between the house and the stream they would sell to Jim at a fair price of $1.50 per acre. This he and Lalani could use as they wanted, for cattle, crops or horses. The remaining 900 acres, those south of the creek and west of the ranch road Katherine and Clay would continue to own. The creek would be a joint ownership, that could not be diverted or dammed without both party's agreement. Clay explained it was one of the sources of water for the cattle on the Taylor's southwest range.

Eric laid out a plot of the property as described for Lalani and Jim to review. Jim would not be required to purchase the 400 acres, but if he did, he could do it on a monthly mortgage basis.

"That won't be necessary, I've been saving for twenty years and $600 is more than a fair price. It's good land, but currently it's set up as paddocks for Kate's yearlings and two-year olds," Jim said running his hand through his hair, almost overwhelmed.

"Jim, we can always move the paddocks to the west property. I just still want the foaling paddock up by the house in order to keep an eye on things," Kate assured him.

"The question is," Eric smiled, "When are you to going to get married? For now, the deed to the house property will be in Lalani's name. Once you are married, I will add Jim's name. Also, when the 400 acres are purchased, then I will add them to the original deed. So right now, Lalani, I need you to sign on this line. As you can see Katherine has already signed the transfer line," Eric said handing her a pen.

Lalani took the pen, took a long look at Katherine, who whispered, "It's always been your home." Then turning to Jim for his look of commitment and love, and seeing him nod with a grin, she signed her name *Lalani*. Later she would add her new last name Baker.

Katherine stood and lifted Lalani to her feet and gave her a hug. "This is going to be such a good place for you, but have you thought of a name yet?"

Lalani smiled, "*Kālua 'ana Hale* – baker house." We will simply call it *Kālua 'ana*, and she took Jim's hand.

~~

Lalani and Jim returned home to Oak Ridge that evening, while Katherine and Clay stayed on in the city for a few more days. As Lalani stepped onto the porch of *Kālua 'ana,* it felt different. Now it was truly her home. She looked out to the north paddock and the large oak tree standing firmly at the front of the house. Now she had finally planted her own roots. Jim came up behind her putting his arms around her. "Thank you for all that you are. In so many ways you have made my dreams come true. I like the sound of *Kālua 'ana Hale*" She smiled and said, "*Ko makou wahi* - our place."

It was now the first week of May, with Lalani busy weeding her vegetable garden and Jim finalizing the planting of the alfalfa field. The Chestnut mare had dropped her foal, a pretty little filly the image of her mother. Lalani had sent her mother's fabric to the dressmakers. Finally, she and Jim set May 28th as their wedding day. Lalani just hoped the furniture she had ordered would arrive before then, including the large mahogany bed that she and Jim had picked out together.

With the men busy branding the spring calves, and Katherine and Jim with the new foals, Lalani kept busy with invitations and other wedding details. The early May weather had already turned warm and the dry hills had become a mix of old and new grasses. It was mid-morning as Lalani sat at the kitchen table when an uneasiness came over her. Makana had not settled by the fire as usual but paced back and forth to the kitchen door. Suddenly Jim came rushing in from the barn.

"Fire, there's smoke coming from the Taylor ranch. I'm going to see. You stay here, and I'll be back."

Lalani took one look at him, and he knew he had said the wrong thing. "Ok, come on. But you're not getting involved."

Jim hitched up the work wagon and they headed toward the main road. About halfway to the Taylor's, Miranda came quickly driving up in her carriage.

"A brush fire on our south range has broken out. The men were branding calves when the wind kicked up and carried some of the embers to the field beyond. I'm going into town to see if I can get more men to create a fireline before it reaches your west hills."

"Where is Kate?" Lalani urgently asked.

"She's at the house. The fire at the moment is not headed that way. Clay doesn't want her involved, especially in her condition," Miranda replied.

"Condition?" Jim commented.

"Jim, I told you Kate was expecting," she said shaking her head.

"Lalani, will you go to the house and make sure she stays out of harm's way?" Miranda asked.

Miranda headed on into town while Jim took Lalani to the Taylor house and then went on to join Morgan and Clay to fight the fire. Katherine stood watching from the study window trying to determine how fast the fire was moving when Lalani arrived. The smoke wasn't coming in that direction, but rather it blew towards the Circle K.

"Lalani, I'm worried about the horses. As the fire gets closer, they will spook and try to jump or break through the fences."

"Now, don't go worrying about the horses. Animals have a natural instinct about danger. They won't panic until it gets close, and the mares won't jump the fence leaving their foals. The men will have it under control before the horses panic."

~~

Jim found Morgan and Clay on the east trail trying to create a fire block. The trail was a narrow ribbon of dirt the cattle had created as they headed to the water hole and stream. Most of the cattle on the eastside of the ranch had crossed the Kikilo stream that ran north to south across the ranch and were out of danger. Now, a handful of ranch hands were strung out with shovels clearing the grass and brush, trying to widen the dirt path to stop the flames from continuing up the hill towards the Circle K. Jim jumped in and joined the effort, smoke streaming up into his face. The fire was at the bottom of a small hill and not moving quickly, but slowly lapping up the dry winter grass as it moved towards them.

Clay came up to Jim with a look of frustration on his face. "Jim, the breeze has picked up. We don't have enough men here to make a big enough gap to stop the fire. We can stop part of it here, but the line of the fire is too long, and it will simply go around us. I can't take any chances of anyone getting surrounded and trapped in the middle. I think it's best to make a stand at the main road into the Circle K. It's wide and the hills from here to there are lower with mostly grass.

I think we have a better chance of stopping it there. I think you and Morgan should go to the ranch road and take the men that mother is getting and work on the fire break there. I know it will be close to the house, but it's the best place to stop it."

"Fine, let me bring Medianoche up to your barn, and Morgan can organize the men when they arrive."

Jim headed back to the Circle K and found the stallion prancing in concern and whinnying along with Prince Philip and Duchess. He led Prince Philip to the north paddock to be with the mares, now standing sniffing the air with deep awareness and their foals standing close by their side. Jim saddled his horse, Buck, and then tied a strong lead to the stallion and another long lead to Duchess that he looped around the pommel horn of his saddle and headed towards the Taylor ranch. He took one last look at the house where Makana stood barking from the window. *I hope the doors and windows are secure and she can't get out.*

As Jim reached the main road, Morgan was coming with a dozen men from town. Miranda stayed in town with several women wanting to help with food for the men. Medianoche pulled at the lead, and Duchess pranced away, Jim instinctively kicked Buck into a trot and continued on to the Taylor's. Katherine saw Jim arrive and immediately met him at the barn, taking Medianoche's lead. The stallion pranced and pulled, almost taking Kate down, but with her quiet whispering way, she was able to calm him and lead him to the barn and a large stall. Lalani had come, taking Duchess's lead and holding her, while Jim dismounted and made sure Katherine was okay. Katherine told Lalani to let Duchess out in the barn corral, that she would be fine there. With the horses settled, both women wanted to know why the horses had been brought there. Jim explained the status of the fire and the plan to make the final fire break at the Circle K main road. They both wanted to go to the Circle K and help, at which Jim firmly said, "Kate, Clay said absolutely you were to stay here. You're in no condition to be shoveling dirt and inhaling smoke."

She started to protest, but Lalani put her hand on her arm, "He's right. It wouldn't be good for the baby. Worrying will be bad enough." Jim walked them back up to the house just as Miranda arrived with two other women.

"Good, you're here and can keep Katherine and Lalani busy," Jim said as he reached for Buck's reins.

"Katherine needs to say here, but I'm strong and have fought my share of fires at the sugarcane fields when I was nine and ten. I'm coming with you. Now, help me up on Buck and don't argue," Lalani said reaching for the top of the saddle.

Jim knew if Lalani was willing to ride a horse, she was more than determined, and there was no stopping her. Jim mounted and then helped Lalani swing up behind him. "Lalani will send word when we have it under control. Don't worry."

The smoke was heavy at the small ranch, and they could feel the breeze that was carrying the fire towards them. Lalani explained that when she was a girl, the burning of the sugar field got out of control. They also chose one of the roads and dug a trench, tossing the dirt onto the fireside edge and then soaking it with water. Once the flames reached it, they stopped unless the winds were too strong and blew embers across to the next field. This had happened only once when she lived there. The wind was so strong, it blew past like a whirlwind. taking several men's lives and a whole village. It didn't stop until it reached the ocean. It flowed like the lava to the sea, and then sputtered and steamed and finally died. I was ten when that happened."

The flames couldn't be seen from the ranch road as of yet, but everyone knew they were coming. Morgan and the men grabbed shovels and began digging a trench and tossing the dirt onto the dry grass. It was about a half mile of road that led into the house, but then another half mile to clear to the creek. While Morgan and the men worked with shovels along the road, Jim went to the back alfalfa field where he had been plowing and brought the plow up to the end of the road. He took a grinding stone and sharpened the edge of the plow in hopes that it would break the hard dirt. Then he hooked the plow to the draft horse and began to plow a furrow into the hard soil towards the creek. The big draft horse pranced at the smell of the smoke as Jim tried to weight the plow so it would dig into the dirt. It was a slow process, but it began to turn a narrow trench that the men then could increase as they worked their way towards the creek. The men still had a long way to go before they reached the furrow row, so Jim turned and made a second pass. This time it went faster.

Meanwhile, Lalani had gone to the barn and collected the water buckets from the stalls and filled them with water from the barn pump. Once all ten buckets were filled, she went to the paddock and retrieved Morgan's draft horse and hitched him to the buggy. She carefully loaded the buckets onto the carriage floor and drove out to where the men had finished digging. She held the horse as Ben unloaded the buckets and poured them onto the edge of the field. Then she returned to the barn and started over.

Jim had returned from plowing the fire break to help Morgan and the others. Clay had sent several of the men from the first fire break to join them, since the fire had reached up around and was closing in on them. Morgan hadn't noticed Clay had not come. "Ben, where's Clay?" Jim shouted.

"He was checking the line to make sure everyone was out before leaving."

Jim and Morgan began to worry. Morgan said, "He should have been here by now." Lalani had just come up with another load of water as Jim and Morgan were mounting up to go find Clay. Jim then stopped and took one of the buckets and tossed it at Morgan, and then another and soaked his own clothes. "Just in case we have to get close to the flames. Clay may be in trouble."

Lalani held onto Jim for a moment and then reached for a blanket in the carriage and soaked it. Jim swung the dripping cloth up over his saddle. He looked at Lalani. Neither needed to say anything. They both gave a look of, I love you and be careful. "Bring him home," was all she said.

~~

Clay had made his way back along the line and was almost back to the main road, when smoke became unbearable and stung his eyes. Not able to see but knowing the need to keep moving, he unfortunately stumbled into a gopher hole. He went staggering down to his knees and put out his hand to stop his fall. Suddenly, he heard it, that distinctive rattle, and then he felt the strike against his arm. He went down and rolled away still holding the shovel he had with him. He still couldn't see the snake, his eyes watery and blurry, but the rattle told him where to send the shovels' blow. Clay swung once hitting the creature firmly in the middle, then he swung again and hit it squarely on the head, smashing it into the hard ground. The rattles stopped.

Clay dropped the shovel and grabbed his arm, now burning with pain. He struggled to retrieve his pocket knife from his trousers and then to open the blade. His aggressive movements had caused the venom to pulse through his veins, but he still knew he needed to cut the vein and see if he could get the poison to flow out of the wound. He made a deep cut and blood began to flow. Removing the scarf covering his mouth to filter out the smoke, he used it to tie off his upper arm, in hopes of not bleeding out. Now he could feel the heat of the fire coming up around him. All he could think of was Katherine. *Clay, you have to get out of here. You can't leave Katherine a widow and your unborn baby fatherless.* He struggled to stand and then began to stagger away from the heat. He hadn't taken more than a few steps when he began to choke from the smoke and went down again.

Jim and Morgan had reached the start of the first fireline and frantically tried seeing through the thick smoke for Clay. They could hear and feel the crackling heat of the fire in front of them. The horses tossing their heads, didn't want to go into the smoke and heat. Dismounting, Morgan insisted Jim stay with the horses. "He's my brother, and Lalani would never forgive me if anything happened to you."

"Morgan there," Jim pointed, as he thought he saw someone, but then he was gone. Morgan called out "Clay where are you?" Hoping Clay would answer, but nothing.

Morgan took a few steps into the smoke and called again. This time he heard the faint reply from Clay, fighting to answer. Jim heard it too, and they both darted towards the sound. Finding him, together they quickly lifted him up and helped him to the horses. Jim took the wet blanket and tore a strip and wrapped it around Clay's cut, and then another for him to use as a filter from the smoke, as he continued to cough. Now they realized they needed to get him to the house. Jim's horse was larger and could carry Morgan and Clay easily. Morgan rode to the house on Buck, while Jim rode to town for the doctor. Clay was still not out of danger.

~~

Lalani now began to worry about Jim, Morgan, and Clay since they had not returned. It had been over an hour since Jim left. She tried to keep her mind on carrying the water, as she brought water for the men who had been working hard for the last three hours. They had the length of the ranch road cleared and were now making their way on the narrow plowed strip to the creek. This was much slower and required twice the area to be cleared in order to create an effective break. Getting the water to this area was difficult, as the dirt was uneven, causing the water to splash out of the buckets, therefore Lalani could only fill them half full. She became more worried about Jim and the other with each bucket filled._Where are they, something must be wrong._

The fire now could be seen from the house porch. It was beginning to reach the ridge just beyond the hill that came down into the ranch and Ben, now in charge, wasn't sure what to do. The road into the ranch would soon be cut off when the fire reached the next hill. The men and Lalani would be trapped, not to mention the horses in the north paddock, as there was no other road out of the small valley. *If the firebreak doesn't stop the fire, where can we go?*

Ben knew it was time to make Lalani leave and go into town to be safe. *Why aren't Jim and Morgan back? Something has happened to Clay.* Just then Lalani arrived with another load of water. Once the water was distributed, Ben took Lalani aside. "It's time for you to go. The fire will be here in the next few hours, and Jim won't want you here."

She looked at Ben, "This is my home and I'm not leaving. If you men stay and risk your lives for my home, I can't leave either. If we leave, we leave together. If I go anywhere, it's to find Jim. He should be back by now."

"Something must have happened to Clay. I'm sure Morgan and Jim got to him and must be taking care of him. But as for you, the road will be cut off soon. You need to go to town where you'll be safe." Ben said trying to reassure her and at the same time impress the urgency to leave.

"I'm not leaving! We can go where the horses go, to the creek, if need be. It won't be the first time I have been knee deep in cold water. But more than that, I have faith that your work will do the job. The winds have not picked up, and as long as they don't, the firebreak will work. I have seen this work in Hawaii, and it will work here," she said confidently. "Jim knows I'll be here, waiting for him.," she admitted softly.

Ben and the others continued to work as they watched the fire race towards them. Lalani started to return to the barn for one more load of water, but instead she went to the porch watching the fire come closer. She knew it must be getting late in the day, but it was hard to tell since the smoke was so thick. She soaked a handkerchief and wore it around her mouth to help her breathe. The horses in the paddock were beginning to trot back and forth at the far east end to get away from the smoke. She worried Camille and Rosie would go into labor and drop their foals because of the stress. *God, please let Jim and Clay be at the main ranch and Katherine not be too worried. Please keep them safe.*

She started down the steps back to the barn and instinctively look towards the ranch road, searching through the smoke, for any sign of Jim. Through teary eyes, she made out a rider coming towards her. She knew that silhouette anywhere. It was Jim. He dismounted quickly as he reached the house. She ran to him, then reaching up, kissed him squarely on the lips, hugging him she was so happy he was safe. After a moment, he filled her in on finding Clay and that he had gone for Doc Newell, who was now on his way to the Taylor's, if the road was still passable.

The men returned from the fireline on the southwest and now felt it best to be at the house to fight any flames that might get through. Lalani told the men to take a break and brought water and towels so they could at least wash some of the dirt from their faces. She brought what cheese and bread she had and handed it out.

She was anxious for the large oak out front and wanted to soak the ground around it. Jim knew that wouldn't help if an ember caught in the canopy, but he placated her and helped carry buckets until the front part was soaked. As they poured the last bucket, they could see the fire had reached the top of the hill west of the ranch road. Now it was time for everyone to man shovels to stop any flames from crossing the line.

Lalani knew too well the danger of holding the line. She had seen men get entangled in the flames and their clothes catch fire, or be overtaken by the smoke when fighting the sugarcane fires. Jim didn't want her on the line. He wanted her down by the creek safe. But she once again refused to budge. She filled a few buckets of water and went and got blankets from the house to soak, in case they were needed. Together Lalani and Jim walked the quarter mile to the road as the fire came flicking down the hill.

Lalani stood back a short distance from the back edge of the fire break, with the buckets and blankets at her side, hoping they would not be needed. She looked to the sky, now a shadowy orange as the sun was beginning to set. The winds had not come up and all seemed still, with only the smell of fire and a faint crackling of burning brush being heard. The line of fire itself was about two feet wide that swept slowly down the hill.

Luke Henry, one of the ranch hands, a Maddock Indian, came up to her. "This is a good fire. We would set fires to burn the underbrush to prevent large forest fires that looked a lot like this. If we are watchful, there will be no problems, and it will burn itself out. No worry." He then grabbed his shovel and took up a spot on the road.

For the next hour, the men shoveled dirt and pounded out hot spots that tried to leap the road. As the sun set, the darkness showed where the flames burned brightest. The flames along the ranch road burned out first. But those to the southwest, along the makeshift fireline, were more persistent. Twice, the flames jumped the line and men scrambled to get them out. Ben sent one man back with a burnt arm where his shirt caught fire. Lalani had brought salve from the house and carefully washed and dressed the burn. The young man assured her he was fine and still needed, then returned to Jim to help.

From out of nowhere Morgan showed up. He had not been able to get through on the road as the fire tried to cross it, and was himself fighting to prevent the fire from crossing over. It was just now he was sure it was out, and he could reach them. He told her Clay was quite ill but out of danger. A short moment later, six of the men began to return from the southwest edge.

"The fire's out. Jim and a few others are going to stay and watch for hot spots that might flame up."

Morgan went to join Jim while Lalani walked back to the house with the men. While they washed up, Lalani got a pot of coffee going, and bacon, eggs, and fried potatoes cooking. It was the best she could do, as she had not thought to put on a roast or chickens to bake. The men didn't complain, but were grateful for the hot food and a place to sit. After an hour they loaded up into the wagon they had come in and headed back into town and to the ranches where they worked.

Lalani wanted to go out to Jim and Morgan, but it was dark and she knew she would only be a worry to them. Instead, she lit the lantern and filled a wheelbarrow with hay and took it out to the north paddock to feed the mares. They were calm again, and Prince Philip came up and nudged her as if he was ready to return to his stall. She opened the gate and took his halter in one hand and the lantern in the other and led him to the barn, first making sure the gate was secure and the foals were safely by their mothers. At the barn she feed Philip, Buck and Clyde, and rehung the water buckets.

Now she went inside and made sure the stove fire was still hot and put on a pot for hot water. Then she went to the parlor and lit the lamps so she could read while she waited. Makana came and curled up next to her chair as she sat quietly thanking the Lord for the protection and anxious for Jim to come home.

As the sun came up Makana began to whine at the door, waking Lalani from her chair where she had fallen asleep. She rushed to the door in hope of seeing Jim at the barn, but he wasn't there. She could now hear the commotion going on in the horse paddock. The mares were trotting up one end of the paddock, and then back. Lalani slipped on her sweater as the air was still chilly. At the far end of the paddock, she could see Camille lying on the ground. She climbed through the fence and ran down to her. A few feet from the mare lay a newborn foal still half covered with mucus. It wasn't breathing. Camille's belly was still bulging and blood lay at her rear. The mare breathed heavily, but didn't move as Lalani knelt by her head. *The foal must have got caught up inside her and has caused her to hemorrhage. I don't think there is anything I can do at this point. Katherine and Jim would know what to do.* Lalani sat stroking the mare's long jaw trying to comfort her. The mare's eye was glassy, and she didn't react to her touch. *I need to get Jim, but I'm sure he would do only what needs to be done now. Having to put down a horse now, on top of the struggle with the fire, just isn't fair. I can't put Jim through that. Lalani, you need to do it, you can't just let her suffer and bleed to death. It could be hours before Jim comes home.*

Lalani patted Camille one last time and then got up. The other mare had moved to the opposite end of the paddock. She looked for Rosie hoping she had not had the same problem. She spotted Rosie, still with her fat belly, standing by the gate. Lalani slowly walked up to Rosie and took hold of her halter. Opening the gate carefully, she led the mare through and relocked it. She didn't want Rosie in the paddock when she put down Camille. Slowly the two walked to the barn and Lalani put Rosie in the stall next to Prince Philip. She looked in the tack room, but no rifle was there. *Jim must keep them in the bunkhouse.* There she found two guns. Jim's big Winchester and his holster with his Colt. She had never handled a gun and was pretty sure she wouldn't be able to hold the rifle straight enough. She took the revolver, seeing it was loaded, and made her way back to Camille. Camille lay still, barely breathing. *Maybe she is gone already and I don't have to do this.*

Lalani laid her hand on her neck and could feel a faint pulsing. Then she stood and pointed the gun at Camille's temple. Her hand shook and she was afraid she would miss the mark and cause the poor mare to suffer more. Finally, Lalani held the gun with both hands and bending closer, took a deep breath and squeezed the trigger. The bullet tore through Camille's temple and blood sprayed back at Lalani's hands. Lalani closed her eyes and turned away, now not being able to look. Lalani dropped the gun and began to run towards the house, when suddenly she was grabbed by Jim, taking her into his arms and holding her tight as she began to sob. Jim had seen it all. He tried to reach her so she didn't have to do it, calling out to her, but Lalani was lost in the emotions of it all and didn't hear him.

"It's alright, it had to be done. I'm sorry I wasn't here. Wait here, I'll be right back," Jim said softly. Jim let go of Lalani, now frozen with her back to the tragedy. Jim walked over and picked up the gun and made sure the mare and foal were dead. Then he returned to Lalani putting his arm around her and led her back to the house.

Jim took Lalani to the kitchen and washed the blood from her hands and kissed her gently on the cheek. This seemed to release Lalani from the horror gripping her, and she now concentrated on Jim being home. "I'm so glad to have you home safe. I'm sorry you had to come back to all that. It's such a shame. You must be tired. I had the bath waterpot on the stove heating, but it's only lukewarm now." She grabbed two sticks of wood to started up the stove fire to reheat the water, as she rattled on. Jim stood at the sink, he was covered in dirt and soot, and he smelled of smoke, not sure what to do. Lalani started to put on a pot of coffee but her hands still shook, causing Jim put his arms around her again and lead her to the table to sit with him. "Ranch life can be hard at times. You sure you don't want to go back to Boston?"

She looked at him with tears in her eyes and took a deep breath, "I've been dealt blows harder than this. As long as we're together we can bounce back." She listened as he talked about the hot spots that came and went during the night, but that they were able to put them out by carrying water from the creek. That around sunrise with the winds calmed, they felt confident everything was out. She asked if he knew anymore about Clay. Jim hadn't taken the time to tell her what happened when he returned, and now explained about the rattler, and that they had found Clay just in time. Lalani knew Katherine would be terribly worried and felt she should go to her. But for the first time, she had someone else that needed her more and who she wanted to take care of more. She would stay with Jim and see Katherine, once things were back in order.

Lalani insisted that Jim use the large tub upstairs to wash and relax in. Together they carried two hot buckets of water up for him to use. She stripped off Jim's shirt and helped pull off his boots. He was so tired. Then she pulled a clean dress from her closet, as hers was covered in dirt and blood, and left Jim to himself. She went out to the bunkhouse and fetched clean clothes for him and took them up, setting them on the chair in her room. She peeked at Jim lying in the tub with his eyes closed. *Thank goodness he's too tall to be able to lie completely down, I'd hate for him drown.*

Lalani had now changed into a clean dress and sat at the kitchen table. She started to hold the cup of coffee in her hand, but it began to shake as she thought of the past day's events. *Am I really cut out to be a rancher's wife? I realize now I have always lived in the city away from nature's cruelties and guns. Can I even stay in one place? I've travelled most of my life. Even with Katherine in Boston, we traveled to New York, Philadelphia and London. We went to Paris, Vienna, Saint Petersburg and more. Am I fooling myself in thinking I could settle in this wilderness on a ranch? The ranch is more than a house, chickens and a vegetable garden. I've never been truly comfortable around horses and I have no idea about cattle. Putting down a steer or finding a dead calf would be just as horrifying as the mare and foal were this morning. I don't ever want to go through that again. And yet if we have livestock on the ranch, I know it will happen again.* She shook her head, trying to get rid of the overwhelming feeling and looked around the kitchen for a distraction. *I do love this house and the sense of home it gives me. I loved the thought of coming here, to home, when I left France. And Jim, I do so love Jim. But will he want to travel? He has been a rancher all his life. What am I to do? What do I really want? I've never really had the freedom to choose for myself and now I just don't know what I want. I want this house and Jim, but with them comes the trappings of livestock and ranching. I'm just not sure I'm cut out for it. Is Jim right I'm better off in Boston? Don't be silly, Boston never felt like home. Nowhere feels like home. Only this house and the people here give me the feeling of belonging - of home.*

After about forty minutes, Jim, clean and more awake, joined Lalani in the kitchen. She had put her thoughts aside and began cooking bacon, eggs and potatoes. Jim told her how proud he was of her for working so hard with him and the men to stop the fire to protect the ranch. "It's our home, Jim. It's our life together I was protecting. I will always want us to work side by side together. It shows our love for each other," she said, taking his hand and trying hard to believe her words in light of the doubts she had just been having about ranch life.

They talked about the damage done by the fire, which was very little. Lalani had not been afraid of the fire as she worked with Jim. It had not raged out of control, and she felt safe by Jim and the other men. The grass would grow back, and the Taylors would be able to graze cattle there by late August. *Kālua 'ana* was not damaged at all. Other than the loss of the one mare and foal, they had been very lucky.

Later, Lalani and Jim together moved the mustang mares and their foals from the north paddock to the barn corral. Lalani didn't want to go into the paddock, but stayed at the gate and opened it as Jim brought a mare, with its foal following close. She kept her mind on the gate and didn't want to look at the mares. Jim sensed she was still troubled by that morning's event. Jim would bury Camille and the foal in the morning. He was too tired to do it that day, and hoped the coyotes wouldn't come in and scavenge the carcass. He hoped the fire had driven them far enough away for a day or two so he would take care of it on the morrow.

Jim went back out to the burnt area to doublecheck for hot spots, and Lalani set to work cleaning the drapes and scrubbing the smell of smoke that clung to everything. By the time Jim had come in from checking on the yearlings in the south paddock, feeding the mares and horses in the barn, and checking on Rosie, it was late afternoon. He came to the house and helped Lalani rehang the parlor drapes she had washed and then sat down and closed his eyes until supper. That evening they sat quietly together in the parlor. Jim wanted to get Lalani's mind on something pleasant and tried to discuss some of the details for the wedding. What suit should he wear? What other things did he need to take care of? What flowers would be available for her wedding crown? Where would they spend their honeymoon night? Lalani tried to hide her looming doubts and said she would be content at the house, as she rubbed her ring fingernail. Jim didn't notice as the fatigue of the last few days set in. His thought was on the honeymoon location and he thought she would want something a little more special. Not being able to get an answer from Lalani on any wedding decisions, Jim gave up. They sat watching the moon come up over the trees for a few moments, then Jim went to the bunkhouse, and Lalani and Makana retired to her room. Exhausted, they all slept soundly.

7

Clearing the Doubts

The second day after the fire, Jim and Lalani thought it was time to go see how Clay and Katherine were doing and to tell them about Camille, as well as bring Medianoche home. They were delighted to see Clay up and around. Katherine whisked Lalani off to their sitting room, while Clay, Morgan and Jim talked in the study. Katherine told Lalani how scared she was when they brought Clay home. She apologized for not being at the ranch when the fire approached. She was preparing to come with food and to be there with Lalani when they brought Clay home. Then all such plans went sideways.

"No need to apologize. I was busy helping Jim with the fire break and you were needed here. The fire really didn't worry me as long as the winds didn't pick up. I'd seen many sugarcane fields burning as a child, and this was similar to that. I just worried about Jim, and if he was alright."

"Of course, you were. I too was so worried. Clay's convulsions during the night were awful. I'm just glad everything has turned out alright and we can get back to happier things."

Lalani wanted to know how Katherine was feeling and who else knew she was pregnant. Katherine was now three months along and had not been able to keep breakfast down most mornings. Lalani reminded her about how ill Kate's cousin Irene had been with her first child. There was always a mess to clean up.

"At least this time someone else has the privilege." It was the new housekeeper Lupe, a young Hispanic girl about twenty years old. Lupe now worked for the Taylors, helping with cleaning and laundry. "She's not as good as you are with my dresses. Perhaps you could give her a few pointers," Kate sheepishly said.

"We will see. So, the baby will arrive in time for Thanksgiving. It will truly be a joyous occasion."

Kate now wanted to talk about when the furniture they had ordered would arrive, and wedding plans. "I told the manager it was imperative your bed arrive before the 28th. That my furnishings could wait if necessary." Lalani blushed, and an uneasy quietness came across her face as she unconsciously fiddled with her fingernail. "Lalani what is it?"

After a moment, Lalani finally got her courage up and told Kate about Camille and the loss of the foal, how she hated doing what needed to be done. But the other mares and foals were fine, and Rosie didn't seem to be stressed, that Jim would keep a close eye on her until her foal arrived.

"I'm sorry you had to be the one to put her down. I know it's a horrible thing. I remember watching my father do it one time when I was nine. To be honest, if we had to lose one, I'm sure Jim and Clay are glad it was Camille. She only gave us trouble, first causing Clay to injure his back and me to be poisoned by that rusty nail. Still, she was a beautiful spirited broodmare. We do have her first filly, which we can keep and use for breeding when she's old enough. But what does that have to do with your wedding?" Kate asked with a great deal of concern in her voice.

Lalani just smiled. "I hoped my dress will be finished on time," she half-heartedly replied as she sat rubbing her index fingernail.

"Lalani that's not it. You can't be having doubts about marrying Jim?"

"Kate, I love Jim and want to be his wife... I ... I just don't know if I can be a rancher's wife. What happened with Camille haunts me.

When I think of it, it makes me sick to my stomach. I've only known life in a big city and traveling. I'm not a rancher. I don't know if I can do it. I want to work side by side with Jim, as we did fighting the fire. But you know I've … well, I've always been afraid of horses."

"Lalani, you don't have to work with the horses. Jim and I will. Clay and I even talked about moving them onto the west property, putting them on Taylor land, building new paddocks and hay barn. You love Jim."

"I do! But I don't know if Jim likes to travel or would want to go hear a symphony. You and I have been here in Oak Ridge for two years, and we still have traveled to Europe and gone to San Francisco often. It's part of me, I realize now, and not running after horses. I'm not sure I'm the right wife for Jim."

"Jim loves music. He sat every evening with us as I played piano. Have you talked to him about this?"

"No, I've just begun to realize it since the fire," Lalani admitted. "He did want to take me somewhere special for our honeymoon, and seemed disappointed when I said we could just stay at the house."

"See, he does want to take you places. Don't you think he has thought about your life and how you have been all over world. That's part of you and makes you special. He has always been attentive when you talk about Hawaii. I think if you talk to him, you will find he's adventurous too… After all, he came to work for two women!" This gave them both a chuckle.

Kate continued to point out how things work out when they're meant to be, pointing out how hopeless her and Clay's relationship was, with her being married when she came and how they could only be friends. But with her husband's unexpected and sudden death, they were free to be together and are very happy. Kate said that Clay only knew ranching, but loved music and was eager to see Europe and all the places she had been.

Lalani's doubts began to subside as Kate rattled on. "Perhaps you're right. Jim wouldn't ask me to do anything I don't want to do. I do love him. I just need to ask him about travelling."

Lalani then asked where Clay would want to go for a night that wasn't too far away.

Kate thought for a moment. "What about the Tallman Hotel up at Upper Lake. It's supposed to be the newest place for getting away out of the city, but very nice, not rustic."

Just then Miranda knocked on the door, "Dinner is about to be served. Are you two going to join me and the men?"

"We're coming!" Kate called back.

Jim and Clay met the ladies at the bottom of the stairs and escorted them into dinner. Kate held Clay back slightly and whispered to him, that Lalani was reluctant about the horses and that they should go ahead with their plans to move them. "What are you two whispering about? Come and sit," Miranda said, as Lupe brought steaks and mashed potatoes to the table. Kate and Clay didn't eat much, as their stomachs were still a little squeamish. Morgan and Jim on the other hand were famished. They had been working hard the last several days.

"Well, Clay, what have you men been talking about? We women are certainly not going to tell you what we discussed," Kate smiled.

Clay came back with, "We were talking about what Jim wants to do with the land. Mostly about cattle. Kate, I think we need to move the south paddocks to the west field, once the grass begins to grow back. The fire didn't do too much damage and the area should be good for horses within several more months and some rain."

"I agree. That way the cattle can have the south pasture and access to the creek. Jim, Lalani told me you came up today to visit but also to fetch Medianoche to bring him back to the barn. But I think he should stay here. He has always challenged you and been difficult when the mares are in heat. He has seldom given me trouble, and up here he will be away from the mares. There's room for him in the stables. I also want to keep Duchess here. She was only there while we were gone."

"Kate, I agree, but Genevieve will be arriving from England soon. Where will we put her?"

"Genevieve?" asked Miranda.

"Oh, she's my mare from the England estate. I just couldn't sell her. Lalani, you remember her. She is such a gentle horse." Kate looked across to Lalani for approval.

"Yes, I remember, she was the only horse that has never tried to eat my fingers as I fed her carrots. I guess she would make good company for Prince Philip and Buck if Medi is gone."

"Then it's settled. Medi will stay here and Genevieve will go there."

Clay then suggested they meet in the next few days to lay out plans for the west field: where paddocks would go, and the need for a hay barn.

Morgan reminded them there was still a lot of work to be done rounding up cattle, and the wedding would be here before they knew it. Lalani and Jim didn't stay much longer after dinner. There was still a half days work be done.

Jim had sensed an uneasiness about Lalani since the shooting of Camille, but now on the way home in the carriage, as Lalani held his arm, she seemed less tense. He was glad she had Kate to talk to, but hoped she would feel free to talk to him about anything. They were quiet most of the way home, only commenting on how good the meal was and glad that Kate and Clay were doing better. As they came down the hill into the ranch, they both spoke up. "We have things to talk about," came out at the same time from both of them, causing them to chuckle. "Yes, we do. Let's sit down by the fire this evening and talk about your plans for the ranch," Lalani said.

"Our plans!" Jim retorted and gave her hand a pat.

Lalani was encouraged by what Kate had said and what had been decided at dinner. She did worry that it wasn't what Jim wanted. Jim liked working with the horses. He always said they were so much smarter than cattle. That evening she made a light supper, but took time to make an apple cobbler with the remaining jars of apples from the pantry. She set the dining room table with fresh linens and candles in hopes to establish a more refined setting for the last meal of the day. Jim washed up and put on a clean shirt and knocked on the back door as usual. "You really don't need to knock anymore," she said smiling.

"I like being greeted and this way I can give you a kiss," he grinned reaching forward and kissing her on the cheek.

They sat at supper, Jim noting it was nice having the candles setting a warm calm mood. He admitted it had been a pretty hectic several days and was relieved the newly planted alfalfa field had not been affected by the fire, or the hay field. But now he wanted to concentrate on Lalani and the wedding. "What do you need me to do?"

Lalani turned and looked at him for a long moment. "I need you to tell me how you feel about a wife that's not a rancher that has grown up in big cities and traveling. Do you think I can be the kind of wife you and a ranch need?"

Jim was caught somewhat off guard. He knew the incident with Camille had affected her quite strongly, but he didn't know she was now getting cold feet again. He pushed the plates aside and took her hand, "Lalani, I know you're a city girl who was looking for a simple quiet life. And I want to give you that life. I gather from the outcome of today's decision regarding the horses, that you don't want this to be a horse ranch. I always knew you were uncomfortable round them. I'm fine with that. I work well with horses but they take a lot more work, and I'm not going to be able to be breaking horses for too much longer. That's why I thought raising cattle would be the best way to make a living." He smiled and took a breath to give her a chance to say what she wanted to say.

"I just have never been around livestock, until coming here. I do like feeding the foals once they're weaned, but they grow so fast and get so strong and big."

"What about cattle?" Jim asked.

"I don't know. I know even less about them, just that you and Morgan disappear for two weeks twice a year to round them up to ship to the market."

"Well, that's a part of it. Making sure they are fed and watered is another big part. Having the right bull for breeding is another. But you don't have to tame a bull and you can't ride a steer," Jim said laughingly. The north horse paddock could become the calf pasture. Calves are fun to watch and you could feed them if you wanted to."

"Would you consider getting a few sheep for the north paddock?"

"What? Sheep! This isn't really sheep country. Cattle men aren't too friendly towards sheep, as they eat the grass down to nothing. Just how many sheep do you want?" Jim said with a leery bite to his lower lip.

"Just one or two, so I can have wool to make yarn for knitting. When I lived in Boston, I had a spinning wheel and got fleece and made yarn for socks and shawls."

"Oh! I think we can get you a couple sheep for that purpose. Good wool socks would be great to have for the cold winters." He was relieved it was only one or two. But Lalani still sat with her napkin, polishing her fingernail and Jim knew there was something more on her mind, something she needed that perhaps didn't involve the ranch.

He got up and took one of the candles and then her hand and led her to the parlor as the sun had set. He sat her down on the settee and then moved to the fireplace and started a fire. Staying with it until it was underway, but also giving Lalani time to gather her thoughts for what was still on her mind, he placed the candle on a table and came and sat with her, putting his arm around her.

"Now, you do know I don't expect you to work cattle or wrangle horses, or plow fields. So, tell me what else is bothering you. I don't want my bride to have cold feet about anything."

Looking at the fire she cried out, "Travel! How do you feel about traveling?" Looking at Jim she rattled on in an excited but leery manner. "I've traveled all my life. I look back and see that about every five years I have ended up in a new country, and within that time at least once a year I have taken a trip to somewhere. Not because I choose to, but because of Kate and Edith. But still I'm afraid come another six months, I'm going to have the urge to pack my bags and go somewhere. And if I do, I want you to come with me."

Jim just smiled a big smile and pulled her close to him. "Wherever you go, I will be there with you. Why do you think I wanted to take you somewhere special for our honeymoon? I'm not sure I can afford to take you on extravagant trips to Europe every year, but someday I would like to take you back to your native Hawaii."

"You would leave the cattle and go on a trip to Hawaii?" she turned with earnest and asked.

"Well, I think we will need to hire a ranch hand that can take care of feeding if we go. And I probably would balk at going during spring and fall planting and roundup, but that leaves us forty-six other weeks out of the year."

Lalani put her arms around Jim's neck and for the first time gave him a deep hug and kissed him squarely on the lips. "I knew I loved you Jim Baker, and now I know why."

"Why?" he said with a puzzled look.

"Because you love me for who I am," and kissed him again. She then settled back into his arms ready to be a wife. The kind of wife she wanted to be: caring, supportive and sharing experiences.

"Jim, promise me one thing. We will make this ranch what we want, not just what I want. I'm willing to learn and do to a point, it will be my new adventure. This is *ko makou wahi*– our place, *Kālua 'ana*. Let's buy the land for the cattle together. I want to use some of my money 50/50 together."

"Clay warned me about independent wealthy women. That when you want something you go ahead and buy it. He told me he didn't pay for the trip to Europe, Katherine did. I assume you don't have millions like she does and I'm pretty sure you won't want to just go out and buy anything you see. Not that I'm saying you can't, if you wanted to. Just promise me you won't go buying things for me because I can't afford to buy them. I don't think my ego could take that. Besides, I'm not poor, I actually have a good amount saved."

"Oh, Jim, no, that's not what I mean. I just want this place to be ours together. We get what we need when we can afford it and with both us buying them. Our funds can go twice as far and keep us going longer, that's all."

"Agreed, except for one thing, I called the bed maker and paid for the new bed myself. I told him to keep your funds on hand for something else you might want."

"Jim Baker, going behind my back is not going to be allowed," she said with a grin.

"Even if it's for a good surprise?" he winked.

They snuggled like young people in love unsupervised and watched the fire until it died down. Then Jim's hankering for her apple cobbler got the best of him, and together they cleared the dinner plates they had left on the table. Lalani warmed the cobbler in the stove warmer, while she washed dishes and he dried. Finally, they settled back in the parlor with the cobbler.

For the next few days things got back to normal. Lalani fed the chickens and weeded her garden as things began to spring up. Jim took care of the horses, and Rosie had a healthy dark bay colt. All the mares and their foals were back in the north paddock for now.

Katherine, Clay and Morgan came down late one afternoon to discuss plans for the layout of the new paddocks and haybarn. They wanted Jim's thoughts since Kate hoped he would still help her. The main idea was to have a haybarn between the two pastures for easy access during winter months. Clay pointed out that it shouldn't just be a hay barn, but should provide a few stalls for mares that might need special care. They agreed that two large stalls at the west end was all that would be needed. The barn's main purpose was for hay storage. They would create a road from the Taylor ranch that would divide the west field in half and join up with the road into the Circle K. The barn and attached weaning corral would be near the bottom of the field towards the Taylor ranch, on flat ground. Water was the biggest problem. How to get water to the new paddocks and the barn. A well would need to be dug. Clay was all excited about putting in a windmill to pump the water into the large troughs for both north and south pastures. Where to place it was the problem. Morgan and Jim thought about how deep a well would need to be dug to reach the water table, and Clay thought about where the wind would be strongest to make the mill work. They could not agree on one place. The top of the ridge had the wind but the well would have to be quite deep to get water during the summer.

Katherine took Lalani to the kitchen while the men haggled over locations. She wanted to know if she had talked with Jim about her concerns. She could see Lalani was happy again, but she wanted to know how it went. Lalani told her they talked, and that they agreed on a cattle ranch and to do some traveling. But mostly they would do whatever together, making compromises when necessary.

Lalani had one thing she needed Kate's help on, that was who would give her away at the wedding. She thought she would ask Morgan to walk her down the aisle, but Jim wanted him to be his best man. "Should I just walk by myself?"

"You could, but what about Eric?" Lalani didn't feel right about Eric as she didn't know him well enough.

"Well, then, Clay would be next best. He would be delighted to do it. He has been here with us ever since we arrived. You should ask him." Lalani said she would think about.

They returned to the men still in conversation about location and cost. Katherine finally set the matter to rest, saying that just below the top of the ridge on the Taylor side, they would hire a crew to come dig a deep well. They would begin digging in late July to make sure they reached the water table at its low point. She would cover the cost and felt every penny would be worth it in the long run. They would run lines from the well to the troughs that the windmill would keep full automatically. Another line from the well could be laid to bring water to the barn. From Lalani and Jim's place, they wouldn't see the mill or the barn, but the field would remain open as it did now. They would only see the horses that wandered over to that side. The plan did have a downside. *Kālua 'ana* would be downwind from the horses and the smell might infringe on their place from time to time. Lalani could live with that if everything else made everyone happy.

With the wedding so close now, these plans would wait until after the honeymoon. The next big thing was the furniture for both houses was due to arrive by train in the next few days. Morgan just laughed recalling the last time he and Clay had offloaded Kate's furniture from the train. It was when she and Lalani just arrived in Oak Ridge and moved to the small ranch. It took all day and three large wagons to move everything out to the ranch. Katherine assured Morgan it would only take half a day and two wagons this time.

Clay chimed in with, "And no piano!" The hour was late, and Lalani asked if they wanted to stay for supper, but Kate assured her Miranda would have supper waiting.

Lalani took Clay's arm as they headed for the door. "Clay, I want to ask you something," she said holding him back. Jim took the opportunity to take Kate's arm, as he had something to ask her.

Clay smiled, "Lalani, the plans are fine to bring the horses up to our west range. It's really what Kate wants." She smiled back, "I'm glad to hear that, but no, I wanted to ask if you would give me away on my wedding day. You and Morgan are the closest I have to family. Jim wants Morgan to be his best man, so would you do me the honor of escorting me down the aisle?"

Clay put his arm around her smiling, "I would be more than honored. You're Kate's big sister. You're family. Of course, I will."

Meanwhile as Jim helped Kate into the carriage, he leaned in and asked. "Kate, is Lalani okay living here on the ranch when we are married? I know you two talked earlier. She doesn't want to live in the city, does she?"

Kate looked at him with a gentle grin. "No, Jim, she wants to be here with you on the ranch. It was really more about me getting out of the way with the horses. As long as you two work this place together in your own activities, you'll be fine. That and she will want to travel from time to time. It's just part of us." Jim nodded and smiled with relief.

Clay climbed up next to Kate, smiling, "I'm going to give Lalani away. Best get my blue suit pressed." Morgan mounted his horse, adding, "I'm best man and already had my blue suit pressed." Clay gave the reins a small crack and they headed for home, while Jim stood with his arm around Lalani waving from the porch.

~~

The week before the wedding was filled with unexpected surprises. On Sunday after church, the ladies held a surprise bridal shower for Lalani. Mrs. Olsen, Carol, as Lalani now called her good friend, had sewn new pillow slips embroidered with the initials: JB and LB. Mrs. Swenson had made a lovely pinwheel quilt in greens and lavender. Miranda had purchased sheets for the new bed that would arrive soon. Kate had ordered a new silky night gown, causing all the ladies to blush. Lalani was overwhelmed with the generosity.

The next day, the train with the furniture arrived and musical furniture once again took place. First, they delivered Kate's things to the main house and then retrieved the settee from Lalani's, all before the noon meal. Miranda and Lalani had to keep after Kate and stop her from lifting things she shouldn't, now being three months pregnant and beginning to show slightly.

Jim and Morgan moved Lalani's new dressing table to her room first. Then they disassembled Lalani's bed and moved it the guest room, taking that bed to the bunkhouse. Lalani didn't want to use the new bed without Jim and would sleep in the guest room for now.

Jim stood in front of the new mahogany bed, now assembled, proud of its strong manly lines. *This will keep us warm on cold nights. Plenty of room for me to stretch out and Lalani to snuggle.*

"Jim, you can hold your horses and stop thinking about the wedding night. The wedding's not for another five days," Morgan uttered loudly.

Jim swung around and shook his head, "Nothing you need to know."

Lalani was happy with the new sofa and chair she had selected for the parlor. Jim still liked the original wingback chair that was there. "It's already broken in to fit me." He was pleased with the new sofa, trying it out to see if it was long enough for him to nap. "You put your dirty boots on there again, and you'll find yourself back in the bunkhouse," Lalani scolded as she pushed his boots back to the floor.

"Yes, ma'am! No boots on the furniture."

By the end of the day *Kālua 'ana* was complete and ready for the newlyweds. Jim placed the hurricane lamp on the new game table, now situated where the piano had been. Lalani stood by her new small Louis XVI chair, content with the new purchases and homey feel of the room.

Midweek, Jim came up to the house dressed in good clothes. "Lalani, you need to hurry and change your dress. We have a train to San Francisco to catch this morning." Jim was taking Lalani to get her wedding dress and to meet with Eric to purchase the land. He had arranged with Mr. Maxwell, the banker, to meet early to obtain the funds before the train left. Jim had not arranged for someone to take care of Makana, so they opted to take her with them. This would be her first trip, and Lalani hoped her training had been enough to keep the six-month pup on good behavior.

Lalani scurried to change and do her hair. They met Mr. Maxwell and then made the train just as the final whistle blew. They arrived in the city just before 11:00 o'clock, in time for her appointment for her final dress fitting. Knowing he shouldn't see the gown, Jim took Makana and departed to do other errands.

Lalani's dress was striking, with the Hawaiian printed fabric skirt and bodice trimmed in black satin to complement the skirt. The small jacket for the church ceremony was gathered in the back to create a slight bustle, but not take away from the skirt. Lalani wished her mother could see the dress as well as Mrs. Crocker. She knew they both would be pleased. Now she hoped Jim would like it.

Jim came back after an hour and they went to Eric's office. He was expecting them and had the deed to the ranch land waiting. Jim presented his bank draft for $300 and Lalani hers for the same amount. Eric smiled, "Partners all the way, I see." Eric had the deed in both their names, but since Lalani wasn't officially Mrs. Baker, it only read Lalani. He would bring it on Saturday for her to add Baker after her name, along with the marriage certificate for signing.

Eric had planned to take them to lunch, but a long-time client had an urgent need, preventing him from going. He assured them Evelyn and he would be at the wedding on Saturday. Jim had made reservations at Tidal Grill and asked if they could leave Makana at the office.

Makana had been quietly sitting at Lalani's side, but when they left without her, she pranced about the outer office, and her excited bushy tail cleared the table of documents. The court filings went flying and Eric's clerk was on her knees gathering them up when the next client arrived. Mrs. Witcomb was an elderly lady, and Makana immediately went to her.

She took one look at the office and said, "My goodness, you have caused a ruckus, now sit," and Makana sat. "Helena, you must take command with young pups or they'll get out of hand." Helena nodded and showed her to Eric's office.

Jim had one more surprise for Lalani. Just after they finished their meal, he pulled out a small box. "Lalani, you have agreed to be my wife, which makes me very happy. Will you wear this ring as a token of our promise to marry?" and he handed her the box. Inside was a splendid emerald and silver ring, not large but not a poor man's ring either. He pulled it from the box and slipped it on her finger, saying, "I will always love you," bringing tears to her eyes.

"Oh, Jim, it's beautiful, but you shouldn't have."

"On the contrary, I should have given it to you weeks ago. I have a simple wedding band for the ceremony that goes with it. But I wanted you to have the emerald green, your favorite color." Lalani reached forward and gave Jim a kiss on the cheek, then blushed, as she remembered she was in a public dining room. They returned home to *Kālua 'ana* that same day, content and happy the wedding was only three days away.

Katherine stopped by after her morning ride, to discuss the final wedding plans and to see the dress. Lalani happily showed her dress and her ring. From outside they could hear Morgan and Jim talking. Morgan led a beautiful roan mare towards the barn. Kate, upon seeing the mare, jumped up and rushed to the barn.

"Genevieve arrived on the early morning train," Morgan said as Kate came near.

Kate took the lead and gently rubbed her forehead. The horse responded with a soft nudge to Kate's face. "Happy to see me, are you?"

Morgan had been telling Jim there was no room at the ranch for another mare, that either Duchess or Genevieve would need to stay with him until the new stalls were built. Kate had ridden Duchess over but now felt Genevieve should be with her at the main house. Duchess was returned to her old stall next to Prince Philip without a complaint. Lalani had come out with a carrot and joined them standing back to stay out of the way. "Lalani, you remember Genevieve from London?"

"Oh, yes, let's see if she is as gracious about eating carrots as she used to be." Lalani walked up slowly, with the carrot behind her back. She reached and patted Genevieve, lightly on the forehead and slid her hand down her muzzle, gently rubbing it. Genevieve watched Lalani intently but didn't move. Finally, Lalani brought the carrot out and Genevieve's eyes widened and her muzzle lifted, but she did not try to grab the carrot. She patiently waited for Lalani to give it to her. Then with a loud crunch, half of the carrot was consumed.

"I guess she remembers you're the carrot lady," Kate said. "Lalani, Genevieve would be the perfect riding horse for you. It would be wonderful for the two of us to go riding."

"I'll keep my feet on the ground, thank you. Anyway, in another month, you're not going to be doing much riding. Your baby tummy will be too big for your britches."

"What do you mean will be. It's already too big. She's wearing my trousers," Morgan chimed in.

Kate rode Genevieve back home, and left Duchess. She liked Genevieve's gait, but somehow Duchess would always be her main horse. *I will leave Duchess there for a few days, but then that will be Genevieve's main home. She really would be a good horse for Lalani. Maybe Jim can get her to ride with him.*

The next day was busy at the church. At the last minute, they decided to hold the ceremony in the garden, since the peonies and iris were in full bloom and the weather was warm. Clay, Jim, and the reverend hunted around and found enough chairs for the twenty guests that would attend. The rose trellis was beginning to bud with small pinkish white blossoms, a perfect setting for the vows.

A small reception would be at *Kālua 'ana* since Lalani and Jim were to catch the 2:00 o'clock train to Sacramento. Miranda and Mrs. Swenson offered to do cake and punch and would bring them to the house first thing in the morning before the wedding.

May 28th was a beautiful clear spring morning. Lalani rose early and watched for Jim from her bedroom window. He came out of the barn, as he still had horses to feed before getting ready, and spotted Lalani standing at the window. He blew her a kiss and shouted, "Will you marry me today? " She nodded her head and smiled back. *Yes, I can't wait to marry you today.*

Kate and Clay came in the carriage shortly and Morgan with the small buggy. Morgan whisked Jim off to the church, almost forgetting his dress boots. Clay sat downstairs with a book and waited while the ladies took their time with hair and dresses. Finally, Lalani and Kate appeared at the parlor entrance. Clay took one look, "You're a rare radiant beauty, Lalani."

She was elegant but simple with a crown of orange blossom and baby's breath on top of her dark shiny hair sweeping down her back. Lalani's gown, with its Hawaiian print skirt and black trim top, created a scene of enchantment. Kate wore a simple satin green empress dress, gathered just below the bust to hide her rounding tummy.

At the church, Jim's friend, Dan, played violin for the guests as they were seated. Jim and Morgan stood at the top of the garden, Jim wearing his best dark blue suit and an open-ended camellia leaf lei representing the traditional Ti Leaf wedding lei.

The violin music slowed as Kate, carrying a bouquet of peonies, slowly walked down the short aisle. Then the music stopped, and Lalani and Clay appeared. Jim looked at her and saw for the first time how truly beautiful she was. Her dress and small crown of orange blossoms in her ebony straight hair caused her Hawaiian features to bloom into an ethereal loveliness. Jim's smile went from pleasant to Cheshire Cat size in an instant. Clay escorted Lalani down the aisle, his six-foot two inches towering over her. But it was Kate that spoke up when asked who gives this woman to married.

The wedding was simple with traditional vows and a double ring exchange, but ended with the tying of a leaf wedding cord around their wrists as they faced their guests, and Mr. and Mrs. James Baker were announced.

The deed was done. Jim beamed with pride as Lalani glowed with a warmth she had never known. Morgan had decorated the buggy with Just Married and a line of cans which bounced along as the small caravan of carriages made their way to *Kālua 'ana.*

The parlor furniture had been pulled to the wall to make room for a small dance area. Again, Dan played violin with a much livelier tune. "Jim, why don't you play something for Lalani?" he said after their first dance.

"Jim, you play violin? What else don't I know about you?" Lalani said with a surprised look.

"I played years ago. It was more fiddle than violin. Irish gigs. I don't think I can remember how."

Everyone insisted Jim try. Lalani took a seat as Jim took the violin. Slowly laying the bow on the strings, he pulled it across, creating a rather catlike yowl. He shook his head and then began to play *I went with him*, as a serenade to Lalani.

Lalani stood and kissed her new husband. "Well, we will have to get you a fiddle so you can continue to serenade me."

"Lalani, how about you doing a Hawaiian dance for us, seeing you have the gown," Morgan urged.

Jim took her hand and escorted her to the floor. Lalani removed her jacket, showing her bare arms and then slipped off the white slippers she wore.

"It wouldn't be Hawaiian if I wore shoes, and without music, it will lose translation." She took a small step forward and then one to the right and then back to left. With her hands she told the story of the sea and waves crashing against the land, the rain coming to the mountains, and rainbows bringing joy to the island. Dan joined with a tapping rhythm on his violin. This was the first time she had danced her native dance in a very long time.

When the applause ended, Kate invited Jim and Lalani to cut the cake, as time was drawing close for them to leave. As the festivities concluded, Lalani changed to traveling clothes, and the newlyweds stepped into their buggy and headed for the train to Sacramento.

~~

The train arrived in the state capital just before sunset. They stayed at the newly built Sterling House and had a quiet supper in the alcove of the dining room. Their room was softly lit and warmed by the graceful white fireplace. Lalani was nervous as she came to Jim in the gown Kate had given her. She didn't look at him at first, as she slid under the covers where he was waiting for her. As she lay back, he tipped her head up so he could see his eyes. A gentle patient deep love gleamed down at her. He took her in his arm and just held her, giving her time to feel comfortable laying by his side. His gentle kiss and her own desire finally allowed her to give herself to him, and Jim was a very happy man.

The next day they wandered down by the river, and then in the evening attended the Woodland opera, enjoying a spirited Gilbert and Sullivan performance of *The Sorcerer.* They walked along the shops and listened to a guitarist playing in the park. Before leaving, they made their way to the Capitol. The gold dome with its bell glistened in the sun, reminding Jim of how his father had come to California in hopes of finding gold in 1852, but never did. Then in 1863 he went to work on the Pacific Railroad as a foreman to help build the transcontinental line. Jim had left home long before then, preferring ranching to working with steel.

By Thursday they were anxious to return home to Oak Ridge and settle into married life. After an enchanting time in Sacramento, they arrived early evening at *Kalua 'ana,* and Jim swept Lalani up in his arms, carrying her over the threshold in his most gallant manner saying, "Welcome home Mrs. Baker," and gave her a lingering kiss to the lips.

Kate had brought Makana over, so she was waiting for them as they came through the door, prancing around them all excited. Once Makana was greeted, Jim retrieved their bags and took them to their room. Again, he stood looking at the bed. *The Sterling bed was fine, but brass beds make too much noise, creaking every time you move. Lalani was wonderful as a new bride, but she will feel much happier in our own bed.*

Lalani went to the kitchen and found a pot of stew and a small bouquet of wild flowers on the table that Kate had left. She lit a fire in the stove to warm the stew and mixed up some biscuits to go with it. They had sat at the dining table many times in the past, but it was different now. He wouldn't leave and head for the bunkhouse. Tonight, they would sit in the parlor by the fire and they would go upstairs together. As the hour grew late, Jim took Lalani's hand and led her upstairs to their room and closed the door behind them.

8

Big Changes

There was lots to be done at *Kālua 'ana*. Jim wanted to get the new paddocks on the west meadow built, in order to move the yearlings from the south paddock, now wanting it for cattle. The first year would not be productive. They would start small and build a herd over the years. A good breeding bull would be imperative and ten to twenty breeding heifers. There wouldn't be any calves for selling for about two years. Until they could make money, Jim would continue to work for Katherine, helping with the horses. She was going to need his help more and more as the birth of her baby got closer.

Lalani and Jim settled in quickly, getting used to the evening discussions about cattle, rather than horses, as Jim searched for a good Black Angus bull. "As soon as we can move the horses to the west paddock, I think we should take a trip up to Rancho Omochumnes, just south of Sacramento. Carol and Dennis Doyle are known for their bulls. You'll like Dennis, a good Irishman. I spent one summer with them when I first started working cattle."

"I'm always up for a trip. But let's not get ahead of ourselves. Don't you need to get the alfalfa and hay cut and stored first? After all, the new baler will be arriving soon. I'm eager to see how it works. Let's plan a trip for early August. Maybe they can sell us a heifer or two, as well."

Jim knew Lalani was right. It was mid-June and the fields weren't as tall as he wanted and the foals too young to separate from their mothers, so he would work with Ben and Dan to clear the road between the two paddocks. The drilling team for the well wasn't due to arrive for another two weeks, giving them plenty of time to cut the road and set the fence posts on the north paddock. The south side with the windmill, well, and barn, they would leave open for the wagons to bring in supplies.

The following week, Lalani wasn't really happy. Jim was busy clearing dirt and rocks, and setting fence posts. It was long hard work in the hot sun, and Jim would come home sweaty and tired. "Jim, I think you need to be here when Kate works with the yearlings. She's way too pregnant to be trying to put blankets on them. You need to help hold the lead and make sure they don't knock her down or worse." *Plus, that will get you out of digging post holes all day. Maybe you won't fall asleep right after supper.*

"I know you're right, Kate needs to let me handle them at this point. I'll talk with her. She can watch from the side while I get them used to the blankets."

"Watch from the side? She'll fight that idea. We will need Clay's backing to get her to agree to that."

Jim added, "She'll protest against the three of us, like a woodpecker knocking against a chimney pipe."

The next evening Lalani had Clay and Kate for dinner and cooked Katherine's favorite meal, lemon rosemary chicken with herb rice. When the topic of working with the horses arose, so did Kate's resistance to letting Jim take the reins. Jim pointed out that currently there wasn't much to do with the horses other than feed and train the yearlings with the saddle blankets. They were still too young for saddles, let alone ride. Still Katherine raised a ruckus, but it was all noise and no effect.

Lalani tried to change the subject to the baby. "Kate, you need to start thinking about baby things. We can go to see Joanna, and I'm sure she will have several things to give you."

"But we don't know if it's a boy or girl, and Joanna only had girls," Kate rebutted.

"Well, I'm sure she has some natural color items. White sleepers. Yellow blankets. You never know."

Clay finally spoke up, "Well, we don't want to take chances with the baby and you, so Jim will handle the horses for now.

"Besides, you need to design the layout of the new hay barn and stalls, and working corrals. The crew working on the well thinks they will hit water within the week. And we need to plan the windmills for pumping and how the pipes are to be laid out. That's going to take most of yours and Jim's time."

"I would like to get the hay barn built before we start harvesting," Jim admitted.

This seemed to pacify Katherine, giving her a new project to concentrate on. *I might as well give in on horses, three against one is unfair odds.*

In the morning, Jim took the saddle blankets out to the yearlings' paddock and laid them on the rail for the mares to sniff. When he came to feed in the late afternoon, he found them on the ground and horse slobber on the corner. *At least they didn't chew on them.*

Kate arrived early afternoon with Morgan. The three sat at the dining table to discuss needs and sketched possible designs for the barn. Jim just wanted a hay barn, not sure why the need for stalls. "If horses needed stabling, it would be best at the Circle K or the Taylor stables, where we can easily watch for problems. Isolated buildings tend to invite thieve to come in and take horses when no one's around. We won't be able to keep an eye on it from either of our places," Jim advised.

Morgan agreed, "Right now, we don't need the added expense. The country is in a financial downturn and buying horses may be low on a rancher's list at the moment."

"But the yearlings won't be ready for breaking for another two years. Surely the recession won't last that long," Kate said with concern.

"You never know, Kate. Back east, there've been various runs on some banks, and they've gone out of business," Morgan added.

It was agreed for now no stalls, just the haybarn. They then went on to figure out how the water pipes to the barn and the paddocks would work best and what size windmill would be needed to pump the water from the depth of the well. Lalani was just happy to have them all sitting inside, out of the heat.

It took them about a week to finalize plans. They had finished digging the well, hitting water at abut 380 feet. The well had a shaft of about 10 inches round. With its depth, they could store a little over 300 gallons and that would be plenty to get them through the dry summers, pumping 100 gallons a day for a dozen horses.

Lalani stayed clear of most of the discussion, bringing coffee and pie when things got heated between Morgan and Kate. By the end of the week, the lumber to build the barn was determined and the order placed with the mill. The paddocks were now complete and the men were reassigned to digging the foundation for the barn. Jim took charge as foreman, but Lalani made him keep his feet on the ground and leave the rafters to the younger hands as the walls went up. Morgan was needed by Clay to help prepare for next month's cattle roundup, saddle breaking some of their own horses, and mending fences.

The end of July came around and the barn was up, with just the finishing touches of windows, doors and hay pullies left to be done. Jim now had alfalfa and hay to cut and bale. The new baler had arrived, and he was eager to see how it worked. He had purchased a draft horse from the Meyer's and would no longer need to borrow one from Morgan. Clyde was a six-year-old Jutland draft, about 15 and a half hands, the typical chestnut with cream color mane and fetlocks. Clyde was already trained to pull a plow as well as a baler press. The fields first would need to be cut and left to dry for a week before baling.

It became clear to Jim, he was going to need help this year cutting
the fields, as the area was twice the acres since planting alfalfa and
hay. Jim and Lalani needed to hire a ranch hand. There were several
young men from various families in the area, but most were needed
by their families to work their own farms. Jim knew that in the city
there would be young men looking for work, but would they be good
at ranching? Clay and Katherine were heading to San Francisco to
arrange buyers for the cattle and to visit Joanne, giving Jim the opportunity to go with them to search for a ranch hand. Of course, Lalani
went along to visit and help.

Jim put an ad in the paper and arranged with the hotel dining
room as the place to interview potential workers. Jim had arranged
for a room for him and Lalani, but once Joanna heard they were in
town insisted they stay with them. Clay and Katherine were staying
with Evelyn and Eric. Several young men answered the ad. Joanna
couldn't understand why Jim wanted Lalani to be there with him.
"She's good at seeing the true character in people," he said. Besides,
Lalani was eager to meet the potential ranch hand, as he would be taking directions from her, as well as Jim.

The first two young men had been shop clerks and had no idea of
farm work. Jim liked the third man. He was just shy of twenty, had
worked on a ranch near Placerville, but came to the city to take care
of his father, who now had passed away. *I can train this young lad to
do things right.* Lalani wasn't certain and wanted to interview the last
man before making a decision.

The fourth man was in his early twenties, had dreams of going
to sea as a child, and now after being at sea for two years realized it
wasn't for him. He had been raised on a farm in Washington and was
quite fit for the task of bringing in the hay. Lalani liked this young
man. He was quiet but confident. "He has an intriguing manner about
him," she remarked. She convinced Jim, "We should hire both of them

to help bring in the fields, afterwards we can decide who to keep on permanently."

"Hire both? What do I do with them while the hay dries?" Jim knew he wouldn't win but needed to ask anyway.

"They can help with the horses. Kate can't, and that way I don't have to help separate the mare from the foals. It will give you a chance to see who can learn new things best."

The young men were glad to have the work, if only for two or three weeks. They would start work at the beginning of the week. Jim and Lalani returned on the evening train to Oak Ridge to set things in order. Evan Pritcher and Peter Thornton arrived at the ranch together. Having met up on the train and not having horses, they began the walk to the ranch when Ben came by with a wagon load for Clay and offered them a ride. "Say hi to Jim for me," he said pointing them to the road into the Circle K. They arrived mid-morning, and Jim showed them the bunkhouse, where they stowed what things they had. He explained Lalani would provide the noon meal, but they would be responsible for their other meals. "Milk and eggs are in the cooler but if you take the last two, you'll be hearing about it from Mrs. Baker."

Jim taught them how to sharpen the scythes and use them without straining their back or cutting their legs. He started them on opposite sides of the field so no competition would get involved, and for safety. Evan picked up the rhythm of cutting quickly, having done it on his family farm. Pete was a little slower at getting use to handling the scythe. They didn't get much done, as the heat was close to 90, and the horses needed feeding. Pete was much better at filling hay bins. They would start again in the hay field in the morning. That evening, Lalani sent stew out to the bunkhouse as a welcome to the ranch. Evan was a tall dark haired young man, quiet. The first night he sat on the bunkhouse porch softly playing a harmonica and whittling on a branch. Peter was lankier, not quite as tall, with sandy brown hair.

He wandered into the barn before dark and sat playing solitaire by the lantern.

The next morning, Jim opened the kitchen door to let Makana out, only to see smoke coming out of the bunkhouse window. Evan hadn't cooked for himself in years and the butter in the pan got away from him and caught fire. He grabbed a towel to put out the flames, but this did not go well, but rather added to the flames. Pete finally got the water bucket, intending only to hit the flaming towel, but instead sent the grease flames splattering as the water hit the pan.

Jim slammed open the door and stomped on a small flame on the floor in front of him. "Flour! You need flour to put out a grease fire!" Pete grabbed a metal tin, hoping it was the flour and pulled it open, tossing the contents on the pan without even looking. To his luck, it was flour and his aim hit the pan and snuffed out the flames. Lalani came in just as the last flames went out. "Oh, my!"

Jim was not happy. "Boys, can't you cook?!"

Evan just shook his head, "My mom always did the cooking and I've been at boarding houses since back from sea."

Lalani looked at Pete and he just looked down, "Canned beans is my forte."

Jim looked at Lalani and she nodded her head. "Get this mess cleaned up and come up to the kitchen," Jim said sternly.

Lalani had bacon, eggs and coffee ready when Evan and Pete showed up at the kitchen door. She sat them down at the kitchen table and told them to eat up, because it was going to be a long day. She and Jim had quickly eaten, while the boys were cleaning up the mess. Jim came in and grabbed his hat, "Let's go boys, there's work to do. Afterwards Lalani will teach you how to cook eggs without burning down the bunkhouse." They gulped down the last bite and sip of coffee and headed out, leaving their plates. Lalani just smiled.

The next day, they managed burnt bacon and scrambled eggs, but the coffee was drinkable. That morning there was a slight breeze, making it easier to cut the hay against the wind. From Pete's side of the field, a torrent of foul words rang out. Then a strong smell caught the breeze. Without warning, Pete had surprised a skunk and received the full blast of its anger. Pete tried to continue to work, but his eyes stung, and he gagged from the putrid smell. Jim finally sent him back to the house. "Now, don't you go into the house, bunkhouse, or barn. Just shout to Mrs. Baker. When she smells you, she'll know what to do. Just stand there until she can help. Now go on."

Evan tried not to laugh, but just couldn't help grinning as he gave the scythe an extra heavy swing. Pete yelled from just outside the kitchen door. Makana barked, and as Lalani opened the door, the dog took one step forwards and then quickly turned around and ran upstairs. "Pete, you need to back up about twenty feet and don't move." Lalani grabbed her vegetable gathering basket and headed for the tomato vines, picking as many large red tomatoes as she could find. Pete just stood and watched. Lalani went back to the kitchen and pulled out the meat grinder. She cut up the tomatoes and put them through the grinder, catching the juice and paste in a bowl as it came out. Once she was done, she went to the porch and set the bowl down along with an empty bucket. Pete still stood where Lalani had indicated, with his bandana over his mouth and nose, trying to breathe.

"Pete, take this and go out by the compost, take and put your clothes in the bucket, we'll burn them later. Take the tomato puree and wash with it. It's the only thing I know of that will cut the smell. Wash thoroughly, including your hair. When you can breathe again, you can come get a warm bucket of water to rinse off with."

Pete gave her a look that wanted to rebel. "You're trying to kill me. Tomatoes are poison."

"I didn't say eat them. I said wash with them, and they're no more poisonous than a possum."

After about an hour, Pete showed up at the kitchen door and knocked. He was now clean but still had a slight aroma to him. Evan and Jim had come back for the noonday meal. Jim took one whiff,

"You can eat out on porch, hopefully by dark you will be able to go inside."

Evan had gone to the water trough to wash up. He removed his shirt and splashed water across his torso which supported muscular shoulders and arms. Lalani stood for a moment watching. *He must have pulled a lot of riggings and anchors over the years at sea. Pete has nothing on him.* Evan was tired by evening and wanted a good night's sleep, which meant Pete needed to sleep outside, as he still smelt like fresh cow pies in the sun.

That evening, Lalani and Jim sat laughing about their hired hands. "More like little boys, one tries to burn down the bunkhouse and the other tangles with a skunk," Lalani giggled.

"True, but Evan has proven to be a hard worker and he learns fast. With his height, he's been able to cut the grass faster, and he's quiet. Pete wants to jabber like a magpie. I don't know if he's trying to give the skunk a warning he's there or that's just the way he is.

"One thing, both boys sure can swear when surprised. Evan was bitten by a wasp today, and he's a sailor all right. The words that came out of his mouth, I'm just glad you weren't around. He shook it off though, and kept on working."

The fields were cut by the end of the week, and Jim paid them their wages. Pete disappeared into town without a departing remark. Evan, now clean, came up to the house and knocked. Lalani opened the door and invited him to join them for a piece of blackberry pie.

"Mr. Baker, I have a favor to ask. First, will you keep this tin for me? It's my savings for my own horse. I like to play poker and have not always been lucky. If I put half my pay in this tin and leave it here, I'm not tempted to spend it on a good hand. A good hand that always turns out to be second best. That brings me to the second ask. Would you mind if I borrow the draft horse to get to town? I grew up riding my father's draft."

"Well, I don't know about that. You might put Clyde up as collateral on a bet."

"Oh, no, I assure you, I only bet my own possessions or money. My father taught me never to borrow something you can't return."

"Your father sounds like a smart man. But why don't you stay here and play poker with me and Jim," Lalani piped in.

"With a woman? I couldn't take your money."

"You don't think women can play poker?" Lalani retorted. "You know, I have a friend Jessie and she's one hell of a poker player. Kate, Jessie and I would sit and play poker for match sticks, when we didn't go to the club to gamble."

"My wife has traveled the world, and done things most women have not. We'd enjoy a good game of cards, but if you have a woman friend in town, don't let us keep you. You could walk to town like Pete. You might even help him find his way back in the dark, otherwise I'm not sure that boy will make it. If you can be reasonable and hold your drinks, and find your way back, you can use Clyde. Just make sure you don't lose him. And I mean that in more ways than one. Make sure his stall door latches and the barn door is closed tight."

"You sure you don't want to stay and play for matches? We can swap sea stories. I've sailed from Australia to London, to Boston. Of course, I was a passenger and not part of the crew, but I've seen my share of storms," Lalani added.

Evan thought about the offer for a moment, but wanted to see what town had to offer. "I'll try to have Clyde back by 10:30, but I don't promise, depending on what or who I find in town."

Jim smiled thinking back to when he was twenty-two, "I'll settle for midnight."

True to his word, Evan had Clyde back in his stall by 10:30, having found a poker game which held him captive until ten. It was Sunday morning and Lalani and Jim were headed for church. Evan declined, saying "never had a ma that insisted on church and pa was, well angry at God for taking ma. I just pray when I need to get out of danger." Lalani just smiled. *I wonder what kind of danger he has seen in his young life. I'm sure storms at sea, maybe pirates, too.*

Monday morning rolled around, and Pete was nowhere to be found. Since he had to burn his one set of spare clothes, Pete didn't have anything other than the clothes he wore. Jim wasn't disappointed. He could see farming wasn't for him, and this way he didn't have to make a decision between Pete and Evan. Evan was far more responsible, level headed, and the harder worker. Jim liked him a lot, and Lalani thought he would make a good addition to her sense of family.

With the uses of the new baler compress, Jim and Evan were able to get the alfalfa and hay fields baled by the end of July. Jim had been so busy with the fields, he didn't put in much work on Kate's new hay barn. Morgan and the Taylor hands managed to finish it off in short order, in time for the hay and alfalfa to be stored there. Jim and Morgan agreed to split the bales 30/70 this year. Seventy percent of them went to the new barn for the horses and thirty went to the Circle K barn for their horses and pending cattle.

~~

Lalani kept herself busy in the vegetable garden, now producing lots of beans for canning and cucumbers for pickling. The chickens were also producing more eggs than they could use, so she would take them to town and sell them to the hotel dining room.

Clay was becoming more concerned about Katherine working with the horses, now that she was five months pregnant. She no longer rode over, but brought the buggy. Jim would send her into the house to visit with Lalani after they discussed what she wanted for the horses. Evan had turned out to be a pretty good wrangler. He and Jim were making good progress with the yearlings' training. The three came easily to them and stood still while halters were put on and now were comfortable wearing the saddle blankets. At least Rosie's filly and Estrella's colt didn't mind. Camille's filly took after her mother, pulling it off after a few minutes, then walking over it several times before she was done with it. Jim called her "Trouble," but she did have her mother's beautiful strong features, and Kate would keep her as a brooding mare, since they had lost Camille.

Finally, the day came to move the yearlings to the newly complete southwest paddock and the mares and foals to the northwest paddock, onto Taylor land. Lalani wasn't sure she was ready to see the mares and foals go. She enjoyed watching the fillies and colt prance and run and nuzzle up to their mothers to nurse. Yet this year the yearlings would not be brought to the north paddock. It would remain open. This she didn't mind. *Maybe I can get the sheep I want, now that the paddock will be empty. Or will Jim want it for the new bull he wants to get? Do sheep and cattle go together? Lalani what are you thinking? Jim has told you a thousand times they do not.*

Kate, Clay and Morgan arrived mid-morning, to help move the horses. Lalani, Jim and Evan met them at the north paddock as they stood watching the foals.

"Lalani, your job today is to keep Katherine at the house. The men and I can handle moving the horses," Clay said in a commanding manner.

"That's fine with me. I was always uncomfortable leading the mares to the south paddock. And more so leading the yearlings here. Wrangling Kate will be a joy, just like old times when she was in school."

"Wait a minute, don't I get a say?" Kate began to protest.

"No!" Everyone said at once, including Evan.

Clay just put his hand on her bulging tummy and then took her hand and gave it to Lalani.

"I'll be watching from the porch," Kate said as they walked back to the house.

Lalani took Kate into the kitchen and set her down in front of a bowl of potatoes needing peeling for potato salad. "It's time I teach you how to cook, at least a few things," she said smiling.

Once the potatoes were on and boiling, Lalani began to teach Kate how to make pie crust for the peach pie she had planned. Lalani cleaned the chicken and would cook that herself. Within an hour, they had the noonday meal ready and cooling. Lalani picked up the breadfruit baby quilt she was making for Kate and they went and sat on the porch waiting for the men to be finished.

"Lalani, you will be happy to know I have finally begun to work on the baby's room. Moving all my gowns was a chore. Clay brought in another large armoire and Lupe helped sort and move dresses. Miranda had the family cradle brought down from the attic, and Morgan is refinishing it for us."

"It's about time. We should pick some fabrics, and I will make some sleepers and gowns to go with the sweater Miranda is knitting."

From the porch, Lalani could see the end of the northwest paddock and Rosie and her colt come prancing over the hill towards them. *I'm glad I will be able to see the mares and foals from here.* Within minutes she could see the men coming down the road. "Looks like they're done and hungry for your potato salad."

Kate was anxious to know how everything went.

"The horses are fine, running about as usual. The barn corral will work out well for the weaning pen, when the foals are ready. We may need to add another lower bar as I think that little bay filly can get under if she tries," Clay assured her, and promised to take her by the new barn on their way home.

With the horses settled in the west paddocks, Jim and Evan started pulling the dividing posts that separated the two south paddocks, turning the area into one large grazing area for cattle. Jim gave Evan more and more responsibility, leaving the daily feeding of the working horses in the barn to him as well as mucking out stalls. This left more time for Jim to check on the mares and yearlings and how they were settling into their new home. The field had grown back quickly with the May rains. But it wasn't high enough for them to feed off completely. Jim still put alfalfa out for them and checked to make sure the water was pumping into the water troughs as expected.

After a week with everything running smoothly, Jim was ready to head to Rancho Omochumnes to look at Angus bulls. On Thursday, Lalani and Jim boarded the afternoon train to Elk Grove, where Dennis would meet them. Dennis was now seventy, and his two sons ran the ranch. He took one look at Jim, "Well, I'm not the only one age-in', look at ya, no longer the scrawny ranch hand. I knew ya would be back one day to buy stock of your own. What took ya so long?" reaching forward and giving Jim a hardy handshake.

"It took getting married to want more. This is my bride, Lalani," Jim smiled and took her arm.

"An' a beauty at that. I always told ya, the luck of the Irish was with ya, Jim."

It was a short ride to the ranch. Carol Doyle had a light supper waiting when they arrived. Dennis had two sturdy young sons that joined them, Caleb and Clem. Dennis teased Lalani for seeing Scotland and not Ireland. "Ya know, they think I have an accent, but at least ya can understand us Irish, them Scots speak as if they have a mouth full of haggis, and ya can't understand a word."

Carol chimed in with, "But they're not full of blarney, like someone I love."

In the morning, Dennis and Clem took Jim down to the corrals where two fine Angus bulls stood.

"Now, Declan here, has a great breeding record, a little ornery but a strong pure Angus heritage. Kieran there, is a year younger and just as pure without the attitude. I have one more I'm willing to part with and that's Seamus, good but he's a bit amaideach." Jim looked a Dennis with a puzzling look.

Clem translated, "Seamus is goofy. He's the youngest of the three and likes to chase magpies. But only when they annoy him."

"He takes his time deciding on which cow to mount, but once he does, he rides her longer than most bulls. Never fails to produce," Dennis added.

Jim took his time looking over the two bulls, and then curiosity got the best of him, and he wanted to see Seamus. They walked out to another corral and there stood Seamus, all 1500 pounds. "He does have a rather goofy expression on his face," Jim teased.

Now having seen all three bulls, Jim liked the strong lines of Kieran and the height and solid build of Seamus. He needed time to see how they reacted to people and wanted to see some of the calves they had sired. Dennis was obliging and let Jim take his time. Jim wanted Lalani's thoughts. *I know she knows nothing about bulls, but she has a natural instinct about things.*

Lalani joined Jim and looked at both Kieran and Seamus. "Who's the better breeder?" she asked Dennis.

"Well, depends, whether ya want fast or thorough. Kieran gets down to business faster getting to 30 heifers in a cycle, but a few times, things haven't taken. While Seamus take his time and can get to say 25 -27 in a cycle, but I've never known him to fail."

"Seems like it comes out about even. Jim, I guess you're going to have to decide. Which one has the better line as a beef cow?"

Jim chuckled, "We won't be eating one of these boys, not at the cost Dennis is going to be charging. But I think I know what you're asking." Jim went back and walked around Kieran one more time. He liked his strong features and his easy manner. Then he thought about Seamus. He looked at Lalani and at that moment she knew he would say Kieran. "Kieran it is," Jim said proudly.

They arranged for the bull to be shipped by train to Oak Ridge and Dennis gave them a deal on two heifers as well. Jim was pleased beyond words, while Lalani was happy for him but uncertain as to what they were getting into. *Are cattle going to be better to raise than horses?*

9

New Arrivals

Jim wanted Kieran and the heifers up in the north paddock where he could observe them, therefore he and Evan set to work reinforcing the fencing to make sure the bull wouldn't break through. Kieran and the heifers arrived at the Circle K within the week and Morgan came and helped drive the cattle from the train to the ranch. With Kieran and the heifers secure in the north paddock, Morgan, Jim, Evan and Lalani stood at the gate observing the start of a cattle ranch.

Clay came riding up to the paddock, wanting to see the new bull. "Looks like you made a good investment there, Jim," he said dismounting. Clay was impressed with Kieran and knew the fledgling ranch was off to a good start. But for now, he needed Morgan back at the Taylor spread. They had their own cattle to round up and get to market.

One afternoon about a week into roundup, Morgan came down the Circle K road, driving two cows. Jim and Evan were in the south field checking fencing.

"What's this Morgan, two strays get away from you?" Lalani asked as Morgan ran the cows into the barn corral.

"Nope! A late wedding present for you and Jim from me and Clay. We wanted to wait until you got your bull before picking them out. They're ready for breeding."

"Oh, my, that's quite a wedding present. It looks like our little cattle ranch is getting off to a big start. Jim will be more than pleased, and you're being far too generous. But thank you." *I hope we don't get too many cows, I'm not sure I'm ready for a herd of cattle yet.*

Jim was elated, and after a few days turned the new heifers out into the paddock with the others. Kieran was true to his reputation. When the heifers came into heat, he was upon them in no time. Now, Jim would just have to wait 60 or 70 days to see if he chose the right bull.

Miranda tried to explain cattle ranching to Lalani, that there were moments like now when there was a lot to do, but during the winter months it was not so demanding. The calves were sold off and the herd was smaller. If there were no heavy snows, the cattle could continue to feed on range grass. "Will you move the heifers to the south range for the winter?" she asked. Lalani didn't know what Jim's plans were for the winter. "I hope so," she replied.

Now that I've had a week to watch the cattle, I think I like watching horses better. Horses run about from time to time and look so pretty. The cattle just stand around swishing their tails. I wonder if I could bring up the purchase of a few sheep for the north paddock? Probably I should wait for spring. There will be enough to worry about this first winter with the cattle.

Lalani now made twice a week trips to see Katherine at home, as the baby was due in a few months. Lalani had finished the breadfruit quilt and several sleepers for the baby, and Katherine had most of her baby things in place. In October Lalani would hold a baby shower for Kate, and after that, it would be just waiting time for baby Taylor to arrive in November.

Lalani harvested the last of the garden vegetables as mid-September came around, canning what she could for the winter. Jim seemed extra busy taking care of the heifers. Lalani was having trouble with the name changes. They no longer had horse paddocks, but cattle ranges. *It's the south range, not the south paddock where the heifers are now. And the north field, not paddock. I do hope Jim will put Kieran in the barn corral, and I will be able to get my sheep next spring. It would have been nice to have fleece to spin this winter and be making socks and shawls. Thank goodness, Clyde and Prince Philip are big enough to go in with Kieran. He doesn't seem to bother them, or they him. Genevieve is still content in the barn corral since Kate's not coming.*

Evan and Jim had now separated the foals from their mothers, and Lalani no longer could see them from the porch. She would wander into the barn and pull a carrot from the bin to give to Genevieve. Buck and Prince Philip would whinny and want their share. Evan and Jim kept encouraging Lalani to ride Genevieve. She could be spirited with an experienced rider, but sensed when one was not and became mild and easy to handle. Lalani stood stroking her long jaw, watching her eyes watching her. *Well, Genevieve, is it time I don a pair of pants and give riding a try? I know Jim would like that. There are parts of the ranch I have never seen because the carriage can't get there. Maybe by Thanksgiving I will get the courage.* "What do you think Genevieve?" The horse just nudged Lalani's hand for another carrot.

Jim wanted to surprise Lalani with a trip back to Hawaii, but knew they would not be going anywhere until after the baby came and the holidays. Jim was glad fall had arrived, and things were calmer. He spent more time with Lalani and let Evan handle the ranch chores. The day before Thanksgiving, as Lalani was in the kitchen making pumpkin and apple pies, she could hear barking at the front door. Makana pranced and whined. Jim came from the parlor as Lalani came drying her hands. It was Brandy. "The baby must be on the way," Lalani let out. "It's about time, I thought it would be here last week," Jim noted.

Jim went to the barn and hitched up Prince Philip while Lalani gathered up a few things. Jim came in through the kitchen door and spotted the pies finished but not baked. "Lalani, we can't leave the pies, they will be perfect to have while we wait." Lalani fetched two pie baskets and they headed out the door. Evan held Makana while Brandy jumped onto the back bench with the pie baskets. "We'll send word when the baby arrives. Don't expect us back tonight," Jim said and he gave Prince a tap with the reins.

Lalani went directly up to Kate, knowing she would be needing her, while Jim carried the pies to the kitchen and told Miranda they still needed to be cooked. Katherine was pacing the floor as Clay sat in a chair looking worried. Kate lit up when she saw Lalani, and gave a sigh of relief.

"Well, Kate it looks like you're doing fine. It's Clay I'm not sure about," Lalani said as she entered. "Clay, stop worrying, everything is going to be fine. Babies always go slow until they are suddenly in a hurry to arrive."

Miranda had come back up, and now added her experience, "You forget about all the waiting and discomfort instantly, as you hold your new bundle of joy for the first time."

Lalani sent Clay to join Jim and Morgan. "Tell Jim to save me a piece of apple pie."

Miranda and Lalani settled Kate back into bed and made her as comfortable as possible. Miranda told stories about Eric and Clay's arrival and how they had been late but not difficult. At one point after a round of contractions, Kate sat down at the piano and played a lullaby, trying to calm herself. But the bench became too uncomfortable as the pressure built. Clay came to check on Kate off and on for the next five hours and Lalani dropped down to the parlor for a bite and to provide an update while Clay was with Kate.

Clay was anxious to send for Doc Newell, and finally Miranda said it was time to get him. Morgan went and returned within the hour. Miranda and Lalani became busy, coming and going with towels and hot water. Finally, around seven in the evening, the cry of a newborn could be heard. Clay raced upstairs and into the room. Kate lay in bed, her hair bedraggled, but smiling. Lalani was just handing her the baby, now clean and wrapped warmly, as Doc Newell was putting his bag to order. "Congratulations, Clay, you have a fine healthy boy," Doc said.

Clay went to Katherine giving her a kiss to her forehead as she pulled back the blanket to show him his son. Lalani and Doc Newell slipped out and downstairs to tell the others the news. Everyone was elated and glad that it was a boy for Clay's sake, and that the delivery had gone without a hitch.

Jim came up to Lalani and put his arms around her, then kissing her on the head said, "Good job, Aunt Lalani. You're too young to be a grandma."

After a few minutes Morgan and Miranda went upstairs followed by Jim and Lalani. Clay awkwardly took the baby from Kate and carefully cradled him in his big arm. "I'd like you to meet Matthew Keenen Taylor."

Miranda was pleased they had chosen her father's name and Keenen to honor Kate's side of the family. The baby had lightly tan skin, bringing out his Indian heritage, but had Clay's deep brown wavy hair and blue gray eyes.

The evening was joyous, with everyone gathering in the upstairs sitting room. Lalani watched Clay and Miranda taking care of Kate's needs and realized she was in good hands. The baby was nursing before long and Lalani had changed the first messy diaper. By ten o'clock Kate and Matthew were sleeping, and Lalani had the urge to be home, in her own house alone with Jim. She tiptoed in and gave Kate a kiss on the head, and whispered that she'd be back in the morning. "Good job, mama."

Jim lit the carriage lanterns and Lalani curled up next to him, taking his arms, and then they headed home. As Jim held her in bed, he could tell she was happy for Kate, but a quietness, almost sadness, but not quite a sad feeling was about her. He turned to her gently and whispered "You're not too old to have your own baby if you want." He could feel a tear drop onto his bare chest, but said nothing more, just holding her, loving her for the wonderful woman she was.

Lalani, Jim and Evan brought all the holiday trimmings to the Taylor ranch the next day. Katherine and the baby were doing fine, in fact so well, she was downstairs sitting by the fire, while Matthew was asleep in his daddy's arms. Evan was glad to be included, but felt a little out of place, as he had never been around a baby. When Miranda asked if he wanted to hold him, he put up his arms and waved her off. "I'm good with colts, but I'd be so nervous, I'd probably drop him. And I don't want to miss dinner, it smells so good. I don't want to be in the doghouse with Makana. "

After an abundant meal of turkey, stuffing, potatoes, beans and more, Morgan put extra pillows on the piano bench and coaxed Kate to play. Matthew seemed to like the soft Brahms, but wrinkled his face and began to cry at the loud Bach. Miranda took great joy in doing grandmotherly things. Lupe was delegated to the messy diaper washing and burp rags. Kate just seemed to want Lalani there for moral support and to share in her joy.

~~

The weather had turned cold by mid-December, but Lalani continued to visit Kate every few days. Lalani had gathered pine boughs and brought them, along with pine cones and ribbons to make wreaths to give to neighbors as they came to see baby Matthew. The week of Christmas, Lalani sat quietly in the rocker by the fire after doing the morning linens. Jim came in and noticed the deep thought she was in. "What's so serious on my pretty wife's mind?" giving her a kiss on the top of her head.

Surprised by his presence, "Oh, hello, morning chores done already?"

"No, but it's cold and the sheets are as stiff as boards, so I brought them in for you. They're on the kitchen table warming up, to be folded. Are you alright?"

"I'm fine, just a little cold and tired from doing laundry." She didn't mention what she had been thinking about. *I must have forgotten when I last washed blood from the sheets.* "You must be ready for dinner. Is Evan washing up?"

Lalani rose quickly and headed for the kitchen. Folding the sheets, she then set pot roast and gravy into bowls, and they all ate. Conversation centered on how to keep the water troughs on the west paddocks from freezing. Evan and Jim disappeared afterwards and were gone for most of the afternoon. About four o'clock, they returned, carrying a small Douglas fir into the parlor. "Where do you want it, by the front window or back corner?" Jim said smiling.

"A tree? I thought we were going to Clay and Kate's for Christmas."

"We are, but we need to celebrate our first Christmas in our home, too. Beside it's a Douglas fir like you talked about when you were little. We can make popcorn and string it for garland."

Lalani smiled, Edith always had a fir tree in Hawaii. She pointed to the front window, and Evan slid the desk to one side as Jim stood the tree up proudly. That evening the three of them strung popcorn and cranberries. Evan had whittled a few ornaments: duck, sleigh, horse, turtle, and small house. Lalani got out some charcoal pencils and sketched Hawaiian designs on them. Jim cut some pinecones that looked like flowers when cut. By the end of the evening the tree was festive. Jim sat by Lalani on the sofa, and Evan played softly on his harmonica.

The next morning Lalani was again tired and not feeling up to going to see Kate. She sat by the fire trying to keep warm and quietly wrapped the last few gifts for Christmas. Jim noticed she wasn't eating much at meals, and by the next morning when she still felt ill, he began to worry. "It will be Christmas tomorrow. I don't want you to miss out on it because of the flu. I think Doc Newell should come take a look. Maybe he can give you something that will help."

Lalani took his hand and led him to the tree. "I don't think Doc Newell can do anything about it at this point," she said, then she reached up and whispered in his ear.

"What! Are you sure?"

"Pretty sure, it's been seven weeks. I've been late before, but not this late. I didn't think about having a baby, but looks like the good Lord did."

Jim picked her up and turned her around, excited with a twinkle in his eye.

"I take it you're pleased, and not terrified," she said with a smile.

"Of course, I'm pleased. I'm so happy for you Lalani, you deserve your own child. You will be a wonderful mother. Now let's get you off your feet and bundled up."

"Jim, I'm fine, no fussing…. Jim, I think I would like to wait to tell people. I don't want to rob Kate of her joy of being a new mother. Can we wait until after the new year to tell people?"

"Lalani, Kate will be overjoyed with this news. Why wait?"

Lalani took Jim's big hand, "Please, I just need time to adjust to the idea. I never thought I would be a mother. I'm a little overwhelmed. Don't get me wrong, I'm happy. But nauseous too, I just don't need everyone worrying about me. You will be enough to deal with. Please, just our secret for now."

Jim agreed for now, but spent the rest of the day smiling and dropping in on Lalani to see if she needed anything. She just needed him out of the kitchen so she could finish her Christmas cake for tomorrow. She had a chicken roasting in the oven and country fried potatoes and cranberry sauce for their own Christmas Eve meal.

Evan ate with them and then joined them in the parlor afterwards. They talked about their favorite Christmas Eves. "In Hawaii, before my father died, our whole village would gather and roast a pig in the ground. We would have a big luau. There would be singing and dancing. My mother would use those gourds on the mantle. She had the smoothest, most gentle step as she danced. Father would play the drum and had a wonderful rich voice. We kids would run around and sneak pieces of pork when it was first lifted from the fire pit. We didn't have a lot, but the comb on my dresser is the one present I remember he gave me. He had a story about the coconut shell and an octopus that used it for a hat. He said the beast tried to sneak off with it and put up a mighty fight for it. But father wacked off his arms and ate him and then made the comb for me. At the time I was terrified of octopus, but now… the poor beast, I hope it was only a story." Evan started to chuckle, "I can just see him fighting with all eight arms, and the beast passing the coconut shell from arm to arm as he tried to grab it." Both Jim and Lalani found themselves also laughing.

Lalani disappeared and returned with Hawaiian sweetbread and cider. Jim and Evan had gone to the barn and returned with Lalani's gift. As she came in with dessert, there by the fireplace stood a small spinning wheel with a large red bow. "Oh, Jim, it's beautiful." She sat down next to it and gave the wheel a spin, and pedaled with her feet for a minute. "It's wonderful, so smooth. It will make wonderful yarn for knitting. But am I going to have wool to spin?"

Just then Evan pulled a bag from behind his chair. "Merry Christmas, Lalani." Handing her a bag of sheep's fleece. "It's last spring's fleece from a friend's ranch. Needs cleaning, but she says it's a great long fiber."

"I will get you your own sheep next spring. But for now, I hope Evan's gift will be enough. I understand you will need these too," and Jim pulled a bag from under the tree.

Lalani was now smiling with plump full cheeks. "Carding brushes for combing the fleece, yes, I will indeed need these." She pulled a small piece of fleece from the bag and laid it across the carding brushes and pulled the fleece into a smooth layer of fibers. There was already a lead yarn attached to the spindle. She placed her feet on the pedals, attached the fiber edge to the lead yarn and began to pedal. The fiber quickly grabbed and spun into yarn. "It's perfect." Lalani stood and kissed Jim in a big embrace, then turned to Evan and leaned down and gave him a kiss to the cheek.

"I have two very thoughtful men in my life. And now it's your turn." She went to the tree and pulled out a package for Evan and then a large long box for Jim. "Evan, you open yours first."

Evan unwrapped a new blue plaid shirt, with something else wrapped up inside it. Suddenly, a big grin came across his face. "A bridle?"

"You're going to need it when you pick out your new horse from Clay's stock. There's a saddle with your name on it at the tack shop in town. We just didn't know which one would fit you best, saddles are such a personal item. I checked your tin and told Clay how much you had saved and he assured me he had several very good horses you could afford to buy."

Evan was speechless, which wasn't saying much, since he didn't spend a lot of time talking. "I'm so, so…Thank you," was all he could get out.

"Evan, you have been such a wonderful addition to our ranch family. You have proved yourself so many times, being here to help, taking care of the place when we're away. Jim and I feel you are *ohana*, family," Lalani said.

"I do feel like I have found my home here. You know I would do anything for the two of you," Evan said graciously. He could see Lalani was pleased.

"Now it's your turn, Jim." Jim sat next to Lalani as he opened his box. Inside in a velvet bag was a fiddle and bow. Jim smiled and shook his head. "I should never have had Dan at the wedding."

"Nonsense! I loved hearing you play, and I have missed having music in the house. Now in the evening you can sit and play just for us, if you prefer. Give it a try," Lalani encouraged.

Jim took the fiddle and plunked at the strings to see if they were anywhere near in tune. "Not bad!" Next, he took the bow and tightened the hairs taut. Finally, he put the fiddle to his chin and pulled the bow slowly across the strings. "Needs a little rosin."

"In the bag," Lalani pointed.

Jim ran the rosin across the bow hairs and tightened the bow again. He pulled the bow across the strings, as the sound resounded through the room. Makana let out a bark. "No comment from the floor, girl," Jim said. At last, he played a soft slow melody, not perfect, but Lalani was pleased beyond words. Evan pulled out his harmonica and the two attempted to play *Away in a Manger*.

They sat quietly eating dessert and thanking each other for their gifts. Then Jim took Lalani upstairs, leaving Evan to close up the fire.

Jim swept her up in his arms and laid her gently on the bed. "The fiddle is great, but you have already given me the most wonderful Christmas gift," and he patted her stomach.

The next morning, Evan opted to stay at the ranch and take care of the horses and check on the cattle, while Jim and Lalani were off to visit friends before going to Kate and Clay's. Lalani was doing a little better this morning, keeping a light breakfast down. She came downstairs in a green velvet dress with a white cotton bodice, feeling excited to visit the Olsens, their closet neighbors to the south. Lalani had made raspberry and blueberry jams during the summer and now had them in decorative baskets to give away. The cake was carefully placed in a box and set on the back bench along with the gift for the Taylors.

It was a brisk, chilly midmorning when they departed. Jim had an extra heavy blanket to place over Lalani, and she wore a heavy wool cloak over her dress and mittens to keep her hands warm. As they left, Lalani called out to Evan, "We will see you and Makana at the Taylors by 12:30 for Christmas dinner – don't be late."

It was a short drive to the Olsens, Carol Olsen was about the same age as Lalani and the two had become close over the past two years. Carol showed Lalani what best to plant, where, when and how. Carol and Lalani had spent many hours discussing seeds and quilting in her parlor. As they pulled into the Olsen ranch, Hattie and Carol greeted them at the door. After an hour of visiting, they left and dropped by the Swensen's house to drop off the jam gifts.

The Swensen's owned the general store and had been so helpful and friendly, making sure they had the best of the goods. Ingrid Swensen was quite pleased to have the jams. About 11:30, they headed for the Taylor ranch. Everyone was there, Eric and Evelyn, Morgan, Miranda, and of course Kate, Clay and baby Matthew. Lalani was thoroughly chilled by the time they arrived, and Jim was concerned, whisking her to the fireplace and asking for warm tea as soon as they arrived. Lalani gave him one of her don't-make-a-fuss looks, that

Kate noticed but didn't say anything. Evan arrived right on time and Makana and Brandy pranced around each other until Kate and Lalani told them lie down. Then both dogs settled by the fireplace, Makana at Lalani's feet and Brandy back by Matthew's cradle.

Miranda announced dinner was served, and the men escorted the ladies to the dining room. Clay told Brandy to stay and watch the baby, as he was now fast asleep. If he cried, they would hear him, or Brandy would alert them. The dining table was beautifully laid out with good china and winter pine boughs and berries. The food looked delicious and smelled wonderful. Lalani took her seat next to Morgan with Jim on her other side. As they began to pass the food, she took one look at Jim, and quickly rose and left the table. She made it to the kitchen waste can, just as she threw up. Jim and Kate were right behind her. She sat down on a chair and Jim gave her a towel. Suddenly she was on her knees bending over the can again. Jim held her hair back as she finished letting go of the rest of her breakfast, and the scone from the Olsens. "Jim, I'll send for Doc Newell," Kate said.

"No need, it's just a bit of the flu. We shouldn't have come," Jim said, helping Lalani back to her chair.

"Flu!" Kate said alarmed.

"Kate, it's okay, it's not the flu. The baby's safe," Lalani managed to say.

"Not the flu?" Suddenly Kate's face lit up.

"Morning sickness? Oh, that's wonderful!"

Lalani looked up at her bewildered, "Not at the moment it isn't. Kate, we don't want anyone to know as yet. Please, just go back out and tell everyone I'm fine. Just too many desserts from visiting friends. I'll join you in a few minutes. Now that my stomach is empty, the odor from the food won't bother me."

"Are you sure you're alright?" Kate asked as she tried to readjust Lalani's hair. "Yes, I'll be fine. Just give us a minute. Now go, before they get worried."

Jim took Lalani in his arms and held her for a few minutes. Then she straightened her dress, grateful nothing got on it, and ran her fingers through her hair. Taking Jim's arm, they returned to the dining table.

"Sorry about that, just too much hot cider and sweets on a cold day. I'm fine. So, Clay, have you told Evan about the horses you have for him to choose from?" Lalani said, trying to get the looks of concern off her.

Kate jumped in, bringing up the two-year-olds as well. Lalani only ate some mashed potatoes, while the others enjoyed the Christmas feast. Miranda, noticing Lalani was still a little pale, invited everyone back to the parlor for gifts instead of continuing to talk around the dining table. She rose and went over to Lalani and took her arm giving her a gentle pat of, I-understand, without saying anything.

Lalani and Jim shared their gifts for Kate, Morgan, Miranda and baby Matthew, now awake. Kate had purchased a beautiful painting of a tropical lagoon for Lalani. It wasn't big, but the artist said it was of Maunalua Bay in Koko Head. "Katherine, it's beautiful. I know exactly where this is. My father took me to played on that beach as a little girl. It's perfect, thank you so very much."

Jim, Kate and Miranda could see Lalani was tired, and it was best to be getting her home. "Well, Jim, I think you should get Lalani home, before it gets dark and any colder. I think she needs a good night's sleep and no more cookies," Kate said smiling. Jim quickly agreed.

"But we haven't had her lovely Christmas cake yet," Morgan protested.

"Morgan, it's all yours tonight. I think I had my fill of sweets for one day," Lalani said, as she got up. Evan brought the carriage around and helped load the packages, while Jim and Lalani said goodnight. "I'll bring Jim and Evan a piece of cake tomorrow and check on you," Kate whispered as she hugged Lalani good bye.

Once home, Lalani snuggled up to Jim in bed, tired but happy. "This truly has been a wonderful Christmas. The first family Christmas I have had in a very long time." Jim kissed her and held her to keep her warm.

Katherine arrived with two large slices of Christmas cake mid-morning the next day. Lalani was feeling a little better, but not up to collecting eggs or being outdoors. Katherine wanted to know all about how she felt about being pregnant, that it was wonderful their children would grow up together. It took a lot of pleading from Lalani to make Katherine keep her secret for now. "I just don't want the fussing. So, let's move on to the painting you gave me. It's lovely, I want to hang it today, but where? I can't decide if I want it over the bedroom mantle where I can see it each morning when I awake. Or here in the parlor for everyone to see."

Kate just shook her head and realized she was not going to win the battle for letting others know about the baby. *After all, it's her body and her baby, others will know soon enough.* "Why don't we take it upstairs and see how it looks on the mantle. You can wake tomorrow and see it. Then in a day you can bring it down here and see if you miss waking to it."

The next morning, she woke to see the painting, and it started her thinking about her mother. *I would so much love to share our blessings with her. In reality I have had such an easy life compared to her. I wonder if I caused her to be as ill as this little one is causing me.*

"Do you want breakfast in bed this morning?" Jim asked, interrupting her thoughts.

"No, No. I'm fine and getting up. Do you like the painting there over the mantle?"

"It's fine, the colors go well with the green wall paper. But what do I know? I like the color of cow pies."

Lalani was happy to have a quiet day at home. She planned to get the large tub out and wash and prepare the fleece Evan had given her. It would take several days for it to dry and then card and have it ready for spinning. She was excited about the whole process and didn't mind the wait.

It took her most of the morning to wash the fleece, doing it in small clumps to make drying faster. Jim rigged a drying rack up in the barn, since the smell was a little too strong for Lalani, and caused her once again to vomit up breakfast. That evening she sat just pedaling her new spinning wheel getting the feel of it. She told Jim she wanted to go to town and get some knitting patterns. "Ingrid will have plenty of baby patterns I can use to make. "

"I thought you wanted to keep it a secret for now," Jim remarked.

"I do. I'll just tell Ingrid it's for Kate's baby, I can tell her about the new wheel. I'm sure she will want to see it, as she spins herself."

Jim just grinned, "Fine, but it will have to wait a day. Tomorrow, I promised Kate to move the mares back to the other paddock, now that the foals are fully weaned."

It was December 30th, the morning was cold and rainy. Lalani once again did not feel well. Jim insisted she stay in bed, and brought her a light breakfast. Jim checked on her several times. By mid-morning, she was up, sitting in the rocker. "Jim, I'm bored, I can't just sit here all day. Bring me some of the dry wool, and I'll sit and card it for spinning." Within minutes, Jim had brought a basket full of dry fleece and the carding brushes. Lalani bent down for a handful of fleece and winced.

"What's wrong?" Jim asked.

"Nothing, just trying to reach the floor from a sitting position was suddenly uncomfortable. I guess my stomach is getting bigger than I thought. I'm fine. Now, go on and finish your morning chores. If I need you, I'll send Makana."

Lalani sat separating the fleece and carding it into neat rolls ready for spinning. As she made one last pull on the brushes, she realized the smell of the wool had kicked up her morning sickness. She stood quickly with a wince once again and rushed to the water closet, making it just in time. "When is this going to end?" Unfortunately, this time the need to vomit continued. Every time she thought she was done, a dry heaving action would ensue. She became fearful as the dry heaves continued. "Makana, get Jim, go get Jim…go," she managed.

Jim, seeing Makana, knew something was wrong and dashed to the house. Evan was just coming up from feeding Kieran. "What's wrong?"

"It's Lalani. Evan, you need to fetch Doc Newell now!" Jim answered as he reached the porch.

Jim reached Lalani sitting on the floor of the tub room trying to catch her breath. Once again, the dry heaving took over. Jim sat down next to her and pulled her into his arms trying to calm her shaking body. "Jim, I can't seem to stop having the feeling to vomit, but nothing's coming up, my stomach is empty. I'm afraid of losing the baby."

"Shhh. It's going to be all right. Evan's gone for Doc Newell. He'll have something to calm your muscles."

With Jim's presence and calm reassuring voice, she began to calm, and the heaving motion subsided. Jim went to get her robe to keep her warm. But as Lalani stood, she let out a gasping cry, and blood and water rushed from her body. Jim grabbed her as she went to the floor. They both knew what was happening. Lalani bent over holding her stomach as tears streamed from her eyes. Jim was suddenly uncertain what to do. *I know what to do for a mare or heifer, but … Lalani. Oh, God please don't take her.*

Doc Newell entered the room moments later, as Jim sat holding Lalani. "Jim, I've got her. We need to make sure she's not still bleeding. I need you to get some cold water and clean sheets we can cut. Jim, you need to do this now."

Jim looked at Lalani, now in a daze, and back at Doc, his words finally registering with him. He leaned Lalani into the doctor's arms and rose, realizing he couldn't do anything for her at the moment, that she needed the doctor's help. Doc examined her carefully. The miscarriage had been quick, but thorough. When Jim came with the water, Doc Newell lifted her into the tub and washed her legs and dried them. Then took the strips of sheet and wrapped her stomach tightly to add pressure to prevent any additional bleeding. Lalani was now aware of what happened, but quiet, with only tears trickling down her cheeks. When the doctor was done, Jim helped get her into a clean night gown and settled in their bed.

Jim sat holding her, as she began to sob. Doc Newell cleaned things up in the tub room and came with a spoonful of sedative to help calm Lalani and to help her sleep. He looked at Jim's worried, disappointed eyes and whispered, "She's going to be all right. Regrettably, older woman often loose the first baby. Their bodies aren't used to trying to keep it. But I see no damage. The next time it will be fine. Just keep her warm and off her feet for a few days. I'll check back in the morning." Jim nodded and could feel the sedative working as Lalani's body became less tense.

Evan had gone to get Kate once the doctor had arrived, thinking Lalani would need her. But upon arriving at the Taylor Ranch, Miranda opened the door. Seeing Evan's worried look, "What's happened?"

"It's Lalani. Something's wrong. Doc Newell is there now, I just thought Kate would want to know."

Miranda knew immediately what was wrong, but didn't say anything about it. "Kate is out with Clay. I think it's better if I go this time." Miranda grabbed her coat and gloves and headed for the carriage Evan had come in. She carefully explained what she suspected to Evan, and he now understood Jim's panic. They arrived at the house just as Doc Newell was coming downstairs.

Seeing Miranda, he shook his head no, indicating she lost the baby. "I'm glad you're here. She will need an older motherly support right now. She's taking it pretty hard. She's sleeping right now. Jim's with her. I think they need a little time alone for now. Go up, say... in an hour. I 've cleaned up the tub room, but it will need a good scrubbing. I'll check back in the morning."

Miranda went up and peaked in. Jim was still holding Lalani asleep in his arms. He looked up, and she could see the tears in his eyes. Miranda motioned for him to stay and whispered she'd be downstairs for now. It was late afternoon when Jim came downstairs and sat down at the kitchen table. He ran his fingers through his hair and looked at Miranda. His whole being had a shaken questioning sense about it.

"It will be all right, Jim. You just need a little time. I see how you two are together, patient, practical, very much in love. As long as you have each other, you will find new joys. Take it from me, Clarence and I lost our little girl when I was four months pregnant. We were devastated, but God gave us two, no three, wonderful boys, who have now given me two wonderful daughters."

"You, Miranda? Did you ever understand why? Lalani feels it's her fault, she keeps blaming herself, saying she's sorry. She has nothing to be sorry for. I didn't marry her to get children, I married her for her."

"She'll know that in time. Right now, she needs to grieve. We know this is no one's fault."

Miranda convinced Jim to take a moment for himself, and she would take soup up to Lalani and be with her. Miranda walked in with a tray of soup and bread. Lalani took one look and sadly gave her a tight-lipped grin as tears filled her eyes. Miranda set the tray down and went and sat on the bed. Lalani immediately grabbed hold of her and between sobbing breaths asked, "Why?"

Miranda held her, stroking her hair and gently said, "Some little ones just aren't ready to come into this world. It has nothing to do with you, or Jim, or even God. Their spirit just isn't ready."

Lalani calmed again, and she sat listening to Miranda's reassuring voice. "I'm glad you came, I'm not sure I could face Kate. Don't get me wrong, I'm happy for Kate. I was still getting used to the idea of being a mother. I guess I don't have to get used to it anymore," she said trying to chuckle and lighten the mood.

"Mrs. Lalani Baker, don't you go thinking or teasing like that. You thinking you weren't ready has nothing to do with what happened.

We both know you and Jim love the idea of family. The idea of *ohana* is part of you. It's an important part of your heritage. You have so much love. You're young and when you decide you're ready to try again, there will be no stopping it. Maybe this wasn't your time after all. Maybe you and Jim needed more time for yourselves or something else has to come first. But don't you doubt for a minute that you won't be a great mother or didn't love this baby. You will always love the idea of this baby. That's why it hurts so much right now."

Miranda explained how she had lost her first baby and how she still cherished the idea, no regrets, only gratitude for the lovely idea. "Give yourself time, take the next few days to grieve and get better. There's a new year just around the corner, and it's full of blessings and challenges, but together you and Jim will find happiness, because you have love for family. Look at the family you have made, Jim, Katherine, Evan, so much love. Now eat some soup, and I'll send Jim up, and no more saying you're sorry. You have nothing to be sorry about. You're not sorry you love Jim, are you?"

Lalani smiled through wet eyes, "No, I'm grateful I have and love Jim."

"Good!"

10

Time to Heal

Miranda told Kate what happened when she returned home. Kate wanted to go to her immediately, but Miranda made her understand it would be hard for Lalani to see her at this time. "You have your baby, and she does not. She needs a little time to heal from the loss."

Lalani was still happy for Kate, but wasn't ready to see Matthew or Kate with her full milky breast. Kate reluctantly understood and sent a note saying she would be there for her when she needed her.

Lalani didn't want to see anyone, even though it was the new year. She sat quietly upstairs, rocking by the fire, with Makana at her feet. She would often just stare at the painting of Muanalua Bay, tears running down her face from time to time. Jim, in his own way grieved, working quietly with the horses, spending more time than usual grooming Buck, Prince Philip, and Genevieve.

It was Katherine and Clay's first anniversary on January 2nd, and Miranda held a small party. Everyone asked where Lalani and Jim were. Miranda would step in and answer, "Terrible flu, can't keep anything down." Kate would smile and fight to keep the tears from welling up. Only a handful of people knew what really happened, and they knew Lalani couldn't handle the sympathy greetings and looks. So, they kept the speculations to a minimum and said she was fine.

As the winter turned bitter cold, but didn't snow, Jim wanted to take Lalani somewhere warm. Somewhere she might find some peace and smile again. After a week Lalani returned to doing things around the ranch: cooking meals, feeding chickens, doing laundry. She sent word to Kate to come visit, that she was ready to talk.

Kate arrived mid-morning with a warm hug and gentle kiss. Lalani had made cranberry scones and had hot tea waiting. Jim said he had business in town, and he and Evan would grab their meal there, so there was no need to cook. He stooked up the fire in the parlor before leaving as Kate and Lalani settled quietly on the sofa. Kate sat talking only about the party and how everyone missed Lalani and Jim, but didn't want to get the flu.

Lalani smiled, "I can't believe it's been a year since you and Clay were married. So much has happened. We were in London at this time last year. How are Thomas, Sophia, Jessie and Jake?"

"They're fine. Thomas says Jessie's homesick for the States, and Jake might bring her back for a visit. But he and Sophia are busy with the Larkbrook estate."

"Jessie here? That would be miraculous. I'm not sure I would be up to her antics at this point. I'm not sure what I should be up to at this point. Kate, I don't know why I'm so shattered about the loss of the baby. It had only been three weeks of knowing and I never dreamed I would be a mother. Even after knowing I was pregnant, I didn't think about it much, except for when I was suffering from the morning sickness. Then I cursed it. Do you think I cursed it out of me?"

"Don't be silly, you didn't curse the baby. All women curse losing their breakfast and not being able to eat what they want. Lalani, no one can answer the question 'why', so don't try. It may have only been a few weeks, but you have such love for everyone. Of course, you loved the baby. Don't ever think you didn't. You will have a little one to love. Just give it time. "

"Time, I've got lots of that now. I've been sitting looking at the painting of Waimea Bay, and I keep thinking it's time I go home. Go back to Hawaii."

Kate had a deep surprised look, and wasn't sure what to say. *Is she thinking for a visit or permanently?* "Are you saying to visit or to live? And what does Jim say about it?"

"Oh, Kate, you don't need me anymore, you have a new family. I don't know. I just have this feeling pulling me home. It's been twenty-five years. I'm sure there's nothing there for me. No one I know, other than the Hawaiian Royals I went to school with, and we were just classmates, not really friends."

"And Jim?" Kate pressed.

"Jim! My greatest grief is having let him down. He was so happy when he found out about the baby. It's hard for us to walk into the tub room at the moment. Jim keeps saying he wants to take me back to Hawaii to see it. Just the timing of everything made it impossible. Now nothing is holding us back from going, and it would be nice to get out of the cold. If we go now, we would be back for spring plant-ing and the calves."

Kate gave a sigh of relief when she heard Lalani say 'back for spring planting'. *Just a visit, a trip might do them good. Lalani's thoughts seem to be all over the place, her emotions are so jumbled, as to be expected. If they go, Matthew will be three/four months by the time they return and not so much of a newborn to remind Lalani of her loss.* "Well, as long as you promise to come home to *Kālua 'ana*, I think it's a great place to go get warm. You always hated the cold winters in London and Boston."

"True, London was the worst. I just want to get back to doing what I used to do. But I just feel if I do, I'm just showing how little I loved...," she said as tears welled up.

"Just stop that! Lalani there's no guilt here, no one did anything wrong. You barely had time to get used to the idea, let alone deeply love a baby. I didn't think much about being pregnant myself, not until I felt the baby kick. It's only then you begin to realize there's a little person inside you. You need to grieve for the loss, because whether you realize it or not, you do love the baby. Don't you dare feel guilty. You did nothing wrong. We all know you will be a wonderful mother.

It will come about. It just wasn't your time. As you said, it's been a very busy year," Kate said, putting her arm around her.

"Kate, I'm afraid I'm too old to have a baby, my body isn't built for it."

"Is that what Doc Newell said?"

Lalani sheepishly, "No. He and Miranda said many older women have healthy babies. "

"Then what are you afraid of? You fell off the horse this time, doesn't mean you will next time."

Lalani began to smile and shake her head, "Kate, this wasn't a horse, and when have I ever gotten on a horse? That's not the right analogy for me. And I didn't fall off, the horse bolted and left me."

Kate looked at her and also began to laugh, "You're right. Did you ever fall out of a canoe as a kid?"

"Okay, I get your point. For now, I just don't want people feeling sorry for me, it just makes the hurt stay longer," Lalani said with a lighter manner.

"No worry. I think only a few of us really knew: Miranda, Evan, Clay and me. At thanksgiving Morgan, Eric and Evelyn believed the flu story. Morgan may know now, but none of us will say anything to friends. You just attend church as usual, and you will see."

"Church? I'm not sure. I want to be mad at God, but somehow, I'm not. I can't believe He would be so cruel. Kate, give me another week and I hope I'll be ready to face the world again. To get back to life."

~~

Jim and Evan returned late afternoon and were happy to see Kate and Lalani working on the wool, preparing it for spinning. That evening Lalani began to spin yarn, "I can at least make you a warm pair of socks and a knit scarf. Jim, I do love having the wheel. It's calming and gives me a new direction, a new project."

Jim smiled with a sense of relief, seeing Lalani content after a long week of unhappiness. "I was talking with Evan about running things while we are away."

"Away?" Lalani said, looking up from the wheel.

"Lalani, I'm serious about taking you to Hawaii. While I was in town I inquired about passage on a ship. Milton at the rail station said the Matson line has a ship that goes to Hawaii from San Francisco. I telegraphed their office and the *SS Lurline* will sail on the 18th and has a first-class passenger cabin available."

"The 18th of this month?"

"Yes. It will also get you out of the cold winter. We could take two months and be back by April for spring planting and the calves. Evan's happy to keep things going here. Don't you want to see Hawaii again? We could go to Mexico, if you prefer," he said with hesitation.

"Actually, ever since Kate gave me the painting of Waimea Bay, I've been thinking about home, how I never returned home. I've been wondering why. It's not like I couldn't afford to go. I do have fond memories, and the warm sunshine would be heavenly. Can we actually be away that long?"

As they discussed the trip, Jim could see Lalani's spirits lighten. He knew it would be good for her to go. The next morning, Jim went and telegraphed the Matson office and booked passage. Lalani became pre-occupied with what to see and where to go. They made reservations at the Royal Hawaiian Hotel on Richard Street, not far from the house that the Crockers owned on Queen Street.

The two weeks passed quickly as they readied things for the trip. They would go to San Francisco a few days before sailing to purchase a few new items. Kate told Joanna about the voyage, and she insisted they stay at their place. The first evening there, Jim watched Lalani playing paper dolls with Joanna's girls. *This is good, she seems content. I'm happy to see her smile return.* Lalani cut out paper dresses, and the girls colored them.

The next morning Joanna took Lalani to The White House department store to purchase a new dress and hat, as well as dress pants and shirt for Jim. As they were about to leave, they passed the glove counter.

"Oh, Joanna, those brown leather gloves would be perfect for Jim. His hands can get so cold. He doesn't notice, but I do when he touches my cheek or holds my hand." Lalani purchased a handsome pair for Jim and a delicate but warm pair for herself.

Kate and Clay arrived late afternoon and would stay with Eric and Evelyn. Joanna invited everyone for dinner that evening. Evelyn wanted to know if they would go to the other islands or just stay on Oahu. "Oahu is my island, with my father's people. We haven't talked about going to the others. Before the islands were united, before the great war, there was a lot of fighting between island nations."

"Great war?" Evelyn asked.

"Yes, I remember my grandfather telling me about the great war with Kamehameha. King Kamehameha was from the island of Hawaii, and invaded Molokai, Maui and Oahu to stop the warring and raiding going on between the islands. My grandfather would tell stories of the war canoes coming into Waikiki Bay, hundreds of them. That was at the end of the last century. Our poor King Kalanikupule and his men were forced off a cliff on Nuumu Pali. To my grandfather, it was no great loss since Kalanikupule was from Maui and had invaded Oahu first, taking it from our native king, Kahahana.

"At the beginning of the century, Kamehameha the First, conquered most of the islands and united them under his rule, Lalani said. "When I was there, King Kamehameha the Fourth ruled. I remember being at his funeral. His brother Lota became king."

Jim smiled, "I guess we will have to visit your old school, so I can tell your teachers how well they taught you Hawaiian history."

"I'm sure they are all gone by now. By the time I got there, all the Royal family's children had graduated and the last king, King Kamehameha V never had children. Only distant relatives attended when I was there: nephews or nieces of the grandchildren of the royal cousins and the like. The school was opened to wealthy families just before I was born. That's why I got to go. I'm sure the school is still there. Hawaiian history was a big part of our lessons," Lalani blushed.

The next morning Jim and Lalani boarded the *SS Lurline* for the six-day crossing. It was mid-January, and storms had been heavy with strong winds and high swells, but today it was clear with the winds changing from the south back to the north. Lalani had hopes of a reasonable crossing. Jim had never been on a ship this size. Only once had he been on the open sea, when he was eighteen, on a lumber boat from Portland to Los Angeles. It was the fastest way to get south to help get a prize bull for a ranch in Pendleton, Oregon.

This voyage he looked forward to, especially the first-class amenities. They stood at the rail and waived to Kate, Clay and Joanna as the ship pulled away. Once away into the large bay, they headed to the bow to view the wide expanse of ocean that lay ahead of them.

Over the past week, as Lalani talked more about her life on the island, and the places and people, she became excited to be going back. Yet she couldn't bring herself to say home. It had been too long. She had lived most of her life off of the island, in the east. Jim put his arms around her, "Now that we're on our way, how do you feel about seeing Honolulu?"

Nestling into his arms, she thought for a moment. "I'm not sure. Parts of me are excited to see the old places. But I know they are not going to be as I remember them. Buildings burn down, and new ones are built. People I knew are probably long gone. I look forward to walking on the sand along the beaches and to feel the warm waters, and smell the wild orchids. These I'm sure haven't changed. I can't wait to take my shoes off and wade into the lagoon. To find a native who knows how to make a Plumeria lei. To eat fresh cut pineapple and coconut."

"Those sound simple enough to accomplish. As for change, it can be good. But I'm sure the old mercantile is still there, the Crocker's house, the school. We have plenty of time to decide when and where we want to go."

"What do you want to see, Jim, besides where I grew up? "

"Well, I wouldn't mind seeing the green valleys and waterfalls people talk about. I'm just not sure I can get you on a horse to go see them. Then of course there are the pretty little Hawaiian dancers," he said grinning.

"Pretty little dancers, huh! I only remember the strong big men dancing," she smirked back. "I do have a surprise for you."

"What?" he said, turning her around to face him.

"I bought a pair of riding boots. Kate said I should show you the back country, and that's accessible only by horseback."

"Really? You won't regret it. I'll take the best care of you. We can plan a picnic out by one of the falls," he said smiling, and then giving her a kiss.

Shaking her head and wondering what she had done, she said, "I know you will take care of me. I just hope the horse will. Just promise we won't get close to the cliff edges."

The crossing had a lot of large swells, but the ship cut through them with ease. Late on the fourth day a storm hit. The captain opted not to go around, but go straight through. The wind howled, and the bow crashed against the high swells. Jim began to get the hang of the rhythm of the crashes and when to expect them, in order to hold onto his coffee. He declined most meals and found baked potatoes and crackers the least offensive. After an eight-hour bout of fighting the storm, the ship finally broke free into clear night skies with calm sea for the next day.

Late the following morning, the ship was to arrive in Honolulu. Lalani was again out on the bow, waiting for that moment when the island came into view. There was something magical about spotting land after being at sea for days, that small dark speck that crops up out of the sea. At first you can't determine if it's the spot of land or a shadow from a cloud on the water. Then you hear the shout, "Land, ahoy!" Your whole being surges with anticipation, you start noticing the little signs: a piece of drift wood, or what you thought was seaweed actually was a palm frond, other birds than the auks or sea birds.

Lalani returned to her cabin and found Jim had most things packed. They had a small breakfast and then headed back on deck to watch the island grow bigger and bigger. The ship swung south, heading for the Kaiwi channel, between Oahu and Molokai. The ship steamed around the southeast part of Oahu and Lalani knew they were getting close to Honolulu as they passed Makapuu point, the winds now blowing into her face. They stood at the rail watching the high dark lava cliffs, passing a blowhole as it shot water twenty feet into the air. "That must be Hanamua Bay. My father took me by canoe there when I was four. That means, this is Koko Head and this is Muanalua Bay."

"It does look like Kate's painting and what that big mountain ahead ?" Jim said smiling.

"Oh, that's Diamond Head to the British but Le'ahi to us natives, meaning 'brow of the tuna'. A soldier thought the quartz crystal were diamonds and Diamond Head just stuck."

Lalani became more excited as she recalled more sites along the coast. Seal lions basked on the rocks as they passed Koko Head. Within a short time, Diamond Head towered above them on the right. "Jim, this is the Le'ahi the old volcano! We're almost there."

As they rounded Diamond Head, a large steam powered tug came up alongside. Honolulu harbor entrance was too narrow for large ships to maneuver, so tugboats were used to bring them through the narrow channel to the docks. Jim watched the men wrangling the large heavy ropes from the tug onto the bow of the ship. Lalani didn't noticed, as she was lost in thought, watching the land and how it had changed. *Where are the fish ponds and the old prison? They've been filled in and torn down. So many new buildings. I hardly recognize Honolulu. Even the smell is changed, but the breeze is still the same. So many more people.*

After about an hour, the *SS Lurline* was snug at the dock and passengers were disembarking. Jim took Lalani's arm as she stepped onto the dock. It had been twenty-seven years since she stood on that dock. She looked at the large Wilder Steam Ship Co. building dominating the dock and the marketplace that stood just beyond. Jim could see Lalani was overwhelmed by it all. "Are you alright?"

"Yes, it's just all different and yet, I feel I know it. Not the buildings but the layout of things. This is Fort Street and that's Market. If we go up a block, we will come to Queen Street. The Crocker's house is on Queen further out. After Queen will be King Street, and the Mercantile was at King and Smith. I wonder if it's still there?"

"Let's go to the hotel and get settled, then we can get our land legs back and go see if it's still there," Jim said as he hailed a carriage.

There were several carriages available to take new arrivals to their hotel. The Royal Hawaiian Hotel was at Richards and Hotel Streets, only a few blocks away. As they rode toward the hotel, Lalani recognized a few places. *All the small thatch huts are gone.* Nothing compared to the grandeur of the hotel except the Royal Palace across the road. The three-story white wood of the hotel glistened with its white porch railings taking up a block in both directions. They stepped from the carriage and up a few stairs onto a wide sitting veranda that looked out over the harbor. Its high ceilings created a cool inviting area for guests to gather. The bellman took their bags and showed them to a room on the second floor looking out onto Iolani Palace grounds.

"Lalani, I'm hungry. We can have the maid help unpack later. Let's get a bite to eat and then we can go wherever you want to go," Jim said patting his stomach. "We can unpack our own things, thank you," Lalani responded.

After a lovely lunch of fresh pork and fruit, they took a carriage out to Queen Street. Lalani wanted to show Jim where she lived. Queen Street was still a small quiet lane, with homes. *There are no more empty lots, everything has been built on. So many quaint little homes.* As they passed Cooke Street, she motioned for the carriage driver to slow. *The old tree is still there, but the lot is no longer empty. Mother and I would come down here and sit under that tree and make flower leis for Edith as a surprise.*

"There it is Jim, the pale green house on the left. Look how big the Monkeypod tree has grown. The umbrella leaves cover almost the entire front of the house. I would climb that tree when I was little."

The house was a mixture of craftsman and island architecture with a large sitting porch. The house foundation was rise in the island style but the steps and porch pillar bases were of black lava stone and basalt. Native flowering plants surround the foundation. The two-story hip roof plantation house with a small upper porch sat nestled behind the large tree.

"Do you want to stop and ask if you can go in?" Jim said quietly.

"I .. I don't know, I have no idea who lives there now. No... not now. "

"Where was your room?" Jim asked

"Oh, you can't see it from here. It was in the back, off the kitchen. It was a rather large room mother and I shared. The kitchen stove helped heat it in the cooler months, but it could get warm in the summer. Being in the back, it didn't get the breeze from the ocean. Still, all the rooms had high ceilings and vents to let the hot air out. The parlor is on the left of the front door and the dining room on the right. That was Horace and Edith's room up there on the right. The one with the sleeping porch." Lalani sat quietly for a moment, picturing what the house looked like inside." *I wonder if they kept the wallpaper. Of course not, it's been over thirty years since they put it up. I wonder what else they have changed.*

The carriage driver interrupted her thought, "Do you want me to leave you here and come back, or should we go on?" he grumbled, as he was getting impatient. Unexpectantly, the front door opened and a young woman stepped out onto the porch. She looked at the carriage and smiled, then sat in one of the porch chairs and began to read.

"You sure you don't want to ask to see it? She looks friendly, here's your chance," Jim said.

Lalani wavered in uncertainty for a moment, then said, "No, not at this moment. But before we leave, we can come back. ... Driver, can you go up to King Street and head back to Punchbowl to the Royal School?"

The driver tapped the horses, and they continued on Queen Street to the next corner, then turned left and went up to King Street, several blocks up. Turning left they headed back towards town. "Look Jim, that's the Chamberlains' house. Their maid and my mother were best friends. I would play with some of their children from time to time. Their daughter Mary and I went to the Royal School, though she was two years older than I was. The Chamberlain family is one of the oldest families on the island. Mary's grandfather was a missionary and helped start the Royal School. He hired Edith to teach English."

"Are they still here? Maybe we can inquire when we get back to the hotel. I'm sure the manager will know all the main families on the island," Jim suggested.

The driver now picked up the pace as he headed up Punchbowl to the school. The sign out front read, Royal School. Here Lalani wanted to stop and get out. "Jim, we can let the driver go. It's only three blocks back to the hotel from here."

Lalani walked up to the main building, a two-story wood building. It was late in the day and the students had all gone home, but several teachers were still in their class rooms, finishing for the day. The building had been added onto since she left, yet she went straight to Edith's old room. A white haired lady was sitting at the desk. "May I help you?" she asked looking up.

"Sorry to interrupt. I was a student here many, many years ago and Edith Crocker was the English teacher. This was her room."

"Oh, I see, well you're welcome to look around, but it's been almost thirty years since Edith was here," she said smiling. "I'm Mrs. Bender and this is now the third and fourth grade math class room."

Lalani was surprised she knew when Edith had taught there. "You know about Edith Crocker? Did you know her? "

"In a way, I was only at the school for one year with her, before she left for the mainland. She had a ward, a pretty little girl in the fifth-grade class. You wouldn't be her, would you?" Mrs. Bender looked at Lalani with a long deep look.

"A matter of fact, I am. What did you teach?" Lalani asked.

"I have always taught math. Back then I taught beginning math to the second graders. Now I teach the advanced eighth grade students. Well, I'll be, you sure did grow into a fine lady. And may I assume this is your husband?"

Lalani turned to Jim who had been quietly standing behind her just watching. Turning to Jim and taking his arm, "Oh, yes, I'm Lalani Baker now and this is Jim Baker. He's brought me home for a visit. We live in California."

Jim exchanged greetings and Mrs. Bender invited them to stay and look around, taking their time, for she was due at a meeting. Lalani looked at the desks, but they had all changed. The desks with separate chairs had all been replaced with desks with attached seats. "Sorry, Jim, I can't show you where I wrote my name on the back of Susan's chair."

Susan was her best friend at school. She lived in Iwilei on the other side of town, so they only saw each other at school. Lalani sat down at a desk by the second window. "This is where I would sit and do my homework, while Edith finished correcting papers. From here I would watch carriages coming and going, but now the trees on Punchbowl Street have grown too tall and thick. You almost can't see the road."

Next Lalani took Jim to one of her old classrooms. Mrs. Lynn was my last teacher here. I liked her because she treated me like I belonged. My first two teachers didn't think I was smart enough to be at the Royal School. When I asked questions, they never answered and spent all their time with the wealthy kids. I had to wait until after school when I could ask Edith. She always answered my questions. All of them, except 'why.' How, what, when, where she always answered promptly. Why, not so much. Edith would look at me and say 'think it out' or if she didn't know the answer, it was always 'because that's the way it is.'"

Jim smiled, "And I bet you asked a lot of whys."

Lalani laughed, "I guess I did. I learned quickly when Edith was going to say 'because', she would get this wrinkle across her forehead. When I saw it begin to form, I would race to say never mind, just so I didn't have to hear 'because'."

"I've heard some of the stories about Kate's school days and her antics. What about you?" Jim asked with a silly grin.

"Me? Antics? I had to be good as not to embarrass Edith. There was one thing. My second year here, I sat behind Ryan Rogers. He would always pull my hair as he passed my chair. One day he pulled extra hard, and I told him if he did it again, I would pull his chair out from him when he went to sit down, so he better watch out. Well, he did it again later in the day. But instead of getting even right away, I waited until the next day. That day I got to my seat early and waited for Ryan. He looked at me and then turned to sit down. As he did, I reached with my foot and pulled his chair back, and he missed the seat falling to the floor. Everyone laughed. I just smiled and said 'I didn't say when I would do it,' and everyone laughed again."

"And what happened?" Jim asked

"Well, of course I was sent to the office. Mr. Brian was very patient and let me explain my actions. He then explained that boys do things like that when they like a girl. Ryan just didn't know how to tell me. All I could think was, yuk!"

Lalani shook her head with disgust. "The funny thing was that Christmas Mr. Brian selected Ryan and me to play Mary and Joseph for the Christmas music program. We both got called to the office and the class thought we had been fighting again. We were mortified when we had to kneel together over a manger while the other kids sang Silent Night."

"Did he stop pulling your hair and did you become friends?"

"After the chair incident he stayed clear of me. But after we did the Christmas pageant, we made a truce. The next year we actually teamed up to do a report on the ocean and got along pretty well. "

"Do you know where he is now or what he does?"

"I have no idea! I have no idea where anyone is. Susan might still be on the island, but probably married with a new name."

They were interrupted by the janitor wanting to sweep and lock up. It was getting late and would be dark soon. Lalani took one last look around and they began their walk back to the hotel. It had been a very long and emotional day for Lalani. After a quiet supper in the dining room, they retreated to their room. As soon as things were unpacked and hung up, they climbed into bed. Lalani was asleep in minutes, while Jim lay holding her. *I'm glad we have come. She seems happy to be here and has so much to show me.*

The next morning Jim arranged for a rental carriage, so they could come and go as desired. Lalani was eager to see if the mercantile was still there. Jim held her off until ten o'clock, and then they headed to King and Smith Streets in downtown. As the carriage traveled down King Street, Lalani pointed out businesses that were still there and others that were gone. "Look, Bishop Bank is still here. Horace did all his banking and investing there. The manager always gave Horace a lollipop to bring to me."

Jim drove slowly following another horse drawn carriage, as a few automobiles maneuvered around them. "There's Samping's, the bakery. Mother and I would go together to get special cakes for Edith's afternoon ladies teas. Mother and I would split a Haupia Cake. You'll like it. It's cake made with coconut milk and arrowroot. It sounds odd, but quite sweet. Many of the stores downtown were owned by Chinese families. The Hungtai family owned the Canton Hotel on Hotel Street, and the Tyhune family the wine shop on Nuuanu Street."

"Did you go to school with their children?" Jim inquired.

"Oh, no, mother just did business at their shops. Back then, the Samping brothers were simple bakers, and I heard the Tyhune daughters had to sell some of their land when their father died. The Hungtai were the really wealthy Chinese family, but their children were only babies when I left." Suddenly, Lalani sat forward all excited. "Look, Jim, there it is. The store!"

Jim pulled up in front of a two-story wood building. The name read Gilbert's Mercantile. "Oh, the name has been changed," Lalani said, stepping down to the boardwalk. She stood looking at the windows and goods. Jim came around and took her arm as they approached the double wood doors. "Horace had those doors made of the local koa wood. It's hard as rock, and they still look splendid." Jim held the door open and Lalani hesitated and then slowly went through. *Oh, things have been rearranged. Nothing's where it used to be. But it looks nice.* Taking a few steps forward, she took in the large space with its high ceiling. *Once again this feels so familiar and yet is so different.* She looked to her right, expecting to see the large cash register, but it was a display case with shawls and lady's gloves. She rubbed her hand over the case. *I think this was the case the watches and fine silver were kept in.* The store was deep rather than wide with several windows along Smith Street. They wandered around for a few moments and then back to the counter in the back, where the cash register was now located.

"Good morning, my name is Kona, May I help you find something?" the young man asked.

Lalani was lost in thought about the old cash register. *Is this the same cash register? Is the ten key still hard to push?* Jim finally answered the clerk. "I'm sorry, but no, we're just looking. You see my wife's father was the original owner and started the store."

"Oh, my goodness. You're Horace Crocker's daughter? I hadn't heard he had a daughter."

Lalani came back to reality and quickly explained she wasn't really his daughter, but *hanai*, growing up in their house and was Edith's companion. The young clerk nodded, with an understanding approval. "As you can see, we have an excellent line of goods. Some of the dresses are the latest French fashion. Mrs. Gilbert likes to go to Europe and purchase them. We have a dressmaker that can make one to fit your size."

Lalani wandered over to the dresses. They were of the fashionable quality Edith liked to stock. The clientele had been the newly arriving American and English businessmen looking for good opportunities in the new sugar industry. Horace stocked goods for this wealthier population, while other stores, like Hackfield on Fort Street, catered to the everyday working people or the increasing Chinese population. "I'm glad to see the quality of goods hasn't changed. Horace would be pleased to see how well kept things are," she commented to Jim, who just stood close, letting her take it all in.

On the far left of the store, Lalani spotted the staircase that went to the office and store rooms. She headed back toward the young man and was about to ask if she could see the office, when she spotted the old regulator clock hanging on the wall. "Is that the original clock that was in the store?" she asked.

"I don't know, I've only worked here for a year," the clerk replied. Suddenly a bell behind him gently rang out.

"I know that bell, it's the dumbwaiter bell," Lalani smiled. "Do you still use it to bring goods down from the upstairs store rooms?"

"Oh, yes. When goods arrive, we send them up to be priced and sorted, and then use the dumbwaiter to bring them down as needed."

Lalani turned to Jim, "You see Horace didn't want to take up space on this floor for a stock room, so he installed the large dumbwaiter and put the storerooms on the second floor. It wasn't the most practical thing, but it gave him more display area."

Kona had turned around and raised the door to find two stacks of stationery there waiting to be put into place. From the stairs came a voice, "Kona, we need to restock the writing goods."

As the grey haired man came to the counter, "Oh, forgive me, I didn't know you were helping someone. Seems like I'm always interrupting Kona when he's busy. I'm Mr. Gilbert, owner and manager of the store," he said reaching out his hand to Jim.

"No apology necessary, we were probably keeping Kona from his work," Jim said.

"Mr. Gilbert, this lady grew up in Mr. Crocker's house and was a companion to Mrs. Crocker," Kona noted.

Mr. Gilbert stood back for a moment eyeing Lalani. "This can't be little Lalani, can it?"

"Yes, I'm Lalani, and this is my husband, Jim Baker. You knew Mr. Crocker and about me?"

"Of course, I purchased the mercantile from Horace. I met you in their home before you left for Europe. I was sad to hear of the Crockers' passing. They were well liked here in Honolulu. Many of my older clients, still speak highly of them. Well, you certainly have grown into a fine lady. What brings you back to Hawaii?"

"Lalani and I have only been married for less than a year and I wanted to bring her back so she could show me where she grew up and the lovely island, I've heard so much about," Jim explained.

"Well, it certainly is a lovely place. Paradise, people say." Mr. Gilbert could see Lalani looking up at the stairs. "Mrs. Baker, would you like to see upstairs? That part of the store really hasn't changed much. Horace's big old desk is still there."

Lalani's face lit up, "Oh, yes, if you don't mind."

You go on up. I'll be there in a moment. I need to talk to Kona about a special order. Lalani took Jim's hand, looking for support and headed up the stairs. At the top of the stairs was a long hall on the left side running the length of the building, back towards King Street. On the right side of the hall were several doors. Lalani walked down to the third door, half wood and half frosted glass, and reached for the door knob and slowly opened it. She peered around the door into the room. *Lalani, don't be silly, you're not a little kid anymore, Horace isn't here to sneak in on.* She opened the door wide and walked in. There in front of her was Horace's large mahogany desk. The wood looked aged, and the surface worn. It was surprisingly neat for a working office. She walked over to the old wood library chair at the desk, and rubbed her hand slowly across the top. *I can almost see Horace sitting here with his spectacles on, poring over papers.* She looked at the desk drawer and started to open the top left and stopped. *Lalani, don't be silly, there are no chocolates in there anymore. Horace did so love chocolate drops and always let me sneak one when I came. I know he always knew. Funny how nice he was to me when I was so little, considering he never had children and seemed so business-like.*

Jim broke her thought, "Does it seem the same?"

"Oh, yes, very much so. I would come up after school and see him sitting here, shuffling papers. He would grumble and say in a gruff voice 'what do you want?' and then look up and wink. Then he would pull that drawer open so I could get a chocolate he always kept there. My first year of school, after school I would run all the way here just to get my chocolate."

Lalani looked around at the rest of the room. There were two more larger wood file cabinets and the chairs in front of the desk were new. On the wall were photos of what she assumed was Mr. Gilbert's family. As she was looking, Mr. Gilbert entered.

"Well, have I kept it in good shape? Would Horace approve?" he asked half teasing and half curious.

"Oh, yes, I think he would. I'm glad to see you kept the desk. It's such a majestic piece."

Mr. Gilbert crossed the room to where Jim and Lalani stood looking at the photos. He pointed to the family photo, "That's my family. The girls are grown and married now." Pointing to another photo on the far end he asked, "Do you recognize that photo?"

Lalani took a close look at the photo of two men wearing cowboy hats on horseback. "Is that Horace?"

"Sure is. He and I rode out to his ranch one day, just after we closed the deal on the store. He said he always wanted to be a western cowboy and raise cattle, but never had the time. He said maybe after Edith was gone, he would come back to the ranch and try. Of course, he laughed and said 'he'd probably go first.'"

"I had no idea. I don't remember him ever talking about a ranch and wanting to raise cattle," Lalani said, most surprised.

"I think Edith wouldn't have anything to do with it, and so he never said anything. I do know he never sold that piece of property. We would correspond on a regular basis at first. He told me if things got too hectic, I could always go to the ranch to escape for a while. I haven't been out there in years. The old house is pretty run down, and vines have overgrown it by now."

Jim was very interested in this bit of news. "Lalani, we should go out and see it, just for fun. It must be a special place if Horace kept it all those years. Do you know who owns it know?"

"I assumed Horace's estate does. As far as I know it was never sold. But you can check with the land office to make sure. Listen, my wife and I are having a little supper party on Friday, why don't you come? The Kanekua's are a little younger, he's one of our leading attorneys, and the Ladds, I'm sure they knew Edith and Horace. Say five o'clock? We live at 442 N King Street. Please join us."

Lalani looked at Jim, and he nodded, saying "We would love to come. We may find it is a small world and know some of the people Lalani knew."

"Great, in that case, please call me Amos. My wife's name is Elizabeth. Please take your time looking around the store. I must be off to the customs house as my ship of goods arrived this morning."

Lalani and Jim stayed for another thirty minutes looking around at various items in the store and then headed back to the hotel via Merchant Street. Lalani pointed out more of the places she knew and others that were gone or names had changed. They caught the last seating for dinner, when they got back to the hotel just after 1:00 o'clock. Lalani talked about the changes to the store and how it used to be laid out.

Jim was intrigued by the ranch Horace had. "We should check with the land office and see who owns the ranch now."

"I'm sure Horace's brother does or has sold it by now." Lalani said, looking at Jim leerily. *I'm sure he knows the road is long gone and grown over. He'll do anything to get back on a horse.* "Are you missing Buck already? I have to admit it does pique my curiosity. Horace having a ranch all that time and he never mentioned it or took me there."

Jim laughed, "He probably wanted some peace and quiet. To get away from all the women and a noisy little girl."

"I was never allowed to be noisy in the Crocker house when I was little. I was the maid's daughter, and mother was afraid of losing her job."

"I don't know, climbing trees and sneaking chocolates. Sounds like you were as much the Crocker's daughter as you were your mother's," Jim smiled.

"I'm sure you're right. Turned out, I had them longer than my real parents. As you know I remember only a few things about being with my father. Yet, my mother had such a beautiful voice, and we did so much together: cleaning the house, cooking, gardening, spending her day off together.

"When Horace took me from her, I think he really thought we would come back here before going on to the States. But when we were in England, the Chamberlains sent word my mother had died. I think he couldn't bring himself to face the promise he had made to me. 'That I would see her again, before I knew it,' is what he said, as we cleared the harbor.

"My understanding is she is buried next to my father at *Kawaiaha'o* Church Cemetery. Jim, do you think we could go there tomorrow? I would like to see her grave. I need her to know I forgave her and Horace years ago for what happened."

"Certainly, we can. We can arrange with the hotel for flowers, if you would like," he said patting her hand.

"I would like that. Afterwards, can we go out to Manoa Stream and find the falls my mother and I used to go to? I know we can take King Street to the end, and then we can hike the rest of the way. I'm sure it's not too far. We could take a picnic."

Jim looked at Lalani and worried it would be too much for her. But he knew better than to say no. "You brought your riding boots, maybe we could ride to the falls instead of hike?"

"You are missing Buck! I'd like to hike this time, like my mother and I did. I promise to take you riding in the back country another time," smiling with a please-don't-mind-this-time, kind of look.

The next morning, they took the carriage to *Kawaiaha'o* Cemetery on Queen Street, passing her old house on the way. When the missionaries first came to Hawaii, they established this church for the Hawaiians. Lalani and her mother would attend every Sunday with the Crockers. The white coral stone building with its square tower hadn't changed. Jim took Lalani inside to inquire where her parents were buried. The church clerk was pleasant and told them how to find it, the graveyard wasn't large and there were only a few trees.

Lalani held onto Jim's hand with the flowers in her other arm as they entered the grave yard. After a moment, Jim spotted the markers. There was no headstone, only a small stone marker with 'Leia, wife of Kakani' on it. Next to it was 'Kakani of *Kewalo* Basin'. Lalani stood for a long moment in front of her mother's marker. *I wish I could remember her face, but I just hear her voice. Her voice calling Lalani... the sweet humming of her voice. Oh, makuahine, I so wish you had come with us all those years ago. I sometimes wonder if you didn't die of a broken heart rather than the fever.* Lalani knelt down and cleared the grass away from the stone edges and gently laid the flowers down. Jim stood aways off and watched, letting Lalani take her time and remember in her own way. She stood again and whispered, *"kala aku nei au iā ʻoe."* *I hope you know I forgave both you and Horace years ago. I guess in reality you saved me from the same fate and gave me the most amazing life for a simple Hawaiian girl. Yet all I can feel right now is sadness, not grief, but sad that we didn't have more time together and that at the moment I can't recall some of those times. Funny I can only remember doing the washing with you and hearing you hum. So many times, you scrubbing and me turning the crank to the ringer, watching the water squeeze out. I so wish you could have been at my wedding and seen my dress made from your cloth. It truly is beautiful.*

The church tower bell let out a billowing ring, breaking Lalani's thoughts. She turned around to see where Jim had gone. He was quietly standing by a small tree watching. He smiled at her, and she knew he didn't mind waiting. She turned back to the markers and looked at her father's stone. She could only remember fleeting glimpse of what he looked like: tall, slim, with strong arms, and his dark hair that reached below his ears. Nothing else, only a glimpse of him sitting in a canoe and then it was gone. She looked back to her mother's stone and again whispered, *"Aloha au ia 'oe makuahine."* For a moment, her mother's round cheeked face with her smile became clear in her mind. *Your smile, what a wonderful smile.*

Finally, she turned and walked back to Jim. "I'm glad they are together. They did have a great love for each other. We call it *e ku'u aloha."* Jim, you are my *e ku'u aloha.* Thank you for bringing me home. *I can't explain it, but suddenly Oahu does feel like home...* How about we go on to the stream and have our picnic?"

Lalani didn't look back, but was content knowing where her parents now lay. They turned north to King Street and then east until they came to a small road that led up into the foothills. The sun was now shining with distant white clouds offshore. But for now, it was warm and the breeze made it pleasant. The small road was well worn, indicating it was used often. They turned north and went until the road petered out at a small clearing surrounded by native Hapu'u fern trees, coral tree with their thorny trunks, and Prince Kuhio vines tangling in the trees.

Jim helped Lalani down and retrieved the picnic basket the hotel had provided. Lalani scampered down a small trail through the lush growth, to the water's edge and stood surveying the stream banks.

The stream was about thirty feet across with about five feet of reasonably moving water running through it. The banks were lined with various ferns, Naupaka flowers and koa trees. Lalani's first instinct was to take off her shoes and wade into the water. But Jim put his arms around her stopping her from doing so. "I think it might be best to stay out of the stream considering what happened last time you waded into one."

"Oh, Jim, that was different. I promise I won't try to wade across. I only want to get my feet wet here by the edge." *That's crazy, those are the same words I used to tell my mother when she brought me here.*

"How about lunch first, and then maybe we both will get our feet wet?"

Jim spread out a blanket in the driest open spot he could find, and they sat quietly talking about what they had seen and done since arriving. After an hour or so, Jim reached down and untied Lalani's shoes and then pointed to a spot where the water was gently lapping the shore. Lalani waded in, holding her skirt in her arms, recalling the feel of the smooth stones and sand under feet. Jim watched the child-like joy she expressed as she walked in the shallow water. He was glad he could give her back some of her happier childhood memories. He stood on the shore, and picking up flat smooth pebbles, tried skipping them across the water. The skips were limited as the water was flowing too fast. *I need a pond, then I could really show Lalani how good I am at skipping rocks.* They walked along a narrow path up stream to a twenty-foot waterfall, cascading off the cliff on the other side of the stream. They found a large rock and sat watching and listening to the channels of water and droplets falling. After another hour they headed back to town. They joined others sitting on the hotel veranda and watched the sky change from blues to golden pinks as the sun set.

11

Reclaiming What Was

The next evening, they had tickets for a concert at the new Music Hall across the street from the hotel. Lalani expected the discussion at intermission to be about the music, but most of the patrons were talking about Queen Lili'uokalani's surrender to the Provisional Government, and that eventually the islands would be annexed by the United States. Jim and Lalani found Mr. and Mrs. Gilbert in the crowd, who were talking quietly about the events that had happened. Mr. Gilbert introduced his wife and granddaughter Sarah, and said they were looking forward to having them to supper the next evening.

"Why has the Queen given up the monarchy?" Lalani asked.

"It's a long and complicated situation. The week before you arrived, US troops landed here in Honolulu. Tempers were running high between the Provisional Government wanting annexation by the US and those wanting to restore the monarchy to full power and stay independent. The Queen was afraid of bloodshed, that innocent Hawaiians would be killed when the troops showed up. So, for the good of the people, she surrendered the monarchy. It's best we not speak of things here. We can tell you more tomorrow if you like," Amos said. with a sense of foreboding in his voice.

Jim had seen the headline of her surrender in a paper, but the article was in Hawaiian. They returned to their seats, a little more apprehensive about being in town than when they had arrived. The chamber music was lovely, but now did not have the calming sense it had in the first part of the program. After the concert, they strolled over to the palace grounds. The iron gates were locked and Hawaiian guards stood at watch. *These gates didn't do any good at holding the enemy out. It's a shame they now prevent the queen from entering her rightful place.*

Jim put his arm around Lalani sensing her melancholy. "She did the right thing. Bloodshed is never the answer. How about we have a quiet day tomorrow, just the two of us at the hotel? Then in the evening we can find out more, if you want."

Lalani nodded her head, wanting to shake off the sad sense of loss before it returned. She wanted to keep the joy of sharing her home with her loving husband. The next morning, they slept late, and Jim picked up some sticks and whittled while Lalani wrote letters to Katherine and Minnie. Since finding out that Horace had a ranch, Jim had been thinking about it. *Can't stop wondering how big it was and who owns it now. Would Lalani want to go see it?*

"Lalani, I'm afraid curiosity has gotten to me. I'd like to find out who owns the old Crocker ranch. Would you mind if we walk down to the land office after dinner?" Jim asked looking up from the small wood ship he was carving from his stick.

"No, I don't mind. I've been wondering if Horace's brother's son owns it."

"Horace had a nephew? Did you ever meet him?"

"Only once, briefly at the funeral. Horace's brother had a son and a daughter, much older than me."

After a light dinner of chicken and rice, they wandered over to the land records office on Punchbowl Street. The clerk was most polite, but hesitated at first.

"Are you a relative?" he inquired.

"I was their *hanai* daughter," Lalani replied

"Oh, I see, then what year and where was the ranch?"

Jim told him as much as they knew. That it was near Kahalu'u on the east coast and he owned it in 1860. The clerk disappeared into the back room and after several minutes returned with a large black bound book. He opened it and scanned an index of names.

"Crocker, Horace. Let's see." He flipped several pages and landed on a deed with Horace's name. "Looks like he bought the ranch in 1849, about four hundred acres in the Kahalu'u Valley."

"Do you know who owns it now?" Jim asked eagerly. The clerk pulled out another large book from under the counter. "Let's see. That's Kahalu'u Valley lots 10-15." Again, he flipped several pages. "Here it is, Martin Shaw is listed as the trustee. He must have been the attorney for Mr. Crocker's estate. He is still the trustee or the receiver might never have bothered to put the deed into his own name, but left it in the Crocker trust."

Lalani looked at Jim with surprise. "Martin Shaw is Kate's uncle. I knew he knew the Crockers, but he never mentioned land when I saw him last year."

"Well, it looks like the estate has been paying the taxes on it. Nothing is due. That's good news," commented the clerk.

"How much are the taxes?" Jim asked reluctantly.

"Looks like, $160 was paid last, that's about forty cents/acre."

"Is that good or bad?" asked Lalani.

"It's pretty cheap, actually," Jim said.

They thanked the clerk and then headed back to the hotel to dress for their evening gathering. Lalani didn't say much about the ranch on their way back to the hotel. *Could it possibly be part of the trust Horace set up for me? Oh, I'm sure it's not, most likely it went to this nephew, otherwise Martin would have said something.* Jim stayed quiet with all his questions and curiosity, knowing Lalani was already wondering herself and would bring it up when she was ready.

~~

They arrived at the Gilbert's just after Daniel and Harriet Ladd, as the sun was setting. Amos introduced them to John and Maria

Kanekua, already there. It started out as a cordial evening getting to know people. John explained that he and Lalani had been at the Royal School together. He was in his first year, the year before she left, and he remembered Mrs. Crocker very well. "She was always correcting my pronunciation of the word 'punctuation.' It would come out 'po-nunaon,' as I was unaccustomed to pronouncing C, R, and T," John shared.

"Well, I'd say she did a good job in teaching. Your English is excellent," Lalani complimented.

They talked about the school for a bit and then the conversation turned to John's legal career. "John's helping Queen Lili'uokalani draft a letter to Senator Cleveland to support reinstating the heir to the throne," Daniel commented, wanting to get the conversation on something more meaningful.

"Actually, the Queen is doing most of the writing," John explained. "The Queen's niece has been in Washington talking to the US Congress and President Elect Cleveland not to annex Hawaii. Since the overthrow and with the American Minister's help, the Provisional Government has demanded that the Queen's petition to be reinstated be put in writing, before any action can be considered. There's just killing time, until they can come up with a way to do away with her, I'm afraid." John said.

"My understanding is President Harrison already approved the annexation, and was just waiting on Congress for ratification," Jim said as he had some knowledge of what was going on politically, though he had no real interest in politics.

"True, but Senator Cleveland, who will take back the office of President in March, is against the annexation, and we hope, will be able to stop it, and demand the queen be returned to the throne," John rationalized.

"But don't the people of Hawaii have to approve any constitutional changes?" asked Lalani.

"Yes, but under King Kalākaua the strong white business men in his cabinet coerced him to make changes to the Hawaiian constitution, to provide more power to foreign business and less to the monarchy. Queen Lili'uokalani, his successor, refuses to accept the new constitution which took more of the native Hawaiian rights away, and proposed her own constitution, but was betrayed by her cabinet who refused to sign it and resigned. Within two days of their resignation the Annexation Group, Samuel Dole, Lorrin Thurston and a handful of other white businessmen formed this Provisional Government and appointed a Committee of Safety. It took them only two days to get John Stevens, the United States Minister to the Hawaiian Kingdom, to land US troops in front of the Palace. That was on the 17th, the week before you arrived. With US troops in Honolulu to protect Americans, the queen surrendered and withdrew to her private resident at Washington Place and began to write the petition to President Elect Cleveland to declare the takeover illegal since there had been no vote."

"But there must be a vote, and the people will reinstate her," Lalani said with a tone of assurance.

"Unfortunately, the non-native landowners will out-vote us. The decline in native Hawaiians caused by European diseases, has caused us to be outnumbered," John admitted.

"Merchants like Amos and I have had little say, and we believe the native people are not being represented," added Daniel.

"So much has changed since I left. I'm sad to think of Hawaii without a royal family," Lalani lamented.

"The Royal family really ended with Kamehameha the Third. Kauikeaouli and Liholiho never had a male heir that survived to take the crown, and their daughters didn't want it. That's how it got to Lili'uokalani, his niece," Harriet informed Jim.

Jim didn't want to get into a political debate, and kept his thoughts to himself. *Having a Republic and not a monarch usually serves the people better. But in this case, it's more like we Americans have taken over as usual and have not considered the native people and their heritage.*

John explained how the sugar plantation owners in the past ten years had become so rich and powerful, there was no stopping them. "We just would like to see some justice and respect for the Queen, for her to be able to serve her people as their representative as Queen Victoria does. There is no reason for her to be banned from Iolani Palace. Thurston's Committee on Safety and his group have taken it over and they're talking about putting her on trial for creating a new constitution. Which I might add she had the right to introduce, but never got the chance to present it to the people for a vote."

They all agreed it was a very uncertain time and the US Congress would regrettably ratify the annexation, and there would be nothing they could do. But hopefully they could restore some of the Queen's rights. But until things were certain, John was going to keep supporting the Queen.

The ladies finally turned the conversation to more cultural topics, asking Lalani how theater and music in San Francisco were doing. She confessed she didn't get to the city often. "I noticed Tchaikovsky's *Iolanta,* his last opera, was coming. The year before, his *Queen of Spades* opera had been performed. "

Elizabeth invited them to join them in their box for the upcoming chamber concert. The conversation then turned to friends and families Lalani knew when she lived there. She didn't recall very many names, but the Chamberlains and the Sumners. "Do you know if Susan Sumner is still here? She was a year ahead of me at school, but always took time to talk to me. Her older sister, Nancy, was part of Queen Emma's court," Lalani questioned.

"Oh, yes, both girls are here. Nancy was married, but is not now. She has three children in their teens, and Susan, is also married and lives here. Mary Chamberlain still lives in the old family home," Harriet confirmed. "Let me arrange an afternoon tea for all of us."

"That would be lovely," Lalani said warmly.

"While you ladies have your tea, Daniel and I will take Jim fishing," Amos added.

~

The next week was busy, meeting with various old acquaintances and visiting places Lalani had known. After dinner one day, they walked the mile down Fort Street and east along Halekauwila out to Kara'ako where the salt ponds used to be. Reaching the water's edge, Lalani stood looking out to Sand Island. "This area is where my father would come to fish. The mahi mahi would gather on the ocean side of the ponds in shallow lagoons, and he and the other men would toss the nets out and pull in the fish. But that's all gone now, filled in with the dirt from dredging the channel. The buildings back there are where the stinky salt ponds were. Jim, so much has changed. I'm glad father and mother are not here to see it. I think they would be sad to see how the *haoles* have so little respect for the land. We need to take care of the land and it will take care of us, not change it to what we want. Mother nature will reclaim it someday. I also think father would be especially sad about the Queen."

"There must be part of the island that's the same," Jim said trying to lift her spirit.

"I suppose, the back side and the mountains of Oahu are the same."

This gave Jim an idea. *I'm still itching to see Horace's ranch.* "Why don't we go find Horace's old ranch house? We can stay the night and camp out. The clerk said it was on the east shore just beyond Kōnāhuanui Peak.

Lalani looked at Jim as if he had lost his mind. *Me camp out, I've never done that in my entire life.* Looking at Jim she could see he was serious. *He has been so sweet about going and doing all the things I have wanted. I did say we would go riding in the back county. Could I possibly manage sleeping on the ground or even worse.* "Jim, if it's truly in the back country, we will have to use horses to get there," she said with anguish in her voice. "Can you really find a gentle horse that I could ride?"

"Yes, I'm sure I can. I would make sure you had the gentlest mare, and we would only go as fast as you felt comfortable," Jim said, with a spirit of hope.

Lalani knew she had opened the door to her least favorite thing. *Seeing how the thought makes his face light up, I guess there's no getting out of it now. He may regret saying as fast as I want – the horse had better like to walk and I hope it's not too far into the back country.* "Jim, you will have to make all the arrangements for cooking and sleeping. Keep in mind I have never slept on the cold ground, not even as a child. Also, I'm sorry, I am not going to wear trousers. I've seen Kate ride with a dress, so that will have to work for his trip."

Jim grinned so big; his cheeks turned red. "That will be just fine, but you may want to get some extra heavy bloomers for protection against the saddle."

Jim set to tasks, making arrangements for gear and finding the right horse for Lalani. Amos recommended a friend's daughter's horse. "His daughter is ten and has a very sweet and gentle horse. I can inquire if she wouldn't mind letting Lalani use her. I know her father very well."

Later that week Jim took Lalani down to meet Princess, a small dark bay, quarter horse. Violet, Princess' owner, showed Lalani how to stroke her favorite spots and the little tricks for getting Princess to do what she wanted. Jim helped Lalani mount, getting her skirts untangled and settled and then walked her around the corral, until she was comfortable. After about thirty minutes Violet thought Lalani and Princess would be good friends and was happy to let the pretty lady borrow her. "I will be away on Maui visiting friends for the next two weeks, so you can use Princess until I get back," Violet smiled.

It was another three days before Jim and Lalani headed out for the Crocker ranch. Lalani had been practicing riding Princess every day and was beginning to feel somewhat at ease. *I'm pretty sure the horse won't run off with me, but I wouldn't say I'm totally comfortable.*

It was a pleasant morning the second week of February when Jim loaded a pack horse with gear. Jim had gotten directions from Amos and a map of the ranch from the land office. Daniel Ladd offered to take them to the trail that led north to Kahalu'u Valley, as he had business on the east coast in Kailua. Kahalu'u was twenty miles from Honolulu and would take half a day to get there.

Daniel played tour guide as they rode on King Street east out of town, pointing out who lived where and when houses were built. Within an hour they were out in the back country. The road had narrowed and became lined with philodendrons, towering to eight or nine feet, ferns and jade plants intertwined. The sky was dappled with clouds but no rain. After two hours Lalani pleaded to stop. "Jim, my bottom is numb, and I need to stretch my legs."

Jim had warned Daniel that it might be a slow trip. Daniel knew all about slow, having a wife and two daughters that also rode slowly when going places. Stopping didn't bother him at all. They took a break and had biscuits and water. Lalani wandered a short distance looking at the Prince Kuhio vines, with their dark pink flowers. "Jim, look, a mongoose," Lalani called out.

Jim had never seen a mongoose. "That's a funny looking weasel. Somebody shrunk it." The little creature scampered off into a thicket of ferns and was gone.

"You must have seen a mongoose as a child?" Daniel asked.

"Oh, yes, I would put out bits of fruit and they would come. But I had to make sure the wild pigs were not around first, otherwise, they would gobble up the fruit first. Father didn't like the wild pigs around the village," Lalani said thoughtfully.

"Are you ready to continue? We still have a long way to go," Jim said.

He helped Lalani remount and they continued their journey through the lush canopy of trees and vines and past small waterfalls. After another hour, they stopped and had lunch at the top of a low mountain. From there, they could see Kaneohe Bay. Honolulu and

Maui were now hidden behind Mount Kōnāhuanui. Once back on the road, they came to a fork. Daniel pointed to the trail that would take them to Kahalu'u Valley. "This is where we part. The ranch is less than two hours up that trail. The small village of Ahuimana is this side of the river. Once you get there, you will be close."

"My understanding is the ranch is just the other side of the river. Amos said we could ask someone in the village to show us to the ranch," Jim confirmed.

Lalani thanked him for his patience and help and said they would have them to dinner at the hotel the following week. Jim and Lalani turned north and the trail narrowed. They passed through a forest of koa trees, and the sounds of the birds was incredible. At one point, a flock of i'iwi took off, creating a streak of red and sounding like a wave rumbling against the shore.

Princess pranced at the sudden flight, and Lalani pulled tight on the reins causing her horse to rear slightly. Lalani grabbed the horn of the saddle in hopes to stay mounted. Fortunately, Jim was close enough to grab the bridle and pull her to a stop.

"Are you okay? Do you want to stop and rest?" Jim asked with some concern.

"No, I'm all right. Are we not almost there?"

"I think the village is within the hour. We are getting close," Jim replied.

They pushed on and came out of the heavy forest area into low lying scrubs. The sun was now on the far westside of the island. Jim gently quickened the pace of the horses, wanting to reach the village before dusk. Within the hour they came over a ridge and Ahuimanu lay ahead of them. They came into the small center of town, to the only public building, a tavern/general store. There were several small hut-type homes and a few wooden homes along the stream. Lalani was now very glad to be off Princess, as the late afternoon sun had set behind the mountains and the air was cooler. They went inside and were greeted by a large Hawaiian man standing behind the bar.

"Aloha, welcome to Ahuimanu. Can I get you a drink? Beer or papa juice?"

"Juice for my wife, and a beer here," Jim said, as he pulled out a chair for Lalani at a small table.

"No, Jim, the bar will be fine. I think I would like to stand after riding all day."

"Sounds about right! I'm Lilpo, owner of this out of the way place. What brings you two all the way out here? From Kaneohe or Honolulu?"

"Actually, we're from California in the United States, but my wife was born in Honolulu. I'm Jim Baker and this is Lalani. We're here to see what's left of the Crocker ranch. Lalani is their *hanai* daughter."

"You're Horace's daughter?"

"Yes, did you know Horace and Edith?" Lalani asked.

"I didn't know Edith. Horace never brought her here. But my father helped Horace build the little ranch house. That would be over forty years ago. I was only twelve at the time but I can remember helping to clear the vines and carrying shingles for the roof. If you're hoping to stay at the house, I'm afraid it's in pretty bad shape. Everything is overgrown, and I'm sure the birds and mice have moved in."

"I knew things would be overgrown, but I was hoping at least the roof was still holding," Jim confessed.

"I haven't been out there in over a year, so I can't say. But I do have a small room out back that you can stay in. It's not fancy, but dry and critter free," Lilpo chuckled.

"Jim, I think that would be a good idea. It's getting dark. We can go see the place in the morning," Lalani said, putting her hand on his arm.

Just then the door opened, and two Hawaiian men walked in. "Aloha, Sam, Kiana. We have guests tonight, Jim and Lalani Baker. Lalani is Horace Crocker's daughter, come to see the ranch," Lilpo said.

Sam and Kiana were born and raised in the Kahalu'u Valley. Their fathers had helped Horace build the house, and as strong boys they carried supplies. Now they were in their late-forties. They sat and talked with Jim and Lalani about building the house, telling them stories of mishaps and Horace knowing nothing about ranching. After a while, Lilpo brought out baked chicken and rice for Jim and Lalani.

Kiana was quite the talker, with a cheery disposition. He had left Oahu and worked on a cattle ranch on the Big Island. "I just didn't like the volcano erupting all the time, and it was so hot and dry on the big island. Good for raising cattle but *hoonawaliwali* – disheartening to someone raised in this lush beautiful valley. So, I returned home and married my sweetheart, Mora." Kiana said he'd be happy to take them out to the ranch in the morning, but for now he needed to get home to his family. Sam finished his drink and offered to put Jim's horses up for the night in his corral. Lilpo showed Lalani to the small room in the back and provided a lantern and clean sheets for the bed.

Lalani had managed to make the bed, and was checking the curtains as Jim walked in. "What are you looking for?" he asked.

"I'm looking for the anole that got away."

"The what?" Jim said, with a puzzled look.

"The chameleon lizard. I was making the bed when it scurried across the wall to the window. I don't know if it went out or changed color to match the fabric."

"I see, or should I say, I don't see it. It must have gone out the window," Jim smiled. *Or I hope it did. Otherwise, I will be awake all night, waiting for Lalani's scream when it tries to climb into bed with us.*

The next morning, they were woken by Lilpo clanging pans in the kitchen and the smell of coffee. After breakfast, Kiana came and took Jim and Lalani out to the ranch. Jim grabbed a few things from the pack horse as there was no need to ride. It was only a fifteen-minute walk from the tavern.

As they came over a small mound, there in the near distance was a small house half covered in vines, philodendron, and two large trees towering behind it.

Lalani stood just taking it all in. It didn't look much like a ranch, certainly not like the Circle K back home. The path to the house was nonexistent. Jim reached into his pack and pulled out a small sickle.

"I thought we might need this," he said, as he began to cut his way through the ferns and grass.

It was about two hundred feet to the house, but Jim was able to clear a path that Lalani could manage. Finally, they reached a small rock wall. Kiana led them to an opening and a stone path that led to the front door. Surprisingly, the door was still on its hinges and the windows still in place, though a few panes were broken, but not all of them. A stephanotis vine clung to the door and covered most of it, while scraggly shrubs towered around the base of the windows and along the path.

Jim cut the final path to the door. "Wow! It smells like your garden, Lalani. What was that plant I just wacked down?"

"Lavender! We plant it around the houses to keep the scorpions and insects out," Kiana replied.

Immediately, Lalani looked around the path for the small brown creatures. *It looks like it's working. I wonder if it keeps chameleons out.*

Jim stepped up and pulled the vines from the door, cutting the roots clinging to the heavy wood mantle. Then he tried the door latch, but it didn't lift. It was rusted shut. There being a crack between the door and frame, Jim took his large knife and worked it through below the latch and managed to tap the latch loose. Pushing against the door, the hinges creaked and barely opened. Together Kiana and Jim kicked the door inch by inch until it was open enough to enter. As Kiana entered there was a flutter of wings, as nesting birds fled through a rather large hole in the roof. There were bird droppings all over the floor where the birds had made their nest in the rafters. Spiders crawled back into the dark corners out of sight.

Lalani walked through the door slowly, taking in the size of the room rather than the foreboding mess. At one end of the room was a large stone fireplace. Two large wood chairs flanked the fireplace, the cushions now in tatters. At the other end was a large table and a small cast iron stove. Lalani noticed a small mouse rush past the stove and under the door at the back of the room. Kiana had noticed the mouse also and walked over to the door and slowly opened it. Inside he could see a wrought iron bed, its mattress covered with dirt and mouse droppings.

Lalani peeked into the room and then looked at Jim, "We are not sleeping here! Nothing you can say will make me change my mind. "

Jim knew not to disagree. The picture was too bleak and dirty. "Fine, I agree, as long as Lilpo doesn't mind us staying with him for a few days."

They headed back outside. Jim and Kiana walked around the house, inspecting the lower half built of stone. Kiana told him his father was a stone cutter and had helped to cut and build the walls and fireplace. Jim poked at the upper wood walls, noting a lot of it needed replacing along with all the roof. The thick dark beams around the windows and door were in good shape, being made of hard koa wood. While Jim talked with Kiana about fixing the place up, Lalani had wandered back to the front short stone wall. She cleared a patch of jade so she could sit and look back at the little house. She sat wondering what it might have looked like when Horace had been there. She sat trying to imagine Horace in a plaid shirt standing in the door. *I just can't see it, he never wore plaid, a Hawaiian print on rare occasion, but trousers and plaid never.* She could imagine him sitting in one of the chairs by the fire, his legs stretched out in front of him, only socks on his feet.

Jim came from the back of the house and joined Lalani. "What do you think?" Jim said, as he sat next to her.

"What do I think? I think it's a mess!" Lalani sparked back.

Kiana came up with a handful of Prince Kuhio blossoms. "For you, to help you see the beauty that is here."

"Thank you, I know there is beauty here, I can imagine a quaint little house. It's just sad to see it in such ruin. What about the rest of the ranch, is it mostly overrun with brambles too? Did Horace ever raise anything here?"

"The majority of the ranch is a pretty little valley, with grasses and small shrubs. That's where the cattle are," Kiana explained.

"Cattle?" Jim was surprised.

"Oh, yes. Horace had about twenty head of Red Angus brought in about forty years ago. Fortunately, for me, when I came back to the valley, I went to work for Sam, who Horace hired to watch over the cattle when he was away. Which was most of the time. We've been doing it ever since.

"Sam and I keep tabs on the herd, culling it down each year to keep it to about thirty head, though some years, a heifer manages to hide a calf. The current bull is pretty wild, but in the last three years he's been a good breeder."

"What do you do with the cattle you take?" Jim asked with a sense of caution.

"When Horace was alive, he gave them to Sam and me as part of his pay for taking care of the place. When no one came for the ranch after he died, Mr. Amos said we should keep the herd small as not to overgraze the land. He said Mr. Horace would want us to continue to take care of the cattle and take the extra beef as pay, to feed our village, or sell it for things we needed for the cattle. I see that the fences are good and the cattle get hay if a winter is bad. The ranch has been under my care ever since Horace left," Kiana said proudly.

"I'm glad the cattle are cared for. Perhaps a little more care could have been taken of the house," Lalani solemnly commented. "Kiana, I think Jim and I would like to take a ride to see the rest of the ranch."

"Wonderful! Sam's place is only a short walk and I'm sure he has the horses fed by now. Sam will go with us. He was up checking on the herd just last week and knows where to find them."

Sam and Jim saddled the horses while Lalani went up to Lilpo's kitchen to make sandwiches for later. They took the small road which led down the hill towards Kaneohe Bay, until they came to a fork with a small trail off to the left, which led to the grazing range where the cattle were. Sam and Kiana kept the barbed wire fence in pretty good shape, especially the section along the road to Kahalu'u and across the valley to the mountain slopes. "We sell a couple of calves to a butcher in Kailua each year to pay for the fencing. The valley fencing is most important to keep the herd from mixing with the larger Kualoa Ranch down valley. Occasionally a heifer will go up into the mountains and get around a broken post," Sam said, making small talk as they rode. They came to a gate and Kiana swung down and opened it. As they cleared the trees, a path opened onto a small lush grassy valley. "This is really the Crocker Ranch. From the mountain base across the way, to half way down the valley and from here back to the Ahuimanu Stream," Kiana pointed out. There were several cows grazing off in the distance. Jim sat tall in his saddle taking it all in.

"Well, Lalani, this is what we hoped to achieve at the Circle K back home. A nice size herd to keep us fed and cared for, "Jim said. "Looks like old Horace had a similar idea."

Lalani didn't say anything. She just observed all the landscape and cows grazing peacefully. "It's beautiful indeed. So peaceful. This is the Hawaii I remember when I lived with my parents. Everyone working together to bring about the good of the land and people. I was always taught if you take care of the land, it will take care of you."

"Indeed, Mālama'Āina, is our native understanding and culture," Sam wisely affirmed.

They rode down the valley to the grazing cattle and Jim dismounted and took a look at a few of the heifers. *Good hardy stock.* Then they rode a short distance up onto the mountainside. Sam was trying to locate the bull, but he was not to be found. "He's pretty wild. We just leave him be, because he seems to be getting the job done and provides us with a dozen or more calves these past years."

They came back out of the trees and again stopped to look out over the valley. "I wonder why Horace didn't build the house here? It has such a lovely view of Kaneohe Bay," Lalani pondered aloud.

"The valley can get pretty windy. Wind in the winter coming off the mountain and in the summer up the valley from the ocean. Horace picked the clearing near town because it was closer to the river for getting water and better sheltered," Sam replied, as he looked at the sky. "It's going to start raining soon, we'd best get back."

Jim took a look at the clouds coming up over the valley. They were gathering into dark thunder clouds. "Bet it rains hard and heavy on this side of the island."

It was only a thirty-minute ride back to Sam's. The rain was just beginning to come down when Jim and Lalani got back to the tavern. Lilpo had a hot chicken stew simmering on the stove. The regular evening crowd showed up, some dripping wet wanting to sit by the pot belly stove, and others not minding being wet at all, because it wasn't a cold rain. Jim and Lalani were joined by Kiana and his wife Mora. Everyone wanted to know if Jim and Lalani were going to take over the ranch. "It's not mine to take over," established Lalani.

Sam had joined them and had been wondering all day who currently owned the ranch. "Who does own the ranch, if it's not you?" he asked.

"I'm not sure, Horace had a nephew, he might have left it to him," Lalani said.

"We checked the land office and it's listed under the trustee's name, Martin Shaw, but he's only the attorney who set up the trust," Jim added.

"I guess I'll just keep on doing what I have been doing for the ranch, until the owner does show up," Kiana concluded.

Lalani and Mora turned the conversation to the fact the house should not have been neglected and allowed to run down. "If Horace were here, he would have made sure the roof was good and kept the rain and critters out," Mora scolded, looking at Sam and Kiana. Lalani laughed, knowing that the cattle were more important to the men than a house. *Especially an empty house. It would be nice to think of it fixed up and Jim and me coming here during the hot California months. Coming to these cool breezes and tropical flowers.*

Just then, three young dark hair heads popped through the tavern door. It was Kiana and Mora's children, Keanu, Kia and little Alana. "Lilpo, can we take a lantern and go crawfish hunting at Ahalamu Point?" the oldest boy asked.

"Fine, just catch enough for tomorrow's meal for all of us," Kiana said. And as fast as they popped in, they popped out and were gone.

Mora could see a forlorn look on Lalani's face. "Oh, Keanu takes good care of his little sister. Alana is only six but keeps up with the boys just fine. Keanu is fourteen and Kia is twelve. Alana was the surprise," Mora said smiling.

Lalani smiled and shook off her momentary sadness. She had only been caught up in the feeling of 'if only' over the loss of the baby twice since she arrived, once when she saw a mother with a baby and the other as she watched small children playing on the beach. "They're beautiful children, you're lucky," Lalani managed to say with a smile.

They spent two more days in Ahuimanu. Jim wanted to see if the roof could be patched, and Lalani wanted some of the overgrowth to be cleared away from the house. Kiana brought a scythe and cut the tall grasses in front of the house. Keanu came also and helped Lalani pull and cut vines and weeds off the front garden wall. Sam had a sheet of wood left over from a project and he and Kiana managed to patch the hole in the roof. Jim was forbidden to climb up onto the roof, as Lalani was afraid he might fall right through it.

"This roof is in pretty bad shape, I put my foot through it more than once," Kiana confessed.

Keanu began to sweep inside the house, sending dust and dirt in all directions. Lalani rescued the broom and suggested Keanu finish pulling the vines off the front garden wall instead. Jim made an attempt to sand off the bird droppings from the wood floor. It still needed a lot of work, but the little bit of care made Lalani happy.

After a day of dirty work, Jim and Lalani rode back down to the grazing range and watched the cattle. The cattle meandered through the tall grass, peacefully feeding and switching their tails. Lalani stayed mounted on Princess watching. *Such a lovely place and peaceful life. I can see why Horace chose this place. I'm glad we cleaned up the house a little, even if it will just go back to the way it was. Still always leave a place better than you found it.*

She looked out to the pristine azure bay and had the need to go sit by the water and listen. Jim was happy to oblige. They rode down past the ancient native holy ruins and tied the horse to a broken stump. Lalani took off her boots and stockings and wandered to the sand. It was cool on her feet, immediately taking her back to the feel of the island. She sat down, with her knees propped up, and leaned forward just watching the aqua blue waves, listening to the sound, and feeling the rhythm of the waves crashing against the reef just off shore. Jim knew she didn't need him there and sat back just watching her, feeling some of the same connecting emotions to the land.

Lalani sat for a very long time, noting the waves coming in threes, first three small rolling rumbling waves, and then a large spill type wave with a resounding crash, followed by two smaller spill waves. Then silence and the rhythm would start again. She could feel herself calming and becoming part of the island rhythm. At last, the wai – the water - was calling her to its edge, and she stood and walked to just where the water came up and kissed her toes. As if saying welcome home.

Jim came and joined her, not saying anything, just holding her hand. Together they watched. Finally, they slowly walked along the water's edge, taking in the serenity and beauty of the bay, ingraining it into their memories.

On the third day, it promised to be clear all day and would be the best day for Jim and Lalani to return to Honolulu. That morning they rode out to the cattle range and took a last look at the cattle and the bay below, and then by the house, still rundown but not so forgotten. Sam said he would try to get a couple of panes of glass to fix the windows, so the place would at least keep the birds out, but he would still leave the old mattress for the mice.

They said their good byes to Sam, Kiana and Mora, and to Lilpo, then headed back towards Honolulu. Lalani was becoming more comfortable with riding Princess, and they picked up the pace, a little faster on the return trip. Jim led the pack horse, now lighter after leaving the provisions with Lilpo, in return for his hospitality. The sun was just setting over the mountains as they come down King Street. Lalani was happy to be back at the hotel, with a hot bath and comfortable bed.

They had been in Hawaii for over a month now. After being at the ranch, Jim was getting antsy to get back to their ranch in Oak Ridge. It would be the beginning of March by the time they returned, if they only stayed for another week and then caught the next steamship back to San Francisco.

The day after their return from Ahuimanu, Jim took Lalani down to the beach in Waikiki. It was a beautiful warm day. He put his arms around her and held her as she looked out at the blue waters. "Are you glad we came?" he said quietly.

"Oh, yes, it's been wonderful to be back. I feel I have regained what I lost so many years ago. Even with all the changes, I feel *pili aina* - I belong to the land.

"Elizabeth, Harriett, Mora have been most thoughtful, and helped make this happen. But most of all, you for bringing me here."

"Mora certainly is lucky, and has her hands full," Jim said, fishing for Lalani feelings about children now. *Is she ready to try again or is it too soon to bring it up?*

Lalani turned around and looked at Jim, putting her hand to his face. "Yes, she is, but I'm lucky to have you. You are the kindest, most loving man."

Jim smiled and kissed her hand, then with a hesitant breath, "Lalani I think it's time to go home to *Kālua ʻana*, if you're ready to be home, that is."

Lalani smiled and looked into his longing eyes, "Yes, I think I am ready to go home. Ready to try again."

Jim put his arms around her and kissed her and held her again for a long moment. Now content, they walked along the water's edge for a while before returning to the hotel.

~~

Later that afternoon Maria Kaneakua sent a note inviting Lalani to tea. The note simply read, "Please join me for tea tomorrow, at 3:00. I will meet you at your hotel." Lalani sent word accepting the invitation, expecting they would be having tea in the hotel parlor. When Maria arrived, she took Lalani's arm and said, "Come with me," and led her out of the hotel and up the street to the main gate of the large white house known as Washington Palace, the Queen's private residence. The guard greeted Maria cordially as if expecting her. Once past the gate, Lalani stopped and looked with piercing eyes at Maria.

"The Queen has asked to meet you. John was telling her about you and how you have traveled the world and met so many interesting people."

"She wants to meet me? But I'm only a maid's daughter," Lalani said.

"No, you are a loyal Hawaiian. Schooled and cultured and in your own way influential," Maria said reassuring her.

They were led into a small sitting room with cream and blue drapes and furnishings. On the coffee table sat sandwiches and scones.

A few minutes later a door opened and in walked Queen Lili'uokalani, wearing a black dress with a white pintuck bodice and sheer sleeves. She was now in her mid-fifties, her face showing the anguish she bore for her people. She greeted Maria warmly as old friends, and Maria turned to Lalani, "Your Ladyship, this is Lalani Baker of whom John spoke." Lalani, not sure what to do or say, curtsied and bowed her head slightly. "Oh, Mrs. Baker, no need for curtsies nowadays. I am no longer royal, so it seems. I'm so pleased to meet you, and please refrain from Your Ladyship, call me Lili. It's so much easier."

The butler came with tea, and after pouring it, was dismissed. They sat talking cordially about what Lalani had seen while she was here. When Lalani mentioned just returning from the Crocker Ranch, the Queen became very interested.

"I was one of Mrs. Crocker's students at the Royal School and was sad to see them leave. Do you know who owns the ranch now?"

That seems to be the question of the year. "No, I'm sorry. I suspect Horace's nephew does. He's an engineer, and I only met him once at the funeral over twenty years ago. At that time, he lived in Virginia," Lalani politely replied and took another sip of tea.

"I see. Lalani, you have traveled the world and met many influential people. The people of Hawaii need your help. We need to convince the United States that we don't need their protection or commerce and to desist with the annexation of Hawaii to the United States. We need you to talk to some of the more powerful people and convince them to influence the Congress not to ratify the annexation," Lili, in a gentle but commanding voice, expounded.

Lalani was uncertain how to respond. *This is the Queen asking me for my help, but who am I? I don't have any influence over people, especially powerful people.* "My Queen, I would love to help, but I have no influence. I know those people, only because I was a companion to an acquaintance of theirs. Yes, I've been in their homes, but it was my friend Katherine that they wanted there, not me. Most of the elite people I do know are not the type to want to give up Hawaii. The Astors and Rockefellers are certainly not going to give up the commerce opportunities. Isabella Gardner, I know well, but she is more involved with the arts. Andrew and Louise Carnegie are the only ones I know that might be willing to help. Andrew believes in the people and is building public libraries in many of the small towns across the United States."

"Good, then you can contact Mr. Carnegie and your friend, to employ them to help. Time is running out, I'm afraid," the Queen said calmly.

By the time they finished discussing the issue, the tea cakes were gone, and the tea had cooled. Maria knew it was now time to go. She had done what she was asked to do. Lalani thanked the Queen for her hospitality and confidence in her as a loyal subject. "I'll do what I can, *Na ke Akua e malama ia 'oe*," Lalani said as she stood to leave, recalling the Hawaiian blessing for protection her mother had taught her.

"*Ma kahi a'oukou e helee aku ai he Akua no!*" Lili replied with a smile. She stood and watched Maria and Lalani depart.

Once back at the hotel, Maria encouraged Lalani to contact those people whom she thought might help, but confessed it would only delay the pending reality of annexation.

While Lalani was at tea, Jim made arrangements for them to take a ship back to San Francisco that would leave in nine days. They spent the final week with the Gilberts and Ladds. Elizabeth and Harriett arranged one final afternoon tea for Lalani, of which they promised no surprises by the Queen. Rather it was a final chance to say farewell to old and new friends, Susan Sumner and Mary Chamberlain and a few others joining in the enchanting afternoon. Most of them had not been away from the islands and in their own way envied Lalani as they pressed her about her time in Europe. Susan took Lalani aside and told her how lucky she was to have left the island, and what a wonderful strong woman she had become. They all urged her to write and let them know what life on the mainland was doing.

Lalani and Jim revisited the mercantile one last time. They walked along the beach in the morning before the breeze rose, and in the evening, they wandered down to the docks and watched the ships bobbing in the harbor. Lalani wanted to say a final good bye to her mother the day before their ship sailed. As they drove down Queen Street, they passed the Crocker house again. Lalani had not wanted to go in and see it, but now as they passed, she pulled on Jim's arm and motioned him to stop. She sat quietly looking at the house, when suddenly the front door opened, and the young woman they had seen the first day came out. She stood looking at them and smiled.

"Lalani, go ahead, go say hello. I'll go with you," Jim said as he started to get down. He came around and helped Lalani, and together they walked up the front steps to the porch where the young woman stood.

"Aloha, I'm sorry for staring at the house and bothering you, but I used to live here when I was a little girl." Lalani said meekly.

Jim stepped up and introduced himself, "I'm Jim Baker and this is my wife Lalani."

"Aloha, I'm Emily Kimioka. My husband and I bought the house several years ago. Would you like to come in and see it? From what I understand the rooms are laid out the same as when it was built. We have done a lot of painting and put-up new wallpaper since we moved in."

Emily held the door open and Lalani slowly went through. In front of her stood the old familiar staircase. *Aloha old friend, how many times I slid down you into my mother's arms.* In the parlor to the right stood the same green ivy embossed title fireplace. *I can't count all the times I cleaned the ash from this fireplace and scrubbed the hearth. It still looks the same.*

"Would you like to see the rooms upstairs? Which one was yours?" Emily asked.

"Actually, my room was off the kitchen. My mother was the housekeeper for the Crockers who built the house."

"Oh, I see. Well, come this way to the kitchen. There have been changes there, a new stove, and my husband built a pantry. But the large room is still there. I use it for my sewing room."

Jim put his arm around Lalani to reassure her as they stood in the kitchen. "This room seems smaller than I remember, but brighter," Lalani commented.

"We painted and enlarged the window by the breakfast nook to let in more light," Emily said, pointing to the large window.

"It's because the counters shrunk, not that you grew up," Jim joked.

Lalani then opened the door to her old room. It seemed huge with no beds or dresser in it. In the corner stood a small pot belly stove. "This room always did get cold in the winter. I see you put in a stove to stay warm."

"Sort of, it's more for heating the iron for the clothes, and keeping my tea warm," Emily teased.

Emily told them to take their time, to go upstairs if they liked. She would be in the garden putting up the towels to dry. Lalani and Jim strolled through the house, Lalani telling him little stories about various rooms. Finally, they went out back to the garden and found Emily. She was hanging towels on a line strung from a tree to a post. "My mother did the very same thing. That tree has seen a lot of laundry in its time." Across the lawn near the carriage house was a tall koa tree. Lalani reached out and touched it as if petting and old friend. "I planted this tree when I was six with Horace 's help. I'm glad to see it's still here, grown into a noble fortress."

After another half hour of talking with Emily, Lalani was ready to go. "Emily, thank you for letting us see the place. I hope it brings you as much happiness as it did the Crockers." Emily smiled and said it has and reached up and broke off a small sprig from the koa tree and handed it to Lalani. "*Pomaika'i ia 'oe*, For good luck."

Lalani took the tiny green branch and held it gently in her hand and smiled. *Wouldn't it be grand if I could plant this back at Kālua 'ana and it would grow into its own mighty tree. But alas it's too dry in Oak Ridge for it to survive. I will press it and tuck it among my postcards.*

Jim and Lalani then continued on to the cemetery to see Leia's grave once more. This time Lalani wasn't so melancholy, but stood smiling, cherishing the fond memories she had regained since her arrival. They didn't stay long, but as they left, Lalani took one long last look wanting to remember how her parents' markers looked under the tree. Finally, she took Jim's arm and said "It's time to go home. Home to *Kālua ʻana.*"

12

Growing Together

Jim and Lalani returned home on a cool brisk day the third week of March. The trees had a yellowish green hint to them as leaves began to bud out. Evan and Makana were there at the train to meet them. Jim started to climb in onto the back bench with Lalani, when she motioned him to the front with Evan. "You two are going to talk cattle and ranch the entire way home, so you might as well sit up with Evan," Lalani smiled. Makana who had been prancing around them since they stepped off the train, jumped up next to Lalani putting her head in her lap. "Missed me? Did you?" she said as she stroked her head.

As they came over the ridge, *Kālua 'ana* lay in front of them. Lalani became overwhelmed and a tear silently rolled down her cheek. *Home... I hadn't realized how much I missed it until now. I'm so glad to be back.* She quickly dried her face before Jim noticed. The carriage pulled up to the house, and Jim jumped out. Before Lalani could step down, he reached up and swung her over his shoulder and carried her up the steps, reaching out and opening the door, Lalani giggling all the way. He slid her down into his arms and happily carrying her across the threshold. "Jim, you silly man, we're not newlyweds."

"No, but this is the day I asked you to marry me and you finally said yes. I love you, Lalani Baker," he said and kissed her. He started to carry her up the stairs, but Evan came in with the trunk just then. "Where do you want this?" he asked.

Before Jim could say anything, "Upstairs in our room, please," Lalani answered. Then seeing Jim's disappointed look, she whispered, "You will just have to wait until later to get me into our own big wonderful bed." Jim set her down and winked, turned and fetched the other bags from the carriage, while Lalani surveyed the house and all that needed to be done. Upon entering the kitchen, she smelled stew cooking and on the table was a loaf of fresh bread. *Kate's been here, or was it Miranda? Whichever, I'm grateful. We will go see them tomorrow.*

The first night home was quiet and Lalani was quite content to snuggle up with Jim in their big bed. In the morning, the sun came streaming in between the east pines through the kitchen window. Lalani was humming as she put coffee on for the men, who were already out checking on the livestock. She looked out to her garden. Evan had added the manure and turned the soil, so it stood ready for planting. But first she needed to pay a visit to Katherine. The thought of seeing Matthew made her apprehensive for some unknown reason. *He must be getting big. I can't believe he will be almost four months. I'm sure I will love seeing him.* After breakfast she couldn't resist getting out to the garden and the chicken coop for a quick survey. The hens came running, expecting to be fed. Lalani reached over and grabbed a handful of grain and tossed it out. She was glad to see her favorite hens were there. Next, she walked out to the garden and stood laying out the rows in her mind of where the carrots, beans, broccoli, potatoes and other things would go. The lavender surrounding the bed seemed to have survived the winter winds. For a instant, she could smell the lavender Jim had cut at the ranch in Kahalu'u.

Jim came out from the barn and joined Lalani, "Now that you are willing to ride a horse, how about I saddle Genevieve, and we go for a ride around the ranch? I'd like to show you places you've never seen before."

Lalani didn't hesitate for a moment, "Alright." *I can wait to see Matthew a little while longer... until tomorrow. He will forgive me, but Kate might not.* She went and put on her riding bloomers and boots. They rode out to the south range where the cattle were and down to the stream. "It's beautiful here Jim. We will have to come often during the summer and picnic." Jim was thrilled to have Lalani riding beside him, seeing the ranch as he did, its hidden beauty, the stream and south range nestled in a small valley of grass dotted with large oak trees.

The following morning Jim came into the house as Lalani stood looking out the window, "What are you doing standing here? I thought you would be ready to go to Kate's by now," Jim said. "You best go get ready. Shall I saddle up Genevieve, or are you going to revert back to the carriage?" he chuckled.

Lalani just grinned and shook her head. *He knows I want the carriage. It's sweet of him to go with me. He mustn't worry about me seeing Matthew, I'm surely ready to have him in my life now.* They arrived just after 10:00 o'clock. Kate heard the carriage and was at the door as Jim helped Lalani down. The two were like school girls hugging each other after being apart for the summer. Kate showed them to the family parlor where Miranda sat waiting. "Where's my honorary nephew? Kate, you mustn't hide him away," Lalani said smiling, trying to reassure Kate and herself.

"Oh, I'm so glad. Clay took him up to change him. They will be here in a moment. But we want to hear all about your trip. Your letters were too brief," Kate scolded. A moment later Clay stood holding Matthew at the parlor doorway. Lalani stood and just smiled and couldn't take her eyes off Matthew. *Oh, my goodness, what a sweet smile, and he has his daddy's dark wavy hair. But those are Kate's eyes. Oh, how he has grown.* Kate stood and took Matthew from Clay. Clay wasn't sure what to do since Lalani seemed to be frozen just watching the baby. Finally, Clay reached out "We're so glad you're back. Kate has missed you more than you will ever know," and gave Lalani a hug, breaking her thoughts. Then he reached and slapped Jim on the shoulder, "Good to have you back."

"He's beautiful Kate. May I?" Lalani said as she gestured to hold the baby. Lalani took Matthew in her arms and sat cooing and talking to him, watching his smile and little hands reach for her long curls. Lalani's reluctances melted away with each of Matthew's smiles. Everyone relaxed and began to share stories, how February rain had been heavy keeping everyone inside, how Matthew was growing more and more each week.

Lalani and Jim told them about how much Honolulu had grown, about the Crocker ranch, and Queen Lili'uokalani's request for US Congress to not ratify the annexation. It was a pleasant morning that turned into dinner with the Taylors. Kate and Jim were relieved to see how happy Lalani was around Matthew. Kate said she would come the next day and discuss what needed to be done with the yearlings and to get ready for the new foals.

The next few weeks went quickly, Lalani getting the house clean and travel clothes laundered and put away. Friends dropped by to visit and find out about the trip. Lalani also took time to fulfill her request from Queen Lili. She contacted Eric in San Francisco and asked if he knew the state senators and congressmen in order to write to them about the annexation of Hawaii. Eric invited Steven White, the Democratic senator, down to the ranch to meet Lalani.

Senator White was most sympathetic about the native Hawaiians. He gave her a few names of other senators that might want to help. Yet he didn't think the annexation could be stopped at this point. The islands were of economic as well as of military interest and advantage to the United States. Lalani went ahead and wrote to the other senators, wanting to do what she could. She carefully crafted her words and urged them not to make the same mistake as we did with the native Indians, sending them off to desolate reservations. She explained that the Hawaiian Islands are an independent nation and would be happy to make an alliance with the United States for military bases in exchange for protection, to work together as separate sovereign nations. Lalani had been home a month and now her carefully drafted letters to various influential people, including Andrew Carnegie and Randolph Hearst, were ready to be sent. She went to the post office and personally sent the letters. She had one other stop she wanted to make.

From the post office she walked slowly down to the general store. As she passed Doctor Newell's office, she stopped. She had been pondering something for a few weeks and had felt more tired than usual. *Do I dare stop and ask him and show him my ignorance. Lalani, it's better to know than not to.* She reached for the door and hesitated for a moment, then forced herself to step in.

"Good morning, Mrs. Baker," said his nurse.

"Good morning, is Doctor Newell in?"

"Yes, he's in the exam room. He just finished with little Terrance Satisk. Would you like to see him?"

"Well, I did have a question, if he has the time."

Doctor Newell emerged from the room. "Of course, I have time, Lalani," he said, as he escorted her to his office. "What can I do for you? I hear your trip was a success."

"It was most delightful," she remarked as she took a seat. "Ah… how do I ask such a private personal question?"

He could see she was troubled over something. She also looked a little paler than usual, though with her dark Hawaiian skin it was hard to tell. "Is it something about the miscarriage? I'm sure you will be able to have another baby just fine," he said softly.

"Well, it's not about the miscarriage. But … about when my menstrual cycle will begin again?"

"Oh, I see. And you haven't had one since the miscarriage?"

"No, not a full cycle. There was a small one in January before we left, but nothing when we were in Hawaii. I haven't really had a full cycle for over three months. Is that normal after a miscarriage?" the concern ringing in her voice.

"One's cycle usually starts again right away. But it's been known to skip. You say you haven't had any bleeding since January. Lalani, it is very possible you are pregnant again," he said reassuringly.

"But I haven't been ill or uncomfortable. I have been more tired than usual, but not ill like before."

"Lalani each pregnancy is different. You can be sick as a dog with one child and healthy as a horse with the next. Is it possible... were you and Jim together in January or February?"

Lalani blushed and looked down trying to remember just when they had first been together. *There was the first week in February at the Hotel, and then again the last week. And then there was the night we came home back in our own bed. Oh, my.* "You mean my menstrual periods started back as usual and that I'm most likely pregnant now?"

"Why don't we do a quick physical. If you did get pregnant in late January or early February, your abdomen should be fairly firm and by now beginning to swell from the size of the baby. You could be three months along."

She agreed to the exam and within a short time, Doctor Newell was pretty sure Lalani was again pregnant. As they talked and from the signs her body was indicating, he suspected she was nearing the end of her first trimester. He reassured her things looked good, there being no morning sickness and being tired was normal. He estimated she was at about ten weeks, this being mid-April now. Lalani sat stunned at the news for a few moments. *Ten weeks, that's just one week more before ... I miscarried. Am I safe or is it going to happen again?* Doctor Newell could see the concern on Lalani's face. "Lalani, everything looks good. I'm sure you are not going to have any problems this time. Just for the next month take it easy and add plenty of liver, fish and eggs to your diet. They will help with being tired. Once you start the second trimester, things go just fine. Really, you have nothing to worry about this time."

Lalani began to smile and stood to leave saying, "Thank you. Now I just have to figure out how to tell Jim without him hovering and worrying."

Another week went by and Lalani still had not told Jim that she was pregnant. She didn't want him to worry until she was sure everything was alright. On Friday mid-morning, Morgan came riding in to *Kālua 'ana* in a hurry. "Lalani, Jim are you home?" Morgan called out.

Jim came from the barn as Lalani opened the door. "What is it Morgan? What's wrong?" Lalani asked.

"Well, the ranchers are all riled up about what arrived for you this morning on the train."

"Arrived for us?" Lalani questioned.

"Oh, it's come already," Jim said.

Lalani, Morgan, and Evan, now there, looked at Jim with a what-have-you-done kind of look.

"It's just a little lamb for Lalani. The ranchers can't possibly be threatened by one little lamb," Jim said.

"You got me my lamb!" Lalani gushed.

"Jim, it's not just one. They sent two. You had best go collect your sheep before they become someone's dinner. And explain you only want them for the fleece for Lalani to spin, that there will be no more coming," Morgan warned.

Jim and Evan hooked up the work wagon and headed for town. When they got to the station livestock pen, there stood a half dozen men including Clay. "Jim. have you lost your mind, bringing sheep into cattle country?" Clay said.

Jim climbed the pen fence and faced the men. "Look, I'm as much a cattle man as the rest of you. I only requested one healthy Merino lamb, so Lalani would have fleece to spin. Why they sent two, I have no idea. But I assure you there will not be any more and they won't be feeding on any open range, " Jim said in a commanding cattleman's voice. Mr. Owen shook his head, "Lalani's got you whipped. Talking you into getting a damn sheep."

"Not whipped, just in love!" Jim smiled back. The crowd disbursed with a laugh and a few grumbles as Jim and Evan loaded the two, not so small, lambs. The men arrived back at the ranch with their two charges, and together Jim and Evan unloaded the sheep crates and carried them to the barn. Lalani and Makana followed eagerly to see them turned out. They stood about two feet tall and scooted to the corner of the stall, staying close together. Their soft woolly coats were a creamy white, as if they had been washed before being shipped. Makana barked, and they rushed to the opposite corner. Lalani slowly walked in and softly whispered to them. They watched her carefully, but did not move. Lalani reached slowing and touched their back. *It's wonderfully soft. I can't wait to shear them and start spinning.* "Jim, how old are they?"

"I requested a two-month old, so I think they're pretty close to that from their size and weight. I'll give them a couple of months to let the fleece grow more, and then we can shear them. Laramie said he'd come up from Modesto and shear them for us."

"That will be wonderful," Lalani smiled, but suddenly her emotions got the best of her, and tears began to run down her face.

"What's wrong, shearing doesn't hurt them," Jim said surprised at the tears.

"Nothing's wrong Jim. I'm just touched by your thoughtful gift. They're wonderful," she said trying to hold the sob in her throat back.

Jim came and put his arm around her. "Well, I'm glad you like them. For now we need to build them a pen they can't get out of. If our neighbors find either of them on open range, they will not be happy with us and you will be eating mutton for dinner," Jim added, not realizing it would make Lalani cry harder.

This second outburst sent a look of worry across Jim's face. "Jim, I'm sorry, I'm being silly. I just can't seem to control my emotions today."

"Are you sure nothing's wrong?" he asked, holding her close.

Lalani knew it was time to tell him. She reached up and whispered into his ear, "Nothing's wrong, pregnant woman always cry when they're happy."

Jim pulled back and with wide eyes looked at her face to make sure she wasn't teasing. "Really?!" Lalani nodded her head, "Really." Suddenly all the interest in the lambs was gone, and Jim had Lalani swept up in his arms and was carrying her to the house, leaving Evan to deal with the frightened little wooly creatures.

For the next week, Jim hovered over Lalani until she finally told him if he didn't stop, she was going to move in with Kate. Kate and Clay were thrilled at the news. Doctor Newell confirmed that she was going to be fine, and things settled into as normal routine as possible for a family expecting a baby.

~~

Lalani planted her garden and Jim and Evan seeded the alfalfa and hay fields. The first calves arrived, three heathy heifers and one bull. Jim had his hands full with the calves and the newly arrived foals at Kate's. Lalani attended to the sheep, now named Sassy and Lulu, and full grown, weighing about eighty pounds.

By late July, Lalani often went to Kate's to play with Matthew, now sitting up and rolling over. This day Kate sat playing piano. "It will be so much fun watching our babies grow up together. Kind of like my mother and Morgan's, watching us grow. Our little ones will be best of friends, like brother or sister." Lalani smiled and thought about Kate's and Morgan's closeness, how it had brought them to Oak Ridge.

"Lalani, now that branding season is done, it's time you and Jim get the baby's room set up. The first of October will be here before you know it." Lalani agreed, but things had been so busy with cattle, horses, sheep shearing and field planting, they just hadn't gotten to it. But August promised to be a quiet month and Lalani was ready to take the next step in preparing for the baby. Especially since this pregnancy was going so smoothly. Only occasionally her back ached and the baby seemingly didn't like broccoli. It gave Lalani indigestion every time she ate it. By fall, the bull calf would be fat enough to sell off for beef and provide the funds needed to purchase all the things a baby needs.

Jim took Lalani to the city in late August to pick out a crib and other baby items. Evan made a cradle for the baby that now sat by the parlor fireplace just waiting. The small room upstairs was redone in pale green, and Lalani made a breadfruit crib quilt in yellows and greens. In the evening, when it was cooler, Lalani sat and spun the fleece wool from Lulu, and during the day, at Kate's, busily knitted booties and watched Matthew crawl from one toy to the next.

By late August, Lalani was quite large and sat under the large oak tree out front, tossing a ball to Makana. *One more month little one, but please don't be in a hurry and come during roundup. Your daddy will be busy and I do so much want him to be here when you arrive. So, let's agree now that you will wait until after roundup. October is a good month to arrive.* She held her tummy as she felt the baby move and once again began to think about names. They hadn't decided on any name yet, since they couldn't agree if it should be an English or Hawaiian name. Lalani wanted English, but Jim wanted to honor her heritage. *Little one, your daddy and I will have to make a decision soon, what is it going to be, Hawaiian or English?* She sat quietly waiting for a sign from the baby, but nothing moved now. All was quiet again.

Lalani was leaning towards Shannon or Jessica and Jim to Leia or Malia. As for boys' names: James after his father or Robert was Lalani's favorite. Jim was opposed to a junior. "He will be his own man, things are changing and he won't be doing what I want. He needs his own name like Hailiki, for thunder and power, or Kia for calm." They would wait to meet the little one before deciding. *Most likely it will be both. Jessica Malia Baker has a pretty ring to it. Hailiki James Baker is a good strong name too. Most likely he will go by James as not to be teased.*

September arrived and the fields had been cut, and the bales were neatly stacked in the hay barn. The garden was harvested and Carol

Owen and Miranda had come and helped Lalani can beans and pickle cucumbers. The calf had been sold off, and Lalani would only have to tend to feeding Lulu and Sassy and the chickens, as plans for roundup had begun. Jim would come home after his shift and feed the horses: Genevieve, Prince Philip and Clyde. Kate, Miranda or Carol Owen would come stay with Lalani during the day, while Jim was gone.

One evening right before the end of roundup, Jim and Lalani sat quietly in the parlor. "It's been a good year," Jim commented. "The summer rains kept the fires away and the livestock had enough water."

"It was a good year. Our trip to Hawaii was a wonderful start, and now the year will end with a new baby. Yes, it's been a very good year," Lalani agreed.

"Well, tomorrow should be the last day of roundup as most of the cattle have been shipped out to the Kansas market. Only the heifers for next year need to be driven up to the south range. There's only about 100 head at this point, so I should be home in time for supper," Jim said as he yawned and closed his eyes. "I'm getting too old for week long cattle drives. Next year our own little herd will be big enough. A dozen head sounds just right to me at the moment." Before Lalani could comment, Jim was asleep in his chair by the fire.

September had been a beautiful month. Indian summer had come with a gentle breeze, for which Lalani was grateful. Jim and Evan were now back at the ranch and getting things ready for winter. The sheep pen had been built next to the chicken coop, so Lalani could feed both in one trip outside, though Evan would probably do it when the cold set in. It was the last day of September, and the air was clear and crisp when Lalani woke. As she came downstairs her back ached, but that hadn't been unusual this past month. *I must have slept on the wrong side last night.* Jim was carrying a load of wood in for the stove, when he spotted her holding her back. "You need a back rub this morning?" Lalani smiled and nodded her head. Jim warmed his hand by the fire and then gently rubbed her lower back. He could feel the tension melt but the ache persisted. "Is it the baby? Is it time?" Jim asked eagerly.

"No, I don't think so, I'm still ten days out and the ache is no different from other times." Lalani then got busy making breakfast as Evan came in to join them. It was late morning when Lalani's water broke while sweeping the front porch. "Jim, Jim," she called, but soon realized he was in the barn. "Makana, go get Jim," and the dog quickly raced to the barn. Jim and Evan came running, and spotted Lalani sitting on the porch bench. "It's time, Jim," she said with an aching smile. Jim carried her up to the big bed, while Evan rode for Doc Newell.

Doc Newell arrived and confirmed the baby was on the way, but it would be hours before the actual arrival. He had several appointments that afternoon, but he would be back shortly after supper, and left where he could be reached if needed sooner. It was a long day of walking around the room, Jim reading poems and playing fiddle to try and make Lalani calm and comfortable. Lalani didn't want Kate or others there until after the baby arrived. She just wanted Jim. About 9:00 o'clock, the contractions grew stronger and closer. Doc Newell was there and was sure the baby would arrive soon. Now, as the contractions grew stronger, Jim became more concerned and didn't know how to help. Lalani squeezed his hand, mangling his fingers against his wedding ring each time the pain heightened. *Now I wish I had sent for Kate. Another woman would understand this better. Jim is such a dear.* With that last thought, another hard contraction began, and Doc Newell knew it was time.

Within a moment, Lalani gave one loud cry, and a small baby girl came out. Lalani held her breath waiting for that inevitable new cry. "Waaaa…" There it was. Doc Newell was smiling as he laid the tiny beautifully perfect baby girl on Lalani's stomach. Jim reached down and kissed Lalani, now breathing again and smiling with tears in her eyes. Doc took the baby to clean her and check her over, then wrapped her up and handed her to Jim. "Congratulations, dad. She's healthy and beautiful." A soft pinkish tan skin glowed with a flat tiny nose and almond round eyes. Tiny thick strands of dark black hair covered her little head. Jim laid his new daughter into her mother's arms, and Lalani unwrapped her feet and counted toes and fingers. "They're all perfectly there," Doc Newell laughed.

Doc stayed for a time to make sure Lalani was alright and the baby could begin to nurse. Once he felt things were good, Doc headed for home. As he reached the edge of town, he crossed paths with Morgan heading home. "Hey, Doc, what brings you out so late?"

"Baby Baker!" he said smiling.

"Lalani had the baby? Was Kate there?" Morgan responded.

"No, Kate, doesn't know yet, Lalani's fine, it's a girl!" he said and turned to continue on to town.

Morgan rushed off at a gallop. Upon reaching home he bursted into the house yelling, "Kate, Kate." It was late, and Clay came down worried something was wrong. "Morgan, stop yelling, you'll wake the baby. Kate's sleeping. What's happened?" Clay said as he put his shirt on.

"The baby's what's happen. Lalani had the baby."

"What? Is everyone okay?" Clay immediately responded.

"Doc says everyone's just fine. Our paths crossed as we were heading home. It's a girl," Morgan explained.

Just about then Kate came down the stairs with a concerned look on her brow, "What's happened? Is Lalani alright?"

"Just fine, but she had the baby. A girl." Morgan reiterated.

"Should we go see her now?" asked Clay.

Katherine stood for a moment taking it all in. *She had the baby and didn't call to have me come? It must have been quick. But she's all right.* "When did the baby arrive?"

"From what Doc said, I'd say about two hours ago. Should I saddle horses?"

"No, Morgan. It's late, and Lalani will be sleeping by the time we get there. If it was a hard labor, it will be better to go first thing in the morning. I just can't believe she didn't send for me," Kate said softly as they headed back to bed. *Thank you God, for keeping them safe.*

~~

At *Kālua 'ana* everything was quiet. Evan had his chance to see the baby and that Lalani was okay and then headed for bed. Jim on the other hand, stoked up the fire in the bedroom and sat in the big rocker holding his daughter, just watching her sleep. *She's as beautiful as her mother. A tiny, wonderful miracle!* He looked over at Lalani quietly sleeping as well and thanked the Lord for her protection and grateful for having her in his life, for the amazing life He had given them. After several hours of watching both, the baby began to stir, her little lips began to suckle. Jim woke Lalani and gave her the baby to nurse as Doc had indicated to do. Jim now sat in bed holding Lalani as the baby suckled her breast. He had never felt such a joy.

The next morning, Kate, Clay and Morgan came riding up to the house, as Evan was coming out of the barn after morning chores. Kate lit off Duchess and was halfway through the door before the men even dismounted. Jim saw them ride in from the upstairs window and alerted Lalani of the whirlwind about to hit. "She'll be mad you didn't call for her."

"Not mad, just a little hurt, but she'll get over it as soon as she sees the baby," Lalani smiled.

Kate came gingerly though the door and stood frozen, looking at Lalani holding her baby. "A girl. A girl for my beautiful big sister. I'm so happy for you. I'm mad at you too, for going through it all without me. But I can see now you didn't need me. And I thought I was the independent one," Kate scolded as she came over to the bed. Lalani uncovered the pink blanket showing the tiny little bundle.

"She is beautiful, Lalani, so petite. I don't think Matthew was ever that small. May I?" she said reaching to hold her.

Clay and Morgan had been downstairs congratulating Jim, and now the three men joined the ladies. "How much does this little filly weigh? Can't be more than a bucket of oats. Let's get the grain scale from the barn and weigh her," Clay said, half teasing.

"Clay Taylor, you bring that dirty old scale near this precious baby, and you'll be sleeping in the barn," Kate warned.

"Well, does she have a name?" asked Morgan. Who won, England or Island?"

Jim reached over and took his daughter from Kate, then looking at Lalani for approval, smiled and announced, "Shannon Malia Baker! Shannon after my mother and Malia means "wished for child, or child of the sea, in Hawaiian." We're still debating if we will actually call her Malia or Shannon. "Shannon," Lalani said and Jim came back quickly with "Malia." Morgan and Clay laughed.

"As a Baker, she will make up her own mind when she's old enough," Kate chimed in.

~~

News of the baby's arrival spread like wildfire among their friends. After a few days Lalani was up and about, and friends dropped by to see Shannon, bringing gifts and food. Jim and Lalani were in seventh heaven. They had a family, a growing ranch, and very good friends. The year had truly been amazing, full of blessings.

Jim insisted visits with Kate needed to be at their place, arguing that Matthew almost one, was sturdy enough to handle the cold weather and bumpy roads. Shannon, on the other hand, was too tiny to take any chances of cold or worse. Kate and Clay understood. Shannon would be the only baby for Jim and Lalani. As for Kate, they were planning for a second child sometime late next year.

The men got back to running the ranches, making sure the pumps were well oiled and ready for winter, the cattle breeding period had come and gone successfully. Jim was confident Kieran had done a thorough job, and there would be four more new calves come spring.

Meanwhile the woman fussed over babies and made plans for the holidays. Lalani tried hard to establish a routine, so meals would be on time, but Shannon seemed to have her own schedule. Lalani wanted to know how Kate got Matthew to sleep at night and be awake during the day. It seemed Shannon had the two mixed up, sleeping a great deal during the day and wide awake until the wee hours of the night.

Some days, Jim was glad he wasn't the one running the bale compressor. He was afraid he might fall asleep and wake up pressed into a bale of hay. But it was Lalani that usually was up at night. Hattie came over and helped keep the laundry from getting backed up, giving Lalani a chance to nap when Shannon napped.

Before they knew it, Matthew's first birthday was upon them. He was now walking and saying da da, mama and dog. Brandy and Makana were big favorites of his, and oh, so patient. Jim and Lalani agreed to bring Shannon to the party, if it wasn't raining. Matthew was enthralled with baby Shannon and always shared his toy with her, and giggled when she cooed or burped. The day of Matthew's party was overcast, helping to keep the temperature from dropping too low, but the clouds weren't big enough for hard rain. As soon as Lalani and Jim came through the door, Matthew came running, "Un ja, Un Ja," as he called Jim, not yet able to say Uncle Jim and Lalani was of course, "Lala." Then he turned to Lalani pointing to the baby, "Baba anon, baba anon." Jim picked him up in his big arms and showed him baby Shannon. "Well, looks like she has her nickname 'Baba Anon.'"

"Oh, please no, she will never forgive Matthew when she's older. Morgan called me sissy, and it stuck for a long time and I hated it. Please let's not encourage him. Baby Shay maybe, but no baba anon," Kate said, taking Matthew and repeating "Shay" to him several times. This he picked up very quickly and then spent the rest of the evening point to Shannon and saying, "Shay Shay."

Matthew was tall like his daddy and had long fingers like his mother. At one point he grabbed Kate's hand and pulled her to the piano and pointed. This was his way of telling her he wanted his favorite song, *Pop Goes the Weasel.* He and the two other little ones stooped down, and when the part of the pop was played, he jumped up and ran around laughing. Before it was too late, the little ones were packed off to home and into bed, including Lalani and Shannon.

Christmas arrived quickly after that. The Bakers came to the Taylors for Christmas Eve. Matthew was such a busy little boy and *Kālua 'ana* was not decluttered to accommodate a one year old. Eric and Evelyn had come down from San Francisco and were themselves expecting their first baby. Miranda thought of the wonderful noise there would be in a few years when all the children would be friends running up and down the stairs together. Evan was there and laughed, "What do you mean, it will be noisy? Clay, Kate, Jim and Morgan are quite loud already." He was right when they got into a debate about something, the room filled with noise. At dinner Eric brought up the news that the plans for a new dam and reservoir were being made. Clay pointed out that for years the valley ranchers had talked about the need for a reservoir and damming a small river near the foothills. Eric pointed out that was still the plan, but a few old haciendas along the upper part of the river were reluctant to give up the water and were pushing to have the dam further down river. Clay chimed in, "Putting it further down river would get the water to more of the ranches, but would flood a large part of the valley. Eric, are you sure about the change?"

Eric confessed it was only a rumor, that the plans he had seen still showed the small foothill reservoir. Jim agreed a dam would be good for the valley. He had seen too many dry summers and too many feuds over water. Miranda wanted to change the subject, since the rumors were getting too close to home. She had everyone move to the parlor for Christmas carols and cake. Kate sat at the piano and played, while the men stood around and sang, *We Three Kings.*

Christmas morning, Jim and Evan made breakfast for Lalani and they sat quietly and opened a few gifts. Later that day, they had several friends come to visit. This year they came to them, rather than asking Lalani and Jim to take Shannon out into the cold. Lalani had made a special Hawaiian Christmas cake served with mulled wine and hot cider. Everyone was still oohing and aahing over the baby and how pretty and petite she was. It was a lovely day, and again that evening Jim sat on the sofa holding Lalani and Malia, as he called her, feeling blessed and happy.

Jim wanted to hold a New Year's Eve party in the barn to celebrate their good blessings. *I also don't want Lalani dwelling on what happened last year and the loss of the first baby. If she's busy with a party she won't have time to remember.*

"Jim, it's too cold to hold a party in the barn in January. Perhaps we could have a small one here in the house," she said softy, then put her arms around his neck and whispered. "Jim, I'm fine! God gave us a wonderful baby girl. It just wasn't our time before to be parents. What happened last year, the thought of that baby will always be with me. But I'm not sad anymore. God took that sadness away by giving me you and Shannon Malia."

Jim looked into her eyes with a grinning smile and nodded. "Ok, no more worrying. I think a small house party would be a nice way to start the new year. Maybe we do double duty and celebrate Katherine and Clay's second anniversary, since we missed it last year."

"That's a great idea. I'll talk to Kate tomorrow and see if she's on board."

13

The Unexpected

The Bakers started 1894 with the celebration of Kate's and Clay's second anniversary. The parlor furnishings had been pulled back to the walls to open up the area for dancing, and the dining table held delicious food and treats along with champagne flutes. Jim joined the fiddlers at one point. Lalani wore her wedding dress and performed a traditional Hawaiian dance showing how the gods created the islands, flowers, and birds and blessed them with the rain and sun. Jim was proud of her and admired the way she still claimed her Hawaiian heritage. Kate watched in awe of the graceful way Lalani told her story. *I never learned my Madi dances. I guess working with the horses is a dance in its own way. But I will never be that graceful, thank goodness I'm married to Clay, who loves me just the way I am.* Just after midnight, friends began to depart. Clay and Kate stayed to help clean up, but Lalani and Kate ended up just sitting at the kitchen table quietly recalling coming to the valley with one plan and how much things had changed for the better. Meanwhile, Jim and Clay put the furniture back in place and came to the kitchen with the last of the dirty glasses. They finished off the last of the champagne with a toast.

"To Morgan, the key to us all being together. To family, to love," Clay toasted, and it being new year's, Lalani added, *"Hau'oli Makahiki Hou!* Happy new year!"

~~

Shortly after the year began, baby Shannon woke with a stuffy nose and breathing difficulty. Jim, being overly protective, sent Evan for Doc Newell.

Doc arrived mid-morning and said Shannon definitely had a cold. "Jim, stop worrying, all babies get a cold at some point. Shannon's strong, she'll be fine in a day or two. Lalani, just keep her warm and make sure she gets enough milk and some water with just a drop of lemon, No honey – just lemon. If the stuffiness persists, grind some eucalyptus leaves in some Vaseline and rub just a very little on her chest. It will help open up her sinuses and let her breathe easier. Just don't overdo it." Lalani thanked him and promised to keep Jim calm. Shannon nursed just fine, but sounded like a little piglet, creating short little snorts as she sucked. Lalani kept the baby with her through the night just to make sure she was breathing easily. The eucalyptus smell kept Jim awake, but he also could hear his tiny Malia breathing and that was reassuring. By morning her stuffy nose had cleared and was just drippy with clear liquid. Within the week, life in the Baker house was finding a basic schedule and sense of what life was going to be.

Winter marched on, with the days slowly growing longer. One early evening in February, Lalani sat playing with Shannon Malia, she turned to Jim. "Jim, we have to pick one name and stick to it or else call her by both. She's becoming more alert and listening more and more. Two names is confusing. So what is it going to be, Shannon or Malia? "

Jim sat watching his daughter reaching and grabbing Lalani's hair. Smiling and watching her mother's face. "Well, I know she is the child of our wishes, but she's so alert and inquisitive, she has a sense of fun and a tight hold on love. I have to concede, I think Shannon fits her best: fun, loving. Her skin is fairer than yours, and Shannon comes from Sionainn meaning 'possessor of wisdom' or 'a wise river'. " Jim picked up the baby and looking at her fair little face, "Yep, you're a Shannon, full of wisdom." At which, she smiled and wet her diaper.

"Yep, definitely a river... Shannon and Matthew also sound like they go together."

"What are you talking about? Shannon and Matthew?"

"Lalani, you know they're going to grow up together and we will be asking, where have Shannon and Matthew gotten off to?" He laughed as he handed a baby in need of a dry diaper to Lalani.

~~

February proved to be a rainy month, preventing the freezing cold. It was a long winter, and everyone was ready for spring. By late March the trees were budding and hills were showing signs of wild poppies and yellow mustard. The hay and alfalfa fields were thick with growth and wouldn't need replanting this year.

Jim and Lalani made plans to enlarge the vegetable garden and to purchase a few more breeding heifers. Jim and Evan would take the trip to see Dennis Doyle to purchase more heifers and arrange for Morgan to check on their stock while they were gone, so Lalani needn't worry. Jim would first prepare Lalani's garden, so she could plant her vegetable seeds, thus keeping her busy while he was gone.

It was the first of April, and calves and foals weren't due for several weeks. Jim knew Lalani's fortieth birthday was approaching and wanted to get her something from a shop in Sacramento they had visited on their honeymoon. Jim hoped she wouldn't have time to miss him if he took an extra day on his way back from the Doyle's. Before leaving Jim arranged with Kate to put together a surprise party on the 8th, the day of her birthday. He would be back by the 6th to help with the final details. On Sunday after church, Lalani took Jim and Evan, to the train catch the train to Sacramento. She stood waving with baby Shannon in her arms as the train slowly left the station. On her way home, she stopped at Swensen's general store and purchased radish seeds and new cabbage seed for planting. They were used to Makana in the store by now, as she sat quietly at Lalani's side. "Jim's off to purchase livestock, is he?" Hank Swensen inquired.

"Yes, he is all excited. Our little herd is growing. We will be up to ten head this spring." Hank grabbed a dry cracker from the barrel and gave it to Makana. "You really shouldn't. She will want to come here every time I'm in town."

"Nothing wrong with that! Just another chance to see Shannon, your little beauty," Mrs. Swensen added.

The five days went quickly and uneventfully. Lalani stood in the garden inspecting the planted rows. *Thank goodness, no storms, fires or calves arriving. I'm happy I got all my rows planted, and I can't wait to see it begin to grow. On the other hand, I think I can wait to be forty. I'm not sure I'm ready to celebrate being 40 years old. I just hope Jim hasn't gone overboard on this surprise party he and Kate are planning.*

Lalani had cleaned up an old wheelbarrow and lined it with lamb's fleece and an old blanket for Shannon to sit in. Now that she was six months old, Shannon was content to sit in the wheelbarrow and watch her mother plant seeds.

Looking up from the garden as she heard Shannon giggle, Lalani wiped her hand on her work dress and then grabbed the handles to the wheelbarrow. Shannon lay back, giggling as they ran back to the barn, bump bump, all the way. "It's time to get cleaned up and dinner on. Daddy and Evan 's train will be arriving in a few hours," she said, lifting Shannon from the wheelbarrow.

Jim was glad to be home, and told Lalani all about the new heifers and Dennis's offer to trade any bull calves for good heifers he had. Jim thought the offer was good for now and didn't want to deal with a young bull as long as Kieran was still healthy. She could tell there was something else on his mind, but he didn't bring it up. *Maybe the details for the party. I'll tease them out of him later in bed.*

It wasn't the party that was on his mind. It was talk he had heard in Sacramento about the new dam. The rumors about changing the location were becoming more than rumors. But until the new location was revealed, he reminded himself he shouldn't get excited or worried.

~~

Kate invited the Bakers to their place to celebrate Lalani's birthday. Jim had her wear her pretty blue satin dress and dressed Shannon in her prettiest pink. Miranda answered the door, and as they walked in, everyone jumped up and shouted "Surprise!" so loud it sent Shannon to crying. Jim took her into his big arms as Kate whisked Lalani into the center of friends. It was a lovely spring evening, the music and people reminded Lalani of the first time they had come to the Taylor ranch for Eric's wedding. Kate had wildflowers scattered about, and Carol Olsen had made camellia leaf leis which hung on the mantle. It was an amazing evening. Kate had a photographer there to take pictures of her and Lalani, then Lalani, Jim, and the baby. This was her gift to her. Shannon wasn't too cooperative and Matthew wanted to be in the pictures, too. They finally managed to take at least one good photograph.

"Baby Shay and me, take baby Shay and me," he kept saying. He finally got his way.

After the pictures and opening of a few gifts, the evening returned to dancing and watching Matthew entertain baby Shay.

It was around eleven o'clock when the Bakers returned home. Shannon was fast asleep, having been rocked to sleep by the movement of the carriage.

Jim had saved his present for now when they were alone in bed. He reached over and gave her a small long box. Lalani slowly opened it and found a beautiful gold locket and chain. The heart shaped locket was engraved with tiny flowers inside a scalloped border. "Oh, Jim, it's beautiful. Now I know why the photographer was there tonight. He did take a picture of just you, didn't he?" she said, as she held it in her hand. She opened it and found a tiny forget-me-not inside. "Jim, I can never forget you! You are the most wonderful thing to come into my life, you and Shannon," turning and kissing him long and gently.

Later that week, the photographer delivered the photos. Jim cut the tiny thumb-sized photo of him and put it in the locket. "There!"

Jim said as he clasped the chain around Lalani's neck. She stood at the mirror smiling, then opened the locket and smiled even bigger. Lalani was also delighted with the photo of her and Kate and another of Jim, Shannon and her. This she would frame for the parlor, the other for her dressing table.

On Friday, they received a surprise visit from Mr. Maxwell, their banker. He arrived shortly after the noon meal, hoping to still catch Jim before he returned to working. Lalani invited him to join them for a piece of cake, left over from the party. They settled in the parlor, and Mr. Maxwell pulled out a large envelope from his case.

"Lalani, this arrived yesterday for you. It is from a Mr. Shaw," he said most seriously. He pulled out a document titled Lalani Trust. As you told me when you first arrived, you had a trust that would come available on your 40th birthday. Well, according this document the trust has matured, and the funds and the interest have been released into your Boston account."

"Oh, my, Mr. Shaw is efficient. I can't recall how much is in the trust? Thousands, if I remember right."

"The trust was set up some twenty years ago, for $40,000."

"That's just like Horace, one for each of my years. Well, that will be more than enough for us."

"Well actually with interest, the account is just over $100,000. Your friend was a very good investor," Mr. Maxwell said gingerly.

Jim had been quiet up to this point, but gasped at the figure and ran his hands through his hair. Lalani reached over and put her hand on Jim's arm. "Don't think of it as mine, but ours. I did nothing to earn it. I only kept Edith company," she said timidly. But Jim knew better. *You gave up your home and family for them.*

"The funds, all or part of them, can be transferred here whenever you want them," Mr. Maxwell added. *Perhaps, sooner than later.*

Jim jumped in, noting, "Lalani, sooner is wiser, the unemployment back east is reaching an all time high and one bank has already had a run on it. There could be more."

"Run on the bank?" she questioned.

"It's when everyone wants to withdraw all their money at the same time. Banks use some savings to invest in mortgages and business loans and don't keep all the funds people have as cash. When everyone rushes to get their money, the bank runs out and usually closes for good," Jim explained.

"So, we should have the money transferred now to Mr. Maxwell? Will people here want to run on the bank?" she asked.

"I don't think we have that problem here. We don't have too many unemployed needing their savings. And with the talk of building a dam, there will be plenty of work. So, Oak Ridge Bank should be safe."

"Jim's right, Lalani, the bank here is in good shape. No need to worry," Mr. Maxwell confirmed.

"Alright, then go ahead and transfer all but $10,000. Leave that in case we travel there. Thank you so much Mr. Maxwell for your help. Is there anything I need to sign or else to do?" Lalani said graciously.

"Well, a matter of fact there is something else. Nothing to sign, but Horace Crocker left you a letter. He pulled out a long envelope and handed it to her. "Again Mr. Shaw has seen that everything is in order." Mr. Maxwell stood, and Jim and Lalani walked him to the door. "I'll be in touch when the funds arrive, and let me know if you need any help with anything else."

Jim sat with Lalani on the porch as she opened the envelope. It was a letter from Horace written in his own hand.

My Dearest Lalani

I hope this letter finds you, and you are well. I want you to know how much you meant to me and Edith. Through the years we came to think of you as our precious daughter, and we had such joy in watching you grow, and in showing you the world.

I have one regret in life, that we never got you back to your native Hawaii. That I was never able to keep my promise that you would see your mother again. I want you to know I tried several times to persuade her to come with us. She just did not have your adventurous spirit and refused. Yet my dear Edith so loved you and didn't want to give you up.

Now that you have lived a life of service to us and I'm sure to others, I want you to have the rest of your life to live and do as you wish. As a father, if you will let me use that term, I want you to have a secure and good life. Therefore, I created the trust for you, the money to come to you on your fortieth birthday. You may do whatever you wish with it. I trust you will use it wisely.

In addition to the financial sum, I have signed over my Oahu ranch property to you. It is in Kahalu'u Valley on the eastside of Oahu. I would go there to find peace and quiet from all the responsibilities of work and noise of Honolulu.

It is perhaps my most cherished material possession and I want you to have it. I want you to be able to return to your island and find the peace and security there that I found. And maybe, you will think of it as me finally fulfilling my promise to bring you home.

With all my Love,

Horace

Lalani sat staring at the letter with tears in her eyes. *I had no idea he loved me so much. Or that when he was away, he was escaping to the ranch. I'm so glad he shared his thoughts with me and that I have seen it. It is a beautiful and quiet place.* Jim reached over and handed her his handkerchief, bringing her back to the present. Lalani smiled and dried her tears. She reached into the envelope and pulled out a deed to the ranch. On the back in the line of transfer was Horace's signature, already notarized, and her name printed waiting for her signature.

"I had no idea he did this for me. When I saw Martin Shaw's name on the property registry in Oahu I thought for sure the land had been given to his nephew. I never contemplated he would leave it to me. I knew they loved me, but never how much until now," she said, as tears welled up again.

"Well, I'm glad we went and saw the place. What will you do with it?" Jim asked.

"I have no idea at this point. Just keep it. It meant so much to Horace. I'm just overwhelmed by all of this. I knew about the trust funds, but had no idea it was for so much. I'm afraid we will spoil Shannon now. Whatever she asks for, I'm sure you won't be able to say no, and now we can afford to give it to her. "

"Wait a minute. *Me* give in? We! We both can say no. I'm sure this won't really change anything. Other than not having to worry about an income, I still plan on raising cattle for our main source, if that's alright with you," Jim said with a seriousness to his tone.

"Of course, you're right. And yes, the cattle ranch is what we want. But someday, when Shannon is old enough, I should take her to Europe for the culture and experience," Lalani responded.

"Just Shannon, what about me? I've never been to Europe," Jim countered back with a grin.

"You can come too!" Lalani gave Jim a kiss on the cheek and sat to reread Horace's letter, as she was still in disbelief. Jim left her to recall memories and headed out to the barn.

Katherine and Clay came to dinner the next day. Clay told Jim how he handled having a wealthy wife, by not giving in on the important things. Also, not to worry if she bought things within reason, as she surely would. Then he added, "I did make her return the Persian rug, not so much because of the cost, more for the fact that it was darn right ugly, and we didn't need it."

"That rug was beautifully made and a good price," Kate said smugly.

"A good price because it was ugly, and they couldn't get rid of it," Clay smirked.

Lalani and Kate cleared the dishes and took a moment to talk privately. "How do you feel about all this?" Kate asked, knowing the mixed emotions she had about Horace.

"I'm dumbfounded, to be honest. I knew they loved me. They couldn't show it much when we were in Boston. I just didn't realize how much regret Horace had for me not seeing my mother again. Of course, he had no way of knowing she would die three months after we left. I've spent a great part of the day just realizing how lucky I've been. If the Crockers hadn't taken me with them, I probably would have died along with my mother of smallpox. I would not have traveled the world, nor met you and come here and found Jim, or had Shannon. If I had survived the smallpox, I would have been sent to an orphanage and ended up working on one of the sugar plantations. I would have had a very different and difficult life. I owe what I have to Horace and you. Again, I'm just overwhelmed by all of it."

"You don't owe me. I would not have had the courage to go to all those places without you. You're the one that told me it was time to come home. I'd probably still be miserable in England, if it weren't for you. Because of you, I came here and I found Clay."

"Well, we both have a lot to be grateful for," Lalani said, as she picked up the cake and headed back to the men.

Jim and Clay were deep in discussion, but stopped short as the ladies came in.

"What were you two so seriously talking about?" Kate asked.

Clay gave her a glance of don't ask, and then said, "Nothing really, just about the new dam and what year-round water will mean to the valley."

"It won't affect us much as our source of water is from the Natoma Creek, and they plan to dam the Cosumnes River," Jim added.

"What about the Taylor Ranch? Is the creek big enough to supply your needs?" Lalani asked.

"No, but we have the Kokila river that comes in from the north. It flows down through the ranch and joins up with the Cosumnes much further south," Clay explained.

"I don't understand why they don't create a dam way west on the river, where the water is needed," Lalani commented.

"The land is too flat in the lower valley. A dam there would flood most of the farmlands. Up here the river runs through various narrow valleys and hills, making building a dam more practical. When water is needed downstream during summer months, they will open the dam flood gate allowing the needed water into the lower valley," Clay further explained.

Jim had been pretty quiet during the conversation with the ladies, rather than let it go on, he quickly challenged Clay to a game of chess. Clay declined as he still had work to do, and they departed shortly after that.

~~

The next month was busy: foals and calves arrived, the two-week branding season commenced, and spring cleaning at the houses took place. There wasn't much talk about the dam. Occasionally, the paper had an article about a land dispute over the catch reservoir.

In May, Lalani and Kate, along with the children, took a trip to San Francisco to see Joanna. Lalani took the opportunity to see Eric and make sure the deed to the ranch was properly in her name, and that it would be recorded thusly at the Oahu land records office. At first, she thought to put it in both hers and Jim's name, but Eric advised not to. This was a gift to her, and if it was in her name only, no one could take it from her in the event of Jim's death. It wouldn't be part of his estate, and no unknown male relative could come in and take it if it was only in her name. "Maybe you're right. Jim does have a sister. But they haven't spoken in years," Lalani admitted.

Kate and Lalani took time to order new dresses for summer and to buy clothes for the children which were growing as fast as the calves. Lalani wanted to get something nice for Jim. "I just don't know what he will appreciate and not think is frivolous. He is such an unpretentious man."

As they walked past a men's shop, she stopped to look at a hat. The sign read 'Stetson Cattleman, the newest style.' Jim has his favorite working hat, but he doesn't have a good Sunday hat. What do you think, Kate?"

"A man's hat is pretty personal. Clay fusses and fusses when he tries on a new hat, to make sure it fits just right. I thought Jim had a black hat for church."

"He does but he doesn't wear it much. He says it doesn't feel comfortable. Maybe you're right. Hats are pretty personal."

"How about a leather band to dress up his hat? I bet they have something," Kate added, trying to encourage Lalani.

"That might work, as long as it's not too showy," Lalani added as she entered the shop. The clerk was more than helpful and showed her several bands. She did know Jim's hat was a Stetson Boss, but not the size. She picked a simple gray leather band with a small round silver medallion. "This is simple, but manly. I hope Jim will approve."

The next morning, they headed for the train station to return home. As they waited, Lalani noticed a newspaper headline, 'Dispute over Dam Location.' As she went to pick it up, the train whistle blew and the conductor called all aboard. With one arm full of baby and the other holding a small case, she started to leave, but turned and managed to snatch the paper up at the last moment. On the train, Matthew and Shannon sat on the floor of the compartment, Matthew showing blocks to Shay Shay. Lalani read the article aloud about the dispute going on with the land owners that would be affected by the new dam. The state had offered to buy the land that would be flooded where the reservoir would form. "Kate, listen to this, 'Long time and influential land owner refuses to sell land and is promoting a location further down the river.' He says, 'the new location would put the water closer to where it is needed.' It continues saying 'currently the state engineers are reviewing his proposed new location.' "

"Well, I wonder who the owner is? And does he have enough power to influence the state? The water is needed in the lower valley, but I thought because of cost, it was being built east of Oak Ridge," Kate remarked.

The article didn't disclose the new location, only that it was further down river. Lalani knew Clay and Jim would be interested in this news, if they didn't already know. Further down the river would put it in or near the Taylor ranch, as the Cosumnes River was the southwest boundary to the ranch.

Upon arrival home, Jim was pleased with the hat band and very glad she had not picked out a hat for him. "They have to fit just right. But the band is handsome and maybe I will wear that black hat to church after this," he said with a smile.

Later that evening Lalani showed Jim the newspaper about the dam location. "What do you think?" she asked.

Jim admitted he had seen a few strangers in town for the past week. *Could they be a survey team looking at a possible site near Oak Ridge?* Jim hadn't paid much attention to the rumors about the dam and a new location. But he did know Carlos Martinez, the "influential landowner." He had worked for Carlos some twenty years ago. Carlos had an old Spanish land grant on which his ranch was located. The Cosumnes River ran along the south edge of the ranch. "He has over a thousand head of cattle at any given time, sometimes more. I'm sure he doesn't want to lose any of his grazing lands to a reservoir. He has a lot of influence in state commerce, too. He owns one of the state's largest copper mines. Knowing Carlos, he has been talking to various state politicians and threatening to limit production or raise copper prices. "

"So, what does that mean for the people of Oak Ridge? Will the town cease to exist because it's underwater?" Lalani asked with great concern.

"No, No. Oak Ridge is too high up and too far from the river area. If they are going to put a dam near us. Well,… most of the land near the river is pretty flat and building would be impossible or too expensive," Jim said, not wanting to worry Lalani. "It's late, time for bed." Turning down the lamp and taking Lalani's hand, they headed upstairs.

Rumors about a new dam location continued throughout the spring, everything from north to south of Oak Ridge to down near

Elk Grove. Clay and Jim just hoped something would be decided soon, as the San Joaquin Valley needed a good permanent source of water. By the end of June, Jim and Evan had cut and baled the first crop of hay and alfalfa. One of the calves born that spring was indeed a bull, and Jim saw no need to keep him. He took Dennis up on his offer to trade the bull for two heifer calves, knowing his value as a breeding bull was worth the trade. *Probably more, can I get three heifers?* By July indeed, three new calves had arrived and all the cattle had been moved to the south pasture. Lalani's vegetable garden was in full production, and canning beans and pickles had begun.

As things began to slow around the ranch, Jim wanted to take Lalani and Shannon to see Yellowstone National Park, having seen pictures of the geysers and hot springs. He made a reservation at the Lake Yellowstone Lodge and booked train tickets for the second week in July. Lalani was excited to go, especially since July had already turned hot with temperatures at 85 degrees. Evan promised to keep her garden watered, and off they went, baby and dog in tow.

The train ride to Yellowstone only took a day. The scenery was like nothing Lalani had ever seen. The tall thick groves of pines, the deep narrow gorge of the Snake River, and the crystal-clear lakes that reminded her of Austria. It was evening as they arrived by carriage at the Lodge, alongside the expansive Yellowstone Lake.

They were welcomed by a friendly bellman who wore a train engineer's cap, a custom since the hotel was built by the Northern Pacific Railroad. The luxury hotel was new and had all the modern touches, including indoor plumbing and private baths to several suites. Jim had booked one of the suites overlooking the lake. Lalani stood at the window looking out at the lake and watching the sun set behind the mountain. Jim came up and put his arms around her. "See, America has some wonderful sights, too." It was spectacular with the lake reflecting the pinks and blues in the evening sky and the mountain in the distance. There was no breeze, so the reflection was like a mirror, smooth and breathtaking. The next morning, they boarded the hotel's private train for guests that took them directly to Yellowstone Park. They could see elk along the river, and as they entered the park, a herd of buffalo.

"They're so big," Lalani said, with surprise in her voice. "I thought they would be the size of Kieran, but they're so much stronger and massive looking. "

The conductor reminded everyone that the buffalo were wild, not docile like cattle, and for everyone to keep their distance or risk being trampled. From one side of the train, a shout of "Bears" came ringing out. Lalani rushed to see a mother and two cubs just for a moment as the train steamed past.

"Don't worry, you will see more of them, but again, don't get close. Stay with your guide and in the carriage," the conductor warned.

The train pulled into the park near a small building where various sizes of carriages were waiting. Again, Jim had arranged for a private enclosed carriage, big enough for all of them and Makana. Joseph was their driver, a native Indian from the local Blackfoot tribe.

"Good morning, ma'am. I will show you all the beautiful sights of the park today," he said as he helped Lalani into the carriage. It was an enchanting morning, with fluffy white clouds drifting slowly in a radiant blue sky. The air was warm, but had a clean crispness to it. "We go to the hot color pool called paint pot, first. Everyone goes to Old Faithful geyser first and it's too busy. We go there later when it's quiet," Joseph said as he climbed up.

The roads were well traveled and not too bumpy. Shannon sat on Jim's lap and giggled and bounced as they went. Joseph slowed and called down, "Bear off to the right near the trees." There he was, a large brown bear standing upright, sniffing the air.

"Oh, he's a big one, wish I had my rifle," Jim called out.

"No hunting in the park, Mr. Jim." Joseph said. "But if you want to go on a bear hunt another day, I can arrange it with my brother Running Wolf."

"That won't be necessary," Lalani quickly replied. She had noticed there was a rifle resting up against the foot board. "And the rifle you have, is it necessary?" she asked.

"Only if something dangerous gets too close. But I never aim at a beast, only near to frighten away," he replied.

After they watched the bear for a few moments, he wandered off into the trees. Joseph whipped up the horses again and proceeded on. After a few minutes, he pulled into an area with steam coming from out of the ground.

"This is paint pot hot springs. The water is boiling hot, so don't go beyond the fence, " Joseph said, helping Lalani from the carriage.

"The colors are amazing. The water's so clear, you don't realize it is so hot. If it weren't for the heat coming from the pool, you would want to step in," Lalani said.

They stood and watched the odd shaped shallow pool with a white rim leaching into a bright yellow and then into a brilliant rust hue. In the center was a deep hole of aqua blue with tiny bubbles ascending.

"It truly looks like someone has painted it," Jim commented. Makana pranced about and at one point stepped into a rather warm shallow puddle, jumping back quickly with surprise at the heat of the water.

Makana ran to a spot at the fence further down and stood barking. "What is it girl?" Jim asked.

Makana had found a beige pool of boiling mud, the bubbles rising in the thick beige ooze to a point and then bursting, sending mud splattering. "Look, Jim, the mud is boiling. That must be hot." They stood and watched the gorgeous colors and steaming landscape even Shannon seemed mesmerized by the colors.

Joseph came up to them as they watched the steaming pool. "The Crow Indian lore says, an old woman was heating rocks and water on the mountain and suddenly a beast came up out of the lake. She tossed the boiling water and rocks into its mouth, and it retreated back to the lake. It is the cowering beast that sleeps below these pools that keep them hot."

"That's quite a story. And what do the Blackfoot people say?" Jim asked.

"We call these mountains 'many smokes'. My people live outside the area because of the evil spirit that inhabited this place."

"And today, are you not afraid of the evil spirits?" Lalani said, understanding native superstitions.

"No. I'm just afraid the sleeping volcano below will erupt someday," he chuckled. "Are you ready to see the puffing buffalo?"

"Puffing buffalo?" Lalani answered.

"That's what Indian lore call Old Faithful geyser. I will tell you that story when we get there."

It was a short ride back through pines where eagles soared and elk could be seen laying below the trees to stay cool. Shannon began to fuss, and Jim asked Joseph to stop somewhere they could have lunch. It was a small clearing with some old logs. Jim pulled out a basket the hotel had packed. Shannon grabbed the crackers and Lalani mashed the peaches into bits Shannon could eat. Makana wandered in the clearing, sniffing all the strange scents. Joseph cautioned Jim to keep the dog close, as mountain lions could be nearby. Jim called the dog back several times before they finished.

The crowds at Old Faithful were small now, only four of five people sat on the bench waiting for the geyser to erupt. To look at it, it didn't seem much, just a small knoll with a muddy white stream running from it. Joseph had timed it so their wait wouldn't be long. "Old Faithful goes off just about every hour, give five minutes here or there. Crow legends says the Grandchild of the Old Woman that defeated the lake beast was a great hunter and killed many animals here. When he killed a great buffalo, the old buffalo refused to die and transformed into the geyser and wouldn't stop puffing out hot air. The hunter then killed a mountain lion and placed it nearby. The lion became a new geyser breathing out steam onto the buffalo to stop it from coming back alive. Today the lion continues to spew out steam, keeping the buffalo asleep."

Just then the small stream of steam stopped, and a slow bubbling of water began until it shot up to create a fountain of scalding hot water over a hundred feet high. Makana jumped up and started barking at the noise. Jim had put her on the leash to keep her from danger. "Quiet, Girl!" Lalani held Shannon, both wide eyed, watching the unbelievable display of water and power. The climax of the geyser lasted no more than a minute or two and then began to lower very slowly. The boiling clear water ran down the small knoll as the geyser sputtered to a stop, and all was quiet again. Lalani, Jim and the others stood shaking their heads. *It's amazing the height it can go and it happens every hour. What a magnificent sight.*

Joseph then took them on to see two other geysers he hoped would be going off soon. One didn't seem to be doing much that day, only a small ten-foot spray. "No good, so unpredictable. But when it is ready, it goes higher than Old Faithful," Joseph grumbled. As time was getting late and they had to catch the train back to the hotel, they made one more stop at a geyser near the depot.

"This is castle geyser. If we're lucky we will see it erupt. The fountain isn't too impressive, but it last longer, and then it sounds like a roaring train for a long time afterward," Joseph said.

They were not the only ones waiting, as several carriages had stopped. Jim and Lalani mingled with other visitors comparing the sights they saw. Then suddenly the steam began to rise. The castle rose to only about forty feet, but it went on and on, filling the air with a warm mist. Everyone seemed disappointed and began to leave, but Joseph stood still. After about four minutes, a rumbling began. It got louder and sounded just like that of a steam locomotive passing by. Steam whistled from its cauldron, but no water flowed this time. Then as it gave a short shrill tweet, it was silent. Jim and Lalani began to laugh.

"What a funny little geyser, all noise and no punch," Jim said.

Joseph took them back to the train, just in time for departure. It had been an incredible day. Baby Shannon and Makana slept on the way back to the hotel.

In the morning Jim rose early and wandered down along the lake and collected several colorful rocks for Shannon to play with. "Jim, they're beautiful, but I'm afraid she will put them in her mouth. They're large but not so large she can't get them in her mouth."

As Jim showed them to Shannon, she picked one up and then the other. Then reaching for a dark red stone, she started to put it in her mouth. "Oh, no, you don't, it's not a cookie," and he grabbed it away before she got it all the way in. She reached for the green stone and Jim realized Lalani was right and swept up all the pretty rocks and put them up out of harm's way. Shannon let out a scream of disapproval, and Lalani quickly distracted her with a real cookie and her favorite toy.

That day they had planned to take a hike and picnic along the river leading into Lake Yellowstone. They came down with a knapsack and hiking boots, ready to meet their guide. "Joseph, what are you doing here?" Lalani blurted out upon seeing him. To their surprise, he was their guide for the day.

"I trade riding tour and hiking tour every other day. If one rides too much, you get fat and lazy," he said with a smile. "I take you to some good places to see flowers and views of big mountains."

Joseph had brought an Indian back carrier for Shannon. Normally, it was for a younger baby, but Shannon was small, and it fit her, with only her feet peeking out the bottom. Joseph led the way, then Jim and Lalani following, keeping an eye on Shannon on Jim's back.

The hike along the lake was easy and Joseph pointed out various water ducks. They reached Pelican Creek and turned to follow it up into the mountains. Joseph knew of an active beaver pond on the river and a place where river otters were often seen. The hike in the low area near the beaver pond was dry in July, making it easy to reach the pond. Joseph planned a long stop in hopes one of the beavers would show up.

"Keep Makana on leash so she doesn't prance into the pond and scare the beavers into their den," Joseph warned.

Lalani and Shannon settled on a small mound of grass where they could observe the beaver's den, and Makana lay next to them. Jim and Joseph scouted for movement in the water.

"Look at the size of those trout, " Jim whispered. "Wish I had my rod and reel with me."

After about twenty minutes of patiently waiting, Joseph pointed to a head just breaching the surface. Jim and Lalani stood looking. He was a large male gliding along. He turned and swam parallel to them. Suddenly Makana caught sight of it and let out a loud bark. The beaver's tail came up with a slap to the water that echoed across the pond, and he was gone. "Oh, Makana, you ruined it," Lalani scolded.

They had been there some time, and Joseph wanted to show them the view of the lake from a nearby peak, so they moved on. This climb was a little steeper and more difficult for Lalani. The trail had narrowed, and scrub caught her skirt again and again. They could hear the hammering of a woodpecker off in the distance and came across bear scat at one point. "No fresh, yesterday," Joseph said.

They came to a narrow point in the trail where the trees were thick with a hundred foot drop on the one side, into a canyon below. Joseph stopped and made sure Jim managed the short distance. Then took Lalani's hand to make sure she too got past. Once past the trees, it opened up to a small round meadow with a view of the river below and looking back five miles at the grandeur of Lake Yellowstone.

They could see the large hotel looming up at the lake, the wind dancing across the lake making patterns in one direction and then suddenly shifting off into another. It was a gorgeous spot. Very few people had seen the lake from this perspective. Lalani took Shannon from the back carrier, then Jim stood with his arms around both of them looking out across the wide valley. "It truly is a beautiful and amazing country," he sighed.

"In Hawaii from this height you see ocean for miles, but here, trees and land stretch out before you. So much land," Lalani said softly.

They had their picnic, and Makana and Shannon played in the little meadow. Finally, the sun was on the down side of noon, and it was time to head back. Going down wouldn't take as much time, but they might spot a deer or a porcupine coming down to the stream. Again, Joseph made sure Jim could pass the narrow trail safely and then helped Lalani.

Makana had picked up a scent and was dawdling behind. Jim called for her, and she came running along the narrow trail. All at once they heard the whelp of a dog's howling and whining as it tapered off. Joseph ran to the narrow trail. Makana had slid off and down the mountain side. He could see her struggling in the stream below. Lalani came alongside Joseph, who grabbed her to keep her back. They watched Makana being swept downstream in the fast-moving current, struggling to keep her head above water. Lalani broke into tears. Joseph forced her back off the narrow path to Jim, where she leaned into his chest and cried.

"Miss Lalani, all may not be lost. If Makana can keep her head above water and swim with the current, the stream slows and widens into another pond. Come, we can see from the trail further down."

They quickly stepped along the trail following Joseph for about a mile and half. Then he turned into some thick trees to the edge of a small cliff. There just below, the stream had widened, and Makana lay on a small narrow part of land against the cliff. Lalani couldn't tell if she was breathing, but Jim could hear her faint whimper. The problem was how to get to her. It was a steep thirty-foot drop to the stream and that was the only spot the river had pulled away from the cliff.

Jim said he would try and climb down, but Joseph said, "No, too steep and difficult. We go back to Lodge and get ropes and blankets.

Only way," Joseph insisted. Lalani hated to leave Makana and called down to her telling her to stay, trying to reassure her friend. "We go now, hurry," Joseph said. They scurried down the trail as fast as they could without falling. As they reached the lake, Joseph spotted his brother and a friend on horseback.

"We need your horse. Miss Lalani's dog has fallen into Pelican Creek and is stuck at No Man's Bend. You take Miss Lalani back to Lodge."

Lalani immediately began to protest, wanting to be with them, to be there for Makana. "Sweetheart," Jim said softly, "You need to take Shannon back to the hotel and keep her safe. We can move faster without you. I promise I will bring Makana home." He lifted Shannon from the pack and handed her to Lalani and gave her a kiss. "I promise," then mounted one of the horses and headed off with Joseph. Running Wolf, Joseph's brother, put his arm around Lalani and began to guide her back to the Lodge.

Tempi, one of the older maids, seeing Lalani's face upon entering, knew something was wrong. She came to Lalani immediately, "What's happened, where is your husband?" she urgently asked.

"Jim okay, dog is injured," Running Wolf said politely. "You take care of Miss Lalani, I go to help," he said and off he went.

Tempi escorted Lalani to her room. At first, Lalani didn't want to put Shannon down as if afraid of losing her too. Lalani had gone to the window and stood staring out towards the road. Shannon began to wiggle and wanted down. "Miss, let me take her. Things will be all right. Joseph is a good scout and knows animals very well," she said.

Tempi took Shannon and changed her wet clothes and placed her in the crib. She went out and brought back a bottle of warm milk and hot tea and biscuits. Lalani had pulled up a chair and was still watching out the window for Jim and Makana. Shannon immediately took the bottle and lay down in the crib.

~~

Jim and Joseph quickly returned to the cliff above No Man's Bend. Makana was now standing. Jim could see she was shaking from the cold, and wondered why she wasn't barking. Joseph brought two ropes from the horse and a blanket. "I will climb down using the rope," Joseph explained. Jim tied one end of the rope to a nearby tree and slowly lowered Joseph.

Makana whimpered softly as he approached her. She was panting in small short breaths. He rubbed his hand along her legs, and she didn't seem to be in pain. Then he ran it across her left ribs, and she gave out a whine and whimper. He again tried with a gentler touch. Makana leaned away, but didn't cry this time. Joseph called up to Jim, "Her legs seem all right, but she may have a cracked rib, or badly bruised from hitting the rocks. Drop down the blanket and I'll make a harness we can lift her up with."

At that moment, Running Wolf arrived and began to help. Joseph took a long heavy limb from the water and tied opposite ends of the blanket to it. Then slid the open blanket under Makana and tied the other ends to the limb. Running Wolf knew what Joseph was doing and dropped down the second rope to be tied to the center of the limb. "Do you think it will hold?" Jim asked.

"It worked before when we rescued injured mountain goat," Running Wolf replied.

Slowly, Running Wolf pulled up Makana as Jim pulled up Joseph, trying to keep them even so Joseph could keep Makana calm and from hitting the cliff too hard. She didn't seem to be injured on her right side, which he had placed toward the cliff. As they neared the top, Running Wolf stopped and let Joseph scramble to safety. Then together they lifted Makana to them. Jim held her gently and was relieved to see she was able to stand. Now they just had to get her back to the Lodge. Joseph and his brother lifted her up to Jim on his mount, and they slowly headed back.

~~

At the lodge, Lalani continued to look out the window. Tempi tried to reassure Lalani things would be all right. "You have had your dog a long time?" Tempi asked as she poured tea for Lalani. The sound of her voice brought Lalani back to the question. "Yes, two years. She was a gift from a friend. Makana means gift in Hawaiian."

"You are Hawaiian and far from home then."

"Yes and No. I left Hawaii as a child. We live in California now. But Makana has been a life saver and best friend. It pains me to think of her hurt and alone."

"I'm sure Joseph and your husband have reached her by now. Running Wolf will know how to get her out of the canyon. You'll see, they will all be here soon," Tempi said with a smile.

"I hope you're right. I just hope she's not too hurt. She wasn't moving when we spotted her." *I hope she was just tired from the struggle. She's a setter and setters are good swimmers. Jim, where are you?*

Lalani went and checked on Shannon. She had finished the bottle and was now fast asleep. The sun had set behind the mountains now and it was hard to make out things along the road. Tempi suggested she freshen up and be ready for when they came. Lalani took one look at her dress. It was dirty and ripped where the scrubs had caught it. She went and washed her face and changed into a simple dress, one she wouldn't mind holding Makana in. As she came out of the changing room, the door opened. Jim came in with Makana in his arms. She was wrapped up in a blanket and didn't seem to move. Jim could see the fear on Lalani's face, "She's still with us, badly bruised, but she's a fighter."

Joseph came in behind him and spoke to Tempi for a moment and then she disappeared. Jim laid Makana on the bed and unwrapped the blanket. Lalani came to her immediately and sat on the bed, patting her head. Makana lifted her head and tried to get up, but Jim held her down. "Shhh, girl. Stay down, it's all right now," Lalani said softly stroking her head, now lying in her lap.

Tempi reappeared with small meat scraps in a bucket of broth in one hand and strips of a dish towel in the other. Joseph took the strips and gently began to wrap them around the dog's ribs. "I think she has some bruised ribs from being thrown against the rocks. But nothing seems to be broken. The wrappings will make it easier to breathe and move," Joseph said, as he tightly wrapped the bandages with Jim's help. Makana's panting seemed to be slower once they were done.

"See if she will take some of the broth and meat, Lalani," Joseph said, handing her the bucket. Lalani slid Makana's head just off the bed and offered her the bucket. She made a slight attempt to lap at it. Lalani reached in and pulled a piece of meat out and gave it to her. Makana took this quickly.

"This is a good sign. If she wants to eat, then all will be okay," Joseph said. "We bring extra mattress for her to sleep on," and he and Tempi disappeared.

Lalani sat patting Makana with one hand and holding Jim's hand with her other. "Thank you for bringing her home, I was so worried. I'm sorry this has happened on such a wonderful trip."

Within a short period, Makana was able to stand and eat on her own. They stayed at the hotel for the next few days, enjoying the lake and keeping Makana quiet. The day before they were to leave, Joseph came with his carriage. "I take you to more special places in park, that only I know," he said. Joseph felt bad about Makana getting hurt when he was guiding and wanted to make up for it. "Tempi will stay with Makana, you no worry."

Lalani and Jim had a wonderful last day seeing amazing sights with Joseph. He took them to see a den of young wolves and the elk herd down by the river, and to several small geysers and more colorful hot pools. He brought them to a bluff overlooking the buffalo herd. These were sights they would never forget. Departing that evening, Lalani told him an old Hawaiian blessing and wished him long life. Jim on the other hand slipped in a twenty-dollar bill and a respectful handshake.

14

Better for Who?

The Bakers arrived back at *Kālua 'ana* the following morning. Evan was there to meet them, and upon seeing Makana bandaged up, reached down to pet her as she greeted him, "Well, girl, what animal did you tangle with?"

"More like a hundred foot cliff into a swift moving river. Just a few bruised ribs," Jim replied.

Shannon, upon seeing Evan, gave out a squeal and reached for him. Taking her and saying, "Glad to see you didn't go for a swim, little one," tweaking her nose as she giggled. "Did you have a good trip?"

"A wonderful trip!" Lalani chimed. "Yellowstone is a land of magic, unbelievable things."

As they drove through town, things seemed busier than usual. "We miss anything important while we were gone? How are the cattle?" Jim asked.

"The cattle are good. The calves are doing just fine, and I believe Kieran has already been busy with a few of the heifers," Evan replied, trying to hide his true thoughts. *I'll wait to tell them about the changes with the dam until after they've had a chance to unpack. No point ruining a good trip first moment back.*

That evening Evan brought in one of the dressed cooking hens for Lalani to fry up for supper. Lalani showed him the post cards she had bought of the paint pot pools and Old Faithful. Evan still didn't have the heart to tell them about the dam. Instead, he let them settle in, and headed out to the bunkhouse.

In the morning, as everything began to come back to routine, Jim asked Evan if he had gotten this week's newspaper. "Need to see what I missed."

"You won't like what's been going on," Evan said.

Jim looked at him, now seeing the concern on his face. "What? What's changed?" Then it dawned on him, *they have decided on a new location for the dam. From the look on Evan's face, it's not good for someone we know.*

Evan handed Jim the paper. The headline read 'Olsen Valley New Location for Dam.' "Olsen Valley!" Jim blurted out. "Have you talked to Bill about this?"

"No, I haven't seen him, but Clay, I know, went to see him yesterday when the news broke," Evan said.

Lalani had breakfast ready as the men came in. Jim sat down without a word, and began to read the article. "What is it?" Lalani asked.

"They have selected Olsen's Valley as the new dam location," Evan said.

Lalani set down the coffee pot and waited for Jim to finish reading.

"Says here they have selected a narrow passage about three miles down the south side of the Olsen's Valley. That the Cosumnes River will be diverted by tunnels until the dam is built. Then the tunnel will be closed, and the river will fill in behind the dam. The tunnel's flow will not affect any towns as it will be directed back to the natural river bed it had used."

"Can they divert a large river like the Cosumnes?" asked Lalani.

"Sure, it takes a lot of digging, but it can be done." Jim answered. "The dam is not the problem for the Olsens, it's the reservoir it will create. It will basically take over most of the ranch's grazing land. We'll ride over to Kate and Clay's after breakfast and find out more," Jim said.

"I'll go with you," Lalani said with insistence.

Jim helped Lalani into the carriage and handed her Shannon. He tied Buck to the back, so he and Clay could ride out to see the location. It was just below the Olsen's ranch. It was also next to the southeast boundary of the Taylor ranch. Evan mounted his horse and came along as well.

Kate was delighted to see Lalani, but from the look on Jim's face, she knew he had read the paper. "Come on in, we're in the study with Morgan and Eric, discussing the legal possibilities." She took Lalani's arm and lead them back to the study.

"Welcome home," Clay said extending a hand to Jim and a kiss on the cheek to Lalani. Matthew was playing on the floor and stood, calling, "Shay, Shay!" Lalani put her on the floor, and he immediately started bringing her toys to play with.

"Sorry you came home to this news," Morgan said.

They had talked to Bill the day before and he was shocked, uncertain as to what to do. Bill's father had started the ranch and he had grown up there. Bill, like the rest of the ranchers, wanted a dam for the valley, but never dreamed it would be on his property.

Clay said that Bill and Carol were in a daze and they were going to have to decide if they wanted to fight or settle. But settling would mean they would lose their land and not be able to raise cattle any longer.

Bill was now sixty-five and had three daughters, none of whom would want to run the ranch. If he sold early when prices were good, they might get enough to retire on. The Olsens had a lot to consider.

Morgan and Clay both pointed out how the dam would bring year-round water to the local herds and badly needed water to the farmers in the central valley. Eric had found out that the three smaller ranches on the south side of the Cosumnes that would be affected had already signed agreements with the state. Eric had come to help figure what price they should get in order to determine if the state's offer was fair. At the moment, the Olsens had not been contacted. "The state tends to offer lower than what the land is worth. And most landowners take it, knowing if they hold out, the offer will go even lower, or the state will just declare eminent domain and take the land anyway."

"We might lose part of the southeast grazing land while the river is diverted through the tunnels. Just how much and how long, we're not sure," Morgan added.

"Will the Circle K south pasture be affected?" Jim asked with concern.

"Jim, I wish I knew. Most likely not. There is a natural small uphill grade between your place and the Olsens. If they let off water from heavy winter rains as they should, your place is way too far north to be affected. Yet if they don't, in years of heavy snowpack, in those years, your pasture may be flooded. That's what I'm trying to determine how much land could be affected, both ours and yours. I want to work up an agreement of compensation with the state for those years the land can't be grazed. Whatever figure I come up with, both of us can use it and we can submit legal documents to the state together," Eric explained.

Lalani had heard enough to know the new location was a possible problem, and didn't need to hear more, until more was known. At least not at the moment, since Eric didn't think *Kālua 'ana* would be affected.

The children were beginning to fuss, so Kate and Lalani took them upstairs to her sitting room. Kate could see the look of concern on Lalani's face. "Lalani, don't worry, I'm sure it won't reach *Kālua 'ana*. If it does, Eric will figure something out. The dam won't be complete, or even started for several years. The reservoir won't possibly fill to capacity for as many as ten years from now," Kate encouragingly said, as she rang for Lupe to bring tea.

"You don't think the water would reach or cover *Kālua 'ana* and the barn, do you?" Lalani asked.

"No, No. The house is way too far up and away. It's only your south pasture that might be affected and most likely not. Now tell me all about your trip. What is Yellowstone like?"

Lalani spent the next several hours talking about what they did and saw and how Makana needed to be rescued. The men did decide to ride out and take a look at the area and didn't come back until dusk. Kate invited Lalani to stay for supper, as they put the children down for afternoon naps. Shannon slept for several hours, but Matthew was up and hungry after forty minutes. The men returned. Lalani and Jim went ahead and stayed for supper, then headed for home.

As summer ware on, Lalani was now glad to be home and back in her garden and playing with Shannon at the creek to stay cool on the hot summer days. On occasion, a heifer would come down and watch them, but Lalani would shoo it a way. She tried not to think about the dam, but could see concern on Jim's face now and then. And she thought about her good friend Carol, and how awful it was for them.

For weeks, everyone only talked about the dam. The men all agreed the location near the Olson ranch was the best place for it, and how much good it would do. They talked about what kind of price Bill should get for his ranch and not how Bill and Carol felt about losing it.

Progress regarding the dam seemed to be slow. The state had not come to the Olsens with an offer yet, and Bill hadn't decided if he would accept it when they did. Carol Olsen was glad the offer hadn't come. She hated the thought of having to move her three daughters from their home. Yet, Hattie was now eighteen and was being courted by a young man. Meanwhile, the younger girls were quite happy at home. Carol and Bill found it hard to talk with the other ranchers, but found compassion when they visited with Lalani and Jim.

In October, the state land manger showed up in town and presented Bill with an offer. Eric had negotiated a price of $3.60 an acre, and also that Bill could stay on his land until the dam construction physically was 50% complete and water would begin to collect in the reservoir area. The bill of sale would only take effect when the construction began, with a leaseback option for the east grazing range. They would be given a thirty-day notice. The Olsens found themselves seriously considering the state's offer. The pressure from the other ranchers had been intimidating, and Bill wanted to retire in another five years, about the time the dam would be 50% built. After considering it for a week, the Olsens signed the agreement.

This meant three or four more years for the Olsens on the ranch and a good income for Bill to retire with. Everyone seemed happy. Jim and Clay still had reservations about the size of the reservoir, but the state land manager was reticent about signing an agreement for compensating the Taylor and Bakers for their land, before the dam was complete. They agreed to wait and readdress the issue once the dam construction began.

Jim and Lalani went ahead and purchased twenty more head which would grow the herd much faster. Kieran was more than delighted to do his part. Kate's three-year olds were ready to be saddle broke, and she would offer them for sale the following spring.

Fall roundup came and went with record numbers and prices. It was turning out to be a good year for the Bakers, in spite of the commotion over the dam.

~~

1895 arrived and the economy of the country drastically took a down turn, and with it, the funds for the dam were reduced. The by-pass tunnels for the Cosumnes had not even begun. The plan to build a substantial dam across the Cosumnes was to be delayed, if not scrapped all together. The farmers in the lower valley were up in arms at the thought of the dam being scrapped. It had been a dry summer for them. Even Jim and Clay were disturbed by the thought of a delay. Many of the local ranchers were demanding that construction start, as they too wanted the water and not have to haul water as they did at the end of August. Clay was worried range wars over water rights would begin to break out. *The Taylor ranch is fine with the Kikilo*

River, but others may try and infringe upon us by bringing their herds to the stream.

The Circle K and the Taylor ranch had natural water sources flowing through them. Seldom had the Natoma Creek gone dry in very hot years. The Kikilo through the Taylor ranch always had some water flowing. The valley ranchers began to talk about a smaller reservoir dam, something that would cost half the amount and could be built in two or three years rather than seven or eight. A group of ranchers and farmers had gone to Sacramento to present their plan. But the state made no promises.

Through the winter months, Jim and Evan helped Kate break the horses that would be sold for roundup in the spring. About mid-February, Jim and Evan didn't show up at sunset, their usual time. Lalani was standing on the porch, about to hike up the west hill to the horses to see why, when Jim and Evan came riding in from the ranch main road. It was dark but Lalani knew those silhouettes anywhere. She went back in and put the biscuits in the warmer.

Jim came through the kitchen door, and Lalani let out a gasp. Jim's head had a large bandage across his forehead and Evan's arm was in a sling. Before she could say anything, "We're okay, just a little run-in with an upset horse," Jim said and leaned forward to kiss Lalani on the cheek.

"A little run in? Looks like you two lost the battle. Oh, my, is Kate alright?"

"She's fine. She was watching from the fence when the black mare got a burr or something under her blanket and reared, twisting to one side and then the other, throwing poor Evan into the fence. I went to grab her reins so she wouldn't trip and break a leg, when she reared again and just clipped me in the head. It looks worse than it is. Don't go fussing. It's only a small cut. Evan's the one needing the fussing. His arm is broke. Doc says six weeks before he gets on a horse or uses it."

Evan sat down at the table, "Damn horse. It won't be any six weeks. I'll be fine in four. Right now, I'm hungry."

The next day was rainy and the men sat around the parlor watching Shannon and complaining about aches and pains. Lalani wasn't sure who was the biggest baby, Shannon or the men. *Right now, the men are winning on that score.* Lalani cooked meals and went about regular chores as best she could. For the next few days, the men sat and talked about cattle, the dam and played cards. They did manage to keep Shannon entertained and Lalani got some wool spun. Once the rain stopped, Clay and Kate came to see how they were doing. Kate felt terrible that she should have been the one in the corral to calm her down. "Oh, no, you don't, not in your condition," Clay said. Kate was again pregnant, the baby due in mid October.

The men thought it was strange that there was no word about the dam. They all agreed it shouldn't be scrapped, that even a small reservoir would be a big help to the valley. Meanwhile Kate and Lalani talked about spring dresses and getting the children outdoors again. Kate admitted she already had interest in the mares. Her reputation for training horses had gotten around and two buyers were already sending inquiries.

Lalani listened politely and was happy for Kate, but that was about as far as her interest went. *I miss the old days of piano practicing and performance. How she worried about the conductors and playing perfectly, which she always did. I wish we had a small piano for her to play here when she visits.* "Lalani, Lalani! What are you thinking about?" Kate said bringing her back to listening.

"I'm sorry. I was thinking how I missed the days when sent hours practicing piano, and we traveled to your piano concerts."

"Oh, my, you miss all those trains and hotel rooms?" she chuckled, "I guess you would. There were no dishes to do or beds to make then. Now we're knee deep in diapers and sweaty shirts."

"Do you miss the performing?" Lalani asked, half knowing the answer.

"Sometimes, but not really. I have my piano and play every day. I do the one concert for the town orphanage each year. That's enough. Though Reverend Miller says we're going to have to hold it in San Francisco at a larger hall. He hates turning people away. Says a lot of people from the city come to hear me."

"That's probably Joanna's doing. Talking it up to her friends. I think a group came down on the train last year. Perhaps performing in the city is a good idea. More people mean more donations to the orphanage," Lalani said with a smile.

~~

By mid-March, Evan was back working almost to full capacity. Jim was busy checking on the alfalfa and hay fields which looked good for an early spring harvest. The hay from last year was almost gone, but if he was careful, what was left would do. Within the next few weeks calves would be arriving, and Kate's four pregnant mares would be dropping hopefully healthy foals.

Knowing the busy time at the ranch was coming up, Lalani and Kate wanted to have a special day just with their men, before they wouldn't see them for weeks. They conspired to have a day in the city, dining and a concert. "NO!" both Clay and Jim said in unison. "You will drag us to shops for hours and then to a boring concert," Clay muttered.

"Boring? You think my piano playing is boring?" Kate said, her dander up.

"I didn't say that. You won't be the one playing." Clay could see he was getting deeper into trouble and looked at Jim.

"How about a romantic picnic by the river, then we go see The Girl of the Golden West opera opening right here in Oak Ridge? We will take you to supper afterwards," Jim offered.

"We accept!" Kate and Lalani said at the same time.

"Jim, I think we have been hoodwinked. I think that was what they wanted all along," Clay grinned.

"Of course, it is. That's why I said it," Jim replied, giving Lalani a wink.

Miranda agreed to watch the children for the day with help from Lupe. Lalani packed the food and Clay brought the wine. Miranda sent pastries for dessert. Kate still wasn't the best cook and Lalani wanted it to be special.

They had a favorite spot along the creek. The weather was warm for March, with only a whisp of a breeze that allowed the fluffy clouds to meander. A few early baby ducklings were in a row behind their mothers. Jim had chosen to leave Makana with Evan after the last water mishap, which allowed the ducklings to linger.

Later that afternoon, they made their way to the new opera house in time for the opening playing of the national anthem. Clay and Jim chuckled throughout the whole comedic performance. "Now, that Puccini knows how to write an opera a man can relate to," Clay said upon leaving. "That Minnie could have been my Sunday school teacher, and I might have come," Jim added.

Clay had made reservations for a small private dining room. He wasn't sure their supper would stand up to Lalani's picnic, but it was romantic with candlelight. A violinist came and played just after the main course before dessert. Lalani was happy that Clay had brought the big carriage, and Jim didn't have to drive, so that she could sit close to him on the back bench with his arm around her. Evan was waiting for them as Clay pulled the team into *Kālua 'ana.* Miranda had brought Shannon home. "She's fast asleep. See you in the morning," Evan said and slipped off to the bunkhouse. Jim picked up Lalani and carried her upstairs, stopping at Shannon's door to peak in, then swung around to their room and closed the door behind them.

The next few weeks were busy. Calves had arrived and three foals. Jim and Evan were busy with horses helping Kate, while Clay and their ranch hands were busy branding. As usual the men would come home in the evening dirty and tired. Lalani would have a hot tub ready for Jim and a warm brandy waiting when he came down.

This year the Olsens wanted to host the spring dance, not knowing if it would be their last at the ranch. Rumors were beginning to spread again that new dam plans were forming for a smaller dam. Again, no specifics had surfaced, just rumors. Couples and friends began to show up at the Olsens in the late afternoon, with food for supper and desserts for later. Lalani was radiant as usual, on the arm of a very proud Jim. Katherine was also radiant with her dark hair done up and tan Indian heritage glowing. She was now beginning to show with her second pregnancy.

Supper was eaten at a long table set up under the elm trees, and everyone shared stories of the crazy cows and calves they encountered this year, and that market prices should be good come fall roundup. After everyone had their fill of delicious food, the dishes were cleared, washed by the women and dried by the men. Desserts and coffee were set out, and then the fiddles came out.

Jim escorted Lalani to the dance floor, gallantly taking her in his arms and beginning to dance. Bill and Carol Olsen, Kate and Clay, Morgan and Amanda his new, but serious interest, and others joined them. The evening was transformed with lanterns hung from the trees. Everyone joined in for a reel and clapping. Those watching were suddenly aware of a rider coming up fast and hard.

Ben from the ranch stood at the door, his big six-foot stature couldn't be missed. Clay and Kate broke off and immediately met him. "The dam is back on, but it's not going to be on the Cosumnes. They plan to dam the Kikilo and Natoma Creek into this valley," he said loud enough for all to hear. A hush went through the air. Everyone knew those were the main sources for the Baker and Taylor herds. Everyone looked at Bill. "No, I haven't been contacted about the change or when building will begin. We haven't been given any notice to vacate," he said knowing their thoughts, since he had already had a signed contract with the state to sell.

"Did you hear when they will start?" Bill asked.

"Soon, according to the Chronicle," Ben said handing the paper to Bill. Clay stood reading the headline alongside him. Everyone was silent, waiting to hear what it said.

Bill handed Clay the paper and walked over to Carol. "Well, my girl, looks like this will be the last party. It says work crews will begin to arrive as early as June." Carol pursed her lips as tears began to well up and she finally managed, "Well, then, may I have one last dance?" Bill took her in his arms and the others gave them room. Dan began to play the fiddle with a soft melody as the others watched.

Jim took Lalani's hand and they looked at each other with a deep concern and slowly joined Carol and Bill. *What will this mean for the Circle K?* Once the dance was finished, people began to leave. Jim, Lalani, Morgan and Amanda stayed and helped clear the tables and things. Morgan went to blow out one of the lanterns. "Please, leave it, Morgan. They're so pretty and give such a magical glow to everything. I think I will sit here and make a lasting memory. Thank you for your help," Carol said softly. Jim and Lalani said they would be in touch once they knew more. Shaking Jim's hand, Bill could see the concern on his face. In the dark, the last two carriages lowly headed down the road towards their homes.

By morning Bill and Carol received a special delivery letter.

Dear Mr. Olsen

A new location for the Oak Ridge dam has been determined. A new smaller dam will be built on the west edge of your property in the small canyon just beyond where the Kikilo Stream and Natoma Creek join. The engineers have determined that the size of the new dam and resulting reservoir will be able to provide the valley with a sufficient amount of water all year round and in the future as the demand grows.

We expect the construction of the new dam to take one year, with work beginning on June 20th. Therefore, according to your signed contract, we are giving you the one month notice, at which time we require you to vacate the property and there will be no leaseback period. Upon departure, the agreed sum will be deposited to your bank according to your instructions.

The project field foreman, Bob Hemstead, will be in Oak Ridge within the next few days and will contact you. Your sacrifice for the valley in providing your property is greatly appreciated.

Respectfully,

Jacob H. Neff,

Lt. Governor

"Bill, that can't be right. Our agreement was we could stay until the dam was half built. The Cosumnes dam was to give us four more years here. And now we have to be out in a month," Carol said, almost not able to get the last words out, because of the anger and sobs swelling up in her chest.

"Shh, Shh… you're right. We had an agreement 50%. With the smaller dam, it's not going to take as long, 50% will be built in seven or eight months, causing us to move sooner than planned. I'll go talk to Clay and see what can be done," Bill said, giving her a pat to her hand.

~~

That same morning, special delivery letters arrived at the Baker and Taylor ranches. Clay's shouts could be heard all the way to the barn. Morgan picked up the letter and read,

Dear Mr. Taylor

A new location for the Oak Ridge dam has been determined. A new smaller dam will be built on the west edge of the Olsen property in the small canyon just beyond where the Kikilo Stream and Natoma Creek join. The engineers have determined that the size of the new dam and resulting reservoir will be able to provide the valley with a sufficient amount of water all year round and in the future as the demand grows.

We expect the construction of the new dam to take one year, with work beginning on June 20th. The new dam location will only affect your west range during a brief six month construction time when water is diverted. We understand a narrow strip of land between the Olsen's ranch and Natoma Creek belongs to you. This property we will purchase from you at $3.60 an acre as we expect the new reservoir will reach that area.

The project field foreman, Bob Hemstead, will be in Oak Ridge within the next few days and will contact you regarding the transfer of title for the land. Your sacrifice for the valley in providing the small lot is greatly appreciated.

Respectfully,

Jacob H. Neff,

Lt. Governor

Before Clay was done fuming, Jim, Lalani and Bill had arrived with their letters in hand. Jim's letter was similar to Clay's, but indicated the land north of the Natoma Creek to the ridge line and from their east and west boundary line. It was basically all of the south grazing land, currently where his herd was.

Once Clay finished reading Jim's letter, Jim burst out, "They think the new dam and reservoir is going to take up the entire Olsen ranch and spill over into ours. Is that possible? Does the Kikilo bring that much water?"

"I suspect over time it could. Depends on the demands for water use," Clay said.

"We never thought the reservoir would cover the house and barn," Bill added. "The original dam site was so far southwest they told us it wouldn't affect the house, just all our range land. Carol's devastated with the thought of the house being destroyed. My father built that house, and our girls have grown up in it."

"The letter sounds like we have already accepted their offer, and it's a done deal. They need to think again," Jim shot back.

Hearing that the reservoir could take up the Circle K, and Jim's anger at this news, Lalani, stunned and not wanting to hear more bad news, took the baby and went upstairs and joined Kate.

Kate told her they had sent a telegram to Eric early that morning, and he would be there on the 1:00 o'clock train. Until they had his advice, they shouldn't give up hope. Kate wasn't going to get upset. But she could see the shock on Lalani's face and knew she was already upset and losing hope. *I feel guilty, it's not our land that will be under water*

now, only hers and the Olsens. I wish I knew what was actually going to hap-
pen and what to say.

Kate tried to reassure Lalani, pointing out again how things had a way of working out for the better. Lalani was calm and knew she would be alright. It was the others, Jim and the Olsens who she was most concerned about. They sat quietly talking about how to help Carol Olsen. That having to pack everything up in a month was going to be difficult and watching the house slowly disappear underwater would be unbearable. Downstairs they could hear Clay's voice rise in disgust from time to time. After about an hour, Bill left, and Clay and Jim joined the ladies upstairs.

"Well, did you get out all your concerns and anger?" Kate said, turning to Clay. Disappointedly, he said, "It's such a mess. There has been talk about a dam in the valley since I was a kid and we need it. I just didn't think it would affect our good friends," and looking at Lalani, added, "and family."

"Have you worked out what we should do?" Lalani asked, looking at Jim.

"Not specifically. We can hold out until we see what the reservoir does. I want to hear what actions Eric thinks we should take," Jim said, now calmer.

Miranda came up and said dinner was on the table, and they should all come and eat. Kate and Lalani tried to keep the conversation on horses and cattle, to keep Jim and Clay from rehashing the earlier conversations. Matthew's asking for more was about the loudest voice heard during the meal.

As Jim and Lalani were just about to leave and heading for the door, Eric came in with his case in hand. "Good you're all here," he said as he shook Jim's hand and gave Lalani a kiss to the cheek.

Before he could settle, they were all in the study asking questions. "Hold on," Eric commanded. "First off, the dam's foreman, Bob Hemstead, was on the train with me and filled me in on their plans. He seems like a reasonable man."

"That's good," Lalani noted.

"But what are their plans?" Clay asked impatiently.

Eric explained the dam would be about eighty feet tall and span the two hundred and fifty yards across the narrow canyon. But it would be made of a new type of concrete, stronger and last longer than an earthen dam. The work crews would be arriving next week, once Hemstead and an engineer by the name of Sam Eastman finished surveying the area.

Clay asked why they were taking possession of Bill's place within 30 days and not giving him until the dam was 50% complete per his agreement, and didn't that violate his contract, so he didn't have to comply? Could he fight it? "Having to vacate now, he can't sell off his cattle. Can't they wait at least until fall for the cattle market to open? "

"It does violate his current contract. But it would cause such upheaval with all the ranchers and valley farmers, Bill refusing to sell would cause a lot of anger and danger for him and the girls. He could renegotiate the contract and insist on a six or seven month escrow, but he wouldn't get the price the current contract offers. A price they are still holding to, I might add."

Clay ran his hands through his hair, not knowing what to tell Bill now.

"Look, I might be able to negotiate a deal where they allow him to leave the cattle on the north range until market. But my understanding is they want the house and barn for the foreman and equipment storage. I can talk to Bob Hemstead and see if he can hold off for sixty days at least," Eric finally offered.

"That would be helpful. You think they will go for it? And what about our south range? Do you know when they want it? Can we prevent them from taking it? " Jim asked, as he held Lalani's hand.

"I wish I could answer that, but until I know more, I won't know how to proceed. My best guess is they want the land for spring overflow. They shouldn't need your land for some time. You should be able to negotiate selling after fall roundup, " Eric said, trying to give them something positive.

~~

Eric stayed in town for the next week, talking with the Bureau of Land Management, Natoma Co. (in charge of the project), and Bob Hemstead. He was able to negotiate a leaseback of Bill's north hayfield and pasture for a dollar a day until the cattle market opened the end of September. It would cost him $120, but he still had to vacate the house in 30 days. They wanted it for the foreman, and the barns to store the concrete coming in on the train cars.

Bob Hemstead called on Lalani and Jim towards the end of the week, after having negotiated with Eric about the Olsen contract. His offer now was for $3.40 an acre for four hundred acres, the length of their south boundary. But they would not have to remove the live-stock until October 1st, but again a leaseback of one dollar a day would be required. They wanted to take possession of the land as of July 15th.

Jim was dismayed, "$3.40 an acre! Why the change? The Olsens are getting $3.60. Our land is just as good and it's our livelihood you're taking away as well," Jim said rather angrily. He also didn't understand the timing of July 15th. Mr. Hemstead agreed with his concern over the pricing and explained the July 15th date. They had plans to divert Natoma creek. It would not run down through the Baker property, but would be diverted across to the Olsen's upper acreage.

"Why?" asked Jim in an argumentative tone. "The creek is the only source of water for the ranch."

Mr. Hemstead explained that the new dam's north ridge tapers off as the Natoma Creek joins the Kikilo. "We want to redirect the Natoma so that it enters the reservoir from the north and not join up with the Kikilo. This will prevent heavy spring runoffs from caus-ing the combined water to overflow the lower ridge. They will divert the Kikilo temporarily at that point, while the dam is being built. Af-terward, the gap will be filled." Experience had shown Mr. Hemstead that dirt filled areas were not as strong as undisturbed natural barriers, therefore, the need to divert Natoma Creek at the top.

"It's unacceptable. First the price, and now the water, " Jim shook his head, amazed at the state's gall.

Mr. Hemstead felt bad for Jim and understood his frustration. "Let me see what I can do, I can't promise both, but they might give in on one area, if the cost isn't too great."

"In reality, Mr. Hemstead, the water being diverted is much more a concern than the price," Jim stated. *I probably shouldn't have told him that, they may try to lower the price in compensation for the water.*

Jim told him they would need time to think about the offer, and what it would mean for their livelihood in the future. "Don't take too much time. This offer is only good for the next five days. I'll talk to them about your concerns, but no promises," Mr. Hemstead said with urgency.

Jim let Evan handle the ranch chores that day and spent the rest of the day with Lalani. They had a lot to decide. "Lalani, you do understand that diverting Natoma Creek means they are taking our water. We won't have the land needed to raise cattle, and in the hot summer months we may have to haul in water if the well goes dry."

"So, we don't sell. They will just have to deal with the creek where it joins the Kikilo," Lalani said.

"I'm not sure they will let us. Right now, they are willing to buy the land and the water rights that go with it. But if we refuse, they can go to court and get a writ of eminent domain, where they can just come in and take the land and give us whatever they want for it, even fifty cents an acre," Jim explained.

"That's not right, it's unfair. So not agreeing is not the answer. Can we get them to divert the creek halfway down the south boundary?"

"We can try, but the most economical point is as it comes onto our property, further down the bank's rise, and it will be more costly. Considering budget is a big factor to this project, I don't see them giving in. But we can ask," Jim said.

"And the house and barn, they won't try to take them?" Lalani said.

"No, the ridge between the house and south pasture is too high. I'm pretty sure the reservoir won't get that high. We might end up with a lake view though," he said with a slight laugh.

"It's not funny. More importantly what about your, ...no, our dream of having a cattle ranch? Without the south pasture and water that's impossible," Lalani replied in a serious manner.

"Sweetheart, as long as we're together, we will have *Kālua 'ana*. We can keep a couple of heifers, and I can continue to work for Kate with the horses. We'll be fine."

"Jim, you can't work with the horses forever and..." Jim put his finger to her lip before she could say more. "As long as you want to stay at *Kālua 'ana,* this is where we will stay. We have enough money to retire, if you don't mind me mooching off your inheritance," he said halfheartedly.

"For now, let's see if Eric can get them to postpone diverting the creek or at least do it further down so we have some water. I think we need to see how we can help Carol and Bill at this point. They have nowhere to go and have so much to pack up and sell in the next thirty days."

"You're right. Carol must be overwrought." Lalani stood, nodding her head, and patted Jim's hand, then reached for a pan to begin dinner. *We have so much to decide. Can I ask Jim to stay here and give up his dream. Should we find another small ranch? What are we to do? .... For this moment, you need to concentrate on dinner. At least Evan will be hungry, I'm not sure I can eat.*

For the next few days, they tried not to think about the dam and decisions, trying to wait to see what Eric could work out. Lalani went to Carol's and helped her sort out and pack things. The Olsens had found a temporary house on the edge of town to stay at, until the herd was sold, and they could find a permanent place.

When Jim went to town for supplies, he was confronted by several ranchers. "Jim, what are you waiting for? Sign the contract so the dam can get underway. You can't hold it up and keep the stream. That water belongs to all of us. You best get on with it or you never know what will happen." Walt Basking went as far to threaten, "A barn may just happen to go up in flames one night."

Later that day, Walt rode into the Circle K and threw a rock at the front door and rode off. Fortunately, it missed the glass and bounced off. Lalani, hearing the bang, found the rock and a note attached.

If you want water, go back to Hawaii, there's plenty water there.

Jim was furious and took the note to the sheriff. He was concerned but didn't have the men to watch over the Circle K. If things escalated, he would do what he could.

The last thing Jim was going to stand for was Lalani, Shannon, or Evan being in danger. Neither Jim nor Lalani wanted to hold up the reservoir that would provide water year round, but threats were not going to be the basis for their decision. Jim had seen range wars over water in his younger days and knew people who were killed because of it. From then on Jim made sure either he or Evan was at *Kālua 'ana* with Lalani at all times. He had a mind to put Makana in the barn at night to warn off any unwanted visitors. But Lalani assured him Evan in the bunkhouse would hear if someone approached. Plus, Medianoche would get riled up and whinny out a warning.

The day before the first offer would expire, Jim and Lalani had supper at the Taylors. Lalani told them how Jim had been threatened, and that several times that week, strange riders had come up to the barn, but Evan turned them away. Eric regrettably informed them he had not been able to get Hemstead to change the point of diverting the Natoma. There just wasn't enough money.

They talked about the situation for a little longer and then let it drop. Jim took Lalani out onto the patio after supper while dishes were cleared and Eric, Clay and Morgan had a smoke. Once they saw everyone was gathered in the parlor, they came in and joined them.

"Well," Miranda said, "Looks like you two have made a decision."

"I think so," Lalani said softly and looked at Jim.

"We will go ahead and sign the darn contract. We don't want any range wars breaking out or losing good friends over this. I'll do as Bill did, pay the lease for the land and sell the herd come fall. Then we will decide what to do," Jim said soberly.

"At least we have *Kālua 'ana* and our own savings," Lalani added. "Now, who's in for a game of poker? If we're going to gamble on life, we might as well play the game."

Kate looked at her as if she was crazy, but then realized she knew it would take their mind off tomorrow and signing. Lalani bet wildly but managed to come out ahead, while Morgan lost everything quickly. Eric and Miranda sat and watched. Finally, by eight o'clock Shannon began to fuss as it was her bed time, and they said their good nights. Eric said he'd go with them to see Hemstead and make sure the contract was as agreed.

That night in bed, Lalani snuggled up to Jim, trying to make him feel better about what was about to happen. "How about we take a long ride around the ranch tomorrow? I'll ride Genevieve, and you can show me all the little hidden places before they disappear underwater," Lalani said. "I think I am going to miss those little calves."

Jim gave her a tight hug, "That would be nice. A last look around. If you do miss the calves, we can always go to Oahu and visit the calves at the Crocker ranch. You know, you should give it your own name, Horace won't mind," he added.

Lalani didn't respond, but listened to Jim's heart beat as her head lay on his chest. She could feel the despair within him. *We can't give up on everything. Jim's right, we do still have the herd on Oahu. At least that's something.*

15

What's Next?

The contract had been signed, and the south pasture would no longer be theirs as of July 15, 1895. It had been a week since they had made the decision. Now it was a clear pleasant morning, and Lalani told Jim to saddle Genevieve, that today was the day to say good bye. Jim helped her and then mounted Buck, and Evan handed him Shannon. Jim wanted her to see the place, even though she was only one and a half and would be too little to remember. *I want to share it with both my girls. To share the dream that might have been.* They rode quietly out towards the southwest boundary, through the trees. The grasses had grown back thick from where the fire had burned. He pointed out a large pine where a flicker had made a hole for her nest. They wandered down along the stream to the big water pool below the large flat rocks and dismounted. Here Lalani had brought Shannon last August when it was so hot. They sat and let her splash in the water, watching her laugh and giggle, making a lasting memory.

Lalani wanted to see where they wanted to divert the creek. They rode east along the creek, coming across Kieran standing in a grassy patch. "Kieran, where will we keep Kieran? We can't sell him," Lalani said emotionally.

"If we keep him, we will have to bring him up to the north pasture. You will have to see him every day. But if we don't have room for a large herd, I'm not sure we should keep him for just two or three heifers."

Lalani could hear the defeat in his voice. "Of course, we will keep him. Don't you dare sell him," she said vehemently. Jim smiled and shook his head. *Well, what do you know, she sure is attached for one who is so afraid of him.* They continued onto the spot Hemstead had indicated the blasting would occur. They would blast to lower the bank and then dig out about fifty feet until it reached the downhill grade. "And how far to our east boundary?" Lalani asked.

"See those trees, see the big oak, it marks the southeast corner."

Lalani kicked Genevieve up to a trot and stopped at the tree. She swung her leg over and held onto the saddle horn until her feet and skirt were free and she could drop to the ground. Jim came riding up with Shannon and dismounted. "What? What are you doing?"

"Jim, do you have your pocket knife?"

"Sure!" He put Shannon down and pulled out his knife and started to hand it to Lalani.

"No, you need to do it. I want you to carve 'The Baker Ranch lies before you', so people when they come to the reservoir will know who made the sacrifice."

Jim looked at her, and smiled. He found a large area where the bark had already been removed by an elk rubbing its antlers and began to carve. Shannon walked around, picking up small pinecones and putting them in her mouth only to be pricked by the scales and then spitting them out. Jim finished carving and put a heart around it. To fit the space, he put -

Baker Ranch

lays ahead

J + L

"Perfect, now Shannon can come back someday and find it," Lalani said.

They mounted again and just sat looking at the land spread out before them. "It is a pretty piece of earth. Poor mother nature has had so much taken from her. One of these days she is going to complain and take it all back. You'll see, she will shake the earth so hard the dam will break, and the water will flow out and she will have her fields again," Lalani smiled.

They made their way past the hay and alfalfa fields that were fenced off to keep the cattle out. "I guess come August I can pull this fence down and just let the cattle eat as much as they can. Next year, this will be underwater," Jim said halfheartedly.

They rode slowly back through the south range past the cattle standing here and there, as they headed back to the house. Jim stopped at a large oak in the middle of the pasture, and pointed to a hole just to the left. "That's the bunny hole. I have spotted baby bunnies every spring darting back to that hole. And on several late afternoons, a large horned owl sits on that branch just waiting."

"Oh, Jim, how sad," Lalani said.

"No, No. We need the owl otherwise we would be overrun by rabbits. And it's here I have caught the rabbits for your stew," he grinned.

Lalani smirked and nodded her head, then gave her horse a kick, and they continued on to the barn. "I'm glad I saw it all before it was gone. Thank you for showing me all its secrets."

The next week, there was an auction at the Olsen Ranch. Farm equipment was auctioned off. The draft horses had been sold to a farmer down valley. Household items were also auctioned off. Bob Hemstead bought the milk cow, and the hens so he could have fresh eggs. Bill kept his horse and the carriage and a horse for Carol and the girls. It was a sad day. Lalani bought one of Carol's quilts she couldn't take and Kate bought Bill's extra handmade bridles. Clay bought the branding equipment, buckets and other items for the barn.

The following day, Jim and Clay brought the work wagons to help move items to the new house and Lalani and Miranda brought food. Finally, everything was moved, and one by one people departed, leaving Bill and Carol and girls alone to say good bye.

Lalani and Jim returned home and stood on the porch, and knew Bob Hemstead would be there tomorrow with the signed contract and a check for the south pasture. "At least we will still have *Kālua 'ana,*"

Jim said putting his arms around her and looking out at the north pasture and Lalani's two sheep.

Bob Hemstead came the next day and informed Jim and Lalani of the planned schedule for activities for the dam construction. He and Sam Eastman would survey and lay out where the dam foundations would be laid. The Kikilo canal would be blasted the next week, and the temporary redirect would begin. Then the following week, the concrete forms would begin to be built. Crews would be arriving within the week. Jim asked about the creek redirection and when it would begin. Bob wasn't sure, but said he would contact him in advance. For the next month, he felt nothing would infringe on them as the base camp was going to be along the Cosumnes near the old dam site.

Jim and Lalani appreciated the information, but were eager to be done with the dam activities and get back to living their life. Jim kept close watch on the cattle, and monitored the south boundary for workers that wandered through. Evan worked alongside Jim, handling the weaning of the new foals for Kate. Lalani's vegetable garden was well underway and beginning to produce. By the end of June, the alfalfa and hay fields were ready for harvesting. Jim and Evan headed out with the scythes to cut the first field, and within two weeks both fields were cut and drying. Back at the barn getting the baler ready, Evan asked if he would be needed come October and what he should do about work. "Evan, I don't want to lose you. I don't know how many head we will have, but I want to keep you with us, if you want to stay. You can always join me in working with Kate and her horses. I still would like to raise some cattle. Lalani and I need to figure things out yet. Do you want to stay?"

"Of course, I want to stay! But I also want to do a good day's work." Evan's youthful pride was peeking out.

Evan shook off his concerns, knowing they still wanted him there, and he and Jim got the hay and alfalfa baled by July. They continued to work and eat meals together without talking about the pending changes. One afternoon Lalani heard a large bang off in the distance and thought it was more blasting to create the diversion channel for the Kikilo. About twenty minutes later, Jim came storming into the kitchen and grabbed the rifle mounted by the door.

"Jim, what's happened?" Lalani snapped.

"They caused the cattle to stampede and two have tangled in the fence. I'm going to run off whoever set off that charge on the creek without warning." As he turned to go out the door, Evan came in and grabbed the rifle.

"Jim, the rifle will only get you killed," Evan argued back at him.

"Jim, Evan's right, please. Are the heifers badly hurt?" she asked.

"I don't know, I didn't stay long enough. I'm so mad at their irresponsibility," Jim bitterly admitted.

"They're hurt, but if we clean up the cuts, and infection doesn't set in, they will be okay," Evan interjected, "Jim, we need to get back to the heifers with bandages and get them to the barn. Not go after the damn workers."

Jim realized he had lost it and Evan was right. He begrudgingly put the rifle back and headed to the barn.

One two-year old heifer had a deep cut along her neck and was still bleeding when they returned. Jim immediately untangled her and began to stop the bleeding. The older heifer's leg was tangled in the lower wire, but she didn't try to pull away, and just stood looking at Evan as he cut her loose. Her cuts were minor, but she seemed to favor her leg. *I think she will be okay if we can get her back to the barn. I hope the other heifer doesn't go down.* Jim continued to bandage the two-year old. *This heifer is too young to be pregnant and could be used for meat if she doesn't make it. Still! This should have never happened. Hemstead said he would give us notice.*

Evan could see Jim getting mad again. "Jim, do I need to get the wagon? Can we get her on?" he asked, trying to distract Jim.

"No, let's see if she will walk back. Have you seen Kieran?" Jim asked.

"Yes, he's fine. He's over just on the other side of those heifers there," pointing to the small group of cattle standing just to their left.

Slowly they walked the heifers to the barn. Lalani saw them coming and came with warm water and alcohol to clean the wounds. The two-year old had gone down, exhausted from the walk and loss of blood. Jim was examining the other heifer's leg when they heard a rider. Evan went to the door to see Bob Hemstead trotting up and dismount.

"Jim, it's Hemstead," Evan said leerily.

Jim got up and pushed past Evan and Lalani and walked up to Hemstead and without a word, sent a pounding blow to his jaw. Hemstead stumbled back, but didn't go down. Jim stepped up to strike again when Lalani grabbed his arm. Hemstead put up his hand to catch the next blow.

"Jim, stop!" Lalani yelled.

Jim's fist went down, and he stood there glaring at Hemstead, now holding his jaw.

"I already passed that blow onto the idiot that didn't follow directions. How bad is it?" Bob asked.

Jim didn't expect this statement and stood sizing Hemstead up. *Hemstead had been a decent man up to this point and he's here asking how bad.* "You didn't authorize the blast at the creek?" Jim finally said.

"Only after you were notified and the cattle were out of the area," he replied. "I had to go to town to receive supplies. I left instructions to tell you we would be blasting late this afternoon. I hoped that would give you enough time to move cattle as they had been grazing near the blast sight yesterday. My irresponsible crew chief didn't want to have to work up until after dark, so went ahead and set the blast. 'Said it would take too much time to notify you and let you move a bunch of mangy cows.' That's when I hit him, hopefully as hard as you hit me, and then fired him."

Jim could see the earnest regret from Hemstead.

"Mr. Hemstead, sounds like you have had experience with cattle," Lalani commented.

"My father had a small ranch, similar to this one. He wanted me to take over, but I wanted to be an engineer instead. I assume the herd stampeded when the blast went off."

"Yes, they did," Jim said sternly, but without anger. "You asked how bad, come see for yourself."

Jim led Hemstead into the barn, while Lalani went back to the house to set coffee going, hoping the two men would sit down and come to an understanding.

Hemstead and Jim did come and have coffee. "Please, call me Bob, and I assure you the company will pay for the loss of the heifer. I am a man of my word, and I expect my instructions to be followed. I ride my crew hard, but treat them fairly. I find you can get more done with respect than bullying."

Jim was beginning to like this man more than he wanted to. Bob explained the need to start the digging of the channel for the creek, but he had intended to start on the downhill side and not the creek bed, waiting until the end of September to make the final break-through to divert the creek. "Jim, I understand you need the water for the cattle until you can sell them. I plan to keep my word. But come October 1st, the creek will be diverted."

Jim didn't have trouble with Bob and his crew after that. The dynamiting continued for another week, but only down by the dam for its bypass canal. The young heifer did not survive and Jim sold it to the dam camp chief for full price. As the summer wore on, Lalani could see Jim becoming more disturbed, snapping at Makana for the littlest thing or not as patient with Evan and Shannon. She also noticed he would have a second whisky whenever they were at Kate's. She worried what would happen once the cattle were sold. They needed to figure out what they were going to do.

August came and Jim and Evan went and pulled down the fence between the hay field and the south pasture, but decided to go ahead and let the alfalfa grow for another two weeks, and then cut it to be stored for Kate's horses. Lalani took Shannon out to the creek rock pool and spent time playing with her in the water and enjoying the lovely spot while they could. After the water play, Shannon curled up on the blanket under the trees and fell asleep. Lalani sat next to her, watching the water flow slowly over the rocks, contemplating what to do about the ranch. *Will Jim be happy without being able to work the fields or taking care of the cattle? He's not going to take care of my two sheep, that's for sure. I just don't believe he will be happy working for Kate for the rest of his life. What is it that we need to do? What will keep us happy? Do we bring the horses back to the north pasture and raise horses? Lalani, be honest, you were quite happy to see the horses go. Bringing them back still doesn't mean Jim's his own boss. He will still be working for Kate. I love her dearly, but we need to make our own livelihood. Jim needs to be able to create our own ranch again. But that means giving up Kālua 'ana. Can I do that?*

Lose my home. Home --- you have had so many homes, when you think of going home, where is that? Certainly not London, or the Crocker or Shaw houses in Boston. Kālua 'ana is the closest thing next to the Crocker house in Honolulu. I guess if I look back that was home. I was happy there. Mother was there, friends were there. I even have friends there now. I guess I could even say I have a home there now. A very rundown overgrown home. But it is mine. There are cattle there too. Lalani's thoughts were interrupted by Shannon's wiggling and waking noises. "Hey, sleepyhead, we had best get back to daddy and make his supper."

Jim was in a troubled mood that evening. He didn't yell or complain, but there was just a quiet uneasiness about him. Time for selling of the herd was quickly approaching. He had decided to sell the breeding heifers when the cattle market opened. They had twenty-one high quality heifers, and he felt they would fetch a good price. The auction for breeding heifers was always at the first week of October, then dairy and beef the last week.

"Evan and I are going to pull Kieran, Agnes and Blanche up to the north pasture this week. I'm keeping Agnes our first heifer. She has produced twins twice now. Blanche is my favorite and I can't sell her. She just has a sweet disposition and comes whenever I'm around."

"That's fine, Jim. We can still sell the calves each year. And it will keep Kieran viable. What about Bill, is he going to sell his heifers?"

"He says no, just going to sell them as beef along with the calves."

"We only have thirty calves, twenty from this year and ten from last, so I'll talk to Clay about running them in with his and taking them to market for us. The larger herds get a better price than the small independent ranches like us. They will all be gone within the month," Jim lamented.

"Then what do you want to do, Jim? Retire and just raise the two head?" Lalani innocently asked.

"Retire! You think I'm old and done and ready to be put out too," Jim snapped back.

"Jim, I… I didn't mean it that way. We just need to figure out what we want to do, what you want to do, that's all," Lalani said meekly.

Jim came over and sat next to her on the sofa, "I'm sorry. It's just hard to give up a dream, especially just as it was beginning to really grow."

Lalani put her head on his shoulder wanting to say something about the Oahu ranch, but not sure that she was ready to give up *Kālua 'ana*.

Just say it, just ask him what he thinks about the idea of moving to Oahu. Doesn't mean you will. He may hate the idea, he's lived in California all his life. Just forget it…

Jim could tell she was thinking about something. She was too quiet. "What is it, Lalani, what else is on your mind?"

Now she was trapped, *Am I ready to ask him my question. Am I ready to answer it myself? You've got to say something.* "Jim, what do you think about the ranch on Oahu?" she blurted out.

"The Crocker Ranch?" he asked.

"Yes."

"I hadn't given it much thought, knowing you didn't want to give up here, or move away from Kate," he said, now curious as to why she asked.

"What if I did? I'm not saying I definitely want to, but just say we did move to the ranch on Oahu," she said tentatively.

Jim pulled back and looked at her, not quite sure what to say. "Well, it would need a lot of work, and I mean a lot of work to get that house livable."

"Yes, I agree, but would you be happy raising the cattle there and living on an island where it rains half of the time and never really dries out. Would you be happy leaving California?"

Jim sat for a moment thinking. *I love the idea of building up the old ranch. But can I live where it rains half the time and in the middle of nowhere. I could live in the middle of nowhere, but could she?* "Uh… restoring the old ranch and making it ours, is very appealing. I don't know about the rain part. As for living in the middle of nowhere? I'll live wherever you are, as long as we're together. I could live on an island and be a cattle rancher. The question is, could you? You have lived in bustling cities all your life."

"You call Oak Ridge a bustling city?" Lalani smirked back at him. "It's just an idea that has been in my mind for the last several days. I just wanted to know what you thought about it. That's all," Lalani said, not wanting to commit to the idea she herself was unsure of.

Jim pulled her close, "I think it's an idea, but let's sleep on it for now. You're not going to want to leave Kate now that the baby is due in the next week or two. She's going to need you. You know that baby is going to come right in the middle of Clay's roundup."

Lalani laughed, "I think you're right about that."

~~

Evan and Jim moved Kieran, Agnes and Blanche to the north pasture. Kieran wasn't too pleased with the sheep, and charged them every time they came near. The third week of September, Jim and Evan rounded up the heifers and made arrangements for a pen at the

Oakland stockyard. Morgan came and helped drive them up through town to the rail pens and load them onto the cattle car. As expected, Jim did get a good price for them, almost a thousand dollars. Evan and Jim only spent two days at the auction and then returned home and drove the calves to join the Taylor herd.

On October 2nd, Jim rode out to the south pasture now empty of livestock. The creek still had some water, but would soon be dry. He came back to the house in a melancholy mood and stood on the porch looking out at Kieran and the two heifers. *Well, Baker, you're back where you started: a bull and two heifers. The dream for this ranch is no longer. Is it in you to start again and in Oahu?* He just stared at the pasture, his mind now a blank.

The next day, Hemstead sent word they would start blasting the final part of the Natoma canal. Jim's mood turned worse at the thought of the creek going dry. The dam's foundation had been poured, and its thick walls were beginning to rise. Natoma's water would not reach the dam for another month or two, depending on the winter rains. It would fill the upper shallow basin first and then spill over towards the dam. Bob's plan was to have the first thirty feet complete and continue to build upward from the dry side of the dam.

Evan went and helped Morgan and Clay with rounding up their herd. It would take a week or more to comb the back hills and sort out the breeding stock from the beef stock. Jim joined the round up on the third day, but he was cantankerous and impatient with the other ranch hands that went after the calf he was chasing.

Meanwhile, Lalani came and spent the days with Kate, very pregnant and ready. About two days before the end of roundup, Kate went into labor. This time was much shorter, and Clay and Doc Newell arrived thirty minutes before the baby. Another healthy baby boy was born at 4:58 pm October 18th . Clay stayed with Kate the next day, but then was needed to help load the large herd onto the cattle cars.

Clay and the other men would be gone for three or four days. Jim had originally planned to go too, but Clay asked him to stay. "I'll make sure we get a good price for the calves. You just take good care of my filly and colt." Kate was not amused about the comparison.

Kate wanted to give the baby a name before Clay left, so while he was packing a few things he stopped, picked up his new son and held him, looking at his little face. "Well, we had Andrew and Jackson picked out. I'm thinking he acts more like an Andrew than a Jackson."

"Andrew Michael Taylor. Andy! Andy and Matt. I like that," Kate said smiling.

"Andy, Matt and Shay Shay," Clay chuckled, giving him back to his mother. Then reaching for the birth certificate Doc Newell left, he wrote Andrew Michael Taylor. "Now it's official." He reached over and kissed Andrew gently on his tiny forehead and Kate on the lips and whispered, "I've got to go, but I'll be back in four days, and I'll be all yours. I love you and thank you for giving me another beautiful son."

"You're welcome. Make sure you say good bye to Matthew, he's going to feel a little left out."

"I will." And Clay shut the door and was gone.

Lalani kept Kate company the next day and Matt was happy to have Shannon as a playmate. Shay Shay followed him around, and he dressed her up in his cowboy hat and bandana and ran around the house, riding stick ponies. Shannon didn't ride hers, but dragged it behind her as she tried to keep up with Matthew.

Jim had no patience for a new baby's crying, let alone Shannon and Matthew's noise, and knew it was best to be out of the house. Lalani was beside herself, trying to deal with it all as she spent the next few days at Kate's, while Clay was away. Jim stayed back at *Kālua 'ana,* trying to keep himself busy with chores and the horses. This year's foals now needed to be weaned from their mothers, so he moved the mare and foals to the barn corral. Then one by one, he moved the three year olds to where the mares and foals had been in the northwest paddock. Finally, he took the mares from their foals into the adjacent southwest paddock. It had been a long day, and it was getting late, and he needed to fetch Lalani and Shannon.

Lalani stood by the piano looking out the window waiting for Jim to come and thinking about *Kālua 'ana* and Jim. *How am I going to get through all this? Jim's unhappy. He's not patient with Makana being underfoot or with Shannon's crying. I'm struggling with Kate's new baby bringing back memories of the loss of our first baby, which is still hard to understand why. And that I haven't gotten pregnant in the past two years. Is Shannon to be my only baby? We have worked so hard to make Kālua 'ana home, don't we deserve more than all the loss? My house is hau'oli 'ole, Not Happy!* Jim arrived at Kate's in a despondent mood, worn out from the day's work and his emotions. Neither of them knew how to console each other on the ride home or the next day.

Lalani was at Kate's when Clay and Morgan finally arrived home on the 25th. They had gotten a good price for the herd, $17.90 a head, thirty cents higher than last year. Clay was now ready to celebrate and spend time with his new son. Jim came mid-afternoon to pick up Lalani. He was still withdrawn and quiet.

Jim politely asked how it went, as Clay offered him the usual whiskey.

"Jim, we got a good price for the calves. And I heard the heifers sold for more than usual. You got a good deal on all of it," Clay said enthusiastically.

"Good deal? I'm not so sure losing your livelihood is a good deal," Jim grumbled as he gulped his drink down.

Lalani was tired and had had enough, then she stood up speaking sternly, "Jim, that's enough. We haven't lost everything. We can start over. We have been fortunate to have good friends and family. I, for one, am grateful and you should be too, for all the help from Clay, Morgan, and Evan." The room went silent, and now no one knew what to say.

Morgan reached over and put his hand on Jim's shoulder. "Give it time, we've been here before. Remember the Edmond's ranch when it went up in smoke. They started over and have a good spread now."

Morgan and Jim had been ranch hands way before either of them came to the Taylor ranch. Jim thought about that disastrous day when the Edmond's house and cattle were caught up in a furious fire that swept through. They had nothing. *At least we have a house and three head. They lost their oldest son too. Such a loss. Lalani knows that loss. She must be hurting too, being around a new baby again.* Jim got up and walked over to Lalani, "I'm so sorry," and kissed her on the top of her head. "Sorry, everyone. I am grateful. It was a successful drive, and we did get a good price. I guess that is something to celebrate." Jim reached over and picked up his empty glass of whisky, "Here's to new beginnings."

Jim was better after that. He had never seen Lalani get that mad at him. Maybe perturbed, but not mad. He and Evan checked the fence line of the old north boundary of the south pasture. This was now the new property southern boundary. They pulled some of the posts from the alfalfa field, since the fence was no longer needed to protect the field from cattle.

"Jim, aren't we going to need some source of hay for Kieran and the heifers? You don't want to be buying hay each winter," Evan said, as he pulled the last post from the alfalfa field.

"Sounds about right, we need to still grow some hay," Jim agreed.

"You know, there's a small field east of the house that has never been used," Evan pointed out.

"That's only about five acres, but it could produce around a hundred, maybe hundred and twenty bales of hay. That's not a bad idea. I bet if we start now, we could clear the field and turn the soil before the ground hardens. Hank Swensen might just have some hay seed left over from last spring." Jim stood for moment thinking. "See, Evan, this is why we still need you here. Let's get these posts to that field and take a look."

Lalani was thrilled to see the men had a project to keep them busy, but was it going to be enough? What next, after it was planted? While the men worked on the field, her thought turned to Shannon's second birthday coming up. Shannon was now talking in short sentences and helping mommy feed the chickens. Lalani wanted something to celebrate after all they had been through.

She went and saw Kate and asked if they could throw the "end of roundup" dance at their place and celebrate Shannon's birthday earlier in the day.

"Lalani, that's a great idea. I have been fretting on how to get everything organized here. I still don't have a lot of energy. Andrew is keeping us up at night, and Miranda is slowing down, too. Are you sure you're up for it?" Kate said with a concerned look.

"Yes. It's what Jim and I need right now. Jim and Evan need to stay busy. Cleaning out the barn and all will do the trick. "

"And after that, have you and Jim thought about what you're going to do?" Kate cautiously asked.

"No, not really. Jim was so emotionally tied up in selling of the cattle, it was hard to reach him as you saw. We can't stay at *Kālua 'ana* and raise cattle, there's no room. Jim's too young to retire, to sit back and do nothing. I know he can help you with the horses, but it's not the same as having your own place, being your own boss. Jim deserves to have that," Lalani said in a forlorn manner.

"You would leave *Kālua 'ana*?" Kate said with surprise.

"I don't know. I don't want to leave it. You and our friends are here. We haven't even looked for another small ranch close by. Don't you go fretting, you have enough in your hands with the boys, all four of them. When is Morgan going to propose to Amanda? Seems he's pretty serious about her," Lalani said, trying to change the subject.

~~

The Baker Ranch was a flurry of activities getting ready for the dance and Shannon's party.

The evening before the party, Lalani caught Jim standing looking out the window, toward the north pasture, watching the cattle. Lalani came up behind him and put her arms around him, in the same fashion he usually did to her. He reached around and pulled her to his side, still looking out. Quietly Lalani asked, "Okay, where are you, and what's on your mind?"

Jim looked down at her, and with a half-pursed lip smile, "The ranch on Oahu."

Lalani was surprised, since Jim seemed to be planning new projects around *Kālua 'ana*. "Really, I thought you and Evan were working on plans for *Kālua 'ana*. Can we talk about it? Oahu has been on my mind, too."

Jim stoked up the fire and then joined Lalani on the sofa. He was quiet for a moment. Lalani waited for him to go first. "I keep thinking about the land and cattle that are there. How we could build up that ranch. It already has a good foundation livestock wise, more than what we had here. But then I think of the house. That disastrous mess. It would need to be completely redone. Probably torn down to the foundation and started over. That would be costly. Then more importantly, there's taking you away from family."

Lalani reach over and put her finger on his lips.

"I've been thinking the same thing. You're right, the house needs to be completely overhauled. But we could redesign it into what we want and need. I've been fantasizing about building it and creating beautiful gardens around the house for Shannon to play in. Building a barn for the horses and watching you ride out to check on the cattle, like before."

"It would be costly to build a new house and barn. Everything would need to be shipped in. And what about Kate?"

"Not everything would need to be shipped. There are good koa trees on the property. They're tough to cut but make very sturdy houses. Leaving the people here is the problem. Yet, we have friends there: the Gilberts and Ladds, Lilpo, Kiana and Mora and the children. As for Kate, I love her dearly, but I love you and Shannon more. You're my family now. A big sister grows up and moves away eventually. I've just waited until I knew my little sister was woman enough to handle things. Kate's thirty and has Clay, as well as Miranda and Morgan. Kate and I need each other's love, but we no longer need to depend on each other for decisions. She will also have Amanda soon to help with things. You and I need to be able to stand on our own. Horace has given us that opportunity." Lalani stood and looked around the room. "I don't deny it will be very hard to leave. This has been my first true home. I can always buy passage and come visit. Kate for that matter needs to come to Oahu and see it. We can build our home there on the ranch." The more Lalani talked about it, the more she became convinced it was the right thing to do. *But is it what will truly make Jim happy?*

"Well, I think we should explore the potential. One other thing. Evan! I would want him to come with us, he's become like a son to me. We understand each other and work well together," Jim confessed.

"Of course, Evan will come. He's *hanai*. We Hawaiians are always adopting older children. He's already part of our family and should be living in the house with us, not in the bunkhouse. The question is, will he want to come?" Lalani deliberated.

Seeing the light come back into Jim's eyes made her realize this was their answer. "Now, Jim, don't get ahead of ourselves. I'm not going to want to leave until the new year. We have Shannon and Matthew's birthdays and Christmas and Kate's anniversary. I'm going to want to be here for all of them."

"No problem. It's going to take more than three months to design and order building materials for a house. There's lots to figure out. I think it best to keep it between us for now. We need to sleep on it and make sure this is what we want. If I can deal with all the rain."

They settled back together and watched the fire die out. There was suddenly lots to think about and to investigate, but first was the dance and Shannon's party to finish planning.

16

Sweet and Sad Times

The Fall dance went off without a hitch. Everyone was glad to see Jim back to his old content self. He played fiddle, danced with Lalani and held his daughter with pride, keeping her finger from the candles as everyone sang Happy Birthday. People asked him, "What's next?" and he simply said, "Sit on my porch and watch the water rise."

During that week, Jim wrote to Sam in Ahuimana about restoring the ranch and building a large house, inquiring about material availability and workers. Lalani also wrote to Elizabeth Gilbert to inquire if there were any small homes on the far eastside of Honolulu they could rent. They were eager to hear from Sam and Elizabeth, but they would have to be patient. Mail was slow between the island and mainland. The more they talked about Oahu, the more certain they were that it was what they should do – wanted to do. They just needed to figured out how much it would cost to do it, if they could afford to do it, and how to get things to Oahu. Jim quietly checked on various building materials, lumber, nails, fixtures and the like. Jim wanted Lalani to have all the modern fixtures such as flush toilets and the new Henry Ford coal burning stove in the new house. Until they heard back from Sam, it was a waiting game.

The next big hurdle was to tell Evan. Recently, he had been spending more time at the bunkhouse just sitting and whittling. Jim was concerned he might be considering finding another job. "Lalani, we need to tell Evan our plans and ask him to come tonight to supper. I think he's beginning to look for another job."

"No, no, we don't want him to do that," she quickly agreed. "I'll make his favorite, beef bites and dumplings."

That evening they sat down with Evan and told him their plans. How much they felt he was part of their family, like a son. How much they wanted him to come with them and be part of building the ranch."

Evan's first response was, "What! Hawaii?" But he sat quietly listening to their plans to build a large house enough for all of them and guests. A barn for the horses. Lalani talked about the deep vegetation and clearing it away from the house and creating a beautiful garden. Jim talked about increasing the herd that was there and bringing Kieran over as a second breeding bull. How they wanted him to be part of all of it.

Evan listened to the sound of their voices as they talked about him being a son, part of their family. His parents were gone, and his older sister was married and living in Omaha. He hadn't seen her in years, but wrote on rare occasions.

"Jim, Lalani, I love being here with you. But I've never been out of California, except for the two years on ship, and I quickly realized it wasn't for me. "

"I'm afraid we have to take a ship for eight days. It's the only way to get there," Lalani smiled. "But once there you will be on solid ground, and the cattle there are the same as here."

"Well, almost the same, they're red faced Angus instead of black. I do plan to bring in Black Angus, eventually," Jim announced, wanting to keep things honest.

"I have to warn you it does rain a lot, but it's warm rain. Ponchos are the required gear," Jim added, not wanting to sugarcoat things.

"We haven't told anyone yet. We're still seeing if it's possible, if I can leave here. But we don't want you leaving us, we would love for you to be part of building it. Creating a home for all of us. But it's your choice. A young man eventually has to make his own way. But perhaps this could be yours. Please, at least consider coming with us. If you want your own place, we can arrange that too." Lalani was almost pleading like a mother does.

Jim felt enough had been said, and Evan needed time to think it over. "Evan, we just want you know, we love you and want you to come and be part of it. But it's your decision, and we will respect whatever it might be and support it."

Evan nodded his head, "It's a lot to think about. But I'm glad you're happy. Can I let you know in the morning?"

"You can take more time than that. It's a big decision. How about a game of cribbage, for now?" Jim said, pulling the board out and giving him a fatherly pat to the shoulder.

The next morning at breakfast Evan had a slew of questions: What was the land like, would he be able to take his horse, were there girls there his age? One by one Jim and Lalani answered his questions as best they could. They could see Evan's concerns beginning to ease. By the next morning, he was on board, as long as Rusty his horse would come too. Lalani and Jim were elated. One hurdle down. Now how to tell Katherine.

They had letters back from Sam and Elizabeth. Sam was thrilled to hear they might come. In his letter he said the company that made the coral block foundation was still in business, and they told him several of the large homes in Honolulu had cost around five to ten thousand to build. Most building materials were available, but specialty tiles and fixtures would need to shipped from the mainland. It would cost them extra for hauling things to the ranch, considering where it was located. Sam also informed him that they got their water piped in from the river, which always had plenty. So, there was no need for a well.

Elizabeth was also excited to hear they were considering moving back to the island, and at the same time, sorry to hear about the state taking their land. Amos wrote 'that's not likely to happen here, too much water here.' Elizabeth thought living that far out of town might be lonely. At the moment, there weren't many three bedroom homes available, but she would keep her eyes open, and write her if something came available.

The news was encouraging. Jim wondered how they would light the house. He was sure the electrical lighting available in Honolulu would not be available to the ranch. He wanted to talk to Sam Eastman, the dam engineer, about it, as Sam had mentioned something called hydroelectricity.

Now that they had some answers that rebuilding the ranch was possible, they felt it was time to tell Kate. They wanted to wait until after Matthew's birthday, but there were so many details to take care of, they just didn't feel they could. Lalani invited Kate, Clay and Morgan to an early supper the first week of November. Kate knew something was up, and they only brought baby Andrew. Jim had cleaned up and met them in the parlor. When Kate heard the news, she was silent and tears came to her eyes. Lalani went to her and put her arm around her. "This doesn't mean we won't keep in touch. I'll write about all the details. You'll come and visit. We'll come back too."

Kate managed to say, "I knew something was happening. You both seemed happier since Shannon's party. I just thought you had found another small ranch in the valley. It never crossed my mind you would go home to Hawaii."

"Kate, it's time for me to go home. Horace knew I would someday and has left us the perfect place."

Jim had to laugh, "I wouldn't call it the perfect place, the house is in shambles, but the land is there for us to build on and the cattle are already there."

The five of them sat discussing all the pros and cons and details that needed to be worked out. The sun began to set and Kate was tired from all the emotions running through her: despair to be without Lalani, joy that they had a place to make their own, fear of losing her sister's advice, and others she couldn't even put into words in her mind. Clay and Morgan, of course, understood and were happy for Jim, offering to help with the move anyway they could.

That night both Lalani and Kate lay in bed in their husbands' arms, soft quiet tears slowly dropping as they realized there would soon be thousands of miles of ocean between them. They had shared everything together for the last sixteen years: the ups and downs of life, their secrets, and the intimacy they shared. Lalani would no longer be at the parties, holidays and children's births in the future. At moments, Kate sobbed.

It took Kate a few days to find herself and be happy for Lalani. Once she did, she knew the move was right for Lalani and Jim. Deep inside, she always knew big sisters eventually grow up and move away. It just took hers a little longer.

Matthew's third birthday came and went. Kate told Matthew Shay Shay would be moving, but he didn't really understand what that meant. Kate worried about how he would do when Shannon wasn't around. Lalani worried even more for Shannon, since she was an only child. "Matty" was her buddy. They spent two or three days together every week, and they ran to each other each time they met.

Both Lalani and Kate wanted this last Christmas to be extra special. Kate would host a big Christmas Eve party so everyone could say good-bye. Christmas morning would be at *Kālua 'ana* with just the Bakers, which included Evan. Then the Taylors would come and join them for turkey dinner.

Now that the herd was gone, and the hay fields no longer needing attending, Jim and Evan went through the ranch equipment and determined what would be cost effective to take, what to leave, and what to buy there. Shovels, picks, buckets and the like, they could get there for a fair price, plows maybe not. The one thing Jim was not willing to leave was the hay baler. It was his toy. It worked well and he wanted it. They took it apart and crated it for shipping. The big question was what to do with the equipment staying. Should they sell it or leave it for the next owners? *Who will take over the house and barn. We need to deed our remaining property back to Kate and Clay.* Jim decided to leave the equipment for the Taylors.

Lalani began to sort out the kitchen, getting rid of an old potato-ricer and a worn out butter churn. *The large waterpot will make a good packing crate to protect my good dishes.* She went through the house setting aside things that actually belonged to Kate, that she never took when she moved, and set them on the game table to return. She sat at the writing desk and rubbed her hand across the inlaid leather top. *This is Kate's too, but I just can't part with it. I will set it at the parlor window of the new house and write my weekly letter to Kate upon it, keeping us close.*

The final packing of house things wouldn't take place until the first week in January. Currently they had passage on a cargo steamer for the 10th of January. Not the finest accommodations, but the ship would take the three horses: Buck, Genevieve and Rusty. Lalani knew she would need her own horse to come and go to the ranch while the house was being built, and the only horse she felt comfortable around and safe on was Genevieve. One afternoon, Lalani got the courage up to ask Kate if she could take Genevieve with them. Kate was surprised but pleased that Lalani wanted her own horse. Kate was very fond of Genevieve, but seldom rode her. "On one condition," Kate said, "You go for a long ride with me to my favorite spots on the Taylor ranch before you leave. That way when I write that I'm sitting by the oak on the south ridge, you can envision me sitting there, or the poppies on the west hills."

"Since you put it for those reasons, I agree. It would be nice to be able to picture you in your favorite spots. I used to do that when you were at Larkbrook in England, sitting in the alcove window," Lalani said, taking Kate's hand and walking out to the barn to see Genevieve.

Sam wrote that he had already begun to clear the vegetation away from the house. Elizabeth had sent a letter saying that a very nice but small house with a carriage house would be available for rent the first of January. That it was on the far end of Queen Street. It was only a two bedroom, but the master had a large alcove area that could be used for Shannon. Jim and Lalani wrote immediately to snatch it up, so they would have some place when they arrived.

Late in the evening as Christmas approached Jim and Lalani would sit at the game table in the parlor and discuss and draw designs for their new house. Jim, Lalani and Evan all had slightly different ideas. But Jim knew it would be Lalani's plan that would actually be built. A fine two-story house with four or five rooms to accommodate overnight guests and two tub rooms. Not showy, but simple in an elegant manner, like its owners.

They would pull down the old structure to the foundational coral blocks. The original large room would become the parlor and entry with the stairs at the far end. The small bedroom on the back would be enlarged for a dining room with doors that looked out to the river. A den for Jim would be added downstairs and a new big kitchen and breakfast area in the back. Upstairs would have a small sitting room for Lalani and Jim with double doors leading to their master bedroom. Jim was definitely taking their big comfortable manly bed. There would be a door to their tub room and another to Shannon's room. Down the other side of the house would be three more rooms, one for Evan and two guest rooms. A second tub room would separate Evan's room from the guest rooms. Jim and Evan figured it would take them ten months to build, if the rains weren't too bad. Jim wanted to promise it would be built in time for next Christmas.

'That would be lovely, but don't promise. Hawaiian time moves a lot slower than mainland time," Lalani smiled.

Jim made arrangements for Clyde, the draft horse, to be shipped to them in February. Horses for heavy work were not available on the island. Lulu, Lalani's merino sheep, and Clyde would come together. Sassy would stay, and unfortunately eventually become mutton stew for the Taylors, but Kate wouldn't tell Lalani that.

Christmas arrived and Kate and Lalani agreed to wear the same color gemstone green dresses. Their dark skin and long black tresses created two images of radiant beauty. Jim and Clay watched the girls throughout the evening coming together and sharing past memories, being true sisters in every way.

Katherine played piano and Lalani sang, something she rarely did, but she had a lovely voice. The game of finding hidden treasures was a hit. Morgan and Amanda turned out to be excellent charade partners. By eleven o'clock, the guests began to depart. Lalani and Kate stood by the fire as it died out.

"This has truly been a magical evening. Thank you, Kate, for making it so. I will treasure it forever," Lalani said giving her a hug.

Jim came with her cloak and Evan bundled up a sleeping Shannon and they headed for home.

Christmas morning, Jim and Evan had cut a small evergreen and brought it inside. Lalani trimmed it with red ribbon, silver paper ornaments and the carved wood ornaments Evan had made. Lalani and Jim sat by the fire waiting for Shannon to wake, meanwhile Evan went to fetch more coffee.

"Well, my love, if it wasn't for this place, I may never have met you. I'm glad your graces and beauty needed my help with the rough and tough things."

"Me too! It's been a good first home to get my feet wet in."

"Ha, Ha!" Jim laughed, thinking back to that terrifying day when Lalani was stuck in the stream.

"But now it's time to let it go, to build bigger, better memories with you," Lalani declared. A small cry from upstairs came floating down. "Ah, sleepy head is awake." Lalani went up and got her from her crib. Evan came in with coffee and gave Shannon a kiss on the head. "Merry Christmas, baby sister," he said quietly but proudly.

They exchanged a few presents, nothing big this year. They took joy in seeing Shannon try to open her gifts. She seemed happier with the pretty colored paper than the rag doll. They sat drinking coffee and eating sweet rolls, content to linger, knowing it would be their last Christmas there.

By noon you could smell the turkey baking in the oven. Lalani had Shannon dressed in an elegant red velvet dress. "You know, that's not going to stay clean long," Evan said teasingly.

"I know, but I want the memory of it for today. Now come help me set the table before they get here."

All the Taylors arrived shortly after one o'clock, bearing gifts and food for the feast. Eric and Evelyn and their baby girl, now four months were there, too. Amanda again joined Morgan and the family. Miranda, the matriarch, sat at one end and Jim at the other.

Jim stood after everyone was seated, "Lalani and I want you all to know how special you all are to us. What a wonderful family you have made for us. That no matter where we are, San Francisco, Oak Ridge or Oahu, we will always be family and always be together in spirit. We cannot thank you enough for all you have done for us and the love you have given us.

We love you all." He took his glass of champagne and raised it, and the others followed. "To family!"

"Hear, Hear, to family," rang through the room.

It was a meal to be remembered, and they all sat and enjoyed it for several hours, talking and laughing about what was and what was to come. Finally, the dishes were cleared. The fathers took the children to the parlor to be entertained while the women cleared, washed and dried dishes. Miranda and Amanda were not needed, as there were already enough for cleanup. Evelyn shooed them out, now wanting to know more about Morgan and Amanda. "Well, has Morgan said anything about proposing? Seems those two are pretty cozy."

"Not a word to me," Kate admitted.

Lalani didn't say anything, but kept right on drying dishes.

"Lalani, what do you know? Morgan told Jim, and Jim told you, didn't he?" Kate queried.

"Maybe. Maybe, he has a little box in his pocket and plans to ask her a certain question, before taking her home to her folks this evening."

"Really?" Evelyn squealed.

"I knew it!" Kate said as Morgan came into the kitchen for coffee.

"Knew what?" He just looked at their faces and knew his secret was out and who had been told. "I knew Jim wouldn't keep it from you," as he looked at Lalani. "At least it didn't get out to Kate until now. Kate, don't go ruining this for me. Promise you won't say a word or a hint," Morgan said in his most serious voice.

"Does mother know?" Evelyn asked.

"Yes, but she can keep a secret. Kate can't."

"Alright, we promise," Kate said, knowing he was right that it was best she didn't know until now.

The afternoon went quickly. Jim played carols on his fiddle the best he could. Finally, Miranda said, "Morgan, it's getting late. You should be getting Amanda home to her folks."

"Yes, yes, Morgan, mother's right," Kate said quickly and received a staring glare back from him. Lalani and Jim waved good-bye as Morgan helped Amanda into the carriage. They then returned to the room buzzing about how he would do it and the date they would marry. They all looked to Jim as he came into the room. He walked over to the fireplace and leaned against the mantle, "He's got the ring in his pocket and will stop at the big oak before her folks. At least that's what he told me."

"When, When?" Kate wanted to know.

"When? Tonight, of course," Jim replied

"No, silly, when does he want the wedding?" Evelyn chimed in.

"Soon, maybe in March, before branding starts. It depends on Amanda and what kind of a wedding she wants," he said, rather perturbed. "That's all I know."

"And that he's had the ring for two weeks. A pretty pink diamond," Lalani added.

"You saw the ring?" Kate said. "And didn't tell me?"

Lalani looked at Kate, and didn't say a word. Kate already knew the answer to that. It had already been discussed. "I had hoped he would have proposed sooner. I'm afraid Jim and I will miss the wedding. Our passage is already booked, and with the horses, we can't change it now," Lalani sighed regrettably.

"Maybe they will get married on January 2nd with a justice of the peace. Then they would have the same anniversary, as Clay and I, and you wouldn't miss it," Kate suggested. "That way I could remind him of his anniversaries, and Amanda could remind Clay, and the men wouldn't miss them."

"When have I missed our anniversary?" Clay indignantly asked.

"Never my love, never," Kate smiled and gave him a kiss.

Christmas was now over, and Morgan was engaged. Lalani stood at the window of the parlor on New Year's morning. *Everyone will be okay. Everyone has the right person in their life and will be in the right place. Perhaps this little house should become Morgan and Amanda's first place.*

Jim came and joined her. "What you thinking about?"

"Oh, who should live here next. I thought maybe it could be Morgan and Amanda's first place."

Jim said he had already talked to Morgan about it. Morgan was definitely considering it. He knew he didn't want his own spread. The Taylor ranch was as much his as Clay's, and he like working alongside his big brother. He thought Amanda would like the house. They could add on if they wanted. It was still close to the ranch main house, but far enough away for privacy. It would depend on what Amanda wanted.

~~

The next week was crazy, with final packing, and getting Kieran, Agnes and Blanche up to the Taylor ranch. It was agreed they would put Kieran in with their heifers, any calves born the next fall would be sold and the profit would be split 50/50 – "No, 40/60. After all, you're doing all the work, Clay. Just keep him healthy until we're ready to have him shipped to us," Jim said, as he shut the corral gate behind the stately beast.

Sunday after church, Lalani and Katherine took the long ride as promised for a private good bye. They rode side by side, Kate showing Lalani her favorite oak tree for writing Jessie, and now it would be her. The spot along the river that was private where she would undress and go wading in hot August. The bluff overlooking the river and valley beyond, where she would sit and contemplate. Kate couldn't help but cry at each stop, but managed not to sob. "I so depend on you, Lalani. What am I going to do without you?"

"You will do what you have been doing these past three years married to Clay. Talk to him, confide in him and you will find all you need," and Lalani kissed her on her forehead. "Remember how we would wait for Jessie's letter to arrive when you were at school. Well, now, we will wait for each other's letters. Just promise you will write each month, not just at Christmas. When the house is built, you must promise to come for a visit. Perhaps for Christmas this year."

They sat and reminisced about all the things they had seen and done together. How Lalani was there for her during her marriage to William. And how Kate was there for her when Aunt Eunice had her dander up and treated Lalani worse than the dog. Kate always treated her like a lady – a best friend.

Early morning on January 10th, Jim and Evan were down at San Francisco's cargo docks with the horses and Makana, helping to load them on board the steamship *SS Georgic*. Lalani and Shannon stayed back with everyone at Eric's place until boarding later in the morning. Morgan and Amanda also came to see them off. Katherine knew she needed to be happy for Lalani and chattered away about the plans for the house and how wonderful it will be, once done. And once again she promised to come for Christmas.

Jim arrived back at the house to fetch Lalani and Shannon. They said their good byes to Eric and Evelyn. "You have the deed as we discussed," Lalani asked Eric, and he reached into a drawer and handed her the house deed now made out to Morgan. Morgan and Amanda stood in the doorway waiting to say good bye. Jim gave Morgan a final handshake and a manly hug. "Thank you for all you have done for us." Lalani went to Morgan and handed him the deed, "We're sorry we can't be there for the wedding. This is an early wedding present, but you will need to rename the house and we hope it brings you happiness." Lalani leaned in and gave him a big hug and whispered, "Take good care of her for me," as a tear swelled up. Morgan knew it wasn't Amanda she was referring to, but Kate. He handed Amanda the deed and with a big smile, "I will. I will take care of both of them. And thank you, I'll miss you," and then put his arm around Amanda.

Eric rented an English hack that was large enough to take Clay, Kate, Matthew, Jim, Lalani and Shannon to the ship. It was a cold foggy morning in the city. Everyone bundled up and off they went. "Just like London with Charles and Abigail," Lalani said, reminding Kate of old friends and good times. They arrived at the ship just before leaving in order to board quickly and avoid a long sorrowful good bye, as well as standing in the cold. Kisses and embracing hugs were shared, but very few words that would lead to tears. Matthew and Shannon didn't seem to know what was happening, they were only happy to be in their daddy's arms.

Lalani smiled and gave Kate one last embrace and kiss to the cheek and whispered, "I love you!" then turned and took Jim's arm and climbed up onto the boarding ramp. They made their way to Evan and Makana standing along the dockside rail.

Lalani now held her breath as she tried to hold back the tears, wanting to be released. She waved to Kate and Clay holding Matthew standing on the dock waving back. She could just hear Matthew's cry - "Shay, Shay!" just before the ship's whistle blew, causing Lalani to shiver. Jim held Shannon as she cried back "Matty...," now wanting to reach him. Evan said, "I'll take her to your cabin where she can be warm," and took her into his arms and held her tight as she continued to call for Matthew. Clay walked back to the hack with Matthew as he too continued to cry out for "Shay, Shay!"

Kate now stood alone on the dock but she didn't feel sad or alone, there was too much to be grateful for. Kate and Lalani stood waving as the tug boat pulled the ship away from the docks. Tears were no longer in their eyes. Only the cool mist of fog pressed again their faces. Lalani stood and watched until she couldn't see Kate's loving smile any more. *Towns may past and fade, but I'll always take the memories and people with me.* At last, Lalani turned to Jim, a calm smile in her eyes, she took a step toward the bow and snuggled into Jim's side for warmth and said "Let's go build a future." *... Let's go home!*

17

Epilogue

The *SS Georgic* steamed into Honolulu Harbor on the morning of January 17, 1896. The sun shone down through white billowy clouds in a clear blue sky. A small breeze blew, but the air was about seventy-two degrees. The town of Honolulu didn't look much different from when Jim and Lalani were there three years earlier. To their surprise, Elizabeth and Amos were at the dock to greet them. Both Jim and Evan were very glad to be back on solid ground. Shannon held onto her daddy with wide eyes. Amos took one look at her and melted, "She's adorable, looks just like you, Lalani."

Lalani disagreed, as Shannon's nose was not as flat and more like Jim's, and she had fairer skin than hers. Evan stayed behind to offload the horses. Amos said he would send a boy from the livery stable to help. "Can I ride Rusty to the hotel? Will they put him up?" asked Evan. Jim looked at Amos, "A boy and his horse. Yes!"

Jim had arranged rooms at the Royal Hotel for the next two nights until their things could be delivered to the rental house. Evan felt like royalty when he reached the nice room, just for him.

Elizabeth had arranged for a welcoming party the next evening: the Ladds, John & Maria, and their daughter, Megan and husband and granddaughter, Sarah. Lalani and Jim felt right at home with the group. This time, little was said about politics, rather they wanted to know all about the house they planned to build.

Lalani settled into the small house on Queen Street, not far from where she grew up. She and the young family that now lived in the house eventually became friends.

Jim and Evan immediately rode out to the ranch. With Sam and Kiana's help they laid out the plans for the new house. Kiana showed Jim where a good old grove of koa trees was on the ranch that could be used for the house. But first the foundation stones had to be purchased and set in place. Kiana insisted the house be raised off the ground, "That's how we do things here on the island, better air flow in the hot months." Lalani rode Genevieve out to see the old house, now cleared of vines. Jim had marked out the house layout on the ground. "It's facing the wrong way. The parlor needs to face down valley for the view, and the dining room, the river." Jim looked at her and frowned, "Lalani, you can't have the parlor facing the valley and the dining room the stream. They are next to each other. The dining room will face the short front wall, if the parlor faces the valley." Evan and Jim painstaking adjusted all the foundation stones so the parlor faced down valley, and the kitchen would view the stream.

Jim, Evan and Kiana spent the first weeks laying the foundation, grateful the rain only hit hard one afternoon. Clyde and Lulu arrived mid-February, and Jim was glad to have Clyde to help bring the heavy koa wood up to the local mill for cutting. Lulu was sent to the rental house and kept in the carriage house. The next several months would be spent cutting koa wood and creating the twenty-four-foot beams and posts for the exterior structure. Sam helped design the roof, so it would collect rain water and send it to a cistern stored on the roof. This allowed for running water to the tubs and flush toilets. The kitchen was piped with water from the river.

Smaller scrap pieces of koa wood were used for the interior lath walls. It was a shame to cover the beautiful wood with plaster. They left the thick header beam over the parlor entrance exposed, as well as the header beams for the windows. In the evening, Jim carved the large koa wood newel post for the base of the balustrade with lei leaves and plumeria. When the koa wood staircase was finished, it was gorgeous, a piece of art. Jim also carved the three fireplace mantles. Coral and shells graced the parlor mantle along with forest green tile for the hearth and surrounding the firebox opening. In the sitting room upstairs, the mantel had hibiscus and stephanotis flowers with coral tile, and for Evan's room the mantel had three running horses with a rich brown tile.

By October, the tile for the fireplaces and the new coal stove arrived. The finishing touches on the house were completed by mid-November, and Jim, Lalani, Shannon, now three years old, and Evan moved into *Mau Loa*. Over the front door in the beam Jim carved the words *Mau Loa* – Forever. This would be there home for the next thirty years. Lalani would create a magical garden of hibiscus, plumeria and other native flowers, where Makana and Shannon would run and play for hours. She would plant koa tree seedlings to replace the trees they had cut down, to give back to the land. Jim got his barn built and put in a hay field down valley by Christmas. The next summer he set up the hay baler and hooked up Clyde and was a happy man playing with his toy.

Kate, Clay and Matthew did come that first Christmas and fell in love with the house and the island. Jim was proud to show him his herd of Red Angus, at that time consisting of forty head and one ornery bull, which Jim named *hana-ino,* Hawaiian for ornery. Kieran was shipped to the island a year later, along with four Black Angus heifers. Over the years, the herd grew to a hundred and fifty Black Angus, but no more, as Lalani did not want to offend the land. As Honolulu grew with tourism, fresh beef was in demand, and the Bakers did quite well.

In 1898 the United State officially annexed Hawaii as a territory. Though Jim was not political, he had more rights to do business and trade than most Hawaiians. Jim, as a US citizen, also had more say in Hawaiian politics than Lalani as a native Hawaiian. Yet Jim supported John Kanekua's fight to reestablish the monarchy's rights and rights for the Hawaiian people. John was able to get Queen Lili'uokalani released from house arrest at Iolani Palace in 1896, and she then lived the rest of her life at her private residence, Washington Palace, just north of Iolani Palace. Lalani would only visit her one more time in 1915 for a birthday celebration along with John and Maria Kanekua, two years before the Queen's death.

For the next thirty years, each time Kate and Lalani met and then had to say good bye, it was bitter sweet. They were happy for each other and knew they had been lucky in life, in having wonderful caring husbands and families. Yet, they would miss each other and would write weekly for the rest of Lalani's life.

Evan stayed on the ranch and eventually took over for Jim. Evan married Sarah, the Gilbert's granddaughter, four years after they met. Jim and Lalani bought them an acre of land next to the ranch down valley, and Amos and Elizabeth helped pay for a small house that Evan and Kiana built. Evan eventually changed his name to Baker, and had two sons Henry and Robert Baker and little Lizzie, who called Jim and Lalani, *tūtū kāne* and *tūtū wahine*, grandpa and grandma. Lalani loved having the children visit.

Shannon grew up at *Mau Loa,* being home schooled until she was twelve, at which time the town of Kailua, down valley, opened a school. Jim made sure Shannon grew up riding horses and would ride her own red roan, Ginger, to school every day. When she was fifteen Shannon attended the Royal School in Honolulu, coming home on weekends and holidays.

When Shannon graduated in 1911, Jim and Lalani took her on a six-month world tour, sailing first to Oak Ridge for their usual visit, while Evan stayed back to run the ranch. From Kate's, they caught the train to see Yellowstone and on to New York to hear the Philharmonic before boarding a ship to London, where they stayed with Thomas and Jessie. After a month, they traveled to Holland to see the tulips, on to Cologne, Prague and Vienna, then back into Paris to see Charles. After a month they took the train to Barcelona and on to Marseille, Rome and Athens. They passed through the Suez Canal, that had long been open, on their way to Bombay and then the long voyage onto Sydney, where they spent three weeks before returning to Oahu. Lalani, like Edith, took great joy in showing them the world she had experienced.

At *Mau Loa* things changed slowly, according to Hawaiian time. Lalani and Jim eventually extended the breakfast area into a covered, but open, lanai on the northside of the house, overlooking the gardens. They would hold wonderful luaus in the springtime with Hawaiian roasted pig, and Hawaiian music and dancers. The Gilberts, the Ladds, Kanekuas, Susan and Mary, and the Greens, the family from Queen Street, would come. Kiana played ukulele and Mora told stories with hand gestures. In the fall, they would hold western style barn dances, after the roundup and the herd had been sold, with Sam, Kiana and Mora, Lilpo and other local farmers.

Lalani rode Genevieve for the next fifteen years, taking evening rides with Jim through the ranch and often down to the beach to sit and watch the waves and feel the rhythm of the island. When Genevieve died, Lalani never found another horse she felt completely safe on. By then the road to town and Honolulu was well traveled by cars, and Jim bought them a Pierce Arrow-48 for trips to town. Lalani never drove it. If she needed to get somewhere on her own, she still had her own horse and carriage. Jim continued to use draft horses and the wagon for hauling things. Evan, finally in 1915, purchased the first truck for the ranch.

Lalani was very happy at *Mau Loa*. She would sit at Kate's writing desk each week and write to Kate about all that was going on at the ranch and how Shannon and the grandchildren were growing. She also wrote to Minnie in Boston and hoped she would come visit one day, but she never did. Kate would send regular letters about the ranch and how the reservoir waters would cover half the south pasture one year and two-thirds the next. How their big tree now stood at the north entrance to the reservoir, where people would come to picnic and see their name.

Morgan and Amanda came twice, and Eric and Evelyn in 1901, just in time to turn on the electric lights in the house. But it was Kate and Clay that came every four years, with Jim and Lalani going back to Oak Ridge every four years in between. Kate had a little girl, Abigail, two years after Andrew, but it was Matthew that Shannon spent most of her time with when they were together. They would both end up going on to the university in Berkeley. He still called her Shay Shay and she called him Matty. Shannon remained on the mainland and, well, that's a story for another time.

Jim loved the peacefulness of the ranch and was quite happy there. He passed away in the fall of 1927 at the age of eighty-two. Evan and Sarah and Lizzie then moved to the big house to be with Lalani. Evan would eventually inherit *Mau Loa*. Evan and his sons would run the ranch for the next sixty years.

Five years after Jim's passing, Lalani bought the old Crocker house on Queen Street and lived there until the year before her passing. In the Fall of 1936, Evan and Sarah moved Lalani back to *Mau Loa* to take care of her.

One clear spring morning, Lalani sat at Kate's desk and wrote one final letter.

May 20, 1937

My Dearest Kate,

For the first forty years of my life, I went where people took me and did what was expected of me to do. It was an incredible education and adventure. Then we came to Oak Ridge, you gave me the freedom to choose what I wanted for my life, and I found the love of my life. Though I struggled to know what my life should become, and circumstances pushed me to grow and make choices, for which I am grateful, they brought me home to my island and along with the decisions, great blessing and joy.

For the last forty years I have been happy at Mau Loa, though now I miss my Jim terribly. We both have been blessed with wonderful families and good friends. You there among your rolling hills and giant oak trees and I here nestled in my lush green valley surrounded by blue ocean. I want to thank you for the freedom to choose and the honor of being your big sister, always caring deeply for you. I hope Matthew will do the same for my Shay Shay. It has been a joy to be your sister. I will always be with you and keep you in my heart.

Lovingly forever,

Your big sister/

& best friend

Lalani

Katherine received the letter on the morning of May 28th, the morning Lalani passed away quietly in her sleep, in the big bed Jim had bought them.

Lalani was buried next to her beloved Jim, and her parents in the church cemetery. Proper headstones now stood over Lalani's parents' graves and a large gray double stone over Jim's and hers. Shannon and Evan made sure everything was as she wanted it on that day, a lovely warm spring morning. The grandchildren were there with her favorite plumeria flowers. Kate and Clay stood by Shannon, and Matthew held her hand. Kiana played soft Hawaiian music, and Shannon read Lalani's favorite poem. Kate stood for a long time, only a few tears now filled her eyes. Shannon stepped forward and laid a lavender orchid lei gently on Lalani's headstone, then Matthew escorted Shannon from the site along with the others. Clay stood quietly waiting for Kate as she said her final farewell.

I shall miss you more than I can bear. My dearest friend and beloved sister. Together in spirit forever.

Aloha au ia'oe mau loa....

Hawaiian Words and Phrases

Aloha au ia 'oe makuahine – I love you, mother

Aloha au ia'oe mau loa – I love you forever

Hale Ke'oke'o – white house

Hanai – adopted

Haole – foreign

Hana-ino – ornery

hau'oli 'ole – not happy

Hau'oli Makahiki Hou! – Happy New Year!

Hoonawaliwali – disheartening

Kala aku nei au iā 'oe – I forgive you

Kālua 'ana – baking

Ko makou wahi - our place

Ku'u'aloha -special loved one – like a wife to a husband

Makana - gift

Makuakane – father

Makuahine – mother

Mālama'Āina – to take care of the land

Malia – wished for a child

Mau Loa – forever

Na ke Akua e malama ia 'oe! – The Great is where you are going!

Ma kahi a'oukou e helee aku ai he Akua no – wherever you go there is God.

Pili aina – belong to the land

Tutu kane – grandpa

Tutu wahine – grandma

Ulu Pono – grow properly- righteousness - Prosper on the right path!

Wai – water

Locations

Ahuimana – location of Crocker Ranch

Iwilei – north of Honolulu where Susan lived

Kailua - two sea – small town on the east coast of Oahu

Kahanlu'u Valley – area of Crocker ranch on east coast of Oahu

About "A Long Journey Home" Series

A Long Journey Home Series is about the life journeys, challenges, and sacrifices of several women around the beginning of the twentieth century, and how these influenced them to be strong and independent, to create their own lives. It tells how women make the hard decisions to do what's right for the sake of love.

Book 1 - *A Long Journey Home ~ Katherine*
Katherine's search for independence and purpose
Book 2 – *A Long Journey Home ~ Lalani*
Katherine's life-long friend's search for a place of belonging
Book 3 – *A Long Journey Home ~ Shannon*
Lalani's daughter's relationship with Katherine's son takes a turn, as her life unfolds
Book 4 - *A Long Journey Home ~ Jessie*
Jessie, Katherine's childhood friend - coming 2025

Other Books by the Author

The Need to Say Good Bye – novel
Kristyn had experienced many losses in life and finally faces them in order to find love.

Wild Things in My Mountain Garden
A memoir about planting a flower garden in the foothills of Colorado

Melody Lavrakas was raised in the San Gabriel Valley in California where she grew up visiting the rolling hills of central California and fell in love with the golden grasses and majestic Oak tree that dotted the landscape. In her late teens she owned her own horse, a bay with silver mane, and rode through the foothill of Pomona. Here she would attend California Polytechnic University, Pomona, and graduate with a Bachelor of Science for Business. In her early years her family moved every three years and she yearned to settle in one place and to find lasting friendship. In high school, she found that sister type friendship which led to finding her true love. Melody married John Lavrakas in 1979. They have three children and lived in Maryland, California, Colorado and Oregon. Together they have traveled to Europe, enjoying Vienna, Prague, London, Paris, Holland and Honolulu serval times. In 1988 they moved to Colorado Springs, Colorado, where John worked in GPS while Melody raised the children, gardened, and dabbled in writing.

Melody wrote her first workbook for an after-school program on Oceanography for Kids and taught it to 4th grader. Fifteen years later she wrote Wild Things in My Mountain Garden. With children grown and married, now settled on the Oregon coast, Melody wrote The Need to Say Goodbye and the first in the series of A Long Journey Home (about Katherine). Now she again combined her love for California rolling hills, the discoveries of travel, her sense of heritage and history, with the beauty of Hawaii and a little romantic fantasy and has written A Long Journey Home ~ Lalani, which reflects the love she and her husband have had over their 45 years of marriage.